Also by Jennifer Hartmann

Still Beating
Lotus
June First

STILL BEATING

JENNIFER HARTMANN

Bloom books

Published by Bloom Books, an imprint of Sourcebooks
P.O. Box 4410, Naperville, Illinois 60567-4410
(630) 961-3900
sourcebooks.com

Originally self-published in 2020 by Jennifer Hartmann.

Cataloging-in-Publication data is on file with the Library of Congress.

Printed and bound in the United States of America.
VP 10 9 8 7 6 5 4 3 2 1

To anyone with a dream: May your dreams
be brave, and your heart be braver.

CONTENT WARNING

I would love for this to be an enjoyable journey for you, so please be aware of the following themes that may negatively impact your reading experience: sexual assault, kidnapping, murder, self-harm, attempted suicide, reference of early miscarriage/non-viable pregnancy, and loss of a pet. While these subject matters were necessary in telling the story I needed to tell, I realize they may be triggering for some readers.

PART 1

THE MATCHMAKER

1

CORA

"Y OU'RE INCORRIGIBLE."

I narrow my eyes at the man I've deemed worthy of my most treasured insult.

Incorrigible. It's a damn good word.

The man in question is Dean Asher—my sister's prick of a fiancé.

Dean laughs, seemingly unaffected by the hostility shooting from my eyes like hot lasers. He must be used to it by now. "What the hell does that even mean?"

"Stupid, too," I say, sipping on my watered-down cocktail with one arched eyebrow.

Fifteen years. Fifteen *goddamn* years is the amount of time I've been subjected to Dean's teasing, ridicule, and bad attitude. He's the stereotypical "bad boy"—surly, well muscled, always reeking of cigarettes and leather. Pathetically good-looking.

Asshole.

My sister, Mandy, fell right into his trap. They were high school sweethearts from the start. Mandy was the epitome of popularity with her Prom Queen title, bleached blond hair, and Abercrombie wardrobe. That was the style back in high school.

I, on the other hand, was none of those things—thank *God*. Despite the fact that I'm only ten months younger than Mandy, we could not be more different. She's athletic, bubbly, and vain. I'm a bookworm who would much rather purchase adorable outfits for our family dog than for myself. Mandy is perky, and I'm prickly. I could recite Shakespeare all day, where Mandy likes to quote the gossip headlines off Twitter.

Even though we have our differences, our sisterly bond has strengthened over the years, and now I'm preparing to be the maid of honor in her wedding next month. I'd like to say that Mandy outgrew everything about her high school years, but, alas, Dean Asher somehow made the cut as she enters her thirties. He's clung to Mandy like a disease. She just can't shake him.

I can't shake him.

So, now I have the divine privilege of being Dean's sister-in-law in four short weeks.

Vomit.

"Pretty sure that's not a word."

I swirl the miniature straw around my glass, raising my eyes to the man staring me down with his signature smirk. His gaze is all iron and grit. I shake my head, ashamed I have to call this guy family soon. "Don't make me Google it, Dean. You know I will."

It's Mandy's thirtieth birthday party. We're at the Broken Oar—a laid-back bar in Port Barrington, Illinois, right on the lake. It's a fun place to celebrate, despite the questionable company.

Dean takes a swig of his beer, his pale blue eyes twinkling with mischief. And *not* the fun kind. "You always were the nerdy type, Corabelle."

"Don't call me that."

He winks at me and I shoot him a death glare. Dean is the only person, other than my parents, to call me by my full name—Corabelle. I *hate* the name. Everyone calls me Cora. Dean knows this, of course, but he's always found immense joy in tormenting me.

Our banter is interrupted by the birthday girl, who is currently bringing the phrase "white-girl-wasted" to remarkable levels. Mandy wraps her arms around both me and Dean, squeezing the three of us together in an awkward, smooshed hug.

"I looooove you. You're my bestest friends. I'm marrying my bestest friend," Mandy slurs, having inhaled at least a dozen Sex on the Beach shots at this point. She turns to me, her head falling against my shoulder. "And *you*, Cora. You are going to marry *your* bestest friend really, really soon."

I push myself free of the embrace. The smell of Mandy's overpriced perfume and Dean's whiskey breath is making me want to hurl. "I'm never getting married, Mandy. Divorce just isn't on my bucket list. Maybe in another life."

I begin to turn away, but Mandy stops me. She pokes a French-tipped finger in the middle of my chest, and I flinch back, scratching at the tickle she leaves behind. "Marriage is sacred. Dean and I are never getting a divorce."

Possibly true. Dean seems like the type who would be content staying married, while enjoying his sidechicks along the way. And Mandy is certainly the type to turn a blind eye. "A fairy tale. Color me jealous."

"Can you guys *try* to get along? Please?" Mandy begs, waving her hands around with an air of theatrics. There is an ounce of sincerity mingling with her intoxication.

I sigh, my eyes darting to Dean. He's still smirking. I tap my fingers along the side of my glass as I pretend to consider Mandy's plea. "I mean, I would… maybe, *perhaps*, but…how am I supposed to get over the spider-in-the-shoe incident? How does someone move on from something like that?"

Dean chuckles as he chugs down his beer, clearly amused with his antics. "That was gold. I'll never apologize for it."

"See?" I shove my glass at him, jutting out my pinkie. "He's uncooperative. I tried."

Mandy smacks her fiancé in the chest. "Dean, stop being a dick to my baby sister."

"What? She can hold her own."

I glare at him, and our eyes hold for just a beat. "Well, he's right about something." Then I storm away, swallowing the last few sips of my crummy cocktail as I approach the bar. I slam the empty glass down and perch myself on a stool, eyeing the bartender. "Another one, please. Make it a double."

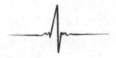

I should have accepted the ride home.

It's a little after 1:00 a.m., and I managed to find the most boring guy in the bar to get trapped in conversation with. My intoxication is dwindling, so now I'm just tired and crabby as my elbow presses against the bar counter with my head in my hand. I'm staring at the idiot to my left as he blathers on about being a lawyer, his cool car, and something about a reality TV show audition. Honestly, he lost me before he even opened his mouth. He smells like my passion-fruit sugar scrub, and it's *really* unsettling.

I feign a mighty yawn, forcing my head further into my palm. "That's great, Seth. Really great."

"It's Sam."

"That's what I said." I thread my fingers through my long, golden strands of hair as I lift my head and force a smile. "Anyway, I should get going. It's late."

Seth/Sam furrows his bushy eyebrows at me, his thin lips forming a straight line. "It's not that late. I'll buy you one more drink."

Nope. I'll puke. I'll definitely hurl all over his ridiculous sweater vest.

"No thanks," I respond, dismissing him with a quick wave. "I'm gonna go."

"Do you need a ride?"

"No."

Actually, maybe. Mandy and Dean drove me here, and I couldn't stomach another car ride with Satan himself, so I turned down their offer to drive me home.

But that's what Uber is for.

I push myself off the barstool, wobbling on my stupid high heels, and snag my purse off the counter. "See ya."

Seth/Sam grumbles as I fling my purse strap over my shoulder and saunter outside. I've successfully ruined his plans for the evening, and I'm pretty much okay with it. I wouldn't mind a night of drunken shenanigans and questionable decisions—Lord knows my vibrator is sick to death of me—but Seth/Sam lost his appeal faster than the Chicago Bears lost their shot at the Super Bowl this year, which was pretty freakin' fast.

Maybe I'm just too picky.

Mandy says I'm too picky.

Oh well. Looks like my vibrator is stuck with me.

The cool breeze assaults my lungs when I walk along the side of the bar, my heels clacking against the pavement. I tug my cardigan around my navy-blue dress, trying to dilute the chill, then reach into my purse for my cell phone. I've never actually used Uber before—maybe calling a taxi would be less complicated. Do taxis still exist?

I continue to fish through the pockets of my purse and locate my phone, but then my eyebrows crease when I realize my purse is feeling a lot lighter than usual. *Huh.* I shine my cell phone flashlight inside to assess further, and a tight knot of anxiety starts weaving itself in the pit of my stomach.

Well, shit.

My wallet is missing.

Did that son of a bitch inside take it because he knew I wouldn't close the deal?

I storm back into the bar, my heart thumping like a wild stampede beneath my ribs. My credit cards, my driver's license, over one hundred dollars in cash. Photographs, my insurance cards, passwords I'll never remember.

Goddammit.

I smack my hand against Seth/Sam's shoulder with a heaving chest. I don't even wait for him to turn around. "Did you steal my wallet?"

He slowly turns in his chair with a look of disgust. "Excuse me?"

"My wallet is gone. You're the only person I was talking to tonight."

Seth/Sam huffs. "Exactly. You were talking to me all night. When would I have had a chance to steal your wallet?" He shakes his head at me, then turns back around and reaches for his beer. "Sleep it off, bitch."

I ignore the insult, too wrapped up in my current dilemma to slap him. The dude has a point. I was literally facing him the whole time I'd been sitting at the bar—albeit, half-asleep and drooling on my hand—but I would have noticed him messing with my purse. In fact, my purse was perched on the bar counter, slightly behind my right shoulder.

That means someone *behind* me would have stolen my wallet.

Shit, shit, shit.

The bar is almost empty at this point. I question the bartender, who only shrugs at me, then puff my cheeks with air, blowing out a breath of frustration. I wander back outside and mentally prepare myself for begging people for rides since I'm suddenly broke.

I start with Mandy, already knowing she sleeps with her phone on Silent.

Voicemail.

I try my best friend, Lily.

Straight to voicemail.

There's no way in hell I'm calling my parents.

I go through my list of contacts, attempting three more people.

Voicemail, voicemail, voicemail.

My thumb hovers over another name, and I scrunch up my nose and pucker my lips, dreading the mere thought. Walking seven miles home in my high heels sounds more delightful than a ten-minute car ride with Dean Asher.

The wind picks up, forcing my hair to take flight. The cold almost chokes me.

I click on his name and immediately begin muttering profanities into the night.

"Corabelle?"

I don't know if I'm more annoyed or relieved that he picked up. "Don't call me that."

"Why are you drunk dialing me in the middle of the night?" Dean's voice is raspy, laced with sleep. I probably woke him up—*good*. A silver lining.

I'm about to explain, but he interrupts. "Let me guess, you had one too many shots of Fireball and you're calling to confess your undying love. I always knew you had a thing for me."

I grit my teeth, totally regretting my decision. I can feel his smirk from here. "You know what? Forget it. I'll walk home."

I'm about to end the call when Dean cuts in. "Wait, wait—you need a ride? I thought you were calling an Uber."

"Yeah, well, some jerk stole my wallet and now I don't have any money. But it doesn't matter. I'd rather walk." I really want to hang up on him.

"Don't be stupid. Your sister would kill me if I let you walk home."

"Your empathy astounds me."

He chuckles. "Sensitive *and* good-looking. I'm a triple threat."

"You mean a double threat. You only named two things."

"What?"

I pinch the bridge of my nose, searching for some semblance of self-control. *Deep breath.* "Never mind. Just hurry up."

I hit the "end call" button like it's my alarm going off on a Sunday morning. These are the moments I wish I smoked. I debate heading back inside, but I don't have any money for drinks and I really don't want to be sucked into another riveting conversation with Seth/Sam, so I lean back against the brick building instead.

Only a few minutes pass before some moron sidles up beside me asking for a light. I glance in his direction and quickly inch away. He's a balding, potbellied man who smells like cooked carrots. I try not to gag.

"I don't smoke. Sorry." I continue to put distance between us, but I can feel the man leering at me from a few feet away. *Ugh.*

"Let me buy you a drink, kitten."

I cross my arms when I catch him staring at my cleavage. "No, thank you. I'm just waiting for my ride."

"I can give you a ride," he sneers, his innuendo thick and not at all subtle.

Cue more gagging.

"Again, I'll pass. Have a nice night."

I never thought I'd be wishing for Dean to hurry up and get here. Even that jerk face is more tolerable than John Wayne Gacy over here, boring his X-ray vision through the front of my dress.

The man prattles on, making my stomach churn. "You're a pretty little thing, you know."

Ew, ew, and more ew. The man is creeping his way into my personal bubble, and before I decide to head back inside the bar, Dean's black Camaro comes careening into the parking lot with its beast of an engine and supercharged tires. He pulls up in front of me and exits the car, tossing his keys into the air and catching them with his opposite hand. He glances at me, waiting for me to "ooh and ahh" or something.

So not impressed.

My arms are still folded defensively as he approaches, his gaze flickering between me and Gacy. My body language screams *I hate you*, but my eyes are sort of pleading for him to get me out of here. "Hey," I mutter with little emotion.

Dean frowns at the man beside me, so I turn my attention to the right and notice the creep is *still* staring at my boobs with a salacious grin on his face. Dean's eyes narrow, then cut back to me. "Ready? 'Cause I'm tired as hell, and—"

"She your girl?"

Gacy interrupts, and we jerk our heads toward him simultaneously.

Dean is quick to reply. Too quick. "Hell, no."

Jesus. As if I have leprosy or syphilis or the bubonic plague. I glare at him, insulted. "Gee, thanks."

"What?"

"Nothing. Let's go."

I stalk forward toward the passenger's side, feeling Dean close on my heels.

Gacy issues us a farewell that makes my skin crawl. "You two enjoy your evening."

I hop inside the car and slam the door, locking it instantly. Dean follows suit, looking over me and out the window at the stinky carrot man.

His eyes are still narrowed and thoughtful. "That creep touch you?"

I flick my gaze across Dean's face, annoyed by how attractive he is. He runs a hand over his bristled jaw, scratching at the shadow of stubble, and I catch a whiff of his musky, cedar cologne and a trace of leather. I chew my bottom lip, leaning back against the seat. "No. Not like you'd care," I mumble, turning to look straight ahead.

"I care, Corabelle. You're in our wedding party. Can't have you chopped into little pieces and hidden under that guy's floorboards before the big day."

I snap my head in his direction, catching the playful smirk on that stupid, handsome face of his. "I hate you."

"You know I'm just messing with you." He winks.

"I still hate you."

Dean's eyes rove over me, assessing me in some way, as he twists the key in the ignition. The engine howls to life. "You know you're just opening yourself up to scary dudes when you dress like that," he says offhandedly, his wrist dangling over the steering wheel as he puts the car into drive.

I snort at the audacity of his claim. "Victim shaming," I supply. "You really are a catch. My sister is so lucky." I blink at him, fluttering my long lashes dramatically.

"That's not what I meant," he counters. "I'm just saying, when you look like that, guys notice."

"When I look like what? Are you saying I look slutty?"

"I'm saying you look good."

Dean issues the strange compliment with such nonchalance, I almost forget who it's coming from. I fidget with the hem of my dress and cross my legs, unsure of how to reply, but then I remember he was still victim shaming and he's still an ass. "Yeah, well, you look like a…bonehead."

What?

A rich laugh mingles with the roar of the engine, and I slink back in my seat. "That's the best you got? The alcohol must be getting to you. Your comebacks are suffering."

"Shut up."

Dean scratches at his jaw again, glancing my way every few seconds. "You're welcome for the ride, by the way. And for saving your life back there."

I snort again. I didn't even realize I was a snorter. "All you did was pull up in your macho car, looking like a tool, and imply that you found me revolting." I smile sweetly at him, placing my hands over my heart. "My hero."

He sniffs. "That guy was one coquettish look away from stealing your panties for a trophy. I definitely saved your life."

"*Coquettish?*"

Dean shrugs, his focus shared between me and the road. "Yeah, so? I got it from the Cora Lawson Handbook. You're basically a walking dictionary."

"I wasn't giving that guy any 'coquettish' looks," I argue, ignoring the jab. "That was me trying not to gag on my own vomit." Then I raise an eyebrow and clear my throat, adding, "You should be pretty familiar with that look."

He tries to hide his smile, but I notice. "No wonder I thought you had a thing for me."

Oh jeez.

I shake my head, forcing back my own smile.

Dean shuffles in his seat, reaching for his cigarettes in the center console. "You know, I was thinking we could squash this little tiff we've got going on. A truce or something."

"Little tiff? You mean the seething hatred I've had for you for the past fifteen years?"

"Yeah, that."

I gawk at him. "No."

"Why not?" he questions, his voice muffled through his cigarette as he lights the end. The embers glow bright, a deep orange and crimson. He sneaks a peek at me when I don't answer right away. "For Mandy. She wants us to be friends."

"Unless you plan on getting a personality transplant, I assure you that hell will freeze over before I consider you my friend." Dramatic, but true.

"Shit, Cora, I'm not *that* bad."

His statement forces me upright in my seat, my neck craning backwards in outrage. Is he being for real right now? I huff my disagreement. "You called me 'Cor the Bore' all through high school because I'd rather study than party every night. You set me up on a blind date with Stinky Steve and videotaped my reaction, then posted it on MySpace. You reenacted *The Ring* the night I watched it for the first time and scared me so bad, I actually fainted. Mandy thought I died, and she had a panic attack. I still refuse to have a TV in my room."

"High school stuff. That was years ago," Dean says dismissively through his laughter.

"You replaced my sugar jar with salt when you came by to pick up Mandy, so I had some pretty interesting coffee to start my morning. *Yesterday.*"

"Well…" Dean scratches his shaggy, brown hair, half-cringing, half-amused. "You give it right back to me, Corabelle."

"You call me 'Corabelle.' You know I hate it." I could go on. I could go on and on and on. I'm tempted to, but it's only boiling my blood further, and I don't have the energy to fight. "We'll never be friends."

I'm looking straight ahead again, but I can see Dean gazing at me from the corner of my eye. I swear there is a hint of softness there. A small, white flag, waving in the wind. "That's your name."

"My name is Cora. Corabelle is the abomination my parents gave me because they already used the pretty, normal name on their favorite child."

Okay.

So, I'm taking this to a very personal place. I need to stop.

"Listen…" Dean is about to respond, but we are both distracted when flashing lights pull up behind us, blinding us with their incessant strobes. He slows down, annoyance etched across his features as he stares into the rearview mirror.

"Dammit, Dean, what did you do? I just want to get home."

"I didn't do shit. I was going the speed limit. My plates aren't expired." He pulls over to the side of the gravel road, smacking the steering wheel with his fist. "This is bullshit."

The car comes to a complete stop, and I fall back against the leather seat with a sigh of exasperation. "There's probably a warrant out for your arrest. Maybe you killed someone. I'm not going down for murder. I'm not your accomplice."

"You think I could kill someone?"

Well, no. "Probably. But you're too dumb to do it right, so now you got caught and you're taking me down with you. This is just great."

"Jesus." Dean swings his head back and forth, scrubbing both palms over his face. "No wonder you're still single."

Oof.

I let the barb sink its teeth in me, seeping into every pocket of vulnerability. He knows my weakest link. I think he gets off on toying with my insecurities and giving them life. "Screw you." There is no teasing or playful banter—only animosity.

Dean glares at me.

I glare right back.

And then the sound of glass smashing against the side of my face is ringing in my ear, and I let out a scream. Two meaty hands wrap around my neck through the broken passenger's side window, and I have no fucking idea what's happening, but I keep screaming on instinct, pushing my feet against the door to keep him from pulling me out as my own hands claw at his arms.

"Cora!"

Dean is on me, over me, punching the guy and trying to release the bastard's hold. I reach for Dean, clinging to his jacket, desperate not to leave this car, desperate not to be taken. I shout through the fear, choking and sputtering, "Drive!"

Dean is still trying to pry the hands from my neck. "I don't have you!"

"Just…drive!"

My vision blurs as the fingers around my throat cling harder, but then one hand releases me and there is a moment of hope—maybe Dean hurt him, maybe Dean scared him away—but the other hand returns. It returns with a shiny piece of metal, and I think it's a gun, oh *God*, I think it's a gun.

More screams.

They are mine, I'm sure.

And then the butt of that gun collides with Dean's head with a sickening *thunk.*

"No!" I shout, plead, *beg.* Dean falls across my lap like a rag doll, and I feel myself being lifted from the seat and yanked through the window as shards of glass tear my dress and skin. "*Let me go!*"

A thick palm that smells like gasoline clamps over my mouth, stifling my cries, and when I glance up, my eyes widen.

It's him.

The John Wayne Gacy look-alike from outside the bar.

No.

My muffled sobs slip through the cracks of his fingers, and I keep fighting as he drags me across the gravel. My legs kick and flail, my nails digging into his fleshy arms until they bleed.

Then I open my mouth as much as I can and bite down.

Hard.

The man wails in pain as blood seeps from his finger wound, and I try to make a break for it. I pull free for a moment, for just a moment, before something strikes the back of my head…

And everything goes dark.

2

---

*D*RIP. *D*RIP. *D*RIP.

    I'm dreaming.

I'm dreaming about the ocean.

We went to Disneyland when I was eight years old—me, Mandy, Mom, and Dad. I'd been so excited. I wanted to put my toes in the salty sea for as long as I could remember. We rented a car and made the drive out to the Pacific Ocean one afternoon, and I can still recall the way my heart was beating inside my chest with wild abandon when the ocean came into view. I pictured Ariel and her sea sisters swimming beneath the surface.

There was magic. There was beauty.

And then I choked. I parked my butt in the sand and watched from afar as my sister and parents splashed and giggled and created memories I so desperately wanted to share.

But I couldn't move. I was frozen to the beach, surrounded by sandcastles and unfamiliar faces. The water had looked so dark and ominous when I'd gotten close. The vastness of the ocean had spooked me, and I was terrified that I'd be swept away.

And then it was time to go.

"Are you sure you don't want to dip your feet in? You were so excited," my mother encouraged, gathering up sand toys and colorful beach towels.

I swallowed hard, my eyes carefully assessing the waves rolling in.

Maybe. Maybe I can do this.

I pulled myself to my feet, my toes digging into the soggy sand. Then I moved toward the howling sea with timid footsteps and trembling limbs. I stopped just short of the shoreline, glancing up at the gray clouds overhead.

"Let's go, Cora!" my father shouted from a distance. "It's about to rain."

Wait, wait, no… I'm almost there. I just need one more minute.

I sucked in a deep, courage-filled breath and continued my sluggish trek forward. That's when the rain started. I watched the droplets pelt the ocean, water mixing with water. My dream washing away before my eyes.

Drip. Drip. Drip.

It started coming down fast and furious. I tried to make a run for it, but a strong hand wrapped around my upper arm, pulling me back.

"Time to go, Corabelle. There's a bad storm coming in."

I gulped, my eyes filling with tears as my father pulled me away. I never did feel the way the water splashed at my ankles. I never felt the seaweed tickle my toes. My father promised we'd go back the next day, but we never did.

To this day, I still haven't been back.

Drip. Drip. Drip.

My eyes flutter open, the steady drips tearing me away from a dream that may forever haunt me. But it's not rain I hear. And I'm not lying in my warm bed, preparing for a new day in the classroom teaching high school English. I'm somewhere else. I'm somewhere cold and dark and frightening. There's a dull ache throbbing at the back of my skull, and I try to bring my fingertips to the source of the pain. It's then I realize that my wrists are chained together behind my back, shackled and bound as if I'm an animal.

Oh my God.

My eyes shoot open, wide and alert. Petrified. I rattle my chains that are attached to handcuffs, trying to gather my bearings, trying to remember how the hell I got here. It's dark, but it's not too dark. My eyes just haven't adjusted to my surroundings yet. I blink rapidly, scanning the room I've been imprisoned in. I'm in some kind of chamber or cell. Maybe a basement. I squint my eyes, noting a small, narrow window across from me with the faintest trace of light.

Sunrise is peeking through my new nightmare, confirming that I am, indeed, awake.

That's when I hear it. A deep, throaty groan.

I twist my neck through the pain and discover Dean Asher chained to the opposite corner of the cement room in the same position, his head lolling back and forth as he brings himself back to reality.

I don't know if there is a sense of dramatic irony in the fact that I've been taken captive with the one person in the world I hate most, or if there is a semblance of relief in the realization that I am not alone in this.

"Dean." My voice is hoarse and weak, hardly a whisper fracturing the heady silence that envelops us. I watch as Dean lifts his head and it falls back against a hard post, prompting another moan. "Dean," I repeat—this time a little louder.

"Where the hell am I," he croaks out, but it's more of a statement than a question. It's a demand. I can see his eyes narrow at me through the hazy darkness, questioning my existence, questioning if his mind is playing tricks on him, questioning *everything*. "Cora?"

"Dean."

His name squeaks out through parched lips. I feel tears begin to bite at my eyes as the fear swells in my gut. I feel nauseated. Hollowed out. I start yanking at my restraints, pulling and tugging, shaking the shackles against a steel pipe.

Dean follows my lead and does the same, shouting for help and clanking his manacles as I scream at the top of my lungs.

"What the fuck is this? Where are we?" Dean is out of breath, his questions heaving out of him with frantic desperation. "Are you hurt?"

I think I should be surprised that my well-being is at the forefront of his concerns, but I'm too overwhelmed with terror and anguish to ponder it. I swallow hard. "My head…" It's all I can manage before more tears well in my eyes and I'm too choked up to say anything else.

"Yeah, me too."

I try to pull myself together, sucking frazzled breaths in through clenched teeth. I feel a panic attack edging its way through me, but I can't let it take over. I'll panic when hope is lost—when everything else has failed, death is imminent, and all options have been exhausted.

Right now, I need to stay focused. Levelheaded.

I need to get us out of here.

I watch as Dean rises to his feet, his hands cuffed behind him and chained to his own pipe. Metal screeches against metal as he stands, then he slams the cuffs against the steel with all his strength, over and over again. "Someone, help! Get us fucking out of here!" he bellows, his voice echoing through the dank basement, mingling with the clanking chains.

I lean the side of my head against the wall beside me. "What do you think he wants with us?"

Dean continues to cause a ruckus, loud and shrill. "Don't know. Don't want to know." *Ding, ding, ding. Clank, clank, clank.* "I'll fucking kill you, mother-fucker!" he shouts.

"He knows you can't kill him. You're chained to a pipe."

Dean ceases his efforts to glare at me from across the cellar. "So, what, I'm supposed to just give up and rot down here? Not a chance." *Clank, clank, clank.* "Help!"

"Do you think he wants you or me?"

I can hear Dean's heavy breaths huffing and puffing from a few feet away. He hesitates before responding, a low hum skimming his lips. "You."

God.

I close my eyes, forcing back a new wave of tears. A few drops slip through, sliding down my bruised cheeks and stalling at the edge of my jaw. I wipe them away with my shoulder. "I guess you're the lucky one."

"The *lucky* one? I'm chained to a fucking wall in a psychopath's basement. At least you hold some kind of value. I'm a dead man."

"I'd rather die than be of *value* to that sicko. You know what that means, right?" I curl my legs to my chest, bile gliding up my throat at the mere thought.

A silence settles between us because, honestly, what is there to say?

Nothing. Absolutely nothing.

We both know what's on the agenda for me, and there's nothing either one of us can do about it. Why he kidnapped Dean, I'm unsure—maybe because he saw the creep's face?

A bitter anger seeps to the surface, and I expel it the only way I know how.

"I can't believe I'm going to die down here with you of all people. The powers that be must really hate me."

"Seriously?" Dean is quick to bite back. "We're probably going to be brutalized down here, and you're holding onto a high school grudge? Jesus, Cora."

I try to balance myself on my high heels with wobbly ankles and pull myself up, sliding my chains up the pipe. My knees are shaking, and I almost collapse back down to the rubble. "Why didn't you drive? I told you to drive." The rising sun continues to spill more light into our hellhole, illuminating the look of outrage on Dean's face. I look away, my jaw tight.

"Are you saying this is my fault? I was trying to save you."

"If you would have just stepped on the gas, he would have let me go, and we'd be safe and warm in our own beds right now." My resentment is spewing out of me, and maybe Dean doesn't deserve it, but it's easier this way. It's easier than accepting the reality of our situation.

I can see him shaking his head at me, clearly insulted. "You're really something else, Corabelle."

I expect him to go on. I want him to say more. I wish he would take the bait and funnel his own fear and frustrations into petty rage and throw it right back at me. *Give me all you got, Dean.*

But that's it. That's all he says, and I feel hollow again.

I slide back down to my butt, the weight of my body, the weight of *all of it*, unable to hold me upright any longer. Dean sits down a few moments later, his legs sprawled out in front of him, leaning back against the pole with closed eyes. My own eyelids feel dry and brittle, almost acidic—like lemon peels. It hurts to blink.

Silence dances between us for a long time. The sun is up, shining its happy, brilliant rays into our dungeon, bringing to light the harrowing truth of our circumstances. I almost wish for the darkness. Most things can be masked in the dark.

My chin is to my chest when a door creaks open and bulky boots pound the steps, one at a time.

Thunk. Thunk. Thunk.

I jerk my head up and glance at Dean, who is looking at me with a similar uneasy expression. Our eyes hold tight as we both rise to our feet once more.

"My pets are awake," the man declares when he appears at the base of the staircase. His belly is protruding from the too-short hem of his T-shirt, and splotches of sweat stain his armpits.

Vomit swirls in the pit of my stomach and I want to retch.

"What the hell do you want?" Dean commands, clanking his cuffs against the pole. "I have money. I can wire you everything in my account."

The short, stubby man gargles his laughter, then coughs until he's bending over and wheezing. When he regains his composure, he straightens and approaches us. His beady eyes hardly spare Dean a swift glance before he's focused on me.

That same leering look from the night before is plastered on his face as he drinks me in, toes to top. His gaze settles on my cleavage, and I try to shift my shoulders to cover myself in some way, but my efforts are fruitless. I'm only making the swell of breasts jiggle, and I think it's turning him on. I inch my way backwards, as if I have somewhere to go—somewhere to hide.

"We're going to have a lot of fun together, kitten," he says to me, puckering his lips like a kiss and making a revolting purring sound.

I feel my resolve crumbling. My heart is racing beneath my rib cage, trying to make a break for it, and I have to tell it to calm down. *There's nowhere to run.*

Dean starts beating his chains again, trying to distract the disgusting pig who is undressing me with his soulless gray eyes. "This is stupid, man. We both have families. Jobs. Friends. They're going to start looking for us. You'll never get away with this."

More gurgled laughter erupts from the man, but he doesn't even look Dean's way. He's still eyeing my breasts, his tongue poking out to wet his thin lips. "Tessie Evans and her clown of a stepbrother said the same dumb shit to me," he says, pacing forward. Getting closer. "Their flesh is compost out in my barn. Their bones make good chew toys for the dogs."

I scream.

I scream and scream and scream, blinded by tears, shaking with terror.

"Please don't do this. I don't want to die," I force out, kicking my legs at the man as he closes in on me. "No, no, no. Please."

"Fuck!" Dean shouts from across the room, still going ballistic on his chains, as if that will somehow help. As if that will get us out of this mess.

"Save the fight for later, big boy," the man hollers over to Dean, his focus pinned on me.

I can feel his foul breath skim my face. He smells like cooked carrots and gasoline mixed with rancid body odor. I squeeze my eyes tight, my shoulders bobbing up and down in time with my sobs. He leans in, further and further…

"Gimme a few hours, kitten, and I'll show you a good time," he mutters with a wink, his nose almost grazing mine. "I have to go make a car disappear first."

Oh God.

He steps backwards, casting his gaze back and forth between me and Dean, then whirls around with a whistle and disappears up the staircase.

I fall to the floor—*hard*, crying and trembling.

There's no doubt in my mind he's going to kill us. He's going to have his fun first, and then he's going to slit our throats and feed our bodies to his dogs.

"Goddammit. God-fucking-dammit. Jesus fucking Christ."

Dean is chanting away beside me, pacing the few steps he's allowed to pace. Then starts pulling forward against the pole, hoping to somehow break free. He tugs and strains through angry growls, and I'm actually worried his hands might separate from his wrists.

"It's no use," I say quietly, my head propped up against the metal post that binds me to this nightmare. This prison. "We're trapped."

"I'm not giving up."

I watch him through blurry eyes as he continues his unproductive efforts, groaning and cursing the entire time. "You're going to hurt yourself."

Tug. Twist. Shout. Swear.

"I'm sure the thought alone devastates you," he grumbles.

I close my eyes as more tears leak out, and I suck in a shaky sigh. "Do you think anybody's looking for us yet?" I wonder out loud, not really expecting an answer—there's no way to know.

Dean eventually stalls his escape attempts, a sheen of sweat reflecting off his face from the morning light. He looks at me, and our eyes stay locked for a few beats, the raw truth of our predicament spearing us right in the gut.

Looking for us.

We're going to be the product of search parties and canine trackers and news reports and gruesome documentaries on Investigation Discovery.

Me and Dean Asher.

Dean inhales with a shudder, leaning his shoulder against the pole. "You know, I used to joke that we'd probably end up killing each other one day," he murmurs, kicking at a small rock near his sneaker. "I guess I always had a feeling we'd go together."

I know he's trying to make light of our ordeal, but his words sucker punch me. They knock the wind from my lungs until I can't breathe. *I can't breathe.*

I sit there on the cold, hard floor, quietly crying until my tear ducts dry up and I'm too exhausted, too weak, to even move.

Dean starts to sing.

I've known he could sing pretty well from family karaoke nights at my parents' house over the last decade. I'd sit on the couch with crossed arms and stony eyes, annoyed by the sound of his rich, gravelly voice. Mandy would swoon. My parents would stare at him with their proud, beaming faces. Even the goddamn dog would watch in adoration, her tail wagging with each perfectly pitched note. Then everyone would clap, except for me, and Dean would take a bow, occasionally shooting a smarmy wink in my direction.

I'd stick my tongue out or flip him off, brimming with contempt. Mandy would jab me in the ribs with her elbow, and sometimes my mother would scold me for being rude.

Ha! Rude.

Wrapping my entire car in plastic before a life-changing job interview is fucking rude.

I try to ignore the sound of his voice and close my eyes, but I find the raspy melodies to be oddly calming. He's singing one of my favorite songs—"Hey Jude" by The Beatles.

And somehow, despite the fear and uncertainty, despite the gravel digging into my thighs and the terror digging into my heart, I manage to fall asleep.

3

"WAKEY, WAKEY."

I jolt awake, thinking for one exquisite moment that it was all a dream.

A sick, horrible dream.

But the man is looming over me with breath that now reeks of tobacco and dirty socks, and his lips are curled up into a grotesque smirk.

I'm definitely in a nightmare, but it's not one I'll be waking up from anytime soon—and it's only just begun.

I slither back on the cool cement, the soles of my heels scuffing against the floor. I try to twist my way around the pole, as if he won't be able to reach me somehow, but he yanks me by the hair and pulls me up to my feet. I shriek in protest, my scalp burning.

"Get the fuck away from her," Dean shouts from the opposite corner.

I use the temporary distraction to knee the motherfucker in the balls. If I'm going down, I'm going down swinging. The man howls in pain and releases my hair, then slaps me hard across the jaw with the back of his hand. The pain radiates through my entire head, and it feels like my brain might start oozing out of my ears.

"Silly little cunt," the man barks, then spits at my face.

His saliva dribbles down my cheek and I almost puke.

"You're a feisty kitten, aren't you?" he continues, plucking my chin between his fingers and forcing me to look at him.

I return the gesture and spit right back at him, watching it hit him in the eye. Then I brace myself for the inevitable punishment to follow.

The man freezes for a solid five seconds, completely blindsided by my actions. He wipes the spit from his eye, gawking at me, his expression unreadable.

And then he laughs.

He doubles over laughing, his voice squeaking and breaking, his butterball hands clasped around his knees. I glance over at Dean, who's watching the scene with cautious interest, a frown etched between his eyes and his arms still tugging at his restraints.

"Kitten likes to play."

The man lunges at me, tearing my dress straight down the middle.

God, no.

"You've been waiting to play with Earl, haven't you?" he goads, his slimy hands palming my newly exposed breasts sheathed in a turquoise lace bra.

Earl. The bastard's name is Earl.

My head falls to the side, my gaze catching Dean's. He's watching in horror, helpless, as Earl fondles me like I'm his science project.

Earl is going to rape me. Nausea swells and swirls inside me, and I force it back, tears trickling from my eyes. "Please don't do this," I whimper, trying to flail my legs to kick him away.

Earl forces his obese body against me, pinning me to the pole so I don't move.

"Such a pretty kitten…" he murmurs, his breath curdling my stomach.

Dean starts growling again, slamming his chains against the pipe with immense force. "I swear to God I will kill you if you fucking touch her. I will find a way out of this, and I will put your fat ass in the *ground*."

Earl chuckles, but doesn't look up. He's too focused on my breasts, as he leans down and jabs his thick tongue between them.

I cry out, squirming back and forth, stomping my stiletto heels against his boots. They hardly make a dent. Nothing is going to stop this from happening.

I've never felt so helpless.

I whack my chains around, stomp my feet, twist and writhe and scream until my lungs physically ache. "*Please*," I beg. "Let us go. We won't tell anyone, I swear. Just let us go…" My God, I sound like a terribly scripted crime TV show. I always thought I'd be more creative if I found myself in harm's way. More convincing.

But there is no reasoning with this man. There's no bond I can form with him, no carefully established connection I can fake. My instincts tell me he is too far gone. He has no conscience, no soul. No trace of sympathy I can try to manipulate.

My entire body tenses up, doing everything it can to resist the vile act that's about to occur.

Dean is still protesting beside me, screaming and yelling colorful obscenities and idle threats. They fall on deaf ears. Earl pays him no mind.

My eyes make their way back to Dean as everything else starts to fade out. I put up a wall, a defense mechanism—a mental block. I completely zone out, staring at Dean, who is trying so hard to lunge at us, to lunge at Earl.

"Look at me, Cora. Keep your eyes on me. Listen to my voice," Dean orders, doing everything he can to maintain my attention. To distract me from the fact that I'm being defiled right before his eyes. "We're going to get out of here, you hear me? I'm going to get us out of here. Just focus on me. I'm the only thing that's real right now. It's just you and me, Cora. Focus, okay? Look at me… Focus on my voice…"

Dean's voice starts to dissolve, my entire mind shutting down and turning to fog. I keep my eyes on him, his movements wayward and clipped. His mouth is still moving, but I can no longer distinguish his words. Everything is murky. Confusing. I think I'm underwater, sinking, drowning, fading away…

I think the ocean has finally found me.

I think I like it here.

Drip. Drip. Drip.

I listen to the steady drips from a leaky pipe as I lie sprawled out on the hard floor. My head is resting against the stone wall to my left, my legs splayed out in front of me.

Seventeen minutes and twenty-two seconds.

That's how much time has gone by since I was desecrated. Used up and tossed to the floor like a piece of trash. I've been counting the seconds as they tick by in perfect time with the drips.

"Cora."

Dean's voice interweaves with the steady drops, and I blink slowly, my gaze fixated on absolutely nothing.

"Cora."

Drip. Drip. Drip.

I don't move. I force myself to breathe, just so I can stay alive.

"Talk to me, Corabelle."

What am I supposed to say? Dean knows exactly what happened. He had a front-row seat to the play-by-play. I finally work up the strength to pull my head upright, and I stare at the foot of the staircase on the far side of the room. I'm dreading the moment those clunky black boots reappear—a prelude to a new set of horrors.

"Are you okay?"

This finally grabs my attention and I force my eyes to the right. Dean is leaning back against his pole, fully facing me, his arms locked behind him. My gaze works its way up from his heather-gray running shoes to the mess of tousled, dark brown hair atop his head. It's starting to curl just below his ears. I remember Mandy complaining that his hair was getting too long and she was about to trim it herself.

I swallow. "I'm fine."

I'm usually a terrible liar, so I'm impressed with how honest that sounded. It's not the truth, of course. It's the greatest lie I've ever told.

Dean is fully aware of this. "You're not fine. You can talk to me."

An eyebrow raises on instinct as my lazy stare continues to assess him. His jacket was removed at some point, so he's only wearing a baby blue T-shirt that matches his eyes and faded jeans. "I can talk to you?" I release a grating chuckle. My throat feels raw from all the pointless screaming I've been doing. "Because we're such good friends, right?"

I take in the way his eyebrows pull together, a look of indignation scrawled across his face. "I'm the only friend you've got right now," he says tightly.

"I'd rather be alone."

Another magnificent lie.

I don't want to be alone. But Dean is here, and I don't particularly like him, so I'm going to take all of my fear and trauma out on him. It's the only sense of control I have right now.

It's my only power.

"Listen," Dean continues, his voice low and splintered. "I know we've had our issues, but we need to work together. Once we get the hell out of here, you can go back to hating me, but this is life and death, Corabelle. Get over this fucking resentment you have with me and let's put our heads together."

"Don't call me that." I pull my eyes away, dipping my chin.

A scathing laugh fills my ears. "Of course that's the thing you focus on." I can see him shaking his head out of the corner of my eye. Then he slams his cuffs against the pole, and I jump in place. "You woke me up in the middle of the night to come pick your ass up, after we already *offered you a ride home*. But I came anyway, because believe it or not, Cora, I do fucking care about you. We're going to be family."

Tears rim my eyes at his words. Funny, I didn't think I had any left.

"I picked you up at almost two in the fucking morning, and I end up here. Chained to a goddamn post, waiting for whatever that asshole has in store for us. And now you're giving me attitude?"

I seethe through gritted teeth, my voice cracking as it rises in pitch. "Do you have any idea what I just went through?" My own derisive laugh slips through as I swing my head to the side. "I can't deal with you right now."

He's quiet for a moment, absorbing my words, and then, "I told you... You can talk to me."

"I don't want to talk to you! I don't like you!"

"Fine!" Dean smacks his chains with a grunt of frustration. "Fucking hell. I'm only trying to help."

I sniff back my tears before they break free. "Maybe if you started helping fifteen years ago—started *caring* about me like you claim you do—I'd be more inclined to open up. But all you've ever done is tease me, hurt me, and tear me down. I have no reason to trust you right now." My chest is heaving up and down, burning and stinging, as my anguish mingles with so many years of bottled-up bitterness.

Dean considers my reply for a long time. The only sounds permeating the space between us are our intermingled breaths and the dripping pipe. Then he scuffs the sole of his shoe against the dusty floor and regards me from the other side of the room. "It's always been our thing," he murmurs. "I give you shit and you give me shit."

"I never had a choice," I counter. "I'm programmed to defend myself around you. My sword is always drawn, ready to fight."

"Because it's fun."

"It's not fun. You were *terrible* to me."

I spare him a poignant glance, taking in the way his eyes dance away from me. Dean scuffs his shoe again, forward and back, and the faint noise of sole against grit sounds so loud in this empty room. It's jarring.

"I was an ass back then," he finally responds, still looking off to the side. "I was a stupid teenager. But it's not like that anymore. I mess with you because you give it back just as good, and it's harmless, and it's *us*." Dean glances my way with his piercing blue eyes. "You can't tell me you don't enjoy our pranks and our banter and all the dumb shit we do to each other."

My reply is quick. "I don't."

"You're lying."

"I'm not lying, Dean. I don't enjoy getting picked on. I don't enjoy always having to be on high alert around you, wondering what 'dumb shit' you're going to pull on me." I pause for effect, simmering on my final words. "Or wondering how you're going to sabotage my next relationship."

His eyes flicker with something I can't exactly pinpoint. It's not guilt or remorse. It's not enjoyment either. "Whatever."

My eyebrows pull up, expecting more than a brush off. "That's it? That's all you have to say for the role you played in ending my four-year relationship?"

"Yeah. Whatever."

I can feel the flames spreading up my chest like wildfire, lighting up my neck, my ears, my tongue. "You're a fucking jerk." I twist my body to the left, trying to get as far away from Dean Asher as I possibly can. I curl my body up toward the wall and retreat into the confinements of my own mental prison.

I hear him let out a sigh from behind me, and I'm not sure what it means. Then he mutters under his breath, "I'm the only jerk you've got."

I was wrong.

I'd rather be alone.

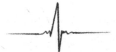

I'm not sure how much time passes, but the sun looks like it's setting in the sky as an ambient orange glow penetrates the dusty window above us. I envision myself breaking free of the handcuffs and climbing the wall, punching the window with a determined fist and squeezing out through the narrow opening. I'll run free, not even caring where I end up.

Anywhere is better than here.

Dean and I have not spoken since our argument, which must have been a few hours ago. He fell asleep shortly after, his back to the pole and his head against his shoulder. He looks peaceful, and I catch myself staring at him every now and then. I'm jealous that he's somewhere else right now. I haven't been able to fall back to sleep. Every time I close my eyes, I can smell my captor's nasty breath against my cheek as he humiliates me.

I also really have to pee, and I'm not sure what to do about it. Are we supposed to just soil ourselves down here? Is getting chained up like animals not good enough for that sick bastard? I squeeze my thighs together, knowing I won't have any choice but to let it out soon. The apples of my cheeks burn just thinking about it.

I thought I'd be hungrier by now, but the hollow hole in my stomach just makes me feel queasy instead. *What I wouldn't give to chug a glass of water, though…*

I daydream about guzzling down ice-cold water, and that makes my bladder tickle. I suck in a deep, calming breath.

And then the basement door swings open and those dirty, steel-toed boots come stomping toward us. It's enough to wake Dean from his slumber, as I hear his chains jangling behind me. I contort myself further into the corner, cowering from whatever horrors are about to unfold.

"Potty break," Earl announces, hiking his khaki pants up over his swollen belly.

I sit up straight as a tingle of hope sweeps through me. My bladder starts doing a happy dance, which isn't exactly a good thing, considering I'm about to burst. "You're letting us use the bathroom?" I scoot my butt around the pole so I can make eye contact with Dean, who is already standing. His eyes flicker my way, then dart back to Earl.

"One at a time. No tricks or I'll shove my pistol down your throat and watch you paint my walls red." Earl pulls a gun out from behind his back and waves it around for emphasis. "Don't want you doing your business all over my floor. Smells bad and takes me out of the moment, you know?"

The moment? *Jesus.* Our pain and terror is a *moment* for him.

But I don't show my disgust, for fear he'll change his mind. I nod and inch my way to my feet, my legs weak and shaky as they try to support my weight. "Thank you."

Earl unleashes a roar of laughter as he advances on me, tucking the gun back into the waistband of his trousers. "Don't thank me, kitten. You're still going to die."

My gaze shoots to Dean. I'm certain my skin has turned ghostlike and my green eyes have dimmed to gray. He stares back at me, looking equally hopeless, equally distraught, as his eyelids flutter closed and a hard swallow bobs in his throat.

Earl clamors over me, unfastening my restraints with boorish grunts. I can't help but contemplate an escape attempt. Maybe if I can get the upper hand somehow, grab his gun or steal a sharp object from the bathroom, I can overpower him. But as soon as the thought skips across my mind, the barrel of the gun is pointed at my temple when my cuffs fall loose. The cuffs are attached to chains, which are secured to metal rings in the wall, and they echo through the cellar when they hit the cement.

"Try anything dumb and you can say goodbye to that pretty little head of yours."

Earl jabs the gun against the side of my face as I massage my chafed wrists. I tug my torn dress together to shield my breasts, hugging myself tight. "I won't."

"Good. Maybe you'll be easily trained, after all." Earl looks at Dean, who is watching us with skepticism and a tense jaw. "You're next, handsome. Don't worry."

Dean and I lock eyes before I'm pushed forward by a husky hand, and I almost trip on my stilettos.

"Cora…"

I glance over my shoulder before I reach the steps. Dean is pulling at his chains like he's trying to reach me somehow. His eyes are swimming with worry and unease. It's the same look I saw earlier when he was talking me through the worst moment of my life, trying to comfort me in the only way he could.

I bite down on my bottom lip as our eyes hold for another beat. Then the cold gun collides with the center of my back, ushering me up the staircase.

I can't help but mull over Dean's words as I'm guided through the small house with olive-green carpet and outdated walls.

Believe it or not, Cora, I do fucking care about you.

4

H E DOESN'T RETURN AGAIN THAT night, and it's a small solace.

The basement grows dark, so dark, shadowing everything around me. It takes a long time for my eyes to adjust enough to see Dean's silhouette perched beside me against his pipe. It must be well past midnight, making it Monday—which means, if people haven't already started questioning our disappearance by now, they will. I rarely call in sick to work, and I certainly never no-show. It would be a huge red flag to staff and coworkers.

And Dean is a well-respected employee in the union doing road construction. He works the first shift. People will definitely start asking questions when he doesn't show up today.

Dean's foot slides against the floor, pulling my gaze in his direction, despite the fact that I can't really see him. I hear him sigh as he adjusts himself and tries to get comfortable.

"You awake?"

His voice is a comfort I didn't know I needed. "Yeah."

I roll the back of my head against the pole, back and forth, and tap my bare toes in opposite time. I slipped out of my heels when Earl brought me back downstairs after the bathroom break. The break was short-lived, unfortunately—he shoved me into a tiny restroom with an oversized T-shirt that reeked of him, then ordered me to change. I climbed out of my shredded dress and replaced it with the white shirt, doing my business, brushing my teeth with a pink toothbrush he left out for me, and joining him out in the hallway a few moments later. He handed me a turkey sandwich and a glass of water and told me I had three minutes to eat. He timed it. Then he dragged me back down to the basement, cuffed me to the pole, and did the same thing with Dean.

He hasn't been back since.

I squint my eyes through the shroud of darkness, trying to make out Dean's outline. It looks like his legs are stretched out in front of him, facing me. I wonder if he can see me better than I can see him. I clear my throat, running my tongue along my upper lip. "I lied to you earlier," I tell him, my voice ragged from crying, yelling, and lack of proper hydration.

Dean makes a low humming sound, then replies, "Which part?"

"I wouldn't rather be alone."

There is a long pause. A resounding silence.

I nibble on the inside of my cheek, wondering if he's ever going to respond. There is nothing to fix my eyes to, so I just stare off into the dark abyss and wait.

Dean eventually sighs. "The fact that he fed us and gave us water is a good sign. It means he's going to keep us around for a little while."

I glance in his general direction, taken off guard by the change of subject. I'm okay with it, though. I'd rather not dive into feelings and grudges and relationship history. I just wanted him to know that. For whatever reason...I wanted him to know.

I nod, even though he can't see me. "I guess. But he's still going to kill us. I'm sure of it."

"Maybe. But we have at least a few days to figure something out. We need a plan."

A plan. What sort of plan can we possibly put together down here, bound and restrained?

My mind wanders, and I can't help but think about the last "plan" we concocted. My mother put us both in charge of Mandy's twenty-eighth surprise birthday party two years ago. She wanted it to be special.

That was my mother's first mistake: thinking *anything* special could come out of me and Dean Asher working together.

"What is it?"

I poke my chin up at the sound of his voice breaking through my reveries. "What do you mean?"

I think I see him shrug. "You got quiet. That usually means you're deep in thought or piecing together a creative insult to throw at me."

I look right at him, and I'm pretty sure we're unabashedly staring at each other—but since I can't say for certain, I don't break away. "I was thinking about the mess we made of Mandy's party a couple of years ago and how any plan we come up with can't possibly go well."

His laugh startles me because it's real and genuine. I'm not expecting it.

"You were definitely in charge of the invitations," he informs me, as if this argument hasn't been dredged up a million times before now.

"Lies. You'll never admit it, will you? I *specifically* put you in charge of invitations because you had more involvement with her social life. Plus, I was already in charge of the catering, cake, and DJ."

"I had alcohol duty. I was clearly overwhelmed with responsibility and under a ton of stress."

My eyebrows rise with skepticism.

"I still don't understand why your mom wouldn't just let us create a Facebook event like the rest of the world," Dean finishes.

I groan and roll my eyes back. Even though no one showed up to the party because *someone* forgot to send out invitations, it was still a memorable night of Chinese takeout and horror movies around the fireplace. A nostalgic smile sweeps across my face. "At least she got to celebrate this year before…" My voice trails off as I look away. The lighthearted atmosphere dissipates when the reality of our situation sinks back in. I pull my legs to my chest and press my cheek to my kneecaps. "I'm going to try and sleep. I have a feeling whatever is in store for me tomorrow will mentally exhaust me."

I shudder at the memory of Earl between my legs, stealing away my faith in humanity. I'm confident my light will be entirely snuffed out if there is ever an end to this persecution. There is no going back to my former self.

Dean whispers at me through the dark after my words leave a foreboding chill in the air. "Good night, Cora."

My breath catches on the inhale. "Good night."

The minutes tick by. I count them.

Six minutes and thirty-five seconds.

It's too quiet, which means my brain is loud and turbulent. It refuses to rest—and I don't blame it, really. I swallow my pride, burying my face further into the valley between my knees. "Dean?"

"Yeah?"

I wet my lips and close my eyes. I can't believe I'm asking him this, but it's easier to be vulnerable in the dark...*and when you have nothing to lose.* "Can you sing to me?"

My belly swims with nerves, and I wonder if my request is too intimate. Too bold. Maybe I'm asking too much of someone who isn't even my friend. But the sound of his voice, all gravel and grit, singing my favorite song, lulled me to sleep earlier, and I'm desperate for a few hours of peace. I need to dream myself out of this prison.

Dean is silent for a few heartbeats, and I'm worried he's going to ignore me. Shut me down. I'm about to apologize, backtrack, tell him to forget about it, but then he replies:

"Any requests?"

A calming sensation washes over me and my body relaxes. "You can sing "Hey Jude" again if you want. It's my favorite."

"I know," he says softly.

He knows? We've never discussed our favorite songs with each other before. I've never cared to know his favorite *anything*, and I assumed he felt the same way. But I suppose when you know someone for fifteen years, whether you like them or not, you're bound to pick up on little things along the way.

When his voice infiltrates the darkness and fills the silence with rich music, I find myself drifting away almost instantly. It's something familiar. Something beautiful. Something good I can latch onto, absorb, and get lost in. I hum the verses into my knees right along with him until sleep eventually takes over and whisks me someplace else.

I dream about the ocean again.

The water is lapping at my toes, pulling me in like a magnet. Beckoning me with its depth and mystery. Tempting me with its life force.

I jump in.

And I swim away.

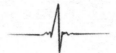

Before I know it, a beam of light is caressing the side of my face and I begin to stir. My neck is stiff and sore, and I almost cry out in pain as I lift my head from my knees. I instinctively try to raise my hand and massage away the kink, but I'm denied the privilege when my cuffs catch against the pole—a sinister reminder of my predicament.

Of my hell.

I roll my neck from side to side, my eyelids peeling open to find Dean staring at me from his corner with the faintest smile touching his lips. I make a sour face. "Were you watching me sleep?"

His chains jingle when his shoulders shrug in reply. "I'm not exactly overwhelmed with better things to do," he quips as that strange, little smile lingers.

It's a curious thing to see, given our situation. I don't think I'm capable of smiling—not until my chains are lifted and I am free.

But…will I ever be free?

I shake away the depressing thoughts, stretching out my legs and straightening, then wincing when my muscles protest. The ground is cold and unforgiving beneath my bare legs, adding to the discomfort. I flick my eyes up to Dean. His smile has dissolved, but his gaze is still soft as he watches me. "How did you sleep?" I ask him. I already know the answer, but I'm not sure what else to say. Our assortment of conversation starters is fairly scarce.

Excited for your pee break today? Ready for Earl to return and terrorize us some more? How soon do you think they'll find our bodies?

My own morbid thoughts make me cringe, so I swallow them down.

"Not as good as you," Dean says. There's a distinct twinkle in his eyes that matches the smile I already miss. "You were out like a light."

"I was drooling, wasn't I?"

"Your secret is safe with me."

I almost smile. *Almost.* Instead, I dip my chin, pursing my lips as I stare at my shell-pink toenails. Mandy and I had gotten pedicures after work on Friday to celebrate the weekend festivities. I realize that today is her *actual* birthday. My sister will likely discover that her two favorite people in the world are missing… on her birthday.

Happy birthday, Sis. I got you a Fitbit.

I wonder if Dean is reading my mind because he tilts his head to the side, studying me almost fondly. "She was excited for that ice cream cone today," he tells me, and there is whimsy in his voice.

Tears well and burn as I nibble on my lip. Mandy and I always celebrate our birthdays together with an ice cream cone at a downtown café. We do our secret handshake, take a selfie in front of the ice cream parlor, and eat our treats on the swings at a nearby park. It's been tradition ever since we were children when our parents would take us. Mandy's birthday is in November, so we're often bundled up like Eskimos, getting strange looks from passersby as we sit on snow-covered swings.

But we love it.

And there's nowhere else I'd rather be right now.

I wiggle my toes as the memories force a few silent tears down my cheeks. I brush them away with my shoulders and try to suck in a calming breath.

Dean is still watching me, taking in my emotions like a film. "You'll get that ice cream cone. I promise you."

I'm not sure why he's being kind to me. It's confusing and unsettling, and I don't know how to respond to him like this. We're designed to fight—swords of steel, heavy armor, and words that sting and draw blood. Letting my guard down feels an awful lot like surrender.

Unsure of what to say, I just offer him a scowl.

Dean lowers his eyes to the slate-gray floor with mild defeat. When he glances back up to me, the twinkle is long gone, replaced by the hopelessness that is hovering inside these four walls, closing in on us. "I'm not your enemy down here, Corabelle." His words carry an unfamiliar weight as they continue to disarm me.

"I don't know how to see you as anything else," I admit.

He stares at me, unwavering, daring me to look away. Then the twinkle reappears, and Dean replies, "Because it's fun."

"No."

My defenses flare back to life and I'm grateful for that—because it's easier. Comfortable.

Not fun.

"You're such a liar," he persists. "And stubborn."

I narrow my eyes at him, my molars grinding together in the way that they do when I'm preparing to rush into battle with Dean Asher. I cross my feet at the ankles and lean back against the pole. "You sure have a twisted idea of *fun*," I shoot back.

Dean runs his tongue along the roof of his mouth, breathing in deep as he prepares to take me down. I can almost feel his dagger poking at my chest. His head cocks to the side, his eyes blazing blue. "Remember when my buddy from college came into town to take me out for drinks? You told him I had a secret crush on him."

Ah, crap.

"Then you slipped me fucking Viagra before we left and I had to hide my dick with a bar napkin the whole damn night. But I'm pretty sure he noticed because I haven't heard from him since, *and* he deleted me on Facebook." Dean is watching my reaction like a hawk. "You can't tell me you didn't love that shit."

Dammit. I completely give myself away when a smile creeps in, pulling at my lips. It's my first smile in days. I'm not sure whether to be angry and accusatory, or to keep on smiling.

But Dean already knows he's won. "I rest my case."

I turn my head to the side in an attempt to hide the evidence, but the damage is already done. He sees right through me.

We are interrupted when we sensed an ugly presence in the room.

Thunk. Thunk. Thunk.

Those boots stomp all over me before they even reach the bottom of the staircase. I rise to my feet as my heart thunders in my chest with resistance. I'm already shaking—quivering with fear. Dean stands slowly, his eyes still pinned on me, but missing the playful spark I had seen only seconds ago.

I want it back.

"Good morning, pets," Earl greets us, wearing some kind of black work polo that stretches out over his large stomach, barely tucking into his pants. "How's my kitten?" His dark eyes shift to Dean. "And the dirty dog."

I swallow. "We want to go home."

Raucous laughter erupts from his mouth, and I feel his spit mist my face. I hold back a gag.

"You are home. I'm your master now," Earl says once his laughter has ebbed. "Is kitten ready to play?"

No, no, no.

Earl descends on me. I inch away, kicking my legs, swinging my head back and forth in protest.

"You sick bastard…you'll never get away with this," Dean shouts, yanking his chains forward as the veins in his neck bulge and pulsate. "When I get out of here, I will beat you into dogmeat if you lay another hand on her. I *promise* you that."

Earl chuckles, unthreatened by the warning. "Don't be jealous, doggie. You'll get your turn."

What the hell? I jerk my head toward Dean, wondering if he is also going to be subject to Earl's vile acts. *Oh God.* The thought makes my stomach pitch.

"Do what you want to me. Leave her alone."

Dean's words only tighten the coil of unease in my gut. Why is this man throwing himself to the wolves for me?

He hates me. I hate him.

But I don't have time to sort through the confusion because Earl is tugging up the hem of my T-shirt with his sweaty palms.

"No…please," I whisper. My voice is weak, my fight futile.

Dean talks me through it like he did last time.

Look at me, Cora. Focus on me. Nothing else is real. It's only me and you.

I sink underwater once more and let myself drown.

"I'm cold."

The sun is setting and our only light source begins to eclipse. A chill has settled in my bones. I'm not sure if it's the cold cement against my exposed skin or my reality stabbing into me like icicles, freezing my veins.

Both, I'm sure.

I'm lying against the pole, listless and paralyzed. The last forty-eight hours, along with all the long, foreboding hours to come, have taken their toll on me. I'm mentally drained.

And so, so cold.

Dean looks ashen and equally run-down, but he's spent the entire day talking to me, telling me stories and trying to lift my spirits. I find that my stone walls are crumbling in the presence of his alter ego.

He casts his sympathetic eyes on me, trailing them along my naked legs. The muscles in his jaw tick. "I meant what I said," he says to me, his tone low and hardened. "I'm getting us out of this. And I'm going to kill him for hurting you."

I'm unsure of what to say to such a bold promise, so I force a tight smile that has no intention of reaching my eyes. "You really think we're getting out of here?" I ask timidly.

"I know we are."

I realize Dean has no way of knowing this and he's only saying it to give me hope, but I let the words soak into all of my susceptible cracks and crevasses. I cling to them with everything I have left.

Before I can reply, I watch as Dean begins to kick off his shoes. One by one, he uses the toe of his left foot to shimmy out of the heel of his right. Then vice versa. When his sneakers are removed, he slides them over to me with his sock-covered feet. "They probably smell like a gym locker, but they're warm. It should help a little."

Our eyes catch and hold, a foreign tenderness traveling between us. I press my lips together, my gaze flickering between the shoes and Dean's vulnerable expression.

He throws me a smile, just as tender, and I wonder how hard it was for him to produce such a thing at a time like this. "I'd give you my socks if I thought you had a way of putting them on."

Maybe this is what my sister has always seen in Dean.

"He's not that bad, Cora. Just give him a chance. He's a decent guy."

I used to laugh in Mandy's face because Dean never showed me his "decent" side. I never understood why.

"Because it's fun."

"It's harmless, and it's us."

"You give it right back to me, Corabelle."

"Thank you," I say as the day turns to dusk and the sunlight abandons us.

I fall asleep that evening, rattled and beaten down. But a tiny pocket of hope lingers inside me, buried deep, trying so hard to claw its way to the surface.

And, above all, I am warm.

5

————————

THE DAYS GO BY SLOW and torturous, but they go by.

We are still alive. I'm holding on to that.

Dean and I play twenty questions to pass the time. He is winning by two games, which grates me. I'm a teacher, and I'm competitive…especially with Dean. I blame it on the lack of nutrition and traumatic circumstances.

Earl returns daily.

I expect it now, so the raw, blinding terror of it has subsided as much as it possibly can. I'm getting better and better at zoning out and turning it off. It's almost like an out-of-body experience. Dean talks me through it every time, and his voice is a solace in the back of my mind as I slip away.

We get our bathroom breaks around 5:00 p.m. each day after Earl gets home from work. We are allowed to brush our teeth, then we have turkey sandwiches with Miracle Whip on white bread and one full glass of water. And then we are sent back down to our prison, shackled to our respective posts, and forced to survive another night in the dark.

Dean sings me to sleep every night, and it's the only thing I look forward to.

Take a sad song and make it better.

6

As THE SUN RISES ON the seventh day and a full week has passed us by, we are no closer to freedom. We are no closer to finding a way out of this barbarous basement and going home.

Home.

Sometimes I forget what it looks like.

I try to picture my lavender bedroom walls, bay window, and the vintage mirror that my grandmother passed down to me. It's a quaint little house with only twelve-hundred square feet and two bedrooms, but it's *mine*. I worked my ass off for it and laid my roots.

I was in the middle of researching local animal shelters to adopt a dog. It has been on my bucket list for a solid year now, but it never felt like the right time. Last Saturday was spent scrolling through furry faces and cute canine bios as I narrowed down my search to find the perfect companion. I found two contenders, though all of them called to me with their sad eyes and heartwarming stories.

But Jasmine and Buffy were the two I was going to meet on Sunday. I printed out their photos and secured them to my refrigerator, excited for this big life change.

I got change, all right. Just not the change I ever expected.

And part of me is grateful I don't have a pet at home waiting for me, wondering where I've gone, relying on me for things I cannot give.

I am the pet now.

Dean's head is back against his pole, but his eyes are on me as I daydream about the two dogs I never got to meet. "Penny for your thoughts?"

I cut him a glance, pulling my legs up until I'm sitting Indian style across from him. "You don't have any pennies. Unfair trade."

He blinks as his mouth quirks into a tiny smile. "Name your price, then."

"You have nothing to give. My thoughts are extremely valuable, you know."

"I'm sure they are." Dean's eyes are as alight as they can be, given the week we've battled through. He dips his head to the side, pursing his lips together and considering the bargain. "All right, Corabelle. A thought for a thought."

I raise the stakes. "How about a confession for a confession?"

An eyebrow arches with interest, his smile blooming. "This could be fun." He winks at me. "And dangerous."

"Dangerous?" I chew on the inside of my bottom lip, my belly doing a forgotten flippy thing. "What kind of confessions did you have in mind? 'I stiffed the pizza delivery guy' or a full-on priest confessional with ten Hail Marys and the act of contrition?"

Dean lets out a gruff chuckle, shifting his weight until his knees are drawn up and shrugging his shoulders. "I would never stiff the pizza guy. Unforgivable." He ponders my question as he studies me, his head still cocked. "But definitely the second one. Let's go all last rites on each other."

I stare back at him, racking my brain for something that is even remotely last rites worthy. To be honest, I'm not all that interesting. I pay my taxes, I drive the speed limit, I don't owe anybody any money. I've never cheated or stolen. And I *always* put the toilet paper roll in the "over"' position. "Fine. But I'm kind of boring, so you'll have to go first. Maybe you'll inspire something sordid and obscene buried deep in my subconscious."

"Okay." Dean's expression turns more serious, the corners of his eyes creasing as he contemplates his confession.

His stubble has grown into scruff over the past week. The dark hair lines his chin and jaw, giving him a rougher appearance. Mandy didn't like the scruffy look when he'd occasionally let a modest beard grow out. She said it made him look like a mountain man. I never paid much attention at the time, but now that his face is the only thing I have to look at, I have to say I disagree with my sister. It's masculine. Rugged.

Maybe a little sexy if the face wasn't attached to Dean Asher.

A few more minutes tick by and the suspense is killing me. He's watching me like he's questioning his truth bomb—possibly regretting the whole thing. "Any day now, Dean."

A sigh escapes him. "All right. Fine." His eyes look even bluer as they hold mine. "I had a thing for you first."

What?

I choke on nothing. I start coughing and sputtering, and I have to force my eyes away from him. "What are you talking about?"

Dean bites his lip with another indifferent shrug. "Before I started dating Mandy. It was freshman year and you walked into Mr. Adilman's class wearing that little denim skirt and purple blazer. Your hair was all long and gold and had some kind of flower clip in it. I thought you were the prettiest girl I'd ever seen."

My heart is doing the Macarena, and my jaw drops like a comical cartoon. I think I'm speechless, which is new for me, but words aren't coming out and even my breathing has come to a screeching halt. Dean looks a little amused as he watches me from a few feet away, his eyes dancing over me while he awaits my response.

I don't respond, though. I'm definitely speechless.

"Your turn," Dean finally says, his voice soft and lilting.

I slow blink my thoughts into actual words, then shake my head. "It's still your turn. It's 100 percent still your turn. What are you even talking about? Was your turkey sandwich laced with all the drugs?"

Dean laughs, sliding his socks across the floor and stretching out his long legs. "I thought I was taking that one to the grave," he admits with a grin. "But I couldn't let you go on thinking I hated you. That's so far from the truth."

"You sure could have fooled me. You could have fooled everyone. Why were you such a jerk to me?"

His grin slips. "I told you. I was a kid, and that's what dumb boys do when they like a girl. They pick on them."

"I'll never understand that."

"Yeah, it's stupid," he says. "Then we both grew up, and giving each other hell was just a part of who we were. There was no going back." Dean is staring at me almost knowingly. "And you can deny it all you want, but you wouldn't want it any other way."

I set my jaw, my emotions spiraling into a frenzy. I'm not sure what to make of Dean's confession. I can't process it. It goes against everything I thought we were.

I gulp back more questions and choose to reroute the subject. Dean's bomb *did* happen to trigger something somewhat juicy. "I lost my virginity to Mr. Adilman."

He gapes at me. "What the fuck?"

I crinkle my nose, not entirely proud of that fact. "I was nineteen. We ran into each other at a bar. Mandy and I had just gotten fake IDs. He gave me a ride home, one thing led to another, and…" My cheeks flush at the memory I've kept to myself for ten years. "I'm sure you can figure out the rest."

Dean fidgets with his cuffs as he blows out a breath. "Shit, Cora. You gave it up to your high-school English teacher? Mandy told me Brandon was your first."

I feel my eye twitch at the mention of Brandon—my first long-term relationship and a huge source of contention between me and the man I'm staring at. "I've never told anyone about it. Not even Mandy." My eyes narrow, irritation with my sister flaring to the surface. "I can't believe she tells you about my sexcapades. Ew."

"She tells me everything."

I huff at him. "Your turn."

Dean parts his lips, about to speak, but he hesitates. His eyes glass over as a mask of uncertainty sweeps across his face. I can see him swallow, and I wonder what else he can possibly throw at me.

"Uh…it's about Brandon."

My body freezes up. "What about Brandon?"

Dean's ankles are swinging side to side like he's nervous. He catches my gaze and replies, "He was cheating on you, Corabelle."

I stare blankly at him, unsure if I heard him correctly. "Excuse me?"

"He was cheating on you. I caught him outside the Oar with his tongue down some floozy's throat. I roughed him up a little and told him to break it off with you or I would break his face."

I continue to stare.

"I knew it would destroy you, so I told him to blame it on me. You already hated me. It was better than letting you hate yourself, or having you think you weren't good enough for that douchebag."

Still staring.

Dean releases a long sigh, closing his eyes for a moment and then braving my stare once more. "Say something, Cora."

I open my mouth to reply, but only a strained squeak emerges. I'm overwhelmed by the truths spilling out of Dean's mouth. I don't know whether to be livid that I've gone three years still pining over a disloyal man, thinking Dean sabotaged my relationship just to hurt me, or touched by the revelation that Dean was trying to protect me in his own screwed up way.

I'm about to tell him that I've gone fifteen years thinking I wasn't good enough for *him*—for his friendship. For his respect. For his decency. But I don't get the words out in time because Earl's boots are making their way down the creaky basement steps. Dean and I turn to the sadistic man who is advancing on us with a devilish leer.

"I have some new tricks up my sleeve for my pets today," Earl tells us, slapping his hands together and rubbing his palms.

Oh *God*. What could he possibly have in store for us?

I feel queasy.

I expect him to saunter over to me like he usually does every morning before work, but instead, he approaches Dean. I stand to my feet, anxiety bubbling in my belly.

Earl snarls at Dean, "Are you ready to have some fun, my dirty dog?"

I start rattling my chains around, sickened by the very thought. "No! Leave him alone."

Dean remains sitting with a straight face. "Go fuck yourself."

"Oh, it's not what you're thinking." Earl throws his hands up, shaking his round head back and forth with a broken laugh. Then he pulls out his pistol and places the barrel at Dean's forehead. "I'm no homo. Now, stand, pet."

Dean rises. We share a perplexed look, both confused. Both frazzled.

"I'm going to unchain you now," Earl says to Dean, his gun still pressed hard against Dean's head. "One wrong move and I'll blow you to pieces. I'll find a new doggie for my kitten. Ya hear me?"

Dean nods.

"Good." Earl pulls a key out of his pocket and uncuffs Dean. I watch as the shackles fall to the floor and Dean rubs his swollen wrists as he awaits more orders.

Earl is quiet for a few moments, taking three steps back so Dean can't make any sudden moves. There is a giddy smile pulling at his fat, red cheeks, and the look on his face makes my anxiety swell and churn. Whatever he has planned cannot be good.

With one satisfied, drawn-out breath, Earl voices his intentions: "Fuck her."

The air leaves my lungs.

The room starts to spin.

I look over at Dean, who is shaken and visibly paling before my eyes.

"What?" Dean questions, his voice hardly more than a taut whisper.

Earl chuckles, his beady eyes filled with wickedness. "Did I stutter?" He points the gun at me, then aims it back to Dean. "Fuck. Her."

Dean is shaking his head in disbelief—in abject horror. "No."

"No?" Earl repeats.

"*No.*"

"Then you die. Three, two, on—"

"No!" I shriek. "No, no, please. Just do it, Dean." My chest is heaving, weighed down by impossibility.

This can't be happening. This can't fucking be happening.

Dean's eyes are wide and conflicted as he looks over to me, his brows pulled together, the veins in his temples ticking with quiet fury. "I won't do that to you. I'd rather die," he says to me. And he means it. I swear to God he means it.

Earl grabs Dean by the front of his T-shirt and starts dragging him over to me, the gun smashed against his rib cage. "Kitten wants it. She's already purring for you."

Dean stumbles as he's shoved toward me, catching himself before our faces. Our eyes unite in a powerful clutch as the palpability of this moment, the terrifying truth, eats right through our withered bones. I can feel Dean's warmth radiating into me as his hands reach out to touch me for the very first time.

He places his palms against my shoulders, squeezing gently. "I can't, Cora. Let him kill me. Please."

"Stop it." Tears brim my weary eyes, and I lean into him on instinct, craving more warmth. More contact. "I'm not letting you die. Just get it over with."

Better you than him.

I can't quite get the words out, though.

Dean lowers his hands, his fingers digging into my upper arms. He drops his head as he lets out a hard, pained breath. "Fuck…"

"Let's go, Romeo. Earl has things to do today. You've got one more minute before I get impatient and trigger-happy."

We both glance over at Earl, then back to each other. The eye contact proves too much for me, so I twist my head to the right as tears spill down my soiled cheekbones.

"Cora." Dean's tone is urgent. Quiet, but laced with heaviness. He takes my chin between rough fingers and forces my gaze on his. "Cora, look at me."

God. The tears fall faster. My lips part, and he glances down at my mouth, his Adam's apple bobbing in his throat. Then he leans in.

Oh, no.

No, no, no.

He's going to kiss me.

I turn my head to the side again, dodging his kiss. "No," I whisper in a cracked voice, my hair sticking to the tearstains. "Don't make this something it's not."

Dean sucks in a jagged breath, halting his forward movement. There is a slight nod of his head, telling me he understands, and then he reaches for one of my chained wrists. A frown settles between my eyes as confusion sets in. He massages his thumb along my pulse point, his gaze still pinned on me.

"Do you feel that?"

I swallow. The lump in my throat is dry and brittle, and it hurts on the way down. "Yes," I squeak out. The gesture is somewhat soothing, despite the circumstances.

Dean continues the circular motion, his calloused thumb grazing my wrist, almost lovingly. "Focus on that. Close your eyes and zone out. The only thing I want you to feel is my thumb massaging your wrist."

I want to cry harder. I want to cry because I'm scared and exhausted and sore and *done*. I want to cry because I can't believe this is happening—with my sister's fiancé of all people.

I want to cry because it's awful, *so awful*, but Dean is still trying to make this better for me.

I dip my chin and squeeze my eyes shut, nodding my consent. I hear Dean's sigh, and it rumbles through me like a white wave. It's followed by the sound of his belt buckle unlatching and his pants dropping to the cold cement.

A familiar, snarling voice penetrates the moment. "Yeah, that's it."

My eyelids squeeze tighter as I try to filter out everything but the feel of Dean's thumb against the sensitive underside of my wrist. His motions are soft and fluid. Constant. Whatever he is doing with his other hand—and *God*, I don't want to know—is not affecting his attention to my wrist. I inhale a rickety breath, long and slow.

"What the fuck is wrong with you?" Earl barks from across the basement. "She's a hot piece of ass. Fuck her, already."

I jolt at the shrill sound of his voice, and my eyes flutter open. I lift them to Dean's face. He's staring at me with a hollow expression. "It's okay. Just do it," I urge him, wanting to get this over with. Wanting to curl up into a ball of shame and cry myself to sleep.

Forever.

Dean's jaw ticks and his nostrils flare. "I don't think I can do this."

Earl interrupts us again. "What's the damn matter with you? You play for the other team?"

Dean whips his head to the right and shoots back, "I'm not a disgusting psychopath who gets off on assaulting women. It just doesn't do it for me."

And then there's a barrel of a gun jabbing Dean's temple, and I let out a scream.

"That's not going to help," Dean seethes, sweat pooling along his dark hairline. He's trying to play it cool, but I can see the fear in his eyes. I can smell it on his skin.

"You have three seconds to figure out what's going to help, or this bitch is gonna be wearing your brains until I get bored with her and put her bony ass in the ground."

A strangled sob escapes me and I rattle my chains, noting that Dean still has not let go of my wrist. I'm not sure what else to say, so I blurt out, "Kiss me."

He glances at me with his ice-blue eyes, troubled and bloodshot.

"Kiss me, Dean," I repeat. "Please."

It's evident our situation is not getting him "in the mood" quick enough for Earl, so maybe some forced intimacy will help. I shift my gaze to the pistol as it slowly retreats from Dean's head. I can't help the tiny sigh of relief that escapes me.

Dean's mouth parts ever so slightly, his eyes drifting to my bruised lips. He looks back up to me, as if to confirm: *Are you sure?*

I nod quickly, gulping down a fear that tastes tangible. "I want you to."

When he leans in, I inhale sharply, my eyes closing in anticipation. I release a modest gasp when our lips make contact and Dean does the same. I told him not to pretend this is something it's not, but maybe we *have* to pretend. Maybe it's the only way to get through this. I feel his tongue poke through, seeking entry, and I oblige. My body bows forward to meet him further, and I open my mouth wider, encouraging him. "Close your eyes and zone out," I breathe against his warmth, repeating his own request to me. "Focus on kissing me."

My words seem to stimulate him in some way, and Dean raises his right hand to cup my face as the other continues its lazy designs against my wrist. We each have a crux. A survival tactic. His touch, my kiss. A kiss that deepens and deepens, taking us over, disguising this moment from what it really is. My tongue is his veil—his black cloak.

But it's also his fuel. Before I know it, his hand has trailed down my cheek, gliding along my waist, my hip, my thigh, until he's gently parting my legs. I feel the tip of him settle at my entrance and everything becomes too real. I make a sound I can't even describe—a mewl, maybe. Ripped straight from the torrent of disbelief spiraling through my core.

"I'm so sorry." He pulls back from my mouth, his head falling against my shoulder as he pushes inside me. "I'm so fucking sorry."

Around, around, and around.

Left, then right. Slow and careful and kind.

Up and down.

He's tracing my vein.

Like art.

I can pretend this is something beautiful.

Dean is kissing me again, his cock filling me, pulsing in and out with hurried thrusts.

Around, around, and around.

Our tongues are battling, desperate to erase everything that's happening—everything that's happened. Just *everything*. Dean's right hand is holding up my leg and perching it over his hip. His fingers are digging into the fleshy side of my thigh, squeezing lightly as he moves in and out of me. In and out. In and out.

Around, around, and around.

I can hear the putrid monster beside us breathing heavily, groaning in pleasure at the display. At the fucking entertainment we're providing.

Around, around, and around.

I need to focus. I need to block out Earl and this basement and the smell of imminent death in the air.

Dean.

There is only Dean.

And it doesn't matter that he's inside me, forcing tiny whimpers from the back of my throat. He's here. He's alive. We're *both* alive.

We're in this together.

He's still kissing me, his tongue getting clumsier as his thrusts quicken and his body tenses. He's going to come.

Around, around, and around.

I keep my eyes closed. I don't want to see his face in this moment. I don't want to witness his pleasure. And it's not because I'm angry or blameful. I'm envious. I'm envious he's able to find a pocket of happiness, of joy, of authentic bliss, in the midst of our shared nightmare. We're in this together, yes, but for a moment—for a few blinding, potent seconds—we will be worlds apart.

Dean's hand slides up my thigh and grips my bare ass, his opposite hand still leaving whispers and apologies along my wrist.

Around, around, and around.

And then he peaks, trying to mask his groan of pleasure as he buries his face into the curve of my neck. Dean clings to me through the aftershocks, holding me like a cherished lover. But I'm not. I am merely a pawn in Earl's game. We are both pawns.

Dean inhales a deep sigh, almost choking on the weight of the breath. "I'm sorry. I'm sorry. I'm so sorry." He repeats it over and over, devastation flooding him. Remorse has replaced the euphoria, and my own envy has faded. I can feel his hot tears fall against my collarbone.

Earl reminds us of where we are and why we're here—as if we could possibly forget. "That was fucking beautiful. I came so hard I saw stars," he growls, his husky laugh making me want to vomit.

Dean is still inside me, softening, yet incapable of leaving me just yet. Maybe he's still pretending.

I don't blame him.

"Time's up, lover boy," Earl snaps.

The repugnant scent of Earl's body odor invades me, and I finally open my eyes to see him approaching us with his weapon. Dean slips out of me, but his left hand is still on my wrist, and his right has glided from my ass and landed on my hip. He's still holding me, soaking me up for as long as he can. I feel him lift his head from my shoulder, but I twist my body to the side, unable to look him in the eyes. Not yet.

Maybe not ever.

"This isn't a romantic morning after, you dumb fuck. Get the fuck over to your corner before I blow you away."

Earl's voice sears me, and I'm left empty and hollow. But nothing leaves a void more than Dean releasing my wrist and stepping away from me. His touch lingers on my skin, and I can still feel him tracing my artery, leaving more of himself behind than he'll ever know. My wrist tingles and hums in the wake of his absence.

When I finally brave a look in Dean's direction, his pants are newly secured around his waist and Earl is fastening his chains.

We have returned to our former positions.

But as sticky warmth drips down my thighs and Dean's tears mingle with the sweat on my skin, I know we are not the same.

We will never be the same again.

7

D EAN."
His name on my tongue echoes loud and grating throughout the quiet room, and yet, Dean pretends he doesn't hear me. He doesn't move or blink or flinch. He just sits there, slumped against his pole, facing as far away from me as he can.

"Dean," I repeat.

Nothing.

I sigh with my chin to my chest, my eyes closing. It's probably been an hour since...well, since it happened. He retreated back to his dark corner, then retreated into himself.

He hasn't said a word to me. He hasn't even looked at me.

"Can you please talk to me?" I try. I can't imagine spending the rest of the day removed and isolated from the only other person who understands what I'm going through.

Dean finally rolls his shoulders with a soft humming sound.

Proof of life, at least.

"I'm not mad, Dean. You did what you had to do, and I underst—"

"I can't, Cora. Please."

The sadness in his tone almost breaks me. He sounds defeated for the very first time. "Don't shut me out. I can't do this alone." I choke on the last word, and my chest burns with a longing to maintain our blossoming connection.

He's all I have.

Dean slowly shakes his head, lowering his eyes to the floor. "I can't even look at you."

I suck in a choppy breath. I can't reach him right now. He is lost to his own demons and regret and impossible decisions.

It's true that I'm not mad. Dean had a gun to his head and both of our lives were hanging in the balance. There was only one way out, and I told him to take it.

And maybe I'm going just a little bit numb.

I close my eyes and lie back, forcing myself to give him the space he needs. There will be time to talk through it—when he's ready.

All we have is time.

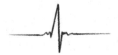

Evening has fallen and our night-light has been extinguished.

It's been hours. *Hours.*

And Dean still refuses to speak to me.

The silence becomes too much to bear, so I decide to break it as we sit alone in the dark—truly *alone.* "I was going to adopt a dog," I whisper into the shadows. I can hardly see him, but I make out a small motion, alerting me he's not asleep. "You wanted to know what I was thinking about earlier. I was thinking about the two dogs I never got to meet last Sunday. I wonder which one I would have fallen in love with."

Silence.

My words linger in the darkness, hovering between us, painfully ignored. I pull my knees up and rest my chin between them. I wiggle my toes inside Dean's gray sneakers that are far too big for my feet. But they bring me a warmth and comfort I so desperately crave, especially now.

I close my eyes and whisper, "Good night."

Dean never does respond to me that night. He doesn't sing.

I fall in and out of a restless, tumultuous sleep, missing the sound of his voice.

8

TEN YEARS EARLIER

*D*EAN, STOP THE CAR!"
  There's an injured dog in the middle of the busy, snowy intersection. She is limping, half toppling over, cowering in fright every time a car zooms past, spraying dirty sludge at her and leaving her to freeze to death.

  "Are you fuckin' crazy, Corabelle? It's a blizzard outside and we're already twenty minutes late to breakfast."

  Mandy perks up from the passenger's side, craning her head to the back seat to look at me with her perfectly lined eyebrows. "Did you forget your purse or something?" she asks me.

  I shake my head, unbuckling my seatbelt and leaning forward, pointing my finger between them. "There's a dog. She's hurt."

  "We can't stop, Sis," Mandy insists, her eyes landing on the pup. "It's too dangerous. Plus, Grandma is probably going into cardiac arrest worrying about why we're late."

  "We can call animal control when we get to the restaurant," Dean agrees.

  Mandy nods and holds up her BlackBerry. "I can even call right now if it'll make you feel better."

  "Are you serious? The poor thing was probably hit by a car. She's going to get hit again!" I argue, my chest pounding with fear. "Stop the car, Dean."

"There's no place to pull over…"

"Fine. I'll get out here." I reach for the door handle like a rebellious idiot, drunk on adrenaline and the need to save this animal.

"Christ, hold on." Dean pulls off to the side of the busy road as the windshield wipers squeak, gathering more and more thick flurries with each hurried swipe.

The car is barely in park when I kick open the back door and tug my hat over my ears, wincing when the icy wind takes my breath away. A car swerves past me and I jump back, wondering if this was a stupid idea after all. I stomp my way through the six inches of heavy snow and pause at the edge of the street, looking both ways. It's rush hour, so there's a steady stream of traffic. The snowflakes are falling down hard, illuminated by the sea of headlights and making me feel dizzy. I decide to make a break for it, thinking I'm probably faster than the cars coming up the hill. I dash out into the highway, my heart in my throat and my blood pumping fast and hot. I almost slip on a patch of ice, but I make it to the median strip in one piece, ignoring the blaring horns and bending over to collect my breath when I reach safety.

The dog is lying flat on her stomach, her wet, shivering body pressed up against the curb.

"Hey, there. I'm here to help. I won't hurt you." I pluck the mittens off my hands and tuck them into my coat pockets. Then I hold my fingers out, slow and tender, watching as the cream-colored dog moves in gingerly to sniff me. *"That's it. You're going to be safe and warm very soon."*

As I inch forward to get a grip on the dog's scruff, I'm startled by a new presence.

"You're a goddamn moron. What the hell is wrong with you?"

I jerk my head to the right to find Dean storming toward me in the snow with a furious look on his face. He pulls his hood up over his head as I glare at him. *"Besides you?"*

"Hilarious, Corabelle," he grumbles. *"You're going to get yourself killed."*

"I guess it's your lucky day, then."

"Will you stop?"

We both look at the dog, who is now trying to stand and escape, likely terrified of Dean and his brutish demeanor. *"You're going to scare her away,"* I scold him. *"I'm handling this."*

Dean huffs under his breath, and it looks like a plume of smoke as it hits the chilly

Midwest air. "How were you planning on getting her back to the car? You barely made it over here without becoming roadkill. And the animal is at least fifty pounds."

Well.

I hadn't really thought that far ahead.

"Just leave me alone. I'll figure it out." I glance across the two-lane street to see Mandy watching us from the car with wide eyes. "I'm sure my sister is losing her shit without you being within arm's reach."

"She'll survive. But you're questionable," Dean replies, his voice growing louder over the howling wind and passing engines.

"You're questionable," I shoot back, and it might just be my lamest comeback yet. I blame the cold. I inch my way closer to the canine, which looks to be some kind of golden retriever mix, and coo out more sweet nothings to try to earn this dog's trust in the middle of a blizzard during Monday morning rush hour.

"I'll get her," Dean intercedes, pushing past me and barreling toward the frightened animal with zero grace and finesse.

"Dean!"

"Come here, buddy!"

He advances on the dog and she bolts.

She straight up books it across the opposite two lanes and almost causes a four-car pileup.

Panic and anger flare as I stare at Dean, slack-jawed. "Look what you just did! I said I would handle it!"

"Ah, hell," he mutters under his breath. Before I can curse him out further, Dean flees across the highway when there's a small break in traffic, chasing the dog down a snowy ravine. I stand there on the median strip with nerves bubbling in my gut, unable to see Dean or the dog. Cars are slowing down to gawk at me—the shivering teenager standing in the middle of an intersection covered in snow. I tap my foot against the slushy cement, slipping my mittens back on to warm my frozen fingers. I watch and wait, anxiety swelling, my chest tightening.

And then I see them. Dean is trudging up the steep ravine, carrying the fifty-pound animal in his arms. My sigh of relief hits the air and my body relaxes—that is, until Dean makes a daring sprint across the highway, not noticing a car speeding right at him with its lights off.

"Dean!" I scream, catching his attention just in time, as the car nearly clips him.

I watch him close his eyes and breathe in deeply, likely taking a moment to process his near-death experience. Then he finishes the trek across the road without injury, pausing on the median to shoot me his trademark scowl.

He's out of breath and his cheeks are stained pink with windburn. "I really hate you, Corabelle."

I can't keep the smile from sneaking across my face. "Hate you more."

We make a safe escape to the car, and Dean lets the dog hop into the back seat with me. I situate myself, trying to warm up, and grin wide when she nuzzles right into my lap like it's going to be her favorite place in the world. The dog releases a long sigh, her chin resting on my thigh. Safe at last.

"I'm naming you Blizzard," I announce to the fluffy dog with matted fur and a sprained paw. "Mom and Dad better let me keep you."

As Dean puts the car in drive and veers back onto the main drag, I catch him glancing at me in the rearview mirror. I swear there is an unfamiliar softness in his light eyes—something akin to tenderness. Something I haven't seen before.

But it disappears as quickly as it came, and the devious twinkle returns.

I stick my tongue out at him.

He flips me off.

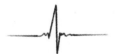

Day eight greets us with warm, tangerine sunbeams—a stark contrast to the murky, muddy feeling of despair living inside my heart.

Eight days.

It feels like longer. It feels like a lifetime.

I wonder when I'll lose track of the days altogether and everything will blur into one prolonged, endless nightmare.

I look over at Dean, and I'm surprised to find him facing me again. He looks worn and run-down. His cheeks are gaunt, his eyes rimmed with dark circles. His skin has turned from a healthy golden bronze to a chalky shade of white. His appearance has shifted dramatically in only twenty-four hours.

But his eyes are still the bluest blue, and they are fixed on mine.

I'm about to tell him "good morning," ask him how he slept, make idle conversation, but Dean speaks up first.

"You would have gotten them both," he says.

His voice sounds frayed as I blink at him, processing his words. They take longer than usual to sink in, and I'm not sure if it's because I'm so exhausted or because part of me doubted that Dean would ever speak to me again. I swallow, my throat cinching.

"You would have adopted both dogs because your heart is too big for only one."

I thought I was too beaten down and dehydrated to make any more tears, but I surprise myself when my eyes start to mist. I keep my watery gaze on Dean, afraid to break this contact, afraid he'll withdraw and leave me all alone again. I offer a small smile. Then I reply, my voice equally raspy, "I didn't think you ever noticed my heart."

It's a heavy declaration, and I hate that it's true.

Dean's weary face grows even wearier as he absorbs my words. "It's impossible not to notice, Cora."

I finally lower my eyes and draw my knees back up to my chin. I don't hear the dripping pipe anymore and idly wonder if it's so cold outside that the pipes have frozen. A cold front was supposed to come through last week.

I lift my gaze back to Dean when the silence becomes too painful. He's still staring at me. Still expressionless. "What are we?" I wonder aloud. I was not expecting those words to come out, but they have been plaguing me for days. Dean has always fit into a very specific box in my life. Dean, the asshole. Dean, my sister's dumb boyfriend. Dean, my mortal enemy.

But...

"You don't feel like my enemy anymore," I finish.

You feel like my lifeline.

I watch a small frown crease his eyebrows as he studies me. Seconds tick by and turn into minutes. Our gazes drift and collide. Drift and collide.

He is thinking. Probably wondering the same thing.

"I don't know," Dean finally replies, a certain kind of sadness lacing every word. "But I think you were right... We'll never be friends."

9

FIVE YEARS EARLIER

W*HERE DID YOU LEARN HOW to do this? Never mind…I don't want to know."
Dean is picking the padlock of an old, abandoned house with some kind of small object—maybe a bobby pin. Maybe a piece of his devil horn.*

Brandon tightens his arm around my waist, warming me up with his body heat. It's only mid-October, but the air is unbearably brisk, giving our haunted house adventure the perfect spooky ambiance.

Mandy is huddled next to Dean, watching him work the lock. She bounces her knees up and down while hugging herself with both arms. "Hurry up, babe. Someone is going to see us," she says in a harsh whisper. "Plus, I'm freezing my ass off."

"Why didn't you wear pants?" Dean asks. "It's thirty-five degrees out."

"They didn't go with my dress. Obviously."

Leave it to my sister to dress up for a very illegal sleepover in a run-down, three-story Victorian. I shake my head with an exaggerated eye roll. "Who are you trying to impress, Sis? The ghost of Mr. Garrison?"

"Ha ha," she barks back. "Unlike some people, I enjoy looking my best no matter the occasion."

Mandy bestows a pointed once-over on my faded blue jeans, baggy hoodie, and scuffed boots. I give my messy bun a quick tug, ignoring the insinuation that my appearance is not up to society's standards.

Breaking and entering was not exactly on my to-do list for the day—or any day ever for that matter. But Mandy talked me into it. The foreclosed Garrison home is the subject of many twisted tales and sordid rumors in our small town, especially this time of year. Besides, Brandon sounded overly enthusiastic about the prospect of spending the night in the creepy house, and I didn't want him to think I was a coward.

I am, of course. I'm practically pissing myself with fear right now.

My eyes zone in on Dean's break-in attempt as I tap the toe of my boot with impatience. "I thought you said this would be easy," I mutter. "You're a terrible criminal."

"Almost got it."

Click.

The lock slips loose and Dean shoots me a victorious wink. "You were saying?"

I crinkle my nose and shuffle past him. Brandon guides me forward with his hand on the small of my back.

"This is wicked," he declares, shining the flashlight on his phone into the darkened entryway. He leans down and kisses the space between my neck and shoulder. "Scared, baby?"

I shiver.

From the kiss—not from the mental image of fifty-thousand spiders scattering into hiding, waiting for us to fall asleep so they can crawl into our eardrums and build villages.

"I'm not scared. Just cold," I lie.

I suck at lying, so Brandon spins me around and pulls me in for a quick kiss. "It's okay to be scared. That's why it's fun."

Dean sneaks up beside us, waggling his stupid eyebrows. "Yeah, it's fun, Corabelle. You've read about fun in your books, right?"

"Wait. You know what books are?"

Mandy swats me on the arm, swaying her bleached-blond hair from side to side. "I was worried about the demonic spirits living in the walls taking us out, but I'm pretty sure you and Dean will end up killing each other first."

I shrug.

She's probably right.

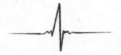

Something tickles the back of my neck, and I'm pretty sure it's a wolf spider or that demon from Paranormal Activity *breathing on me.*

I swat at my neck, then swing my head back and forth as goose bumps cover me from head to toe. Yuck. When I glance down to finish unrolling my sleeping bag, I see three huge, hairy spiders pop out of the cotton material, ready to suck my soul.

I scream.

Loud.

Then I feel another tickle on my neck and I jump to my feet, stomping my legs, shaking my arms, my hair, my clothes. I kick the sleeping bag with a shaky foot and back away, ramming right into a hard body. I scream again.

Familiar laughter assaults my ears.

I fly around and spot the feather in his hand, then immediately begin pummeling his chest with furious fists. "You asshole!" I shout, my heart jack-knifing beneath my hoodie. "I hate you!"

Dean grabs my wrists, putting a quick end to my attack. "Yeah, yeah, yeah. Hate you more."

My chest is still heaving as I narrow my eyes at him. "No, you don't. There's no possible way you could hate me more than I hate you." I yank my arms free.

He doesn't respond to that. He knows I'm right.

Dean's smile is broad and devilish. "You didn't like the spiders?"

I twist my head around to look at the hideous fiends, only to realize they are, indeed, fake.

Jerk, jerk, jerk.

I turn back to glare at him, and he throws his hands up. "You make it too easy for me, Corabelle."

I don't spare him another glance as I storm away to join Brandon in exploring the second floor. I'll get him back later.

That's a promise.

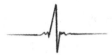

"*Want one, Corabelle?*"

I'm sitting in front of a plethora of candles, trying to stay warm with whiskey and fleece blankets. Mandy is in the bathroom fluffing her hair or something, and Brandon is playing on his new HTC phone in the other room.

"*Don't call me that.*" *I look over at Dean, who has appeared on my left as he holds out a box of powdered doughnuts.*

I love powdered doughnuts.

My eyes narrow in his direction, but his face remains stoic and unreadable. There is no mischief or nefarious intent gleaming out of those blue eyes. I remove one of my arms from the red-and-black-checkered blanket and pluck a doughnut from the box.

I take a bite, then instantly spit it out when I inhale a mouthful of cornstarch.

This motherfucker.

Dean busts out laughing, and I'm about to shout obscenities at him, maybe start punching him again, but an idea pops into my head and I act quickly.

I wrap my hands around my neck and start coughing, my eyes watering, my entire body shaking. "*I—I'm allergic…to cornstarch…*" *I sputter, clawing at my throat and wheezing, doubling over with impressive realism.*

Dean's face goes white as he kneels down beside me and starts patting my back. "*Shit, Cora. I didn't know. Are you okay?*"

I shake my head, violently gasping for air. "*I…can't…breathe…*"

"*Fuck…shit!*" *he yells, shaking my shoulders, his eyes popping with terror.*

I fall backwards onto my sleeping bag, my fingers still curled around my neck as I pretend to give up the fight. My eyelids flutter closed and my head drops to one side, my body going limp.

Don't laugh. Don't laugh.

"*Holy shit…Cora!*" *He keeps shaking me.* "*Cora!*"

I wish I could see the look on his face right now.

"*Mandy!*" *he shouts, and I hear multiple footsteps stomping into the room, joining us.*

Dean cradles my face in his hands, lifting my head upright as his thumbs caress my cold cheeks. The gesture is strange and gentle, and it unnerves me as I lie there holding my breath.

"She just passed out, Mandy. I fucked up. Jesus Christ," he stammers. "Cora!"

"What the hell happened?" I hear Brandon say as he approaches.

Mandy starts to panic, and I picture her flapping her arms like a bird in the way that she does when she's freaking the hell out. "Did you kill my sister?" she demands of Dean.

"I didn't know she was allergic to cornstarch!"

All of a sudden, a hot mouth descends upon mine, and it's not Brandon's. I've memorized the feel of Brandon's lips, chapped and rough with a thin upper lip.

No, these are full and soft and taste like mint and bourbon.

Dean is giving me CPR.

As much as I'm relishing my prank, I have to draw the line at Dean Asher's mouth on mine, no matter how entertaining this is. Besides, Brandon and Mandy are involved now, and it's not fair to them.

I open my eyes.

Dean starts pressing against my chest, puffing bursts of air into my mouth, his forehead glistening with perspiration. My parted lips turn up into a smile against his and he notices, pulling back to look at me.

My grin widens and I start laughing uncontrollably. "Gotcha."

Dean leaps off of me, rising to his feet and scrubbing his face with both palms. He runs his fingers through his hair as he stares down at me while I roll onto my side, drowning in my own amusement.

"Are you fuckin' serious?"

I can't stop laughing.

"I thought you were dead!"

A few snorts break through and I can't catch my breath. I worry that I might actually pass out. For real this time.

Mandy speaks up, crossing her arms over her ample chest. "Not cool, Sis."

"Yeah, babe, you scared us." Brandon is crouched down beside me, his hand on my shoulder.

I allow my laughter to subside as I lift myself up on my hands, my eyes finding a highly unimpressed Dean. "I got you good, and you deserved every minute of it. Your face was priceless."

Dean stares back at me, spearing me with callous eyes, his shoulders heaving. It's apparent he is not sharing in my hilarity. In fact, I've never seen him look at me like this before—frazzled, outraged, maybe even a little hurt.

Whatever.

I'm not sorry.

"I need a fucking smoke," Dean says in a gruff tone, fishing through his pockets and pulling out a pack of cigarettes. He shoots me a final dirty look before disappearing into one of the adjoining rooms, the old floorboards creaking beneath each step.

The evening proceeds with far less excitement as I snuggle into Brandon's chest and sip on a cocktail. We tell ghost stories around the candle arrangements, munch on popcorn and chocolate chip cookies, and allow our minds to play tricks on us as we giggle and squeal at every strange, spooky noise.

It's a fun night. A memorable night.

But something is off.

It could be the uncomfortable sleeping arrangements. It could be the chill in the air. It could be the tummy ache from all the junk food I've consumed. It could be the spiders lurking in the shadows, waiting to breed inside our brains.

Or…it could be that Dean doesn't say a single word to me for the rest of the night.

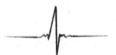

Over a week drags by in this house of horrors.

Sixteen sunrises mock us from the frosty window.

Twenty questions. Turkey sandwiches. Earl. Hunger pains. Heart pains. Singing. Stories. Despair. Sex with Dean.

Sex with Dean.

That is something I'll likely never wrap my head around. It's happened four times now. *I've had sex with Dean Asher four times.* And it's not rape—I will never call it rape. Every time, he waits for my consent. Every time, he is willing to die in that moment if I choose to say no.

And every time, he dies just a little bit anyway.

My body is not my body anymore. Earl treats me like a piece of trash, tainted and disposable, but Dean massages my wrist to help me cope, whispers his shame into my ear, and spills his tears against my neck before being dragged away and chained back up.

Dean is holding my wrist between his fingers and thumb, circling around and around and around as he thrusts in and out of me. He doesn't look at me. In fact, he hardly looks me in the eyes at all anymore. I think he's afraid of what he might find there.

"That's a good dog," Earl sneers from a few feet away, giving orders in between his disgusting moans. "Kitten loves it."

I suck in a breath and keep my head turned to the other side. Dean pulls back, dropping my leg and raising his hand to the side of my face. I fall to my feet due to our height difference, and he slips out of me. He could hold me up with his opposite hand, but he doesn't. He won't let go of my wrist.

His touch is delicate and kind on my cheek, and my skin sprouts with goose bumps that I hope he doesn't notice. "Are you okay?"

Earl interrupts. "I didn't say to stop railing her, you dumbass dog."

I spare Dean a quick glance, nodding and swallowing down the real answer: *I'm not okay. I will never be okay.*

Dean sighs, blinking slowly. He's unconvinced, but also aware that there's nothing he can do about it. He lifts me back up with reluctance and situates himself inside me once again, and I release a small gasp when he fills me. There is a strange, disturbing sense of relief at the feel of him between my legs. Maybe it's a twisted case of Stockholm syndrome. Maybe I've gone mad. Or maybe Dean is warm and safe and familiar, and that's all I have to cling to.

I'll take what I can get.

When he finishes, Dean pulls out of me and buries his face against the curve of my neck like he always does. "I'm sorry. I'm so sorry, Cora." His breath tickles my ear and his tears dampen my skin. "Please forgive me."

I do. I always do.

Dean is shoved back into his corner and shackled like an actual dog. This is normally when Earl leaves for work, but he pauses as he turns around, pinning his dark eyes on me. I shudder.

"My turn, kitten."

What?

No. Please, no.

"No…" I inch back, wishing I could disappear into the pole.

Earl lunges forward and backhands me, forcing a cry from my lips.

"Hey!" Dean shakes his chains, anger radiating from him in waves.

"I take what I want when I want it, you stupid bitch. Understand?" Earl hisses.

I nod, tears leaking from my eyes, my jaw throbbing.

Earl rips off his belt…and as it slides roughly through the loops, I notice a tiny piece of the latch fly loose. It's so small, it hardly makes a sound as it lands by Dean's foot—but Dean notices. I try not to make a scene or give us away, but my eyes widen as they lock on Dean, and I watch as he hides the metal clasp beneath his sock.

I don't know what it means or what its purpose may be, but it's something. It's all we have.

10

D O YOU MISS HER?"

The sun pokes through the window on the eighteenth day, teasing us. We are facing each other from our respective corners, our legs sprawled out in front of us, our toes *almost* able to touch. Dean is slouched back against his pipe, his eyes fixated just over my shoulder.

"Who?" he wonders absently.

He knows who, but I answer anyway. "My sister."

Dean blinks, slow and lazy. There is a far-off look on his face as a wave of silence passes between us, and I wonder if he's going through memories in his mind like a film reel. He finally nods his head one time, just as slow. "We were supposed to get married in two weeks. Mandy wanted a winter wedding with velvet shawls, a horse-drawn sleigh, and white Christmas lights."

A nostalgic smile breaks through as I reminisce wedding planning together with Mandy. We had ruby-red bridesmaid dresses with snow-white shawls. It was magical.

It would have been magical.

I glance at Dean, silently begging him to look at me. To *see* me.

To assure me I'm still real.

"She was really excited to marry you," I say, my voice a small whisper.

Amanda Asher.

My last memory of Mandy was her practicing her future signature on the bar tab that fateful night.

I watch Dean's jaw clench in reaction to my words, his eyes closing as he accepts the fact that he might never marry Mandy. He might never get married at all. He might never have children or watch another football game or eat a medium-rare steak or pet a dog or sleep in a goddamn bed with an alarm clock waking him up to tell him, "*Good morning. It's early as shit and you have to spend ten hours at work today doing hard labor, but at least you get to breathe in the fresh air and feel the sunshine on your skin.*"

Dean's head falls back against the pole, his eyes still closed. But when he opens them, he finally finds my face. My sad, jade eyes. My pasty skin and matted hair. He *sees* me, and it feels like a tiny miracle.

I'm real. *We're* real.

"We're getting out of here today."

As soon as he says the words that make my heart skip a dozen beats, Earl's boots are clunking down the wooden steps.

"Rise and shine, pets. Ready for a new day?" Earl exclaims, his face beaming with evil joy.

He paces over to Dean, the sound of his steel-toed boots against the cement always so loud and antagonistic. Earl unlocks the cuffs, then steps away with the gun pointed directly at Dean's skull.

But instead of walking toward me like he usually does, Dean remains where he stands. He is completely still, his expression blank, as he stares Earl down with a scathing glare. "You're a fat, fucking bastard," he says, his tone low and leveled.

Earl stands stock-still while I watch the scene in terrified silence, my fingers curling around my pole and gripping tight.

Then Earl slugs Dean across the jaw with his fist.

I flinch, crying out in protest, yanking at my chains to draw Earl's attention back to me. When Dean slowly pulls himself up from his knees, his fist is closed tight, hiding a small treasure.

Earl presses the barrel of the gun against his back and shoves him toward me. "Don't fuck with me, kid. Next time it's a bullet in your face instead of my fist," Earl warns. "You're on borrowed time."

My breathing is ragged and quick as Dean approaches me, face-to-face, blue eyes on green. My gaze drifts to his busted lip, already swelling and smeared with blood. I inhale, almost choking when the breath reaches the back of my throat. Then Dean leans in. He presses those full lips to mine, and I immediately taste the metallic, coppery blood on my tongue, mixed with sweat and a trace of mint from the toothpaste. I part my mouth, allowing his tongue to slip inside, and he breathes in deeply, *so deeply*, as if he's sucking up my life force for survival.

As he continues to kiss me, I feel him reach his arm around my body, finding my cuffed wrists. But instead of placing his thumb against my pulse point like he usually does, he pauses. His mouth breaks away from mine, and Dean grazes his lips against my right cheek until they are pressed up to my ear. The tickle of his hot breath makes me shiver.

Then he whispers in a scratchy voice, "Don't let go of your cuffs. Don't let them fall."

Another breath gets caught in my throat as I instinctively curl my fingers around the metal, gripping as tight as I can. Dean takes a moment to unbuckle himself and push his jeans down to his ankles, then lifts me up with both hands.

"Wrap your legs around me," he orders.

I ignore the tingly sensation those words cause and do as he says, holding myself up so Dean can try to unlock my cuffs with the belt clasp. It feels like an impossible feat, but *my God*, I've never wished for anything more.

Dean enters me, averting his eyes like always, unable to witness my reaction to what he considers a horrifying violation. I should agree, I really should, but my guess is that my eyes tell a different tale.

It's better that he doesn't look.

When we get into a comfortable rhythm, Dean finds my wrists again, pressing his chin into the curve of my right shoulder and hiding his face from Earl. From the other side of the room, it probably appears that he's really into this— when really, he's trying to set me free. I don't miss him massaging my wrist today because I'm too distracted by the notion of escaping and finally getting out of this prison.

Please work. Please, please work.

I count the seconds in my head, trying to keep my face focused and unreadable. It feels like more time is going by than usual and a stir of panic rumbles in my belly. I attempt to keep my breaths even, my eyes closed. I wait and wait and wait.

And then Dean pulls his lips back to my ear and says softly, "I need you to moan, Corabelle."

Moan?

I swallow with uncertainty.

"Please," he whispers, the plea muffled against my ear and creating more goose bumps.

I nod and conjure up my most convincing moan, masking the sound of the cuffs releasing behind me, hiding the evidence of our monumental win.

Holy shit, he did it. Dean did it.

I clutch the metal in my hands for dear life, making sure they don't hit the ground and give us away. Dean takes a moment to focus on his "task" and finishes inside me a minute later. He doesn't say he's sorry this time. He doesn't cry or beg for my forgiveness.

He pulls back and winks.

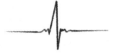

We wait for what feels like an eternity, which in reality is probably less than an hour. We wait until we're confident Earl has gone to work.

Earl has a routine. He works Monday through Friday, leaving in the morning and returning shortly after sunset. Today is Thursday, so he should be well on his way to work by now, giving us less than eight hours to get the fuck out of here.

My heart is about to burst inside my chest with anticipation and anxiety. There is a lot riding on this—there is *everything* riding on this. I have no idea how to get Dean out of his chains, so it's going to take a while to figure it out. I've never picked a lock before in my life, let alone professional-grade handcuffs.

"He's gotta be gone by now," Dean says to my right, prompting the nerves in my belly to do the mambo. "You ready?"

I let out a hard breath. "I'm ready." I finally let go of the metal and feel the cuffs slip from my wrists. It doesn't seem real at first, so I just sit there, forgetting I can move. I can walk. I can do a freakin' happy dance if I want to. I pull myself up to unsteady feet, pinning my gaze on Dean.

Then I run to him.

He's standing in front of me, his eyes wide and expectant, his chest heaving with fretful breaths. I catapult myself right to him, slinging my arms around his neck and touching him for the first time in weeks. Touching *anyone*. My hands are my own. My body is mine.

I skim my fingers through his hair, tugging gently, reveling in the feel of the soft strands. Dean doesn't tell me to hurry up and get moving. No, he gives me this moment. He lets me run my palms down his neck, over his shoulder blades, then back up and around to his chest. I plant them there for a few moments, taking in the hurried beats of his heart.

He feels warm and safe and alive.

This is really happening.

I lift my eyes to his, overcome with emotion. A similar sentiment is staring back at me, and it almost stops my breath.

I find my bearings and pull my hands away from Dean's chest, taking a small step backwards. "I don't know how to get you out of those," I tell him.

"I know. I'll walk you through it. I dropped the pin behind your pole—bring it over here and I'll tell you what to do."

I nod, making my way back to my corner of nightmares and sliding the front of my hands over the dusty floor, my eyes casing every inch as I search for the little gold pin. When I spot it, I pick it up, pinching it between my fingers, and I dart back over to Dean to await instruction.

I settle behind him as he returns to a sitting position and take his hands in mine. He starts walking me through the steps, but my mind feels foggy and unfocused, and my hands are trembling, so I keep dropping the clasp. He mentions single locks and double locks and stopping points. Clockwise, counterclockwise, springs and bars.

It's so much. It's too much.

"I–I can't get it, Dean." I feel myself panicking, the metal shaking in my inept hands. "I suck at this. I'm so sorry."

"Hey, hey. It's not easy to do. You're doing great."

I keep going, cursing under my breath as sweat lines my brow. At least thirty minutes drag by, causing my anxiety to swirl and spin. I fall back onto my butt with a cry of defeat, swiping my damp forehead with the back of my hand. "I can't do it."

Dean is silent for a moment as I watch the way his shoulders sag slightly. He must be so disappointed in me.

"It's okay, Cora. Don't worry about it," he tells me, trying to find me over his shoulder. I scoot forward so we can see each other. "Just get out of here and bring back help."

I gape at him. "And leave you here alone? I—I don't even know where we are. What if I get lost? What if I can't find help and he discovers I've escaped?" I ramble, out of breath. "He'll kill you!"

"I'll be fine," Dean says. "Just get the hell out of here. Find a main road and have someone call the police."

"What if—"

"Go, Cora. Please."

Our eyes stay locked as his words trickle in and stick to every piece of me. I gulp down my fear and worries and self-doubt, nodding with concession. "Okay." I climb to my feet, Dean following suit. My knees are weak and shaky as I lean in for one more hug, memorizing the scent of his skin. "I'm getting you out of here," I whisper against his neck.

We hold eye contact for just a moment longer, then I turn away and jog over to the staircase.

"Cora."

I pause at the sound of his voice, spinning around to face him from across the room. "Yes?"

Dean pulls his lips between his teeth, mulling over whatever he's going to say. I watch his throat bob as he swallows, his grown-out hair sticking to his forehead. "I know I said you can go back to hating me when we get out of here," he says in an angst-ridden voice. "But I really hope you don't."

A solemn silence hangs between us, thick and palpable.

I blink.

Then I smile and reply, "But it's fun."

Dean's mouth tips up into his own smile, taking in the words I've adamantly denied for so long. I cling to that smile, using it as fuel as I make my way up the wooden steps, hoping and praying the basement door is unlocked. If it's not, I guess I'll be squeezing myself through that tiny window that has taunted me for the past two-and-a-half weeks. I bite my lip, reaching out a tentative hand toward the doorknob.

It twists. The door squeaks open.

There is a God. There is a freakin' God.

I blow out a slow breath, my body relaxing just a bit. I've made it out of the basement. Out of the dungeon. Out of *hell.*

Now…to feel the crisp November air against my skin. I want to swallow it down and let it cleanse me, washing it all away. Every rape and sleepless night. Every stab of hunger and insatiable thirst. Every teardrop, every nightmare, every hollow thought.

I take cautious steps down the narrow hallway, passing the small bathroom on the left and heading toward the main living room. The house reeks of mold and urine. There are a few crooked pictures lining the walls, showing me that this monster isn't an *actual* monster. He's human. He has a life. A family. They have no idea what he has become.

I keep walking, noting a 1970s kitchen on the right and a musty living room on the left. There is an oak door off the living area. An escape.

But before I make my exit, a calendar catches my eye. It's pinned to the wall in front of me with a red thumbtack. There are large X's in black Sharpie across the dates starting from November 8 and ending yesterday, November 25. There is a scribble next to the number eight that reads: *New Pets.* A shiver crawls up my spine as my feet make their way toward the calendar. It's surreal to think that almost the entire month has been wasted in captivity.

I flip through the preceding months, my curiosity getting the better of me. Nine days prior to the eighth are blank—the last X is etched onto the square of October 29. My stomach coils with dread at the realization that another couple likely died that day. I count the previous X's: *there are twenty-two.* The couple before us survived twenty-two days in that basement.

Our time was almost up.

A strangled sound escapes me as I bring a hand to my mouth, holding back my queasiness. My insides feel sick, and I want to puke. And cry. And scream.

But I don't. I'm almost there. I'm almost *out.*

On instinct, I snatch up a few envelopes lying in a stack of mail on the kitchen table.

They are addressed to *Earl Hubbard.* His address is listed.

Perfect.

I spin around, uncaring that I'm only wearing Dean's too-big shoes and a T-shirt that barely touches midthigh. All I care about is finding help for Dean. All I care about is ending this nightmare and putting Earl behind bars for the rest of his life.

I run to the front door and whip it open. The cool air assaults me, and it's much colder than I anticipated. Probably freezing. I look around, realizing we're tucked away on some kind of farm, far, far away from civilization. The acreage stretches farther than my eyes can see. Part of me wonders how long I'll even last out here before succumbing to hypothermia.

No.

Dean is counting on me. His life depends on me.

I can do this.

I dart out the door and start running straight ahead, hoping there is some kind of road or town behind the line of trees. The icy leaves crunch beneath my feet as the cold wind already begins to freeze my limbs.

But my escape is cut short when I feel a hand wrap around my mouth, while a thick arm encircles my waist, pulling me back. The envelopes fall from my grip.

No, no, no.

Earl snarls against my ear as I kick my legs and scream into his filthy palm. "Nice try, kitten. You're going to pay for this."

"*No!*" I scream and scream and scream, my efforts muffled by Earl's hand. As he hauls me back toward the house, I notice a charcoal grill off to the side with a turkey sitting atop the grates. I blink, struck by a cruel twist of fate.

It's Thanksgiving.

It's a national holiday.

We blew our escape attempt on the one day he didn't have to work.

Tears rim my eyes as I fight with everything I have left. When Earl pulls me through the threshold and into the living room, I spot a landline phone on the far wall.

Oh my God.

Why didn't I think to look for a phone? I'm so used to my cell phone. No one has landlines anymore. But if I'd paid attention, I could have called the cops and waited for rescue, avoiding this utter disaster of an escape attempt. Soon, we'll be back at square one.

Soon, we'll be dead.

As he yanks me forward toward the hallway, I swing my head back and forth until I'm able to open my mouth. I take the small window of time to chomp down on his hand, drawing blood. Earl howls in pain and releases me on instinct, giving me an opportunity to race toward the phone.

I reach it.

I pick it up and start to dial with quivering fingers.

9–1-

"You fuckin' bitch." Earl smacks the phone out of my hand before I get the last number in, then clubs me over the head with some kind of metal pipe. I drop to the kitchen floor in a daze and he begins kicking me in the ribs. I scream in pain, in fear, in hopelessness. I can hear Dean yelling for me from down below as I lie across the stained yellow tiles, curling my body into itself while Earl's steel toe breaks my ribs.

When I feel myself on the verge of passing out, Earl grabs a handful of my hair and drags me down the hallway. I twist and resist, digging my fingernails into his arm, but it's no use. He opens the basement door and throws me down the flight of steps.

I hear Dean shout my name right before my skull hits the cement and everything goes black.

11

I THINK THE WAVES ARE WHISPERING my name.

Maybe they are singing to me and my name is the ocean's favorite song.

"*Cora.*"

It sounds so beautiful coming from the mouth of the magnificent sea. Every letter is a perfect note. Every syllable is a melody, harmonious and pure.

But as the water kisses my toes, a howling wind blows through and plucks my name right from the ocean floor. The song turns hard and loud, like a bass drum pounding in my ears, stomping on my ribs, and squeezing my head until I cry out. It hurts...*it hurts*.

It's not supposed to hurt.

"Cora."

I open my eyes with slow, painful blinks as my surroundings begin to take shape. My reality.

The evidence of my failure.

I start to cry instantly, my cheek pressed against the gritty cement, my hands locked behind me in a position that is all too familiar. I sob, hysterical and weak, realizing my eyes are unable to produce tears.

I can't even fucking cry.

"Cora...fuck, Cora, I thought you were dead," Dean says, his voice threaded with impetuous relief. "Talk to me, Corabelle. Tell me you're okay."

I continue to wail, shake, and moan, my body racked with hopeless defeat and more pain than I can even process. "I failed. I failed you. I'm so sorry," I choke out through tearless sobs, drawing my knees up to my aching chest. I'm not sure what's more broken—my ribs or my heart. "I'm so sorry, Dean. I just want to die."

"Don't you dare say that," he tells me in a desperate plea. "It's not your fault. It's not over. Please don't give up, Corabelle. I need you."

I can't bear to look at him. He's living proof of my fatal fuckup.

"Remember the day Blizzard got hit by a car? Remember what I said to you?" Dean continues.

I sniffle, my chin to my knees, as I lie sideways on the ground. "You said if she dies, I can always get another dog."

"Not that part." Dean's sigh travels over to me and I hear him adjust his chains. "I told you her heart was still beating. As long as it was beating, she was okay."

I do remember that.

It was four years ago. I had stopped by my parents' house on my lunch break to take Blizzard for a walk. Somehow, her collar broke loose and she darted out into the street chasing a squirrel. The guilt I felt almost destroyed me. I was certain she would die and it would have been all my fault.

But Dean was the first person to arrive at the animal hospital. I figured it was because he'd always had a soft spot for the fluffy, ivory dog he'd carried to safety in a snowstorm all those years ago, but I remember him being unusually kind that day. He sat with me until my sister and parents showed up, trying to calm me down. He even rubbed my back, shushing away the tears. The foreignness of his disposition was enough to distract me from the grief, and his words always stuck with me: "You just need to stay in the moment," Dean told me in an unfamiliar, soothing voice. "Her heart is still beating...as long as it's beating, she's okay. Just take it one second at a time, Corabelle. Blizzard is okay and there is no reality where she's not okay."

Blizzard survived and Dean returned to his usual obnoxious self the following day. We slipped right back into our familiar banter and old, combative routine. Compassionate Dean was a distant memory, quickly forgotten, and I figured he was only being nice because Mandy had been giving him extra shit that week for almost sabotaging my teaching interview by wrapping my car in plastic.

I swallow down my spastic breaths, trying to apply his comforting words to our current situation. It's not over yet. We're both still alive, and as long as we're alive, there is hope.

I need to be present—stay in the moment.

It's not over.

I force myself into a sitting position, wincing through clenched teeth as the pain engulfs me. I'm certain I have cracked ribs, along with a concussion.

But I'm not dead. I'm still okay.

I finally glance at Dean, breathing heavily as I try to block out the burning discomfort sailing through my shipwrecked body. I don't speak, but I notice his eyes soften as I stare at him...*renewed hope*. I don't need to say anything for him to know. I got up. I pulled myself together.

We're going to fight until our last breath.

12

DAY TWENTY IS UPON US and our time is running out.

Earl didn't feed us or give us water the previous day. All he did was allow us to use the bathroom, brush our teeth, and then I was subjected to a beating with his leather belt, amplifying my already broken body.

It was a punishment for my "misbehavior."

I sucked up giant handfuls of water as I brushed my teeth over the sink, so I won't be dying from dehydration just yet, but I feel my body getting weaker every minute.

I keep thinking about how the couple before us only made it twenty-two days, and I wonder if that's the deadly number. Then I force myself to push those unproductive thoughts away because it's not day twenty-two. It's day twenty.

We're okay.

Dean and I are in the middle of discussing a possible escape plan during our bathroom break later when those boots make their way down the stairs and stomp over to us, each step sending a wave of nausea right through me.

"Is my kitten ready for her doggie's bone?" Earl snarks, then bursts out into hoarse laughter, entirely amused with his sick, stupid pun. "Hope my pets enjoy it today—might be the last time. My own dogs are hungry for some fresh meat."

Oh God.

I hold back my terrified cry.

It's not over. We're okay. It's not over.

Dean approaches me after his restraints are removed, looking weary and haggard and so unlike the man I once knew. I used to loathe that mischievous gleam in his eyes, the one that loved to instigate me and push my buttons. Now, I would do anything to get it back.

Something tells me that even if we manage to make it out of here alive, I'll never see those eyes again.

Earl barks his orders from the other side of the basement, as if we don't know what to do by now. He waves his shiny gun around, but I don't hear any of the words coming out of his mouth. Everything sounds muffled and far away, like I'm underwater.

I'm only focused on Dean.

Nothing else exists.

Dean closes in, reaching for my wrist and beginning his slow, circular motions over my skin. He then presses his opposite hand to my chest and lets his forehead fall against my own. I inhale a sharp gasp, not expecting the gesture. There is something intimate about it—something different. I force my eyes shut because I find myself unable to look at him while we're in this strangely personal position.

Odd, considering he's been *inside* me. It doesn't get more personal than that.

He pushes his hand against the crown of my breast, but not in a sexual way. He sighs so deeply it resonates right through me. "It's still beating," he whispers, his words a soft kiss against my lips. "As long as it's beating, you're okay."

With his hand to my heart and his thumb trailing along my pulse point, he leans in. I meet him halfway, eager to feel his warmth, desperate for that human contact—that *connection*. His tongue invades me, and our kiss feels hungrier than usual. It's more than routine. It's more than survival. Maybe he's craving that connection just as much as I am.

Dean trails his hand down my breast slowly, splaying his fingers along my abdomen. His touch is gentle and soft against my sore ribs, merely a tickle. A small whimper escapes my throat, and I instinctively raise my leg to wrap it around his waist, our tongues in a frenzy and our lips devouring one another.

Dean's hand leaves me to unbutton his jeans and yank them down his hips, and then I feel him at my core, seeking more of my heat. We're both warm and breathing and alive, and it's intoxicating. *Life* is intoxicating when you're on the brink of death, day after day.

I inhale a tapered breath when he pushes inside me, my hands gripping the pole. My eyes are still closed as I try to zone out to my usual, happy place—the one that's far, far away from here.

But I keep being pulled back to Dean.

I'm too aware of him today, too drunk on the feel of another human body breathing life into me. His forehead touches mine again, but I keep my eyes shut, too scared to look at him. Too scared to see if his blue, blue eyes are reflecting everything I'm feeling right now.

His movements are slower than usual. Slow, but steady. Intense.

Usually he's quick and hurried, eager to get this over with. But not today. Today, it's different—almost like he's savoring every inch of me. And I'm not sure why, I'll never know why, but my body starts to respond. I block everything out, except for Dean, and I feel a pool of heat surge between my thighs…an ancient buzz of pleasure.

Pleasure.

What a thing to feel when you're chained in a basement with a madman waving a gun at you in one hand and beating off in the other.

But I go with it.

I go with it because it's better than feeling like I'm dying inside.

I think Dean notices, too. He palms my ass with one hand beneath my T-shirt, my unwashed hair falling over our faces like a curtain. I'm dirty and gross, and I probably smell like a sewer, but that doesn't stop Dean from burying his face into my neck and breathing me in, inhaling my scent like it's sweet, beautiful oxygen. He picks up speed, and I realize my other leg has wrapped around him, holding myself up and pulling him close as his cock drives in and out of me.

He lifts his head.

I can feel him looking at me. Watching me. Begging me to open my eyes.

I do.

My eyelids flutter open and the air catches in my throat when our gazes meet. He's staring at me like I'm the only goddamn thing in the world, and I suppose, right now, I am.

A soft moan passes through his lips and I want to know what it tastes like, so I lean forward to capture his mouth in another searing kiss. He kisses me back with everything he has left, every last ounce of life and hope, his tongue tangling desperately with mine.

Then his thumb halts its calming designs along my wrist.

My security blanket is gone. My way out has turned to dust.

And I hardly notice.

I don't even care because I'm so wrapped up in all of the strange, powerful feelings coursing through me, swallowing me whole.

Dean trails his hand up my arm and cradles my neck, pulling back from my mouth to find my eyes again. He doesn't want to give me an escape this time. He wants me to be *here*, in this moment, with him. My breathing is heavy as tiny sounds crawl up my throat with each hard thrust. I want to reach for him. I want to touch him like he's touching me. I want to feel his skin beneath my fingertips, assuring me he's real.

I'm not alone. I'm not alone.

Dean's hand disappears from my neck and falls between us, and I almost choke on a gasp when I realize what he's doing. The thumb that has been tracing my wrist, giving me comfort, is now pressed up against my clit, massaging me as our bodies crash together. His eyes don't leave mine. My eyes don't leave his. We're locked together, something silent and unspoken but all-consuming passing between us.

It doesn't take long before the telltale sparks begin to scatter and climb, an orgasm building. My breath hitches with tiny gasps and whimpers, and my God, the look on Dean's face when he realizes what's happening—when he realizes I'm going to come...

Shock. Disbelief.

The space between his eyes creases, his brows furrowing, pupils blown. His gaze is wide and full of something I can't even begin to unravel.

And then I feel myself peaking, bursting, so he kisses me, devouring my moan with his mouth and plunging into me three more times before his own orgasm takes over. He lets out a primal groan, shuddering and digging his fingers into the underside of my thigh as he comes.

And then it's over.

We both come down, our lips and teeth pressed together, our breathing low and heavy. Dean's grip on me loosens, and my legs fall from his hips. I'm absolutely terrified to look at him, partially disgusted by what just transpired, but mostly confused. I duck my head the moment our mouths separate, forcing back the hot tears of shame.

What the hell was that?

A slow clap rings out beside us, echoing right through me, and I realize I had forgotten he was even there.

"Well done. My little playthings put on quite the show," Earl sneers, a gurgling laugh erupting from him.

Dean quickly pulls out of me, and I can see that his chin is to his chest as he steps backwards. He can't look at me either. He's shuffling with his pants when Earl lurches forward and pushes him to the opposite corner with the barrel of the gun.

"Intermission time," Earl says as Dean pulls up his zipper.

"Fuck you…you vile, filthy, *inhumane* piece of shit."

A beat.

Oh no, Dean. What are you doing?

Dean must have a death wish because he continues. "You're a sick, twisted piece of garbage. You'll never get away with this because you'll keep doing it. You'll keep kidnapping women because there's not a single fucking reality where you could even *pay* a woman to touch your tiny, impotent dick. You're going to get caught, and then you're going to rot in a prison cell until you drop dead, you fat, fucking *fuck*."

Earl is silent for a moment, his pistol positioned right at Dean's chest. My heart all but stops as I wait, my insides twisting with dread.

He's going to kill him.

He's absolutely going to kill him.

I can't let that happen.

Before the trigger is pulled, before a shot rings out and Dean drops in front of my eyes, I let out a mighty, shrill scream and shake my chains at the same time. It's enough to pierce the silence and force Earl's attention in my direction for the briefest moment.

It's enough to give Dean a tiny, pivotal window to make his move.

It's our one and only chance of getting out of here alive, and Dean takes it.

He follows through on his promise.

With a guttural growl, Dean lunges at Earl and knocks him right off his feet. They both tumble backwards onto the hard floor, Dean on top, Earl grabbing for his pistol that slipped from his meaty paw. Dean gets to it first and shoves it away with a quick swipe of his hand, and I watch it slide across the floor and out of Earl's reach.

"You motherfucker," Dean spits out, sliding one palm around Earl's neck as he rises to his knees and straddles our captor, beating him with his opposite fist. Dean pummels him. He's violent and angry and completely zoned out. "You sick piece of shit. This is for laying your *disgusting* fucking hands on her."

Thwap. Thwap. Thwap.

The sound of fist against face is sickening as blood spatters up at Dean and all around us. I'm holding my breath, squeezing the pole with all my might, watching the horrific scene in front of me.

"You bastard. You fucking bastard." Dean is focused. Determined. He's using both fists now to wreak havoc on Earl's face until the monster becomes unrecognizable. "How dare you fucking touch her. I'll fucking kill you."

Thwap. Thwap. Thwap.

Blood, flesh, bone. It's everywhere. Earl's limbs quiver in shock as he loses the fight and goes limp on the cement.

"You're dead. You're fucking *dead*," Dean seethes, spitting through his teeth, his punches hard and brutal. He's an animal—out of control. "I'll *kill* you."

But he already did. It's done.

It's over.

I hear skull cracking, and I clench my eyes shut, shouting, "Dean, stop!"

"Fuck you, motherfucker."

Thwap. Crack. Thwap.

"He's dead, Dean!" I cry. "He's dead. He's dead. Please stop."

My voice finally infiltrates the vengeance-fueled haze that has consumed him, and Dean stills his fist midair, his chest surging with weighty breaths, his body shaking with rage. His eyes widen as he takes in the gory scene in front of him—a horrifying, ugly mess he created with his own bare hands. A life taken.

End scene.

Dean propels himself backwards when the image sinks in, scooting himself away from the blood-spattered body and pulling himself to faltering feet. "Fuck…oh, Jesus…" He holds his hands out in front of him, staring at the bloodbath, his breathing intensifying and becoming unhinged.

I want to run to him, console him in some way, but I'm still chained to this goddamn pole. I tug at my manacles. "Dean, please get me out of these. I want to go home."

He snaps his head up, and the look of incredulous horror on his face will be ingrained in my mind forever. Dean looks back down at his hands, then starts scrubbing them against the front of his jeans. "Yeah, okay. Fuck… Okay…" He's out of sorts, pacing around in a circle, tugging at his hair.

"Dean." His name breaks on my tongue, and I bob my knees up and down, desperate for freedom. "Please."

He swallows, blinking at me and nodding his head. "I'm sorry… Yeah, okay…" Dean jumps into action, putting the grisly truths aside until we are out of here.

He pauses to glance at Earl's body, and I think he's going to search him for the key to the handcuffs.

Instead, he runs back to his pole and slides down to his knees, his hands roving over the cement to find the pin of the belt. He locates it, then stumbles over to me with wild eyes and bloodstained skin. "This might take a few minutes."

I nod, closing my eyes so I don't have to look at the mangled body lying in front of me. I can feel Dean's breaths beating against my hair as his hands shake and quiver while they try to unchain me.

It takes a long time. Ten, maybe fifteen minutes. But when the cuffs finally slip loose and clatter against the cement floor, I pull my arms free with a cry of relief. I hear the pin follow with a tiny clank, and Dean's forehead falls against the pole beside me while he takes a minute to regroup. I turn to him, watching his eyes close as he tries to control his breathing. His sticky hands cling to the pipe—the same piece of metal that has held me captive in this hellhole for almost three weeks.

I reach out my own unsteady hand, placing it against his shoulder, stepping forward until we are almost fully touching. Dean's jaw clenches and unclenches as he twists his head to the side, still leaning against the pole, finding my face. I rub my hand along his back, much like he had done at the veterinary hospital that dreary afternoon with Blizzard. Our eyes hold as I try to quiet the demons so clearly wreaking havoc on his mind.

And then, in one fell swoop, Dean tugs me toward him as he stands up straight, crushing me to his chest, his arms wrapping around me and holding tight.

My own arms slink around his middle, my face buried against his racing heart. I can smell blood and fear and terror and victory. I feel him trembling in my embrace, his body coming down from the massive adrenaline spike. He hugs me tighter and tighter, and I don't even care that my ribs are screaming in resistance. He could never hug me tight enough.

Our emotions begin to settle and we slowly pull apart, our eyes lingering for one potent beat before he takes my hand and pulls me to the staircase.

I don't spare Earl, or whatever's left of him, a final glance as we race past his body. He's not worth another second of my life.

We won.

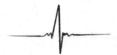

Dean is scrubbing his hands and arms in the kitchen sink with a bristled brush, erasing all remnants of Earl from his skin. He's relentless and harsh, washing and cleansing until his flesh is pink and raw. I watch the water run red as Dean's eyes stay laser focused on his task. Even when all of the blood has disappeared down the drain, he keeps scrubbing.

Swish. Swish. Swish.

"Dean," I say gently, coming up behind him in an attempt to distract him. He doesn't hear me.

Swish. Swish. Swish.

"It's okay, Dean."

He keeps scrubbing. Dean is trying to cleanse more than just his skin.

Tiny specks of blood begin to form along the surface of his arms, and I finally reach my hand out and place it against his shoulder. "Dean, stop. You're hurting yourself."

He pauses his movements, turning around and glancing between me and the blood-tinged bristles. He swallows. "Sorry, I just…" His voice trails off, but he doesn't need to finish the sentence.

We both know exactly what he's doing.

I jump in place when police sirens sound in the distance, and I waste no time running to the back door off the kitchen.

"Cora, wait. They'll come inside to get us," Dean says, trying to keep me from darting out into the subzero weather in nothing but a bloodstained T-shirt.

But I can't listen to logic or reason right now. Safety is roughly four hundred yards away, and I'm desperate, reckless, *aching*, to have a taste of humanity. I can't wait.

I'm done waiting.

The door slams against the wall as I whip it open, and the icy air blasts my face. I gasp at the intensity of it, but it doesn't stop my feet from launching me forward, pulling me closer to freedom. There's a dirt road behind the house, and I try not to think about the fact that if I'd gone out this door two days earlier, I probably would have made a successful escape. We'd have two extra days with our families in our warm beds, eating real food.

I could have spared Dean from committing a grisly crime that he will likely carry with him for the rest of his life.

But I try not to think about that. There's no room for what-ifs right now.

As I stumble forward, I clutch my throbbing ribs as they scream at me to go slowly. My head is pounding, my body is crumbling, my limbs are numbing from the cold, and I realize I've barely made it a few feet. I see the flashing lights ahead, though, and that's too tempting—too seductive. I need to keep moving.

I press on, holding back my cries of pain as I push forward across the crunchy leaves and frost-tipped grass. It's then that I feel him behind me, his warmth touching me before his hands ever do.

"I've got you." Dean throws a jacket over my shoulders and picks me up off the ground, one arm around my back and the other tucked under my knees. We pause for a moment, our eyes catching, and I wrap my own arms around his neck, allowing him to carry me the rest of the way.

I lay my head against his shoulder, and I swear I could fall asleep. Even though I'm half-naked with broken bones, caked in blood and dirt and semen, being trekked through an open field in the arms of my sister's fiancé—I'm at peace. I feel safe. I'm exhausted.

My soul is exhausted.

I listen to Dean's arduous breaths as he totes me through the property in his strong arms. I concentrate on his heartbeats, quick and steady. I can't help but wonder what the future holds for us now. It's impossible to go back to the way we were because we aren't those people anymore. We've been through too much. We've *seen* too much.

I've witnessed the deepest, darkest parts of Dean. I've seen him cry and kill and come.

He's been inside me.

When we finally reach the dusty, blocked-off road where police cruisers, ambulances, FBI, media, and firetrucks are all lined up, I burrow my face deeper into the crevice of Dean's shoulder. After three weeks of surviving the bowels of hell with this man, I realize I don't even know how to process life beyond our nightmare.

Dean sets me down, gingerly and carefully, and we stand there for a moment facing our new reality together.

A fresh start. A second chance.

Flashing lights, noise, cameras, faces attached to people who will never understand.

I inhale a splintered breath, closing my eyes, feeling overwhelmed and panicked and relieved all at once.

And then his knuckles graze against my own like a soft kiss, a knowing touch, a *promise*. I feel his fingers interlace with mine. We stand there, hand in hand, watching as EMTs and police officers move toward us like in a slow-motion movie scene. I hold on to him. He's still my lifeline. He's still all I have.

We're in this together.

PART 2

TIES THAT BIND

13

DEAN

I STARE AT A BLACK ANT crawling along the toe of my shoe.

It's weaving itself into confused circles on the dark suede, looking lost and unsure. It dances across my interwoven laces, likely searching for food and warmth. I can't help but wonder how it's surviving these brutal winter temperatures. It's so small and fragile—so insignificant. It doesn't stand a chance.

"Dean."

Cora and I were ants. Small and fragile, lost in a cold, scary world. Set up to fail.

We had each other, though.

The ant is all alone.

"Dean."

I register my name catching on a sharp gust of wind that sails by, almost knocking me off my feet. I look up from my place on the sidewalk to find Mandy spearing me with those worried eyes I've become so familiar with over the past two weeks. "Yeah?"

"Are you ready to go inside?"

Her microbladed eyebrow arches with concern, and I realize I zoned out in front of her parents' house, sympathizing with an ant. I glance down at the insect, only to find that it has since left my shoe and disappeared into the cement cracks.

I hope it beats the odds.

Mandy plants a smile on her crimson lips when I nod, then steps over to take my hand in hers. She is warm, and yet, a chill sweeps through me.

"It's going to be fine," she says idly, sensing my resistance as she threads our fingers together. "It'll be good to have a little normalcy again."

Normalcy. Nothing about the last five weeks has been normal, that's for sure. And I can't imagine this forced family dinner with her parents will feel anything close to normal. "Yeah. I guess."

Mandy blinks her fake lashes at me, trying to mask her apprehension with another smile. "Do you need a minute?"

"No." A minute won't change anything. A minute doesn't erase the damage done. A minute isn't going to teleport me back to the safety of my own bed, where I can comfortably avoid my current reality and battle my demons in private. "Let's go inside."

I move forward because it's the only choice I have. We walk up the cobblestone pathway to the bright-blue Colonial-style house in a picture-perfect neighborhood. I've walked this path thousands of times before, but today I spot a little gnome statue next to the row of shrubs lining the front of the house. He looks rusted—worn from the elements. "Is that a new statue?" I inquire of Mandy as we reach the porch step.

"Richard the Gnome?" She scrunches up her nose. "He's been there for, like, two decades, Mr. Observant." Mandy shoots me a wink, attempting to be playful. "Cora named him Richard because she said he looked like Richard Marx."

I nibble on the inside of my cheek. I can't help but wonder how many other day-to-day things I walked right by without ever affording a glance or a thought.

We step inside the all-too-familiar home and are greeted with the smell of garlic, rosemary, and a hint of pine. I turn to see a magnificent, fresh tree in the sitting room to our left, decorated in golds and reds and priceless, homemade ornaments.

Most of the time, I don't even know what day it is, let alone the fact that it's almost Christmas.

"Oh, Dean."

My head snaps up to find Bridget and Derek Lawson rushing toward me from the kitchen. Bridget's long, brown skirt trails behind her as tears well in green eyes that bear a striking resemblance to Cora's. Her blond hair is cropped into a pixie cut, her crow's feet creasing as she casts her worry and love all over me.

Derek is behind her, his salt-and-pepper hair telling his age despite his youthful appearance. He has Mandy's eyes—hazel, more slanted, adorned with thick, brown lashes.

They are my second parents. My own father passed away almost twelve years ago from a heart attack, and my mother is in the dementia ward at Sunrise Assisted Living. I spent most of my high school afternoons here, studying with Mandy, playing board games, laughing our way through karaoke nights, and eating home-cooked meals. Bridget and Cora loved cooking together. Their meat loaf was one of my favorites.

Bridget places her kind hands against my cheeks, cradling my face like I'm her very own son.

I should have been five days ago. December 5 was supposed to be our wedding day. Instead, I spent thirteen hours buried beneath my bedcovers, ignoring Mandy's phone calls and only getting up to take a piss and munch on stale saltine crackers.

"You look better," Bridget says, her watery smile impressively veiling the obvious lie.

The Lawsons visited me at the hospital in those strange, hazy forty-eight hours post-rescue, but I haven't seen them since. I haven't seen anyone except for Mandy, who stops by my town house unannounced more than I'd like her to. She has a key, though, so there's not much I can do about it.

I'll never tell her I thought about stealing that key and flushing it down the toilet.

"I feel a little better. Still adjusting." I go with the lying theme. It feels simpler. "Thanks for having us over tonight."

"Mom, give him some space. He's not an exhibit," Mandy scolds, pulling her snowy-white hat with a furry pom-pom off her head, sending her hair into a static-infused mess.

Bridget reluctantly steps away and Derek paces over to me, squeezing my shoulder with a firm, affectionate hand. "It's great to see you up and about. The girls made meat loaf—your favorite."

The girls?

I hear the patio door slide open from the back of the house, squeaky and familiar, followed by the sound of exuberant paws skidding across the hardwood floors.

Blizzard must sense my presence because she careens toward me in the entryway, all sixty-five pounds of her, and promptly lands on my feet, rolling over for a tummy rub. I crouch down to scratch her belly, releasing my first genuine smile in weeks. Blizzard's tail wags furiously beneath her. I can't believe this old girl still has so much energy. She's got to be twelve or thirteen by now. But her excitement at seeing me walk through that front door has never wavered over the last ten years. Not even a little.

As I rise to my feet, my eyes land on the figure standing in the kitchen and my breath hitches in the back of my throat.

Corabelle.

Mandy hangs her coat up on the nearby coatrack and clears her throat, leaning in close to her mother. "You said Cora wasn't coming tonight," Mandy mutters in a low voice as she tames her flyaways, her eyes dancing over to me with apology.

It's true I wasn't ready to face her yet.

Maybe I'll never be ready.

"Sorry, sweetie, but your sister texted me a few hours ago and said she changed her mind."

Their conversation begins to fade away as my eyes lock on Cora's from across the foyer. Memories flow through me, making me feel itchy and slightly panicked, but there is also a profound comfort that stabs at my heart. She is a vision of life and light and survival. Her hair is golden blond, shiny and healthy again, curled loosely over her thin shoulders. She's always been petite, but her frame looks even more frail and willowy in a deep-purple dress that probably fit her better five weeks ago. The neckline hangs low, revealing her bony collarbone and remnants of a few lingering, faded bruises.

Cora twists her hair over one shoulder and my eyes drift to her exposed neck. The same neck I peppered with sorrowful kisses and soaked with my tears of shame.

My jaw clenches and my heartbeats accelerate, my hands turning clammy as I swipe them along the front of my blue jeans. I'm not sure what to do, so I merely acknowledge her with a quick nod and swallow down all the things I cannot say.

But I don't miss the flash of hurt and dismissal in her eyes before she spins around and busies herself in the kitchen.

I flinch when Mandy's fingers begin tugging the sleeve of my winter coat, yanking me out of my messy thoughts. "Take your coat off. Stay a while." She beams at me, then follows her parents into the family room, chattering on about her shift at the hair salon like it's another ordinary day in Normalville.

I stay rooted to the snowman welcome mat, staring at Cora's back as she leans over the kitchen counter, facing away from me. Her head is bowed, her shoulders taut. She is gripping the edge of the countertop as her hair falls over the sides of her face in waves.

I want to run to her. I want to take her in my arms and whisper into her ear that everything is going to be okay. We survived. It's over.

But I don't.

I can lie to Mandy and her parents and my friends and my boss and my therapist…but I can't lie to her.

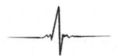

We all sit around the formal dining table, and for a moment, everything feels like it used to. It's easy to pretend between four walls adorned with pretty paint colors, lace drapes, recessed lighting, and holiday decorations scattered throughout. It's easy to pretend in the company of the family I've come to care about over the past fifteen years while they discuss politics and trending Netflix shows as if nothing is amiss.

But the facade cracks when my gaze floats over to Cora, sitting across from me, smashing her meat loaf into something unidentifiable with the tines of her fork as the candlelight illuminates the dark circles under her eyes. I push my own mushy meat loaf into my mashed potatoes, realizing I'm doing the exact same thing. I reach under the table to give Blizzard my dinner roll so it appears that I'm actually eating the meal that probably tastes delicious.

"About the pregnancy."

Mandy's voice pushes through my fog, and I lift my head, turning toward her. *Pregnancy?* A silence washes over the dinner table, and I feel incredibly out of the loop. "What?" I glance from face to face, but everyone is looking down at their plates like they're in the midst of a riveting crossword puzzle. My eyes shift back to Cora, but she's not looking at her plate. Her eyes are wide and accusatory as she stares down a sheepish-looking Mandy.

Mandy presses her lips between her teeth, flipping her hair over one shoulder. "Sorry. I–I didn't mean to blurt that out. We were talking about our cousin's new baby, and it just triggered… You know. I suck at thinking before I speak."

I blink. Cora's fork clinks against the dinner plate as she folds her hands in her lap, but she refuses to meet my eyes. I don't think she's looked at me once since our stare-down from earlier. I run my tongue along the roof of my mouth, putting two and two together with a hard knot twisting in my gut. "Are you pregnant, Cora?"

Her head finally jerks toward me, alarmed by the sound of my voice addressing her for the first time in weeks. I watch her haunted eyes swirl with grief and confusion and sadness and everything in between. But the eye contact doesn't last, and she ducks her head with fluttering lashes. "I was," she says softly, so soft I almost don't hear her. Then she pins her eyes back on Mandy. "I didn't want to talk about this. I didn't want to talk about any of this."

Cora pushes back from the table and stands up, scratching at her wrist and making a quick escape from the dining room to the staircase.

I follow, not caring if it looks strange or inappropriate. My instincts tell me to follow her.

I can feel their eyes boring into my back, trying to understand why I'm chasing Mandy's sister up the stairs, but they have to *know*.

They have to know we're different now.

The image of Cora and me standing together, our hands interlocked, dappled in bloodstains and dirt with an identical far-off look in our eyes, has made the rounds on the internet. In fact, it went viral as soon as the photo was released by the media. It has over two million shares and hundreds of thousands of comments ranging from "Sending prayers to those poor souls" to "This looks like the movie poster for the next Quentin Tarantino film" to "Following for future wedding announcement." Mandy delicately questioned me about the photo, hoping for insight into our shared nightmare. Hoping for answers I wasn't able to give her. She doesn't know all the details of what transpired in that basement—only what she's seen in news articles and TV broadcasts.

All I told Mandy was that we formed a friendship out of survival and fear and boredom and loneliness. It was necessary. It was inevitable. It was all we had.

She'll never know the things I was forced to do, the lines that were crossed, or the guilt I'll carry with me until the day I die.

And she'll certainly never know how those lines blurred inexplicably on that final day.

I take the stairs up two at a time, passing through the loft and poking my head into each room. I find her sitting on the edge of the guest bed of her old bedroom, pinching the bedcovers between white-knuckled fingers. Her breathing is labored and her hair is blocking her face.

"Cora."

She looks up, surprised that I followed her. I watch the complex emotions flicker in her eyes as she tries to read me—tries to make sense of why I'm standing in front of her, looking just as lost and vulnerable as she is.

Cora rises to her feet, smoothing down the fabric of her slightly too-big dress, then tucking her hair behind her ears. My eyes dance across her face, drinking in her pink cheeks and those soft, full lips that I should not be so familiar with.

Then we each take a step forward. Then another. Then one more.

And before we've thought anything through or had time to ponder our next move, our arms are wrapped around each other, her hot breath against my neck, her hair that smells like daffodils tickling my nose. I pull her close, breathing in every ounce of her, savoring her warmth.

She feels like home.

"Dean," she whispers, her voice breaking on my name like it split her in half.

I squeeze her tighter, my hand cradling the back of her head, my fingers tangling in her hair. I breathe in and out, slow and deep, trying not to go back to that basement where she was all I had to hold on to. "I'm sorry I haven't called you," I apologize, and I truly *am* sorry. "I didn't know what to say."

I've spent an embarrassing amount of time over the last two weeks just staring at my phone, telling myself to dial her number or send her a quick text. Just to check in. Just to make sure she's okay. Instead, I've been a coward, getting my inside information from Mandy and avoiding Cora just like I'm avoiding everything else in my life.

Cora's hands land on the back of my neck as she pulls back, our eyes bound, our connection still palpable. The look on her face is too familiar, too reminiscent of that last day—the moment everything shifted. The moment our relationship or friendship or whatever the fuck we were was stripped down to bare bones and raw truths and more questions than we'll ever have answers to.

I break away. I turn away from her, my hands linked behind my head as I try to sort through the murk and muck swirling around my brain. When I spin back around, Cora's arms are folded across her breasts, her armor up, her gaze pointed at her freshly painted toenails. I inhale sharply. "You were pregnant?"

Cora sucks her bottom lip between her teeth as she scratches at her wrist and spares me the smallest glance. She looks flustered as she replies, "Yes."

I crack on the exhale. "Jesus. Are you okay?"

A shoulder shrug. That's all she gives me.

"Cora…"

"My hCG levels were high enough to indicate a pregnancy had occurred. But there was nothing on the ultrasound, so they told me it was either a chemical pregnancy or I miscarried early—likely when Earl kicked me until he broke six of my ribs, then tossed me down a flight of stairs like I was a bag of trash."

She keeps scratching her wrist.

"Fuck, Corabelle…" I run a palm over my face, reeling from the knowledge that our three weeks of hell created a *life*—as fleeting as it was. A thought pokes me and I add, "Do you know if it was…mine?"

I watch her cheeks burn as she stares off behind my shoulder, bobbing one knee up and down. "No. There's no way to know," she says, refusing to look me in the eyes. Refusing to acknowledge what that question implies. "It wasn't viable."

I look down at the cream-colored carpet, zoning in on a matching tuft of dog hair. "You should have told me when you found out."

I feel her eyes on me again, but I don't look up.

"Told you? When, Dean?" Her tone is strained, accusatory. "When you were shutting me out? When you decided to abandon me after everything we went through?"

"I just needed time, Cora."

"How much time? I noticed the look on your face when you saw me standing in the kitchen tonight. You looked like you saw a ghost," she says, heated and ready to break. "You didn't want me to be here."

"That's not true…"

"It is true. You probably would have avoided me forever."

I spare a quick glance over my shoulder to make sure no one is standing outside the door. Then I take a step forward and whisper harshly, "I *raped* you."

Cora presses her lips together, her eyes glossing over. "You did what you had to do to get us out of there. I told you to do it. That's not rape."

"You didn't want it. That *is* rape," I counter.

We avoid the elephant in the room: the fact that maybe we both wanted it that final day.

"I wanted to *live*," Cora insists, taking her own step closer to me, her voice low. "I would have done almost anything to survive at that point."

"Everything okay?"

We spin around, moving away from each other in the process, to find Bridget standing in the doorway, her hand against the frame as she leans into the room. I swallow, bowing my head.

Cora clears her throat. "We're just catching up, Mom. Sorry I bailed… We'll be out in a minute."

I raise my chin, watching as Bridget gives us a tight-lipped smile and that worried-mother look before retreating back down the hallway.

Catching up.

Like we're two old friends reconnecting over margaritas.

Nope—just chatting about rape and abuse and miscarriages, wondering how the fuck we're ever going to move past this and just be *us* again.

Cora releases a long sigh, dropping her arms to her sides and glancing up at me. "We should get back to dinner. I'm sure Blizzard is eyeing my dissected meat loaf."

I'm about to ask her, *What now? Where do we go from here? When can we talk again?*

But she sweeps past me, daffodils and passionfruit and so many unknowns lingering on my skin as she disappears out the door. I watch her go with gritted teeth, hopelessness swimming through my veins.

We are bound, chained, tied—to our trauma, and to each other.

We're in this together.

And yet, I've never felt more alone.

14

I ZONE OUT AS I STARE into my refrigerator, eyeing the assortment of fresh groceries Mandy just dropped off. I told her she didn't need to do that—I'm more than capable, and I sure as shit don't have anything else to do since I'm not back to work yet. But she insisted, carrying inside two brown paper bags filled to the brim, tucked under both arms.

Mandy is now wiping down my countertops as she fixes me a sandwich. "How are you feeling? Did your appointment with Dr. Dryden go well?"

I blink into the yellow light, not fully registering her question even though I heard it. I stare at the head of broccoli, fairly certain I can make out a vague outline of Pat Sajak. If I just tilt my head a little to the left…

Is he still alive? Is Wheel of Fortune *still a thing?*

"Dean, did you hear me?"

I glance up. Mandy is standing in front of me, holding out a sandwich on a paper plate. Her heavily painted eyes are narrowed, slicing me with concern. I close the refrigerator and force a smile. "Yeah, it went okay."

She sighs with relief, her worried lips turning up into a toothy grin. "Good. You're being honest with him?"

Honest?

Well, I'm not outright lying. But I'm certainly not revealing everything. Dr. Dryden knows I killed a man, but he doesn't know it was her face I envisioned, the images of her dignity being dismantled, that drove my fists into those savage, fatal blows. He knows I was forced to watch Cora get raped and abused, but he doesn't know that I, myself, was forced between her legs with a pistol to my head.

Dr. Dryden knows a lot, but he doesn't know about the real ghosts that haunt me and keep me up at night.

So, I guess I'm lying by omission.

"Yeah," I reply, taking the plate from Mandy's outstretched hands. "I'm being honest."

Now I'm lying to my fiancée.

Mandy nods her head, her perfectly coifed hair bobbing over her cashmere sweater. More relief. More smiles. "I'm proud of you, Dean. I know it's not easy to—"

I spit out the bite of sandwich as soon as it touches my tongue, dropping the plate and wiping at my mouth with the back of my hand. "This is turkey?"

Mandy gapes at me, her glossy lips parted with alarm. "Y-Yes. You love turkey."

"I don't love turkey."

"I thought…"

I close my eyes, shoving the painful flashbacks away as I shake my head. "I don't love it anymore." I trek backwards out of the small kitchen, trying to control my breathing. "I think I need a nap."

"Dean…" Mandy follows me to the couch, sitting down beside me, closer than I'd prefer, and grazes her supersized fingernails that resemble talons along my knee. "I'm here for you, babe. What can I do?"

I think over all the things she can do, but she won't like any of them.

Go home.

Stay home.

Give me some fucking space.

I pinch the bridge of my nose, guilt soaring through me in waves. I hate that I'm pushing away my girlfriend of fifteen years. I know she's only trying to help. I know she cares and wants me to get better. But I feel like an entirely different man, and I'm not even sure this man wants to marry this woman anymore.

I'm fucking broken.

The thought stabs me like the edge of a dagger as I lay my head back against the leather couch cushion. I feel Mandy slide up even closer, her hand trailing higher and higher until…

I grab her hand before it reaches its destination, trying not to crack under the weight of the rejection in her eyes.

"Dean…please. We haven't been intimate in almost six weeks." Mandy's eyes begin to mist, her nails digging into my palm. "I miss you."

Jesus, I feel like the biggest goddamn asshole. Mandy and I always had a pretty normal sex life—a little vanilla, but I had no complaints. She's sexy and willing and mine, and yet…I can't fucking do it.

I'm not ready.

"I just need a little more time," I say, letting her down as gently as possible. I have no idea how much more time I'll need. All I know is that it's too soon.

I just can't.

Mandy scoots backwards, dropping her chin to her chest as the rejection manifests into anger. "I figured after weeks of celibacy, you'd be all over me."

A prickling heat crawls up the back of my neck and settles in my ears. *Fuck.*

"You were only down there for three weeks, Dean," Mandy continues, still avoiding my eyes. "I thought you would…you know, bounce back by now."

Only three weeks.

Mandy and I once took a vacation to Cancun for three weeks. It's funny—I hardly remember any of it. That could have something to do with the unlimited drink packages and the spoiled posole that knocked me on my ass for a few of those days, but…the memories are vague and fuzzy. Only bits and pieces stand out.

I remember every vivid detail about that basement.

The dripping pipe. The cracks and ridges in the stone wall on my right. The pink foam insulation overhead, peeking out of the wooden beams in the ceiling. The way the sunrise cast a radiant beam of light into our dungeon, magnifying all of the little dust particles in the air. I tried to count them one morning, but the light kept shifting and I'd lose track.

I remember the daddy longlegs spider in the cobwebbed corner that never seemed to move. I thought he was dead until I caught the tiniest twitch of one of his thin legs. I wondered how long he could go without food.

I bet he wondered the same thing about me.

I remember the gaudy floral wallpaper in that moldy bathroom and the way it peeled from every corner, revealing decayed walls and water damage. I recall looking in the dusty mirror, not recognizing the man reflecting back at me.

Cora.

I think about the way she chewed on her lip while we played twenty questions to pass the time. She took the game seriously, like she was up for the grand prize on a cheesy game show.

I remember the golden glints in her emerald eyes that seemed to fade with each passing day.

I recall the occasional smile I would pull out of her. They felt so magical—so beautifully out of place. Her smile was the closest thing I felt to being rescued over the course of those twenty days.

I remember the goose bumps on her skin when I'd gently caress her cheek, or her hip, or her thigh, trying to bring as much tenderness to the moment as possible. *It's just the cold*, I told myself. But sometimes a small sound or squeak would accompany the goose bumps and she'd give herself away.

It was only three weeks, but it's burned into every cell, every vein, every tainted pocket of my soul.

Forever.

And so is she.

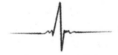

I break down the following Saturday morning and send her a text message.

Me: Can we grab coffee? We should talk.

I pace back and forth through my living room in just my sweatpants, staring at my phone screen and scratching the back of my neck, noting that I really need to get a damn haircut.

She reads the message fairly quickly, and I hold my breath, bracing myself for a shut down.

Cora: I suppose. But only because I'm standing at your front door right now.

I blink at the response, processing her words.

Well, shit.

I jog over to the front of my town house, pulling open the door to reveal a bundled-up Cora, sprinkled with snowflakes, her hands in her pockets. Her eyes drift downward as the icy wind blasts me, and I remember that I'm shirtless.

She brings her gaze up from my naked chest with a sharp swallow. "You forgot your shirt."

"You forgot to tell me you were dropping by unexpectedly."

"Then it wouldn't have been unexpected."

Faint smiles creep onto both of our faces, almost as if we'd forgotten how but we're trying to remember. I take a step back, encouraging her to enter. Cora hesitates for a moment before moving forward and stomping her snow-covered boots against my welcome mat. I watch her shake the flurries from her hair and notice that one sticks to her eyelashes. I want to lean in and swipe it away, but I keep my arms at my sides. "What brings you by?" I stuff my hands into the pockets of my sweats, rocking on the heels of my feet.

"Same reason you texted me, I'm guessing." Cora unzips her coat and slips out of her boots, sweeping her fingers through damp hair as she takes tentative steps through my entryway. Her eyes dance across the messy living area littered with empty potato-chip bags and beer bottles, random piles of laundry, and my bed comforter I've been using for when I fall asleep on the couch at random hours watching mindless television shows. Her eyes are brimming with sympathy as she cuts them back to me, pulling her arms out of her coat sleeves.

I take the jacket from her and hang it over the back of my recliner. "Sorry for the mess." I scratch the scruff along my jawline—I still haven't shaved. "I wasn't expecting company."

Cora shrugs her shoulders, a gray, oversized sweater dipping off one of them, and continues her idle perusal. "My house isn't any better." Her gaze lands on my side table where a book is being used as a coaster for my Miller Lite. "*Of Mice and Men*," she mutters quietly.

We make eye contact and it lingers, and the longer it lingers, the harder it is to break away. But I'm the first to lower my head, massaging the back of my neck with my hand. I reach for a stray T-shirt that luckily only smells like my cedarwood deodorant, then pull it on while Cora watches from a few feet away. I clear my throat. "Coffee?"

She nods. "Sure."

I bring two full mugs out of the kitchen a few minutes later and find Cora on my couch with her feet pulled up. She's flipping through the book, but sets it back down when I approach.

"Thank you," she says, cradling the warm ceramic between both palms. She stares down over the rim for a few moments as I situate myself beside her. "It's the little things I missed the most, I think. Hot coffee. Slobbery dog kisses. My music playlist. The sun on my skin." Cora takes a sip, sighing as she leans back against the cushions.

I face her, resting my mug on my thigh. Her words are all too relatable. "It's weird," I muse. "I thought the first thing I would do after I got home was gorge on cheeseburgers and french fries. Greasy fast food. I was craving a fuckin' Big Mac something fierce down there." I watch her mouth tip into a soft smile as she turns her head toward me. "But I'm finding I don't have much appetite for anything. I munch on shitty snacks and drink beer all day. I'm always hungry, but I also feel kind of sick inside…you know?"

"Same here. It's this strange, hollow feeling—like a hungry hole that needs to be filled, but food isn't the answer." Cora averts her eyes to just beyond my shoulder, drifting away before I can catch her. She finds her way back after about ten seconds, shifting on the couch and picking at the hem of her sweater.

"Are you seeing a therapist?" I wonder.

She nods, still avoiding my gaze. "I'm pretty sure my therapist needs a therapist at this point."

I observe the way she gnaws on the inside of her lip, scratching at her wrist as she stares at the far wall. "Have you told them…everything?"

Have you told them your sister's fiancé was forced to fuck you six times, and one of those times you got off?

I keep the fucked-up truths to myself as she nods and replies, "Mostly."

I want to know which part she omitted, but I'm pretty sure I already do.

Cora changes the subject. "Did they ever find your car?"

My motherfucking car. If I could kill that piece of shit all over again, I probably would. I spent two years saving up for a down payment on my dream Camaro with all the bells and whistles. I only had it three months before Earl "made it disappear." I shake my head, my anger simmering. "Nope. I'm going back and forth with my insurance company, seeing if there's anything they can do. I've been taking an Uber to my therapy appointments."

"That sucks. I'm sorry."

"Yeah, well, it's replaceable. Eventually. He took a hell of a lot more from you."

We both let that dark cloud hover over us for a minute, and I kind of wish I could take it back. I didn't mean to give her wounds life. Cora seems to mentally retreat, and I can only imagine what she's thinking about.

I hope she's thinking about me talking her through it, begging her to focus on me, to only see me, to only hear me…

But I know she's not.

"They're searching for more bodies," Cora says in a low, shaky breath. "They've uncovered a bunch of bones buried on his property. They're trying to identify the victims."

I close my eyes. "Fuck…" I haven't been keeping track of the story unfolding. It's too much for me to deal with. It's too soon, too fresh, too personal. I've already recounted the story to the police, the doctors, my therapist. I was grilled by detectives who were wondering if they had a goddamn murder case against me. While it was obviously self-defense, there wasn't a clean bullet wound or a quick stab to the heart. No, I fucking *pulverized* the bastard with my bare hands. It was violent and savage and out of control.

He had to be identified by dental records.

But given the circumstances, there were no charges brought against me. Thank *God*. The last thing I wanted was to leave one prison and go straight to another.

Then again…I have to wonder if I'll always be in some sort of prison.

"It's so messed up," Cora continues, setting her coffee down on the wooden table beside her. She lifts her teary eyes to me as she twists back around. "That was almost *us*, Dean. That was…"

I hear the panic in her voice and I see it in her wide, green eyes, so I inch my way closer to her on the couch. "Shh, hey…it wasn't us. We got the fuck out and we survived." I reach out to graze my knuckles against her cheek, watching as a tear slides down and collapses on my finger. Cora's eyelids flutter closed as she sucks in jagged breaths. "We're alive, we're breathing, and we're never going back."

Cora raises her hand to touch mine, cradling my fingers. The contact makes something inside me spin and buzz and squirm. I grind my teeth together while she brazenly nuzzles her face against my hand like it's the most natural thing in the world. She kisses the heel of my palm, and I almost fucking lose it.

"I go back there every night."

Hell.

I pull her in, clutching her to me and letting her head fall against my chest like a lost lover. I wrap both arms around her, twining my fingers through her silky strands of hair, inhaling her familiar, calming scent. "Is this okay?"

She nods against my T-shirt, sliding her own arm around my midsection. "It's okay." Cora is silent for a long time, her breathing more even and steady. I almost wonder if she's fallen asleep until she murmurs, "It doesn't feel like Christmastime."

I continue to stroke her glossy locks, massaging her scalp with the tips of my fingers as I try to alleviate her pain the best I can. I slide my opposite hand into the pocket of my sweatpants and pull out my phone, scrolling through the stations until I find the one I want. I turn the volume up and lean back, holding Cora in my arms as Christmas music begins to serenade us through my cell-phone speaker.

I feel her relax almost instantly, burrowing her tearstained cheek further into my chest.

Cora falls asleep a few moments later with "I'll Be Home For Christmas" echoing in our ears, warming us up, taming our tortured souls…and I know I'll be perfectly content if this is all I get for Christmas this year.

15

ONE YEAR EARLIER

*Y*OU'RE PROBABLY GOING TO THINK *I'm a weirdo, but I sorta got you a Christmas present."*

My brow furrows in confusion, my eyes glazing over with equal parts curiosity and spiked eggnog. Then I feel like a giant dick because I didn't get her anything. Cora and I have never exchanged gifts before—well, except for that one year I gave her a vibrator shaped like Santa Claus that said, 'Ho, Ho, Ho' as it vibrated. She, in turn, gifted me with a sharp punch to the shoulder. "Shit, Corabelle. I didn't get you anything."

Cora sits on the couch, one bronzed leg draped over the other as a champagne flute dangles from her hand. I'm sitting across from her on the floor, leaning back on my hands. The sequins of her red cocktail dress sparkle against the Christmas lights, a festive complement to her bright, green eyes.

It's honestly annoying how pretty she looks.

"It's probably for the best that you didn't."

I'm certain we're both thinking about the Santa vibrator when a rosy blush kisses her cheeks.

I shoot her a sly grin. "Well, hand it over. Is it a car? Tell me it's a car."

Mandy shoves her pointy fingernail into my arm. "Why would Cora get you a car?"

"Because she loves me."

"Ew." Cora sets her champagne down on the coffee table in front of her, bending over just enough to reveal a dangerous amount of cleavage. I look away. "Only you would confuse love and hate. I'm sure it's very complicated for your itty-bitty pea brain to keep straight."

"You two are ridiculous," Mandy mutters through a slow breath. "I need more brownies."

She stands up on her wobbly heels, and I can't help but wonder why she's been wearing stilettos all night in her parents' living room. She disappears into the kitchen, leaving me alone with the more aggravating sister.

Not that I mind. Sparring with Cora Lawson is pretty high on my list of preferred activities.

She thinks I'm an idiot, and I let her think it. I get a rise out of the incredulous look in her eyes when I say or do something stupid. It's part of our game.

"Whatever, Corabelle. Show me what you got."

"Don't call me that." Cora delivers her classic irritated glare, then leans over the armrest of the couch to retrieve a gift hiding underneath the tree. "Catch."

She tosses me the present wrapped in colorful twinkle lights, and I catch it with skillful ease, winking at her as I start to open it. "You're pretty good at wrapping. Did you take a class on it?"

Another glare.

I continue to peel back the paper and discover a book. I'm not a reader. I prefer podcasts and audiobooks. But I suppose it's the thought that counts.

"Of Mice and Men," Cora states, reaching for the stem of her wineglass and bringing the rim to her lips. "It was required in sophomore English class, but I think it's safe to assume you never read it. It's a good one."

I purse my lips together. She's right about that. I never read it. "Well, thanks. That's actually kind of nice of…" My voice trails off as I start flipping through the pages.

They're all blank.

Every single one of them.

My head snaps up and I twist the book around, feeling bad that she ordered a defective one. "Uh, slight issue," I tell her.

Cora sits up straight, blinking slowly. She stares at me in what looks to be utter confusion before replying, "Crap. I didn't think you'd notice."

Ah, hell.

Next Christmas? It's on.

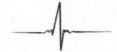

"Good night, Mr. and Mrs. Lawson. Merry Christmas," I say, waving to my second parents, my arm slung around Mandy's waist. "Thanks for the great dinner."

And for the delicious eggnog with a fantastic amount of rum.

I sway from one foot to the other as Mandy tries to hold me steady. I see her mouth "I'm driving" *to her parents as we head toward the front door.*

I notice Cora slipping on her winter coat, gathering her bag of gifts as she follows us out. Before she sweeps past us, she pulls something out of the giant bag and slaps it against my chest.

"For you," she mutters, her face unreadable.

I look down at the book—Of Mice and Men. Only, this time there are words.

"Read it. You might like it." Cora spares me a final glance, then blows a kiss to Mandy as she moves to the door. "Merry Christmas."

She disappears outside, her sugar-cookie-scented body mist trailing behind her.

Mandy puckers her lips, studying the book in my hand. "We can donate it. She'll never know."

I trace my fingers along the cover, smiling at my very first Christmas present from Cora Lawson. I shrug. "Nah. I think I'm going to read this one."

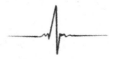

I stare at her across the kitchen island while Cora helps her mother slice the ham for Christmas dinner. Her hair bounces back and forth along her back in champagne waves, her emerald dress landing midthigh, and a serrated carving knife shaking in her right hand.

"Want me to finish up, sweetheart?" Bridget proposes, and I wonder if she sees what I'm seeing.

Cora dismisses the offer with an abrupt shake of her head. "I got it."

Slice. Slice. Slice.

Back and forth. Careful and slow.

I want to slide up behind her and wrap my arms around her petite waist, whispering in her ear that it's okay. Everything's okay. But I can't do that because my fiancée is standing beside me posting Christmas memes on Facebook and she wouldn't understand.

"Oh my God. Allie is engaged!" Mandy announces, beaming with excitement as she taps away at her keypad, reindeer ears bobbing atop her teased head of hair. "She better ask me to be a bridesmaid."

Slice. Slice. Slice.

"Ooh. I forgot Allie's brother is recently single. Do you think Cora would go for him?"

My eyes shift from Cora's careful cuts to Mandy sipping on a glass of holiday punch. "What?"

"Jason. Remember we went to his Super Bowl party? He was dating some chick then, but I *swear* he kept checking my sister out." Mandy slurps her punch through a red straw. "Cora thought he was cute."

I don't realize I'm tensing my jaw until it starts to ache. "It's a little soon, don't you think?"

"She's been single for three years, Dean, and she's almost thirty."

"Yeah, but she's still recovering from a trauma. She's probably not looking to date." I chew on my cheek as I avert my eyes back to Cora, who successfully finished carving the ham and is now transferring the slices to a festive serving plate. "She needs more time."

Mandy glances up from her phone and her cocktail, a knowing grin blooming on her face. "You're protective of her now, aren't you? That's so stinkin' sweet. You're like a worried big brother." She releases a whimsical sigh. "I always knew you two would work out your issues."

Fuck. The term *big brother* makes me want to gag. "Yeah, I guess."

"Well, as her sister and primary wing-woman, I'm going to set something up. Maybe we can do a double date to ease her into it."

My jaw keeps ticking, and I want to slap it. "I don't think I liked Jason."

Actually, I don't even fucking remember Jason, but I'm confident I don't like him.

Mandy gives my chest an affectionate pat. "You don't have to like him. You're not the one who's going to get naked with him." She shoots me a teasing wink and chugs down the rest of her punch.

My stomach feels queasy as my mind flashes with images of Cora getting naked with some douchebag. It's way too soon. And maybe I am protective, but how can I *not* be? I'm the only one who understands what she endured during those three weeks in hell. If anyone is going to have her back, it's me, and I won't apologize for it.

I make my way over to the alcohol cart adorned with a bowl of spiked punch and rum-infused eggnog. Mandy and Cora's little cousins are running around, chasing each other with red and green glow sticks, while the adults mingle in the living room awaiting supper. I spoon myself some punch with the ladle and chug back the entire glass in four gulps. Then I serve myself another glass, then another, until I'm feeling well past buzzed by the time dinner is over and we've made our way to the Christmas tree for the gift exchange.

I'm sitting on the floor with my back to the front of the couch, my legs splayed out in front of me as Mandy sits behind me and rubs my shoulders. I'm nursing my sixth, and hopefully final, glass of punch, watching with bleary eyes as Cora unwraps one of her gifts across from me.

It's a sweater.

She forces a smile that doesn't reach her eyes. No one seems to notice but me.

It's my turn to open a gift.

It's a sweater.

I also force a smile.

When one of the little cousins tears through a gift bag and pulls out a police officer costume, he jumps up and down with excitement. He keeps digging through the tissue paper and shouts, "Cool! Handcuffs!"

My stomach pitches and my gaze settles on Cora, who starts scratching at her wrist and fidgeting in her chair. Her eyes dance over to me, but only for a moment before she excuses herself from the festivities and disappears up the staircase.

Shit.

I wait a few minutes until it doesn't look obvious that I'm following her, then announce to Mandy that I need to use the bathroom. But Mandy is too absorbed in a conversation with her aunt about weighted blankets, so my escape goes unnoticed.

I find Cora in the same place I found her the night of our reunion—sitting on the edge of the guest bed in her childhood room, squeezing the covers between her fists. She notices my presence before I speak, and I wonder if she anticipated me following her up here.

"I'm fine, Dean."

I click my teeth together as I stand in the doorway, noting how she doesn't look up at me. I decide to approach, stepping into the bedroom and closing the door behind me. The sound makes her flinch. "Merry Christmas," I say in a low voice.

I can almost feel some of the tension leave her as I sit down beside her on the bed, the mattress sinking beneath my weight. Cora finally glances up at me, finding my eyes with a tiny frown. "You smell like vodka and Skittles."

A grin pulls on my lips. "You didn't try the punch?"

"No. But I can see that you did." She assesses me up and down, as if the stripes on my shirt will give away the number of glasses I've inhaled over the past two hours. "Be careful. You look like a hot mess."

I run a hand through my mop of brown hair, noting that the top two buttons of my dress shirt are unhooked and only one sleeve is rolled up past my elbow. I think Mandy made me wear a Santa bow tie, but I have no idea where that went. "You look sad," I counter, taking in her vacant eyes that are missing the sparkle I've come to love so much.

"I said I'm fine."

"Well, maybe I can help you be more than fine." I nudge her shoulder with my own. "I sorta got you a Christmas present."

Those eyes widen in surprise, her lips parting, pink and glossy. "What? Why?"

"Because you got me something last year. It's my turn."

Cora lowers her chin to her chest, picking at the threads on the comforter. "I didn't do much shopping this year, so I didn't get you anything. I feel like a jerk."

"It's okay. One of these years the stars will align, and we'll both get each other something at the same time."

She nibbles on her lip. My gaze drifts to her mouth on instinct before I redirect it back up, suddenly very aware of the way her bare thigh is smashed up against my slacks. I should probably scoot away, but the alcohol keeps me rooted in place.

I reach into my pocket and pull out a small box. "The wrapping isn't as good as yours. Don't judge."

"I always judge." Cora finally allows a smile to slip as she takes the gift from my hand. "Well, it's too small to be an embarrassing holiday vibrator, at least."

"Is it, though?"

She laughs. She fucking laughs and it's the best gift ever.

"Is something going to jump out at me?" she questions, twisting the box between her hands as she studies it over her lap. "Does it bite?"

"No and no."

Cora doesn't look convinced, but she begins to peel away the paper, corner by corner, with careful fingers. When she pulls the top off the little white box, her breath catches as she stares down into the cotton stuffing. She's staring at the gift inside, but I'm staring at her. I'm watching the emotions climb up her chest, then her neck, landing in her throat and releasing with a squeaky sigh. Her red-tipped fingers graze the heart pendant attached to a gold chain.

"It's beautiful, Dean. It's...too much." Cora glances up at me with misted eyes, then looks back down at the necklace. She removes it from the box, letting the delicate chain dance over her fingers as she holds it up and gazes at the gilded heart.

"Open it. It's a locket."

Cora blinks, surprised. I can see her fingers tremble as she unclasps the two pieces of gold and fixes her eyes on the inner contents.

Still Beating.

She doesn't say anything. I wonder if maybe she doesn't understand, so I start to explain. "I was thinking you can wear it over your heart as a constant reminder of everything you survived. As long as it's still beating, you're okay."

She is still silent.

I'm starting to doubt the gift, thinking maybe it *is* too much. Maybe it's too personal. Too triggering.

But then Cora throws herself into my lap, her arms around my neck, and I feel her tears slip underneath my shirt collar. "Thank you," she whispers in a ragged breath. "It's perfect."

The necklace remains clutched in a tight fist as her tears continue to fall, hard and relentless, racking her body with everything she tries so hard to keep inside.

She doesn't need to pretend with me, though. She doesn't need to hide.

I'm here, and I see her—every scar, every flaw, every broken, hollow piece.

And I understand.

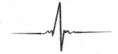

Blood. Blood everywhere.

So much goddamn *blood*.

I feel it spatter my skin and I taste it in my mouth, but I keep going. Flying fists, cracking skull, brain matter. Dreadful, painful moans…*death*.

He needs to pay for what he did to her. He needs to die. I promised I would snuff his worthless life for touching her, and that's exactly what I'm doing.

No remorse. No going back.

It's over.

I think I hear her voice, far away, calling for me to come back to her.

"Stop. He's dead."

Cora breaks through, and reality sinks its teeth into me as I stare down at the grisly crime I've just committed. Dear God, it's like something out of a horror film.

A fitting end to a gruesome tale.

I did this. I fucking did this. I murdered a man in cold blood with nothing but my tattered, dirty knuckles.

The motherfucker deserved it.

I'm about to jump back, get as far away from this bloodbath as I can, but then his eyes fly open. Terrifying white eyes with irises so black, so barbaric, they almost skin me alive. Earl lifts himself up on his haunches, his wide, bulbous eyes sunken into mangled flesh.

Then he reaches out his hands and curls them around my throat, his grip viselike. Impenetrable. He snarls through broken teeth, blood misting my face as he smothers me. "That's a very bad dog."

It's not over. It's not over.

It will never be over.

I launch myself into a sitting position, slicked head to toe in sweat, my breathing coming quick and uneven. I throw my legs over the side of the bed, my hands squeezing the bedsheets, and I vaguely hear my ringtone going off in the distance as my thoughts begin to find their way back to reality. As I search for my cell phone, lost amongst the dampened sheets, I realize my head is still spinning from the alcohol. Mandy dropped me off at home around 11:00 p.m., and I promptly chugged a quarter bottle of vodka before passing out well after midnight.

Fuck, I feel like shit.

I locate the ringing phone and see that it's Cora's name lighting up the face. It's also two o'clock in the morning.

My heart starts to race as I accept the call and slur into the receiver, "Cora? Where're you?"

"Dean."

Oh, hell. She sounds like she's crying. "Are you okay, Corabelle?"

Her sniffles are evident on the other end, accompanied by small whimpers. "I had a horrible nightmare. I can't shake it and I'm scared."

"Do you need me?"

I don't even hesitate to ask. If she needs me, I'm there.

There's a catch in her breath, and then, "Yes."

"Gimme fifteen minutes."

Fifteen minutes later, I'm stumbling out of an Uber in front of her small bungalow, almost tripping over my feet as I jog clumsily up the stone walkway. My forehead falls against the turquoise door, and I start pounding my fist against it as I call out, "Cora, it's me. Open up."

I hear her footsteps on the other side, and when she flings the door open, I almost fall forward. I catch myself on the frame, drinking in the sight of her standing there in nothing but a braless, white tank top and cotton panties. But she doesn't seem to give a shit that she's half-naked in front of me, because she steps backwards to allow me inside, her eyes red and bloodshot, her feet as unsteady as mine. I close the door behind me, unable to keep my gaze from roving over the body I've come to know so well.

She doesn't try to hide from me.

She knows I've seen her far more stripped down than this.

But it's her eyes that do me in. They look glassy and lifeless and utterly haunted. "Corabelle…"

Her bottom lip quivers as we stare at each other, only a few feet apart. "I took sleeping pills. They're supposed to help me pass out and forget, but…the nightmares, Dean. I can't even… God, they're so horrible."

I start to move forward, her tears a magnet to my aching heart. "Come here."

Cora doesn't falter. She runs toward me, closing the gap between us and weaving her arms around my neck.

I don't hesitate either. Like instinct, like it's the only thing to do, I reach under her thighs and lift her up until she wraps her legs around my waist and buries her face into the crook of my neck. I start walking. I carry her through every darkened room, down the short hallway, and into her bedroom. We collapse onto the bed, still holding on, still desperate for that spark of warmth that only seems to ignite when we're together.

We situate ourselves on the queen-sized bed, and I only let go of her to pull the blankets up over our bodies, then my arms envelop her once again. She's stoned on sleeping pills and I'm drunk off my ass, and we're messy, damaged humans clinging to each other as we battle through the storm together, but it's okay because we're *together*.

Cora curls herself in to me, close enough that I'm certain she can feel my heartbeat radiate right through her as she drifts to sleep. I wonder if she can feel how broken it is.

As the alcohol haze consumes me and I begin to fade out, I lean down to kiss her forehead, chasing away a rogue strand of hair with my fingers, then grazing them down her cheek, her neck, and the front of her chest.

I fall asleep with her heart pendant clutched in my hand.

16

EARL TIMOTHY HUBBARD.

I finally find the strength to research the case.

My case.

Our case.

It has made international headlines, branding Earl with the nickname of the Matchmaker. He'll be going down in history as a renowned serial killer after eleven bodies were discovered buried beneath his vast acreage. His victims were taken in pairs—male and female, with no blood relation or romantic connection. Earl had boxes and boxes of trophies, trinkets, and evidence stored in his attic, including Cora's wallet and my leather jacket and car keys. He had journal entries devoted to each "couple," though none of the detailed contents have been released to the media. It's been alleged that, based on the diaries discovered, Earl groomed his victims into developing feelings for one another—and when he felt like they had successfully fallen in love, he would murder them in cold blood. He got off on watching his victims mourn their lover being tortured to death.

Sick fucking shit.

I think back to that fateful night, dwelling on every little thing I did wrong. Each wrong turn and fatal slip of the tongue.

"She your girl?"

Earl's question seemed harmless at the time. I had no idea I'd be sealing our fate when I replied with a firm *"Hell, no."* I should have fucking lied, but getting under Cora's skin was more important. Pissing her off was more fun.

I had no idea I put the nails in our goddamn coffins.

Turns out the guy was a run-of-the-mill sales clerk for a company that makes power tools. I had thought at first he was a dirty cop, but the flashing lights on his vehicle were only there to trick his victims into pulling over. You hear about this shit in crime show documentaries, but you never even dream about it happening in real life.

I close out of the news articles as my skin heats up with prickling anxiety. I feel physically ill. I'm cursing myself for reading this crap—I'm clearly not ready, and the wounds are still too fresh. Too raw. And I sure as fuck hope that Cora isn't reading any of it.

I lean back against my couch cushions, closing my eyes as I try to get a handle on my breathing. Two dogs were confiscated off the premises and are being held at animal control. One was a German shepherd and the other was a Yorkie mix. Neither dog looked threatening from the photographs. In fact, they looked terrified and malnourished—a far cry from the rabid beasts I'd pictured gnawing on our skeletons. I wonder what kind of horrors Earl subjected those poor animals to.

At least they had each other.

I grab my cell phone off the side table when it starts to vibrate, not overly excited to see Mandy's name staring back at me. And that makes me feel even shittier than I already do.

Mandy: Can't wait to see u later babe! Pick u up at 7 :) :)

Mandy is hosting her annual New Year's Eve bash tonight. Usually, we host it at my town house because it's bigger than her modest two-bedroom apartment, but given my current state of harrowing misery, we both agreed it would be better if she took care of the festivities this year. I honestly had no intention of going—ringing in the new year with a handle of vodka and my progressive rock playlist sounded far more appealing.

But Cora will be there.

I haven't seen her since that confusing, hangover-infused post-Christmas morning, but we've talked on the phone every night since.

We don't talk about how we woke up in each other's arms, spooning, our legs impossibly entwined and my hand up her tank top.

The timeline of those early morning hours is hazy at best. I vaguely recall an Uber ride with a driver I was convinced was Kurt Cobain, and I kept asking for his autograph, followed by the smell of Cora's daffodil hair quieting my demons and her warm breath against my neck lulling me to sleep. I remember a nightmare forcing me awake. And I remember eventually falling into the most comfortable sleep I've had in almost two months…despite the raging migraine I woke up to at almost noon the next day.

When Cora finally untangled herself from my arms and our eyes met, there was an unspoken promise that we would never speak of it again.

So, we haven't.

And sometimes we don't speak much at all—simply knowing the other one is on the opposite end of the line, breathing and alive, safe and warm, is a solace in itself.

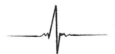

"Oh my God, Dean!"

"You look good!"

"Thank goodness you're okay!"

I wouldn't say I look *good*, but I did manage to find a clean shirt that didn't smell like last week, and I finally made the effort to shave, leaving just a shadow of stubble along my jaw.

And I wouldn't say I'm *okay*. But I'm here with a fake-as-fuck smile on my face, so I suppose it's a step in the right direction.

As familiar faces and curious strangers crowd me with questions and compliments, I clench the spout of the beer in my hand, wondering if I could crack the glass with just my fist.

After all, my hands have broken far worse.

Mandy slides up behind me, snaking her arms around my midsection and holding tight. I feel her press kisses into the middle of my back, and I raise my unoccupied hand to pat her clasped palms. "Good party," I mutter.

I'm lying. The party is awful and my head is pounding, and I feel like everything is spinning. There are people here I used to consider good friends that I haven't given a single thought to over the course of the last seven weeks. Are they even my friends? Am I completely desensitized to human connection?

I turn to see Cora walk through the door with her friend Lily, bathed in sparkly silver and skinny jeans, her hair glowing with fresh highlights and a look in her eyes that resembles a cornered animal. My heart does a funny flip inside my chest, and I know that I'm not *completely* desensitized.

Cora puts the brakes on after stepping through the threshold, grasping Lily's hand and tugging the brunette backwards. The music is too loud to hear what they're saying, but Lily scrubs her hand up and down over Cora's arm, comforting her in some way. Likely telling her that it's not so bad. It will be just fine.

She's a liar, Cora. It's a trap.

Mandy notices her sister's arrival and unlinks her arms from my waist, making a tipsy, enthusiastic jog over to Cora, who still appears frozen and ashen in the entryway. I sip my beer, watching the scene from afar, taking in the way Mandy pulls Cora in for a hug like life is raining down sunshine and puppy dogs.

Cora's eyes meet mine over Mandy's shoulder and I lower my beer, offering her a small, understanding smile. She sends the same one back to me. But before I'm able to approach her to say hello, I'm sucked into a conversation with one of my good friends, Reid. He slaps my shoulder, looking genuinely happy to see me, and we spend about fifteen minutes catching up—well, he catches *me* up. I'm certain Reid has no desire to hear what I've been up to since we last saw each other in October.

When I break away to grab another beer, I find Cora in the kitchen clinging to her red plastic cup, engaging in conversation with Lily and a familiar-looking guy I presume to be Jason. I pull a fresh beer out of the cooler and glance in their direction, deciding that I was absolutely correct: I don't like Jason.

He's wearing a turtleneck, for fuck's sake.

And he keeps reaching out to touch her—her arm, her hand, her hip. He even pulled a piece of invisible lint out of her hair. Cora is all smiles and niceties as she nods at him, but I can see her grip on the cup is tightening and her knee keeps bobbing up and down. Lily is laughing at whatever bullshit he's spouting off, and hey, I think Lily and Jason would be perfect for each other now that I think about it. *Let's make that happen.*

I decide to insert myself into the conversation.

Cora's eyes dance over to me, lighting up when I push my way into their little three-way circle. "Dean," she greets, a big smile pulling at her perfect, cherry-stained lips.

"There you are," Lily says, leaning in for a one-armed hug, while her other hand clutches her own beverage. "Cora said you'd probably be here. How are you?"

"I'm doing good. Things are getting better." It's easy to lie when it's all you ever do. "What's new with you?"

Lily chatters away about her job as a pharmacy technician, but my eyes keep darting over to Cora. Jason is playing on his cell phone as he nurses a beer, occasionally looking up to nod and smile. I'm only half listening to Lily when I decide to blurt out, "Cora's not interested."

Lily stops talking. Everybody stares at me.

Jason clears his throat, sucking down the rest of his beer and tossing the bottle into a nearby trash can. "If that was directed at me, I'm pretty sure the woman can speak for herself."

"I'm sure she can, but as her soon-to-be brother-in-law, I have a responsibility to look out for her, and she's in no way ready to jump back into the dating pool. So, it's my strong recommendation that you take your flirtation elsewhere."

Jason lets out a laugh that sounds anything but amused, while Lily tries to stifle her own laughter. Hers definitely sounds amused, though.

Cora crosses her arms over her chest, glaring daggers at me. Her cheeks are flooding with color, her jaw tight. "What the hell, Dean? I'm standing right here."

"I know."

Jason turns to me, his hands planted on his hips. "Listen, man. I know you two went through some shit together, and I get that you're looking out, but—"

"Some *shit?*" I repeat, twisting around to face him. This flippant mother-fucker. "We were chained up like dogs for three goddamn weeks, kept alive with turkey sandwiches and well water, forced to do fucked-up shit, while Cora—"

"Dean!" Cora interrupts.

Jason holds his hands up. "I'm not trying to downplay anything. I was just talking to the girl."

Before I can get another word in, Cora snatches my hand and starts dragging me away from the kitchen. "Excuse us," she says over her shoulder.

She pulls me into Mandy's bedroom and slams the door shut, pressing her back up against it. "What. The. Hell."

I let out a sigh, feeling a little regretful. Maybe those four beers hit me harder than I thought they would. "Sorry, I was just trying to protect you."

She sets her cup down on Mandy's dresser and takes a step closer to me, her eyes stony, her features taut. "You *embarrassed* me."

"I wasn't trying to."

"Jason is a nice guy. He's always been polite and respectful. Besides, my sex life is none of your damn business."

"Sex life?" I arch an eyebrow as my insides spike with something that feels like jealousy. "You want to have sex with him?"

Her cheeks tinge brighter, her gaze floating away from mine. "Whether I do or I don't, it doesn't concern you."

I swallow. "You looked uncomfortable. I was trying to help."

"I don't want your help, Dean. You don't need to protect me anymore." She releases a slow breath, tipping her gaze to the ceiling. "And maybe I was uncom-fortable. Being *here* makes me uncomfortable. I'm still trying to get acclimated to people and noise and *living* again," Cora explains, her tone strained with tell-tale emotion. "But I don't need a babysitter. I just need to rip the Band-Aid off."

"You think of me as a babysitter?" I try to downplay the audacity in my voice by looking at my feet.

Cora is silent for a long time, prompting me to glance up. I find that her eyes are fixed on me. We hold for a beat before she replies, "I have no idea what you are to me."

At first, I'm offended. I'm outraged. *After all we've been through.* I'm about to respond, flustered and angry, when I realize…she's absolutely right. What the fuck are we?

We'll never be friends. We're no longer enemies. We can't be lovers.

Where does that leave us?

Soldiers at war. Kindred spirits. Two lost, wandering souls with nothing, and everything, in common.

Or…maybe not.

Maybe we aren't something meant to be labeled. We transcend titles.

And that, I fear, is the most powerful thing of all.

I lower my gaze to Cora's chest, noting the locket dangling between her breasts. She carries a piece of me with her.

She carries a lot of my pieces with her.

I chew on my cheek, scuffing my foot against the tan carpeting. "Have you seen the recent updates on the case?"

Cora looks taken off guard by the change of subject and starts scratching her wrist, her knee bobbing once again. "Yeah. It's all over my newsfeed."

Dammit. I was hoping she hadn't seen it. "It's all sorts of fucked. He was grooming these couples to fall in love or some shit before he killed them… It's sick and twisted."

Her eyes are wide and glazing over, her breath hitching on the inhale. "He said our time was almost up. Did he think…?"

Our eyes meet.

And I'm dead certain we're both thinking about what happened against that pole before I tore Earl's face off.

We both jump, startled, when there's an incessant pounding on the bedroom door. "Cor? You in there?"

It's Mandy.

"Be right out," Cora says, her voice clipped.

"You little hussy! Are you with a guy?" Mandy teases, then barges in, apparently not giving a crap if Cora is getting it on with some guy. She stops in her tracks when she spots me. "Oh. Hey, babe."

I stuff my hands into my pockets. There's a flash of suspicion in her eyes and it makes me feel itchy. I know Mandy has seen the news reports about

Earl's true motives, but she hasn't interrogated me yet. I gulp. "Hey. We were just talking."

A weird, awkward silence settles between the three of us, and I kind of want to just fall over and play dead like those goats do.

"Sorry, I didn't mean to interrupt," Mandy says, coughing into her hand as she tugs down her hot-pink dress with the other. "We're about to play flippy cup."

I used to love flippy cup.

I used to love a lot of things.

"Okay, that sounds fun," Cora says, reaching for her discarded beverage and sparing me a glance. "Count me in."

The women walk out, and I stand there alone in the middle of the bedroom—in the middle of *my fiancé's* bedroom—confused, rattled, and out of sorts.

What the hell did Earl see?

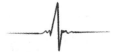

It's almost midnight and I can't find her.

I know it's wrong, I know it's twisted, I know I'm beyond wasted at this point, but it's almost fucking midnight. It's almost a new year. And I know, I *know*, I should be looking for Mandy right now, the woman I've rang in the last fifteen years with.

But I need to find Cora.

We went to hell and back this year—*together*. When the clock strikes twelve, it's a clean slate. A metaphorical new beginning.

"Ten…nine…eight…"

I scan the partygoers who are chanting and smiling, their drinks splashing around in their hands as they wave their noisemakers.

"Seven…six…"

I turn to the small balcony off the kitchen, and that's where I find her. She's leaning back against the rail, facing me.

"Five…four…"

I make my way toward her, pushing through a mass of bodies, and reach for the sliding door handle, pulling it open.

"Three…"

A wave of cold air hits me, and I watch as her hair is set in motion from the wind. The sparkles on her blouse twinkle beneath the moonlight, her eyes doing the same.

She's waiting for me.

"Two…"

I'm about to step out onto the balcony when I feel fingers curl around my elbow.

"There you are!"

I'm spun around in a circle.

"One!"

A mouth meets mine as celebratory cheers ring out around us. Mandy links her arms around my neck, pulling me in for our traditional midnight kiss, and my body wants to protest, push back, disengage…but I just stand there, my arms at my sides, and I allow her to kiss me. I'm too drunk to put up much of a fight, and besides, what would be the point?

Sorry, babe. I kind of wanted to have some one-on-one time with your sister instead. Maybe next year.

I'm a fucking asshole.

Mandy smiles as our lips part and she taps our noses together. That was our first real kiss since her birthday party on that fateful Saturday night.

"Happy New Year, Dean. This one will be better…I promise." She leans in for one more peck before adjusting the collar of my shirt and stepping back. "Want another drink?"

I want to say yes, but I'm already seeing double. "I think I'm good. I'm going to get going."

"Okay, I'll drive you."

"No, I'll call an Uber. You're the party host, Mandy."

She's about to argue, but Cora is suddenly beside me, her shoulder brushing up against my arm. "I can drive him. Lily's hitching a ride with Todd, and I'm getting tired anyway."

Mandy puts on her gossip face. "Ooh, scandalous. I'll need details." Then, as if remembering our encounter in the bedroom earlier, her face falls and her eyes dart between us. "Are you sure, Cor? I don't mind."

"Don't be silly. You can't leave your apartment unattended."

Mandy nibbles her lip, looking conflicted, until one of her friends starts calling her over for Jell-O shots. "Yeah, okay. That works." She glances over to me. "Call me in the morning?"

I nod.

Cora fishes through her purse for her car keys, then tips her head to the door, encouraging me to follow.

It's a silent ride to my town house, five miles on the other side of town, and I almost fall asleep. But I'm too preoccupied with thinking about the last time we were in a car together, and every time we hit a stoplight, I half expect the window to be smashed open and for a new nightmare to begin.

She helps me into the house a few minutes later because things are starting to spin at this point, and I make my way to the bedroom on stumbling legs, unbuttoning my shirt as I walk. "Come on," I say to Cora, who is lingering in the doorway, quiet and unsure.

"I should get going. It's late."

I pause to face her. She looks nervous, but not the uncomfortable nervous—not the Jason nervous. It's something else. "Lie down with me."

A bold request. Goddamn alcohol controlling my tongue.

"Dean…"

"It's not like we haven't before."

She blinks. "That was a mistake."

I take a step toward her, my shirt hanging open. "I guess if you want to call the best sleep we've had in almost two months a mistake, then sure. Okay."

Cora ducks her head, lowering her eyes to the gray rug in my entryway. "You know what I'm talking about. It's not appropriate. Especially because we've been…" She clears her throat. "Intimate."

"Those were fucked-up circumstances. We didn't have a choice."

"I know, but we have a choice now. We have our free will back, and it's telling me it's not a good idea to get in bed with my sister's fiancé. It's wrong, Dean." She lifts her eyes back to me. "I'm sorry."

I can't argue with her. I can't argue with any of that. I'm being torn in two directions, my mind telling me it's not right and that Mandy would never be okay with it, and my fucking soul wanting nothing more than to feel Cora pressed up against my chest, the sound of her beating heart singing me to sleep like a goddamn lullaby.

I'm so fucked.

I nod slowly, pressing my lips together. "Yeah, you're right. Happy New Year, Cora." I shoot her a jaded smile and begin to turn around…but something stops me. Something that has been bugging me for weeks. I stop her before she slips out the door. "Hey, wait a sec."

Cora turns to me with curious eyes. "Yeah?"

I scratch the back of my head. "That thing I said in the car that night… about the way you were dressed. About opening yourself up for unwanted attention…" I force my eyes up, noting a perplexed frown etched between her brows. "That was shitty. I don't ever want you to think that what happened to us was your fault or that you brought it on yourself. It was a fucked-up thing to say, and it's been bothering the hell out of me. I just… You looked so fuckin' pretty, and I guess I've always felt this weird protectiveness over you. I see the way men look at you and it drives me crazy."

Cora is wringing her hands together, biting her lip so hard I'm afraid she might draw blood. "Oh. Um…thank you."

"Yeah, you're welcome." I massage the nape of my neck, my chin to my chest. "Well, good night."

"Good night, Dean. Happy New Year."

I look up at her just as she shoots me the sweetest smile that makes my heart do things it *really* shouldn't, and then she's gone. I think about that smile as I crawl into bed a few minutes later, and I know I won't sleep well tonight, but I'll definitely sleep a little easier.

17

*M*ANDY'S *FINGERS ARE DANCING ACROSS* my knee under the table, making their way up my thigh. I catch her hand before it makes contact and shoot her a wink.

Little minx.

The Oar is noisy with rowdy patrons watching the game, slinging back beers, and shouting obscenities at the big-screen TVs. Cora and Brandon sit across from us, making googly eyes at each other as they try to decide on an appetizer. My friend Reid stops by the table with his new girlfriend to chat, while a waitress appears to collect our orders and refill our drinks.

Life is good.

I have a beautiful woman who I think I want to marry someday, job security, a new town house, and pretty damn good friends. I'm not sure why it hits me in that moment, hanging out at our favorite bar on a random Friday night in the middle of winter, but as laughter fills my ears and Mandy's hand presses warm against my thigh, I feel content.

"Do you think the waitress is hot?"

Reid says his goodbyes and I turn to Mandy, who is leaning on her palm and twirling a piece of light-blond hair around her finger. "Huh?"

"Her boobs are really big. And her extensions look great." Mandy puckers her lips with a sigh, deep in thought.

"You're crazy. I didn't even notice her."

It's true—I didn't. Cora is convinced I sleep around because I'm a "giant jerk face," and I guess cheating goes along with being a giant jerk face, but the truth is, I've only ever been with Mandy. We were each other's firsts when I was a sophomore and she was a junior, and we've been together ever since. We took a three-month break in college, but I still never strayed. It didn't feel right.

Honestly, the only other woman I've ever even thought about in that way is Cora…which is a secret I'll take to my grave. Neither of them can ever know I had eyes for Cora Lawson first when she ambled into English class as a doe-eyed freshman, radiating innocence and lavender.

The Lawson sisters are still the two most beautiful women I've ever laid eyes on, and one of them is currently glaring at me from across the table.

"What?" I question, leaning back in my chair. "Is my breathing getting on your nerves?"

"That's a given." She shrugs. "And you're such a liar. You obviously noticed the waitress."

"I didn't, and why would you assume that?"

"Because you're a straight male." Cora pauses, a wicked gleam settling in her green eyes. "Well…that's up for debate, I suppose. We can't forget that embarrassing incident with your college buddy last year."

I can't believe she went there. "You mean when you slipped me your dad's Viagra after I mentioned I had a headache? Real cute, Corabelle. I thought it was Advil."

She almost spits her drink out as she erupts with laughter. Damn her. That was the most humiliating night of my life, and I still have no idea how I'm going to get her back for it. Everything I think of falls short.

The waitress returns with our wings and cheese fries, and I keep my hard gaze on Cora, refusing to humor her with even the tiniest glance in the waitress's direction. But I can see Brandon out of the corner of my eye practically drooling into his craft beer.

"Anything else I can get for you guys?"

"Nope," I say, still staring at Cora.

She narrows her eyes at me.

The waitress walks away, and I reach for the wings, dipping one of them into the little cup of ranch dressing that was set in front of me. I take a big bite…

And literally almost Exorcist vomit all over the table.

"What the fuck? Is this mayonnaise?"

I hate mayonnaise. Despise it. Even the smell of it makes me want to puke.

Cora's laughter reemerges, and I zero in on the culprit. She's getting way too good at these pranks.

"Cor, you're such a bitch," Mandy says beside me, but her own laughter breaks through as she tries to hide it with her hand.

I fold my arms across my chest with payback in my eyes as Brandon leans into Cora, kissing her head and muttering, "That's my girl."

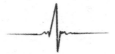

Mandy and Cora left about fifteen minutes ago. Brandon and I decide to stick around and have a few more beers since the game is still going on, and we're both eager to see who wins.

"I'm gonna take a piss. Be back in a few," Brandon says, sliding off his stool and weaving his way through the busy bar and grill.

I take a sip of my beer, my eyes on the game, when I notice the faint scent of flowery perfume floating over to me. I glance to my right. Our waitress is leaning her elbow on the bar, holding up her notepad and tapping it with her pen.

"Can I get you anything, sugar?"

There's no mistaking the flirtation in her tone, nor the intent in her eyes as she checks me out, biting on her bottom lip and thrusting her cleavage in my face. I look away, bringing the rim of my glass to my lips. "Pretty sure you saw me with my girlfriend all night."

"She's not here now," she replies boldly, tilting her head to the side and fluttering her long lashes.

I respond by pulling out my wallet and slapping a twenty-dollar bill on the bar counter, then rising from my stool. "Have a nice night." I don't indulge her with *a parting glance. I breeze right by and head out the doors to have a smoke before I leave. I can finish the game at home.*

I pull out my cell phone to text Brandon that I'm taking off, when I hear a familiar male voice coming from the left side of the parking lot. I squint my eyes through the darkness and spot Brandon leaning back against his Jeep…with his arms around a mysterious raven-haired woman. He laughs as he leans in and starts making out with someone who clearly isn't Cora.

I see red.

I waste no time in storming over to the cheating bastard, my hands forming into fists at my sides. Brandon pulls away from the woman when he sees me closing in, looking flustered and fucking caught. *I glance at the brunette and nod over my shoulder. "Leave."*

"Excuse me?" she demands, hands on her hips.

"Or you can watch," I shrug. "That's cool, too." I grab Brandon by his shirt collar, yanking him forward, then throw him back against the hood of his Jeep. "You slimy piece of shit. Four years—four fucking years with her, and you're throwing it all away for shiny, new coed pussy?"

Brandon raises his hands in defense. "Shit, man, I was just messing around. Don't tell her, okay? It'll kill her."

I slug him across the jaw. "You're going to tell her."

Brandon grabs his face in pain, howling into his hands. "I think you broke my damn jaw." He tries to push me off of him, but I hold tight. "You don't even like Cora. Why the hell do you care, anyway?"

I slam him against the car and he cries out again. "I always knew she was too good for you." I watch the mystery brunette scurry away in her high heels, and then I return my attention to Brandon. "You scumbag. You're going to end things with her or I'm going to break your jaw for real. I promise you that."

Brandon finally shoves me away and pulls himself up, breathing hard. He shakes his head. "It'll break her heart, man. The last guy she was with cheated on her and she hasn't gotten over it. C'mon, just let this go. It won't happen again."

I run my tongue along my teeth, letting his words sink in. Then I blow out a slow breath. "Say it was me."

"What?"

"Tell her you're breaking up with her because I threatened you. She already hates me. She'll believe it."

Brandon stares at me, dumbfounded. *"You're fucking crazy. Are you secretly in love with her or something?"*

I lunge at him, slamming him back against the hood. "Do it, or I swear to God you'll be at the plastic surgeon's office tomorrow getting a new goddamn nose." I lift off of him, slapping at his already bruising jaw as I stand. "Then I never want to see your face again."

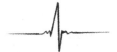

A double date.

Fantastic.

Things are just as awkward as I expected them to be, considering what transpired with Jason at Mandy's party last week. I tried to talk Mandy out of setting up this disaster, but she insisted it would be "good for Cora."

I'm not sure going back to the same bar that Earl hunted us down in with the intention of setting Cora up with a guy only six weeks after she was raped for twenty days straight is what's *good* for her, but there was only so much protesting I could do without looking suspicious. Besides…Cora agreed, despite my grievances.

And now we're trying not to make eye contact with each other over the table as she sits across from me, only pretending to eat her mozzarella sticks.

"So, when do you go back to work?" Jason asks Cora, leaning back with his hands on his knees, looking far too interested in the way the spaghetti strap of her camisole top slips down her shoulder.

Cora pulls it back up, tucking her hair behind one ear. "Monday, actually. I'm a little nervous, but it'll be good to get back to normal and have a routine again."

Mandy and I share a flatbread pizza, and I return the smile she sends me when we reach for the same piece.

"Do your students know what happened to you?"

My eyes cut to Jason, then Cora.

Cora makes designs in her marinara sauce with the end of the mozzarella stick, clearing her throat. "I'm sure they do. It's still the number one trending story."

"Shit," Jason says in a low breath, shaking his head with sympathy. "That's so rough. Well, the upside is maybe you'll get a movie or Netflix deal out of it. You know Hollywood is going to want to tell your story." Jason reaches for his beer and takes a few sips. "Have you been asked to do any interviews yet?"

Cora is scratching at her wrist, and I notice the delicate skin looks raw and irritated.

"Yeah, but I'm not ready yet. Maybe someday."

We share a look, but she glances down by ducking her head. Without thinking, I stretch my leg out under the table until I find her foot, linking my ankle around hers and prompting her eyes to go wide. I stare at her with a soft expression, grazing my ankle up and down her calf, trying to soothe her anxiety the only way I can. She doesn't pull away.

And she stops scratching her wrist.

Fuck. I think we're playing footsie under the table next to our dates.

"That's pretty cool, though," Jason says absently. "You're basically famous."

My head shoots up and I drop my foot. I'm done with this train wreck. "Cool?" I repeat through clenched teeth, trying to keep my voice calm and collected.

Mandy reaches out to touch my thigh, a gentle warning not to make a scene. I can see Cora's eyes spearing me with her own warning as she tucks both feet underneath her chair.

Jason cringes at his choice of words. "Sorry, that came out wrong. I was just trying to find a little positive in the negative."

"There is nothing positive about what happened to us. *Nothing,*" I bite back. I realize I'm gripping my fork like I'm about to use it as a weapon. I don't even remember picking it up. I drop the utensil with a clank, then fall back against my chair while everyone goes quiet.

I tap my hand against my thigh and bob my leg, desperate for a cigarette. I haven't had a smoke since the night of the abduction. I figured I had gone three weeks without it, so there was no point in starting up the habit again. But I'm finding myself easily agitated and low on patience lately, and the nicotine always helped calm me. Maybe I should just start smoking. Hell, I'm already a borderline alcoholic at this point… What's another vice to add into the mix? I decide to pick up a few packs after this shitty double date, and in the meantime, I'll just try to get drunk.

The night goes on painfully slowly with Jason asking dumbass questions, Cora playing with her food, and Mandy trying to seduce me with coy winks and thigh grabs. I sling back five beers over the next hour, grateful when I finally feel the telltale buzz creep in.

Jason and Cora are talking about some book I've never heard of, and Cora looks into it. She's relaxed and engaged, laughing at something he says with a genuine smile. At one point, Jason wraps his arm around her shoulder and leans in to kiss her on the cheek.

"You're such a sweetheart," I hear him whisper against her ear.

It takes all of my lingering willpower to keep my ass in my seat and refrain from lunging across the table to throttle him.

Jason announces he needs to use the restroom a moment later and ventures away from our table. Mandy immediately perks up.

"Oh, my God, Sis. He loves you." She beams, reaching over to squeeze Cora's hands in hers. "What do you think?"

I don't miss the way Cora glances at me before replying. "He's nice. I think there's potential."

"He seems like a douche," I mutter under my breath in between chugging down my sixth beer.

Cora jerks her head toward me. "Why? He's been a total gentleman."

"It's obvious he just wants to screw the damaged local celebrity."

I regret the words instantly, closing my eyes and waiting for the well-deserved comeback. But all I feel is Mandy ramming her elbow into my ribs. I wince. When I open my eyes, Cora is simply staring at me, wounded and teary-eyed. *Fuck.*

"Is that what you think of me, Dean?" She swallows, her hands trembling. She hides them in her lap. "You think I'm damaged, and men only want me for one thing?"

I try to backpedal. "No. Shit, I'm just…feeling drunk and out of my head right now, and I don't like Jason. I just meant that *he* probably sees you like that."

"Because I have no other redeeming qualities…"

There is still no anger, no bitterness, no animosity in her words. Only pain. Which is so much fucking worse.

I can't say what I want to say with Mandy sitting next to me, watching the scene unfold with questioning eyes, and I sure as hell can't stand to see that look on Cora's face for a second longer, so I push myself from the table and rise to my feet. I storm away, not looking back, and head toward the bathrooms. Jason is exiting as soon as I'm about to enter. He pauses, looking somewhat rattled by my presence.

I hadn't planned on starting anything, but fuck it. "Just stay away from her, okay?" I get in his face, watching a frown crease his brow. "She's been through too much. She doesn't need you fucking her all up again."

Jason swings his head back and forth, folding his arms defensively. "You've got balls trying to cockblock me from a woman you're clearly in love with, while your fiancée—her goddamn *sister*—sits right next to you."

What the hell? I almost choke on his words. They send me into a frenzy and I feel myself spiraling, so I snatch his T-shirt between my fists and spin him around, slamming him up against the opposite wall. "You don't know what the fuck you're talking about."

"It's clear as day, asshole, and I want no part of it." Jason shoves me away, smoothing out the wrinkles in his shirt. "You can have her."

I try to get my tapered breaths under control and reply, "I'm not in love with her. You're delusional."

"Keep telling yourself that." Jason slaps my shoulder, then runs a hand through his dirty blond hair and turns away, mumbling under his breath, "*Fucking dick.*"

I watch him leave, my blood boiling, and notice Cora standing there at the end of the hallway, clutching her purse strap in a firm fist. Her eyes dart between us, looking upset. Confused.

I'm a few feet away, but I hear Jason mutter before he breezes out the front door, "Sorry, but I'm not up for a competition. Take care of yourself, Cora."

And then we're left staring at each other from across the hall, both of our chests heaving, our eyes locked and loaded, the words on the tips of our tongues. But Cora walks away, pushing out through those same doors and disappearing into the night.

I follow her.

"Cora," I call out, watching as she makes a quick escape to her car, hitting the unlock button multiple times until her headlights blink to life.

"Leave me alone."

I catch up to her and slide into the passenger's seat as she enters the driver's side. "I'm sorry."

She doesn't look at me. "Get out of my car, Dean."

Cora turns on the ignition, mascara streaks etched across both cheeks, and even though my head is starting to feel loopy from the beer, I realize I fucked up. Big time. I made her question her worth *and* I sabotaged her date.

And for what?

Why?

"Corabelle, please. Talk to me."

Her shoulders are trembling as she plants both hands on the steering wheel, squeezing until her knuckles go white. More tears spill from her eyes. "Fine." She sniffles, looking up at me with eyes made of emerald flames. "We're done. Whatever this is, whatever is between us—it's done. Over. I thought I needed you to heal, but this is toxic... All you're doing is holding me underwater and I can't breathe. I can't heal when I'm constantly reminded of my trauma every time I look at you." Cora inhales sharp, ragged breaths as she finishes. "I thought you could fix me. But you're killing me, Dean."

I'm stunned into silence, my heart shattering into a thousand fucking pieces. All I can do is gawk at her, and I know she doesn't want this, I *know* she's just upset and pissed and confused. I find myself feeling entirely vulnerable and at a loss for words. I glance down at the center console, swallowing my pride. "I don't know how to get through this without you."

"You need to try. We're not in that basement anymore. We're on our own now."

"No, Cora, we *are* still in that basement. We never got out. And we'll stay down there, trapped, chained to steel pipes, drowning in darkness, until we can fix our shit. *Together.*"

"No!" Cora slaps one hand against the wheel, releasing a gasping sob. "No… *not* together. I can't be calling you in the middle of the night to come over, we can't be sharing a bed, we can't be talking on the phone every night until we fall asleep." She shakes her head furiously. Adamantly. "I can't let you hold me and touch me and look at me the way you do. It's not fair to Mandy. I feel like my soul is *rotting.*"

"We haven't done anything wrong," I insist, trying to get through to her.

"We've done *everything* wrong."

I gaze at her through the dim-lit car, her tears illuminated by the dashboard. She looks worn down, defeated, and lost. All I've tried to do is build her up, put her pieces back together, and quiet the ghosts that haunt her day in and day out.

I had no idea *I* was the reason for the look in her eyes right now.

It guts me.

I glance down at the chain around her neck, the heart locket hidden beneath her red camisole. Her top matches the color of her mouth, even though her lipstick is smudged from the tears still raining down her cheeks. While staring at her lips, I'm reminded of the last time I was pressed against them and how warm and soft they felt—something good and pure poking through the ugliness. I find her eyes and ask, "What happened between us that last day?"

I finally said it. I brought life to the single most confusing moment of my existence, and up until now, up until this very second, I could still pretend it was a dream. A mirage. Maybe a fucked-up fantasy. It wasn't *real*—as long as we never acknowledged it, it never happened.

But it's real now. And it's hovering between us, thick and potent, tearing away our armor and walls and carefully assembled layers.

Cora's breath hitches as she locks her eyes on mine, blinking back more tears. "I wasn't myself. I zoned out and my body was confused. It didn't mean anything."

I frown, taken aback by her words. *Bullshit.* "You're lying. You were *there* with me, one hundred percent. I saw it in your eyes."

"No."

"Yes, Cora."

"*No*," she grits out, her chin quivering. "Please go."

I lean forward until our faces are only inches apart and I can smell the flowers in her hair. I clench my jaw and say in a low, low voice, "You can lie to yourself all you want, but I was there. I *know* you felt it. And I'm not saying I understand it, or can explain it, or know what the fuck to do about it, but it was *something*, Corabelle."

She pulls her bottom lip between her teeth, her breathing uneven and her body still shivering, but not from the cold—no, not from the cold. Cora leans in to me, her eyes dancing to my mouth for a fleeting moment, then right back up again. She sucks in a breath. "Don't call me that." Her voice is deadly calm and full of icy warning. She falls back against the seat, still cutting me with her sharp gaze. "Now…get out of my car."

The flickering light I've carried with me since the day this all began, the hope of better days, the glimmer of promise that someday, one day, everything will be bright again, extinguishes right then and there. I feel cold and dark and empty.

And so very alone.

I nod, slow and sure, silently admitting my defeat, then turn to exit her vehicle without looking back. If this is what she wants—if this is what she *needs*—I have no other choice but to walk away. And even though I hear her crying, sobbing her heart out into the starry night through the cracked car window, I keep on walking.

I walk straight toward Mandy, standing in the middle of the parking lot hugging herself, her own tears of betrayal slipping down flushed cheeks.

"Mandy…" I say, picking up my pace so I can reach her, get to her, try to explain something I can't even explain to myself.

But she whips around, her hair flying over her shoulder like a curtain closing. Mandy gets into her own car and speeds out of the parking lot as Cora's car follows behind a few moments later. I'm left abandoned in The Broken Oar parking lot on a frosty January night.

It's fine, I say, stumbling back until my foot hits a curb, and I collapse onto a patch of grass.

It's okay.

I've slept in worse places.

18

My head is pounding when I wake up the next morning to a muted light trickling in through a nearby window. At first, I think I'm back in that basement. It's day number sixty-three, and the endless cycle of torture and mind-numbing madness continues. I instinctively begin tugging at chains that don't exist, and when I snap back to reality in a cold sweat, I realize that the chains *do* still exist. They are the invisible kind.

Those might be the worst kind.

I rub the sleep from my eyes with the heels of my palms, sitting up on my elbows and taking in my surroundings.

I'm in Mandy's bedroom.

"Good morning."

My head flicks to the right. Mandy is sitting beside me, holding a glass of water and a bottle of Advil, her expression somewhat melancholy. Mandy drove back to the bar to pick me up five minutes later, too racked with guilt to leave me there. I was grateful…though, I wonder if I truly deserved the courtesy. She brought me back to her apartment, and I plowed through the leftover alcohol from her New Year's party, passing out a few hours later.

I sit up all the way, leaning back against her blush-pink upholstered head-board. I pop three pills and drink the water she hands to me, then set the glass down on the nightstand, sighing as I run a hand along my face. "I'm sorry."

I've been saying that word a lot lately.

I'm sorry I'm still fighting a battle I can't win. I'm sorry I'm a mess, drinking away my problems. I'm sorry my head is filled with dark, depressing thoughts that often consume me. I'm sorry I can't touch the woman I'm supposed to marry. I'm sorry I can't fix the woman who won't let go of my heart.

I'm sorry I keep fucking up.

I'm sorry I'm wasting my second chance.

Mandy looks over at me with her raccoon eyes and mess of blond hair. "You left me alone in the bar, stuck paying the dinner bill, to chase my sister into her car, Dean."

Shit.

I'm *really* sorry for that.

"It's not what you think, Mandy. It's not…it's not like that. We're trying to get through this shit together, and I'm not handling it well." I puff my cheeks with air and let out a hard breath. "There's no handbook, or guide, or *Surviving Life after Earl's Torture Chamber for Dummies*. There's literally no one else out there like us because he murdered them all. We're an anomaly—we're not supposed to be here—and it's fucking me up."

Mandy reaches out a tentative hand, resting it atop my own. "I'm trying to be patient, I really am. But when you're always running to her and away from me, it hurts. I should be the one helping you through this. I should be your anchor."

"I know," I say, my voice pitching. "Trust me, I know."

She squeezes my fingers in her warm hand, offering me a wistful smile. "Maybe you need medication…" she suggests.

"I'm not sick, Mandy."

"You *are* sick. You have PTSD. You were tossing and turning all night, sometimes yelling and shaking the bed. You haven't figured out your car situation, or when you're going back to work, or how you're going to pay for anything when your savings run out. You drink all day, every day. You haven't said a word about the wedding. You won't touch me or kiss me. In fact, it seems like you don't even want me around." Mandy ducks her head, biting back tears. "You're not okay, and I don't know how to help you."

I don't know how to help me either.

"I think I just need time."

I can see her scanning my face, trying to read me, out of the corner of my eye. Mandy pulls back and starts wringing her hands together, inhaling sharply. "Do you need time away from me? Do you need space?"

I run my tongue along the roof of my mouth, rolling my jaw. "I just need time to think, I guess. I don't know."

"To think about if you want to spend the rest of your life with me or not?" Her voice sounds scared, edging on panicked.

I glance at her. "I don't know, Mandy. I don't know what I want anymore."

I thought I knew what I wanted. I had my future all set up, locked in, ready to go. Mandy and I have always been good together. It's been easy and low key. No drama. Minimal fighting. Maybe a little stale at times, but that's bound to happen when you're with the same person for one-and-a-half decades.

But now I feel like something's always been missing.

That *spark.*

A profound connection.

Fun.

I feel like I'm a different person and Mandy hasn't changed at all. I'm evolving, and she's stagnant. I'm picking apart all the things that make us different, all of our flaws and missing parts. I care about Mandy, absolutely, but do I *love* her?

I think so. Maybe…but it's always been comfortable and carefree. Surface-deep. Not that it's lesser or defective in any way, but it's different. We've never pushed ourselves to grow; we've never peeled apart our layers and uncovered what really makes us tick.

Something feels like it's missing now.

We have no scars, no battle wounds. We haven't been to hell and back, or clung to each other in the shadows, crying, shaking, expelling the dirtiest pieces of our soul together.

Cora and I were forced to grow together, to connect on a deeper level.

Our survival was at stake.

Fuck.

I throw my legs over the side of the bed, feeling mixed up and shaken. I bury my face in my hands, flinching when Mandy places her fingertips against the small of my back.

"Think about what you really want, Dean. I'm not going anywhere." She rubs my back in soft and steady motions, up and down, back and forth. "I have a bridal party coming into the salon for updos in an hour, so I'll drop you off at home on the way. Feel free to take a shower or eat or something. I'm going to get dressed."

I feel the mattress lift up as she stands, her footsteps making their way out of the room, the door shutting gently behind her. I tent my fingers and stare at the wall.

What the fuck do I want?

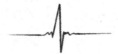

I'm sitting in front of the television that evening, keeping my eyes away from the kitchen where a brand-new bottle of vodka beckons me from the top of the refrigerator. I'm torn between throwing it over my balcony into the wetlands and polishing off the whole damn thing, just so I can go numb and pass the fuck out.

Or die.

I'd probably die, and it's concerning how unaffected I am by that prospect.

Maybe Mandy was right about the medication thing.

I'm still deciding what to do when I hear my phone buzzing beside me on the little wooden table. I reach for it, surprised to see Cora's name attached to a long string of text messages coming through.

Cora: I'm sorry about what I said.

Cora: I think.

Cora: The truth is I had a few glasses of wine so now I'm a little loopy and confused and normally we would be talking on the phone right now but we're not because I told you to leave me alone and I kind of regret that.

Cora: Don't judge me for that awful run-on sentence. My eyes are bleeding just looking at it. Please delete it.

Cora: Anyway, I'm going to try and sleep. I don't hate you. I know I said you're holding me underwater but you're the only thing keeping me afloat.

Cora: Good night.

Cora: Delete that run-on sentence please.

I find myself smiling down at my phone, debating if I should reply, or if I should call her, or if I should Uber it over to her house and hold her until she falls asleep.

Maybe I should ignore her.

Maybe she was right about everything.

I tap my thumb against the side of my phone, pursing my lips together as I consider my next move.

Then I shoot her a quick reply:

Me: Good night, Cora.

I head to bed, minus the vodka.

19

My first day back to work the following week is a train wreck. I'm a heavy-construction-equipment operator for the roads, which basically means I need to be lucid and clearheaded as fuck. I operate tractor trailers, bulldozers, cranes, and a variety of other big-ass vehicles to patch concrete, repair highways and bridges, and haul toxic materials around. The heavens decided to rain down an ice storm today in honor of my first day back, so I had triple the anxiety. It was nearly impossible to stay focused as I tried to remember controls and protocols, while also having to fake-smile my way through the day and answer a thousand questions pertaining to my close encounter with a serial killer.

But I survived.

The weather is clearing up as I pull off my hard hat and hop into the rental car provided by my insurance company. It's a shitty Hyundai, but it'll do for now. I let out the sigh it feels like I've been holding in all day and collapse into the driver's seat, drained and exhausted. I'm also fidgety and edgy from my alcohol detox. I haven't touched a drop of liquor since the double date from hell over a week ago at the Oar.

I'm trying. I'm really fucking trying.

As I'm about to put the car in drive, my phone starts to ring, and Cora's name and number pop up on my Bluetooth screen. I squint my eyes to make sure I'm seeing correctly and that impaired vision isn't a side effect of the withdrawals. Cora and I haven't spoken much over the last week, aside from a few casual text messages and some Facebook engagement. She filled me in on her first days back to work teaching at the school, and I told her about my upcoming start date, which was today. Basics. Normalcy.

Nothing that would indicate we barely escaped death two months ago, and certainly no reference to our emotional encounter in her car when she told me to leave her the hell alone because I was killing her.

Even though she took it back, I'm still giving her space.

For her, and for me.

I click Accept, thinking she's calling to inquire about my first day back. "Hello?"

I can make out the faint sound of sniffles on the other end of the line. "Dean?"

"Cora?" My heart goes into overdrive, my chest flooding with thousands of harrowing scenarios. "Are you okay?"

"I—I'm sorry to call you. I know it's your first day back to work, and I was just going to leave you a voicemail, but…" She tries to catch her breath, small sobs breaking through. "It's Blizzard."

I blink, absorbing her words.

Oh, shit.

"Blizzard? What happened?"

"She had a seizure or something. It was bad, Dean. We couldn't snap her out of it. I'm at the emergency clinic and they say she's totally unresponsive." Cora starts crying, hiccupping through her words. "They said we need to consider euthanasia."

Fuck. This can't be happening. I pinch the bridge of my nose, then trail my fingers through my hair, tugging at the roots. "Shit, Corabelle. Tell me which hospital and I'm on my way."

"Are you sure? I know you're working…"

"My shift is up. I want to be there."

Her sigh of relief kisses me through the Bluetooth. "We're at Care."

"I'll be there in twenty minutes."

I disconnect the call and drive at least ten over the speed limit, my mind reeling, until I career into the lot and park like a jackass, taking up two spaces. I run through the main entrance and find Cora and her parents huddled together in the waiting room. Cora stands as soon as she spots me coming toward her and we're yanked together like magnets, pulling each other into a tearful embrace. I smile at the Lawsons over Cora's shoulder. Derek has his hand on Bridget's knee, while Bridget blows her nose into a tissue.

"I'm so sorry, Cora," I whisper against her ear, feeling the way she tightens her hold around my midsection in response. "How much time do we have?"

"They're waiting for us in the…room." Cora sniffs, pulling back to glance at me through red-rimmed eyes. She swipes at the tears along her cheekbone. "Mandy's at work. She said it was too hard to be here. Mom and Dad are going to wait out here, but…did you want to come in with me? To say goodbye?"

"Of course."

I don't hesitate. We rescued this dog together, and I'll be damned if I'm not with Cora when Blizzard takes her last breath.

Goddamn.

Cora gives a tight nod, then alerts one of the staff that we're ready to go in. I follow her, a solemn silence settling between us. It's a quiet, peaceful room, adorned with electronic candles and soft music. Blizzard is lying very still on a dog bed in the center of the floor, her fluffy chest heaving ever so slowly with each breath. I feel my emotions get stuck in my throat when I lay eyes on the dog that has felt like my own for the last ten years.

I'd dog-sit her when the Lawsons took family vacations. I'd take her to the dog park with Mandy and Cora, watching her chase tennis balls and make new friends. Blizzard always greeted me first when I'd walk through the front door with Mandy, collapsing onto my feet and rolling over for belly rubs. She always sat beside me at the dinner table, waiting for the snack I'd inevitably offer her, and she always wagged her tail in adoration as I sang karaoke in the Lawsons' living room.

Her tail never seemed quite as enthusiastic when everyone else sang.

The technician talks us through the process in a kind voice, letting us know to take as much time as we need. There's a button we need to press when we're ready.

When we're ready to let her go.

Cora kneels beside her dog, resting a shaky palm against Blizzard's ivory fur. I kneel down next to her, doing the same, our shoulders melding together as our own respective memories sail through us.

"She was acting funny the night Mandy and I were getting ready for her birthday party. Bumping into things, walking in circles, panting more than usual," Cora whispers, our fingers brushing together as we stroke Blizzard's tummy. "Do you think she was sick and waited for us to come home?"

Cora looks up at me with big eyes as tears track down her rosy cheeks. I swallow, holding back my own grief, trying to be strong. "Yes. She couldn't go without saying goodbye to her favorite people."

Cora links her index finger with my pinkie, resting her head against my shoulder as her body trembles with fresh tears. I snake my other arm around her, bringing her as close as I can, then twist my head to plant a kiss against her hair.

"I'm glad you're here," she murmurs, wiping her tears away with her sleeve.

"I never thought I'd hear you say that."

I relish in the small, hoarse laugh that escapes her as her finger squeezes mine.

I press the button a few minutes later and the veterinarian steps inside with her cart. It's a cart of death. The doctor explains what's going to happen, that it will be peaceful and painless, that the medicine will stop Blizzard's heart and she will fade away.

I can't help but feel like that's a perfect way to go.

It's an emotional few minutes as we watch the dog's chest rise and ebb until she releases her final breath, surrounded by her rescuers—surrounded by love.

Fuck, I think I might lose it.

The doctor issues us her condolences and begins to drag the cart out of the room. "Blizzard was a wonderful family member, Miss Lawson. I'm very sorry for your loss. I'll let you and your boyfriend say your final goodbyes now. Feel free to step out whenever you're ready. There's no rush."

Boyfriend.

I suppose we do look like two grieving lovers, pressed up against each other, fingers intertwined. Cora doesn't correct the mistake as the door clicks closed.

When an eerie silence fills the room and I glance down at Blizzard, lifeless and unmoving, something in my heart clenches. My bones physically ache and my lungs fill with impossible grief. I lean back against the wooden bench behind me, inhaling a few shuddering breaths, and then I let go. I press my palm over my face as tears sting my eyes, spilling out, depositing into the cracks of my fingers. Cora immediately scoots backwards on the floor, sliding up beside me and leaning in. She wraps both arms around me and presses her cheek to my chest, holding me as I cry my fucking heart out over this fluffy little friend I'm going to miss the hell out of, and so much more.

"Shit, I'm sorry," I breathe out, hating the way my voice splits and wavers as I scrub a hand over my face.

"You loved her," Cora whispers against my neon work vest, her fingers clutching the shirt underneath. "It's nothing to be sorry about."

She raises her head to look at me and our eyes lock together, something heavy and potent and commanding passing between our souls. Cora touches the pads of her fingertips to the side of my face, which is still damp with my grief. I grit my teeth together, unsure of how to process the moment or the strange, bewitching energy hovering in the air. I stare at her, taking in her runny makeup, glossy eyes, and pink mouth. Her cheekbones are flushed with sadness and her hair is a mess, sticking up like she just got zapped by something.

Maybe she did.

Cora leans up on her knees, then ever so softly, without warning, presses her lips against my mouth...just barely. It's a featherlight kiss.

A flutter, a buzz—like hummingbird wings. Beautiful and curious.

She pulls back, her eyes widening slightly, a frown creasing her brow as if she's dazed and bewildered. Her tongue pokes out to wet her lips and she breaks eye contact, falling back to the floor and clearing her throat. "Sorry. I don't know why I did that."

I draw my knees up to my chest and scratch at my shaggy hair, running my palm down the back of my neck. We're friends, in a way—I think—and that's what friends do sometimes during life's shitty, heartbreaking moments.

Right?

I glance down at Cora, who is leaning against the bench beside me, her eyes closed and her lips pressed together as if she's replaying how they felt against mine. I let my fingers dance their way over to her hand and I lace them through hers, grateful she doesn't pull away from me. Her hand squeezes mine as I look back to Blizzard, so peaceful and loved, and say, "It's nothing to be sorry about."

I offer to drive Cora back home as the snow starts to fall.

It's Martin Luther King Day, so she didn't have to work today. She was grading papers at her parents' house when Blizzard had the prolonged seizure she wasn't able to recover from.

I asked her before we left the hospital, just to be certain, "Are you sure you don't want to go with your parents? I don't want you to be alone when you're so upset."

Cora shook her head. "I won't be alone," she said.

I took that to mean she wanted me to stay with her for a while, so when we pull into her driveway, I follow her inside. The snow is falling hard now, having only been coming down in soft flurries when we pulled out of the emergency clinic parking lot. Fat snowflakes blanket our hair and jackets as we make our way up the snowy pathway to her front door.

I pause in my tracks before going inside, glancing up at the sky, blinking at the sheet of white raining down on my face. I can't help that a smile breaks through my somber haze. "It's a blizzard."

Cora falters on her porch step, twisting around to look at me with the widest, most enchanted eyes I've ever seen. She steps down to join me on the walkway, holding out her arms and looking up with me. "Oh my God. Do you think…?" Her voice trails off and she starts to laugh. She *laughs*. Delirious laughter pours out of her as she spins around in circles, her nose pointed toward the heavens. "It's her, Dean. She's saying goodbye."

I think my goddamn heart might explode.

I suck in my emotions, blowing them back out into the chilly air. I'm not sure what's got me more choked up—Blizzard's parting gift to us or watching the way Cora is floating around and around in clumsy circles, sheathed in white, looking utterly enraptured and lost in the moment.

Healing.

She looks like healing.

We find our way inside and strip out of our soggy winter wear, collapsing onto the couch, mentally and emotionally drained. Blizzard always used to sit right between us on the couch—*always*. It became a running joke that she was trying to prevent us from killing each other.

Now I wonder if she was trying to tell us something.

I shake the thoughts away and lean my head back against the cushions, my eyes closing on instinct as the long, tiring day takes its toll. I've almost completely passed out when I feel a hand squeezing my knee.

"Go lie down. You look exhausted."

I make a *hmmph* sound, which is code for *That sounds great, but I don't want to move.* Cora seems to decipher the noise and starts tugging on my legs, stretching them out until I'm sprawled out, taking up the full length of the sofa. Fleece envelops me and I tuck the blanket around me, noting the faint aroma of daffodils as I tug it up to my chin. I'm starting to drift away when I feel her lips against my cheek, just as light as before. A tickle, a whisper, a fleeting kiss.

Healing.

She feels like healing.

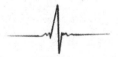

A scream forces me upright on the couch, disoriented and bleary-eyed, as I try to figure out where the fuck I am.

Mint walls, a coral couch, a shag rug beneath my feet.

Daffodils.

Cora.

I'm on Cora's couch.

Cora is screaming.

I jump to my feet and sprint down the hallway to her dimly lit bedroom, where I find her tossing and turning, kicking at the covers, gripping the bedpost between both fists behind her head.

She screams again. "*No!* Please, no…"

Her eyes are closed, squeezed tight, but I know she can see.

She sees all the same horrors I see when I close my eyes at night.

I rush to her bedside and cautiously slide myself onto the mattress, careful not to startle her. "Cora…Corabelle, you're dreaming." I slip my arm around her waist and pull her close, whispering into her ear, "Come back to me."

She's still writhing on the bed, her expression pained and terrified, so I try again.

"Cora…"

She whacks me across the jaw.

"Fuck," I mutter, massaging the side of my face as Cora whips herself into a sitting position.

Cora's eyes fly open, her chest heaving with strained breaths. "Dean? Dean… oh my God…" She grabs my face between her hands and starts peppering kisses along my tingling jawline. "I'm so sorry. I was dreaming. I'm *so* sorry."

"It's okay. You're safe."

Cora slings her arms around my neck, pulling me as close as she possibly can, and sobs against my shoulder. "Are you real?" she cries, tilting her head until her warm lips are pressed to the side of my neck.

I freeze for a moment, a shiver sweeping through me. I'm unsure of what to do or say or how to console her, but instinct takes over, and I lower her back onto the bed, cradling her in my arms as I situate myself beside her. "I'm real. You're real. Everything's okay, Corabelle. It was just a dream."

Her arms are still linked around my neck and her tears are still flowing. "I feel like I need to keep touching you… It was so vivid…" Cora slides her hands up and down my back, then over my chest, much like she had done the first time I released her from her chains. "Did I hurt you?"

I shake my head, planting a soft kiss on her forehead. "I'm fine."

"God, Dean…I'm so sorry. I'm such an idiot."

Her face is cupped between my palms in an instant as I force her eyes on mine. "You are *not* an idiot. You're the strongest fuckin' person I know."

Cora's chin quivers as I swipe her stray tears away with my thumbs. "I'm not strong. I'm falling apart."

"You're strong as hell. You *amaze* me." How can she not see what I see? How can she not know? "Don't you ever say that again, you hear me?"

She sniffs, still trembling, still misty-eyed and vulnerable. "I feel like it was all my fault. On top of all the flashbacks and nightmares and madness, I have this coil of guilt in the pit of my stomach. You shouldn't have been there, Dean." Cora sucks in a fractured breath, her leg sliding up over mine. "I shouldn't have called you that night…"

I frown, thrown by her admission. Rattled by the absurdity of it. "That's crazy talk. I was the one who set it in motion. That bastard asked if you were my girl and I should have fucking lied. I should have said, 'Hell fucking yes, she's my girl' because I'd be lucky as shit to have you."

She stares at me with the most astonished look swirling in her emerald eyes, and her lips part, her gaze slipping to my mouth for the tiniest second.

"Cora, listen to me," I say, still holding her face in my hands, still clinging to her like it's the very last time. "Those were the worst three weeks of my entire goddamn life and they will haunt me forever." I swallow. "But I'm glad I was there. And I'd do it all again, a thousand times over, just to keep you from going through that shit alone. I'm *glad* I was there with you."

A gasp-like whimper escapes her. I've never seen her look at me like this before.

I close my eyes, dropping my forehead to hers. "And don't ask me what that means, Corabelle, because I don't have a goddamn clue. All I know is that I'd kill that son of a bitch over and over again just to keep you safe. Hell, I'd kill a hundred men if I thought that would chase away your nightmares and bring you peace. And I know how fucked that sounds. Trust me, I *know*, but I can't let you go another minute feeling guilty or responsible or *weak*. You're a warrior."

Jesus Christ, I'm spouting out these raw, unfiltered truths like I'm delirious, drugged—out-of-my-mind *drunk*.

But I've never felt more sober or clearheaded.

Or *terrified*.

Cora is gaping at me, speechless.

"Ah, shit… Say something, Cora." Our foreheads are still melded together, our noses touching. I feel her peppermint breath against my mouth as I close my eyes, waiting for her to tell me that *I'm* the idiot.

Cora is silent for a long time. The woman who has always been quick to bite back, sling her insults at me, use her words as ammo, is uncharacteristically quiet. Her hands are on my chest, one right atop my heart, and they fist the material of my shirt as her leg entwines with mine. Our bodies are close, too close, our groins almost touching, and my hands are cupping her jaw like she is something to be cherished.

Why isn't she talking?

Cora finally takes a long, unsteady breath, then inches down the bed until her face is smooshed against the front of my chest. "Sing to me."

For a moment, I'm brought back to that basement. I travel back to those dark November nights when I could hardly see her through the black hole between us. It killed me that I couldn't touch her. I couldn't reach out and grab her or hold her in my arms, bring her comfort, or whisper into her ear that it was going to be okay.

My voice was all she had.

I sing "Hey Jude" as I cradle the back of her head with one hand, feeling her tiny hairs tickle my chin with every breathy note. We fall asleep curled up together, clinging to each other, heartbeats aligned, but this time there are no sleeping pills. There is no alcohol. There are no vices or excuses or things to blame except ourselves and the confusing feelings that have burrowed inside our hearts.

And while there are still so many questions swimming around my brain, I finally feel like I have an answer to one of them.

I know what I have to do.

20

FIFTEEN YEARS EARLIER

*M*R. ADILMAN IS SUCH A *douche-nozzle.*

I flick the eraser side of my pencil up and down against the blank page of my notebook with a giant yawn, resting my head on my opposite hand. Mr. Adilman is prattling on about some book we were supposed to read as he simultaneously checks out Miss French when she stops in to give him a message about a new student. Gross.

"Listen up, everyone. We have a new student joining us today. Let's make her feel welcome here at Cary-Grove High," Mr. Adilman announces.

I glance up from my serious lack of note-taking and my mouth goes dry.

In walks an angel.

Seriously. I think she's a real-life angel with wings and a halo and maybe even a harp.

There's definitely a harp.

Her hair is spun with gold, partially pulled up with a flower barrette. Her denim skirt almost touches her knees, and a lavender blazer sits over her baby-blue tank top. She's wearing chunky sandals and the sweetest smile I've ever seen.

I'm blatantly staring, possibly drooling, as Mr. Adilman directs the petite blond to a desk much too far away from mine. She clutches her books to her chest with nervous hands, quietly taking a seat.

"Class, say hello to Corabelle Lawson. Her family just moved here from Rockford."

She clears her throat. "Um, it's Cora."

"Oh." Mr. Adilman looks down at his notes. "I'm sorry. This says Corabelle."

"Yeah, but I go by Cora."

The class mutters a bored hello as I continue to plan out our future in my mind. Homecoming and prom are a given. It would be great if we end up going to the same college together, but long-distance relationships aren't so bad. We'll make it work. We'll be married by thirty, buy a big house in the suburbs, and have three blond-haired babies by thirty-five. We'll travel a lot, then move right by the ocean when we retire.

I wonder if she likes the ocean.

Cora glances over in my direction and our eyes meet for the very first time.

Green.

Angels have green eyes.

She smiles at me, that same sweet smile, and this one is all mine. It fills me up and lights me on fire, and I know, I just know…

I'm going to marry this girl one day.

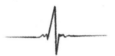

I'm sitting on Mandy's couch after work that Friday, guzzling down water from a bottle as I try to collect my thoughts. I squeeze the bottle in my fist, listening to the crinkling plastic mingle with the sound of Mandy's chipper voice floating through the apartment.

"And I can't believe Margo is retiring…"

I open and close my hand around the empty bottle.

Crinkle. Crinkle. Crinkle.

"She's basically our mama bear…"

Crinkle. Crinkle. Crinkle.

"Definitely going to… Dean? Are you listening?"

I snap my head up as Mandy saunters into the living room, wiping her hands on a dish towel. "Yeah. Sorry."

"Everything okay?" She cocks her head to one side, her hazel eyes shimmering with concern. "You look a little pale."

That's probably because I've been holding back my vomit for the last fifteen minutes.

My throat bobs as I swallow. "We need to talk, Mandy." I set the bottle down next to me and wipe my hands along the front of my denim pants.

Mandy stares at me for a moment, registering my words. She nibbles on her top lip as she wrings the towel between her fingers. "About what?"

She knows about what. I can see it all over her face.

Fuck.

"Shit…this is the hardest conversation of my life."

"Dean." My name comes out as a tiny cry, a plea. "Don't do this."

I stand from the couch, stepping toward her with outstretched hands. She moves back to avoid my reach and I pause, my arms falling at my sides, defeated. "I don't want to hurt you…"

"Then don't. I don't want you to hurt me." She folds her arms across her chest, her body already trembling. "We can work through this."

"We can't. And it's not because I don't care about you. We've had an amazing run, and I don't regret a single moment of the last fifteen years."

"Please stop…"

"But I feel like a completely different person right now. I know it was only three weeks. I get it, but I can't explain what happened to me. I just… I don't feel that connection, that spark, and you *deserve* that. You deserve so much more than what I can give you."

God, I hope that didn't come off like I'm feeding her bullshit because it's the fucking truth.

Mandy closes her eyes, holding them shut as her emotions begin to peak. I see her hands curl into fists, and she asks, "Is it because of her?"

"What? Who?"

"My *sister.*"

The word spits out between clenched teeth, like it was nearly impossible to say.

My jaw ticks in reply. This isn't about Cora. This is about me and Mandy. We're not well suited. It doesn't *work.*

Not anymore.

"No," I say.

"You're a liar. Something happened between you two in that basement," she says. "That guy was called the Matchmaker, Dean. I've tried to tell myself that you two hated each other and nothing would have happened, but now I'm just feeling like a huge idiot…"

I sigh. "I'm not saying I don't have a strong connection with Cora. I do. We went through a horrible trauma together, and it's impossible not to come back different from that." I run a hand along the nape of my neck, scratching at my hairline as I try to piece together words and sentences that make sense to both of us. "We were forced to do some fucked-up shit, and…it bonded us."

She swallows, almost choking on the words. "Do you have feelings for her?"

Feelings.

God, of course I have feelings for her. She makes me feel a lot of things. She always has.

But I realize Mandy is referencing something more specific.

More destructive.

She wants to know if I have romantic feelings. Sexual feelings. *More- than- friends* feelings.

"It's complicated."

Mandy glares at me. "It's not complicated, Dean! You either want to fuck my sister or you don't."

Jesus.

I look down at my work boots, realizing I should have taken them off at the front door. I probably tracked mud and sludge through her apartment.

"I'm going to be sick."

I glance back up as Mandy's hand hovers over her mouth, holding back her horror. I shake my head. "This isn't about Cora. I told you that."

"Then what is it? You just fell out of love with me in a matter of twenty days? All the other thousands of days didn't mean anything?" she demands.

I hesitate before blowing out a breath. "You don't feel like there's always been something missing between us? Like, we just haven't been able to dig deep enough?"

She grits her teeth. "What the hell does that mean? You asked me to *marry* you, Dean. I assumed you had done your digging."

"Fuck, I don't know. I think I was just comfortable… Everything had become routine and easy, you know? Your parents became my only real family, we have the same friends, Blizzard…" I let my voice trail off, closing my eyes for a moment to regroup. "Change is fucking scary, Mandy. I cared about you, we had history, and on paper we fit just fine. It didn't seem worth it to throw it all away."

"So, what's different?"

"Change was *forced* on me. I was forced to rot for three weeks in a serial killer's basement, and it really put shit in perspective."

Mandy taps her foot against the carpet restlessly, her long nails digging into the flesh of her arms. "It's great to know you were down there thinking about how you couldn't wait to break up with me."

"You know that's not what I mean." I take a small step closer to her. "Jesus, Mandy, I've *tried* to give this time. I thought I just needed to clear my head and work through all the bullshit. I've spent countless hours wondering how I can fix this and make it work. I *want* it to work, but…" I throw my hands up with defeat. "We don't fit anymore."

Tears spill from her eyes, smudging her perfectly applied makeup. Her eyes are level with my chest, unable to meet my guilty gaze. Mandy runs her fingers through her hair, tugging it back and cradling the nape of her neck as she tries to control her grief. "Fifteen years. *Fifteen years* of my life wasted on you."

God.

I'm an asshole.

A giant, fucking asshole.

"You want to know what I was doing while you were down in that basement, thinking about how much we don't fit and 'bonding' with my sister?" She finally lifts her eyes to me and they narrow with disdain. "I was making flyers. I was leading search parties. I was on the phone with police, with friends and relatives, with your mortgage company and utility providers letting them know your payments might be late…with fucking wedding coordinators begging them not to cancel our date because you were coming *home*." Her cheeks are bright red, flushed with scorn. "I was driving around town looking for your car *every single day*. I didn't eat. I didn't sleep. All I did was cry and look for you, praying for you to be okay…picturing you standing at the end of that aisle."

I squeeze my eyes shut, cupping a hand over my mouth and breathing deeply. I know there's nothing I can say to make this better. I know there's nothing I can do to lessen her pain or make her understand. I can't go back in time and tell her to stay the fuck away from me because I'm only going to break her heart one day.

All I can do is trust that this is the right thing for both of us and hope she sees it, too. She deserves better than this. She deserves more than half-assed kisses and hollow conversations. She deserves better than *me*.

"I'll always care about you, Mandy. *Always.* And I know you'll fall in love again and walk down that aisle someday. I know you'll find someone who sees the scariest, darkest parts of you and loves the shit out of you anyway. Someone who presses your buttons, gets under your skin, makes you crazy in all the best ways. Someone who makes you feel so alive, you can't imagine going back to the shell of a human you were before you met them. Someone who sees you, really *sees* you, stripped down and raw, and wants to collect all your broken pieces and cherish them like they are something beautiful."

I take a deep breath. Then another.

My heart is pounding against my ribs, my vision blurring. Mandy is staring at me like I was momentarily possessed by Nicholas Sparks.

Fuck.

I close the gap between us and grab her face between my hands, pulling her forehead in for a kiss. "Mandy, Mandy, sweet as candy," I whisper, echoing the rhyme I'd sing to her when we were teenagers. "I don't regret you. And I pray you can forgive me someday and we can be friends, because my heart won't be the same without you in it. But I understand if you can't, and I respect that." Her eyes are shut tight, weighed down by the burden I am handing her. "I know this isn't the happily ever after you imagined. I'm so sorry for that. But I *promise* you'll get it, and when you do, you'll look back and this will all make a hell of a lot more sense."

I place one last kiss against her hairline, watching as her tears silently dampen her cheeks.

Then I pull away and walk out her front door.

21

Cora: I did a thing.

I'M SITTING AT MY KITCHEN table that Saturday afternoon, eating one of those frozen macaroni and cheese dinners, when Cora's text comes through.

Me: How outrageous are we talking?
Cora: Hmm. Upper medium?
Me: On a scale of "I cut my own bangs" to "I bought a llama farm"
Cora: Let's just say I bought the llama from the farm. Two of them.
Me: Wtf?

I'm about to just call her when a picture text comes through and I almost choke on a noodle. It's a selfie of Cora holding a scraggly Yorkie mix in one arm, while her other arm is draped around a German shepherd, hugging the animal to her chest.

Me: ......
Cora: I sort of adopted a serial killer's two dogs. Meet Jude and Penny Lane.

Twenty minutes later, I'm standing in her living room.

"Are you nuts?" I glance at the two dogs curled up together in one giant dog bed as the miniature bed sits empty. "You adopted Earl's dogs? The ones who were going to eat us?"

She stands up straight after refilling their water bowls, pulling her hair up into a ponytail and raising an eyebrow at me. "I doubt they were going to eat us. Earl was just trying to scare us."

I blink. "The guy was pretty honest and forthcoming, if I recall."

"They needed homes, Dean. Nobody else wanted them. I already planned on adopting a dog, and this just seemed like the right thing to do. Look at them."

We both turn our heads to admire the undeniably adorable display. Penny Lane, the little one, is curled up into a tiny ball against Jude's chest. They are both fast asleep and content.

"Fine, they're fuckin' cute. I'm not a stone-cold monster. I'm just confused." I scratch my head, cocking it to the side as I try to process it all. "Aren't they… messed up?"

I realize that was the wrong terminology when Cora's head snaps back over to me. "Not any more messed-up than us. Are you saying we don't deserve to be loved and cared about because of what happened?"

Shit.

She's got me there. I fill my cheeks with air and shrug my shoulders, letting out a slow breath. "Yeah, I guess you're right. I just thought they might be aggressive or have some issues, you know?"

Cora swings her head back and forth, glancing at the resting animals. "They had a full assessment and the vet doesn't think they were abused. Just severely neglected. They're very attached to each other, so they came as a bonded pair."

A bonded pair.

They aren't the only ones.

She smiles wistfully. "I guess you were right about me getting two dogs."

My own smile stretches across my face. Her heart is even bigger than I thought. "I guess so."

"They're the sweetest. I've only had them for a couple of hours, but I think they knew everything was going to be okay the second they stepped inside the house," Cora says. "It's like they knew they were home."

My smile turns contemplative as I watch her, her bare toes curling into the shag rug, a far-off look in her eyes. It's funny how home can mean one thing one day and something entirely different the next. I think that's because home isn't a place—it's a feeling.

"Have you talked to Mandy lately?"

My daydreams disintegrate at the mention of Mandy's name. I chew on my tongue, realizing Cora doesn't know yet. "Uh…yeah."

Cora begins busying herself around the living room, fluffing pillows and folding a blanket. "She was supposed to come over last night to watch a movie with me, but she never showed up. She hasn't replied to my texts either, which is weird. She's usually glued to her phone." Cora breezes into the kitchen for a bottle of glass cleaner and starts spritzing the coffee table, wiping it down with a fresh rag. "Maybe she had to work late and forgot."

"She didn't tell you?"

Cora stands up straight to face me, adjusting her tunic that dipped down her chest. "Tell me what?"

Damn. I was hoping I didn't have to have this conversation twice. I'm still recovering from that look of utter devastation in Mandy's eyes, and I have no idea how Cora is going to react to the news. "I broke up with her yesterday."

Cora stares at me, unblinking, and the rag slips from her hand.

"I figured she told you. It was a rough night, and she didn't handle it well—obviously. And I just think—"

"Undo it."

I frown as I meet her eyes. "What?"

Cora pulls her cell phone out of her waistband and storms over to me, slapping the phone against my chest. "Undo it."

I catch it and hand it back to her. "No. What are you talking about?"

She spins away, her shoulders heaving up and down as emotions consume her. Cora is silent for a few beats, her ragged breaths the only sound permeating the air around us.

I reach out to touch her shoulder. "Cora…"

Cora flies back around on her heels with wild eyes. "Is it because of me? Did you break my sister's heart because of me?"

"No." I have no idea why she's so pissed off. "This has nothing to do with us."

"You're lying."

I stare at her, confounded. "Jesus, Cora, what the hell? I just... We don't work anymore. I can't pretend there's something there when there's not. It wouldn't be fair to either of us."

She hugs her arms around her chest, stepping toward me with icy purpose. "You're so stupid."

"Excuse me?" Cora storms away down the hall, and I follow, my anger flaring. "Cora!"

"I said you're stupid!" she repeats over her shoulder.

"Why are you acting like this?" I call after her, pushing against her bedroom door just before she slams it in my face. I barge inside. "You're being ridiculous!"

"Fifteen years!" she shouts, whirling around, her ponytail following and catching on her lip gloss. She shoves her hair aside, tears brimming in her eyes. "You just gave up fifteen years."

"You'd prefer I give up twenty? Thirty? If I *know* it's not meant to be, why would I string her along when she can start over and find happiness?" I counter, throwing my arms up.

"You're a coward."

"What?" I shake my head with a contemptuous laugh. "First I'm stupid, now I'm a coward. Thanks."

"Yes," she spits out, stepping right up to me until we're toe-to-toe. "You're a stupid coward, too scared to put in the work. Did you go to couple's counseling? Anything? Did you even *try*, Dean?"

"Fucking stop it. You don't get it."

"You were supposed to marry her! How could you do this?" Cora cries as the floodgates open and her tears begin to fall. "You were happy. You were happy before..." She lets her voice trail off, rolling her jaw and dropping her eyes to the floor.

I scrub my palms over my face with a sigh. "I was happy, but I wasn't *happy*. When you spend three weeks convinced your life is about to be over, you tend to do a lot of soul-searching and reevaluating. Mandy and I were getting by, but we weren't thriving. There was no *passion*."

"Passion? You're throwing away fifteen years for *passion*?"

"I didn't throw away shit!" I yell back. "They were a good fifteen years and I have no regrets, but we ran our course."

"Because of *me*."

"No, Cora, because I'm not in love with your sister anymore."

"Stop lying!" she shouts, her voice laced with desperation, almost panicked. "I was right about what I said in the car that night. This is toxic. This is *wrong*. We shouldn't even be contacting each other. Mandy's life is ruined and it's all my fault." Cora starts to sob into her hands. "I can never forgive myself."

"Corabelle, stop…" I try reaching for her again, but she pulls away like I'm going to burn her.

"Don't touch me. I can't even look at you."

"Why not?"

"Because it's true, okay?" Her voice breaks, shuddering and quivering and full of defeat. "Something happened between us that last day. I felt it, too. And I thought it was just some screwed-up defense mechanism that I'd leave behind in that basement…but dammit, Dean, it followed me. I still feel it." She looks up, boldly finding my eyes. "It's destroying everything, and I *hate* you for it."

My hand cups her face as my heart constricts inside my chest. "Corabelle…"

She slaps my arm away. "Don't call me that. Don't *touch* me. Just leave me alone."

"You don't hate me."

"Yes, I do!" The pitch of Cora's voice rises as new tears break through, and then she shoves me backwards. "I hate you. I always have."

"No."

"I *hate* you!" She shoves me again, her palms planting against my chest, causing me to stumble. "I hate you… I ha—"

"*No.*" I grab her wrists and walk her back toward the far wall until she's pressed up against it, shaking and crying. I cradle her wet cheeks between my palms and plant a kiss on her mouth, tender and soft. "You love me. You fucking *love* me, Cora."

Her cry becomes a gasp as her body arches into me, and I kiss her again—just as softly, just as sweetly. Then again, lingering longer, and again, until she curls her fingers around the nape of my neck and pulls me hard against her mouth.

I *kiss* her, and this time, there is no mistaking what it means.

There are no apologies.

Our lips fuse together with madness and chaos, missing and yearning, our tongues tangling like we're starving for each other. I angle my head to taste her deeper, but it's still not enough—*never enough*. Moans mingle together, becoming one, and I grasp her thigh, yanking it up and around my waist. So familiar…so instinctual. Cora sifts her fingers through my hair, then drags them down my neck, my chest, my abdomen, forcing a groan from the back of my throat. I trail my lips along her jawline, still christened with tears, my tongue tasting her as I find the curve of her neck.

Cora grinds her groin against my erection as her hands claw their way up my shirt. "I don't love you, Dean."

I kiss my way back to her perfect mouth, warm and soft, and she whimpers when I tug her bottom lip between my teeth. "Yes, you do."

"No," she breathes out, a strangled sob, like she's begging for it to not be true. *Please don't be true.* "I can't…"

"It's okay," I whisper, framing her head between my hands when she starts to twist from side to side, rejecting the very thought. "It's okay."

Cora yanks my face back down and our mouths crash together, teeth colliding, tongues hungry and violent. I grasp the side of her face, then force her jaw open by pushing my thumb between her teeth. She squeaks in surprise, and I take her mouth in mine, filling her with my tongue and tasting every inch of her. It's sensual and erotic, and I can't get enough. I'm fucking *drowning*.

She pulls back to catch her breath, crying out as if she's still trying to deny what seems abundantly clear. "This isn't real," she gasps, grazing her ankle up and down the back of my thigh. Her fingers are fisting my shirtsleeves with white knuckles, scared to let go.

"It's real." I kiss her forehead, then her nose, then her heart-shaped upper lip, as I intertwine our fingers and raise our hands above her head. I press our foreheads together, feeling the way our bodies meld so effortlessly. *A perfect fit.*

I'm about to kiss her again, I'm about to lose myself to her mouth and tongue and glorious heat, when my eyes catch sight of her wrist peeking out of her long sleeve.

It's been scratched raw, swollen and irritated, possibly infected.

Reality hits me like a bucket of ice water, and I grab her arm, cradling her wrist between my fingers and inspecting the damage. Cora tries to pull away, tries to erase what I've already seen, but I hold tight. "Corabelle, you're hurting yourself."

"Don't…" She sighs, her voice hitching. Her tears inevitable. "I'm fine. It's fine."

"God, Cora." I graze my thumb over the marred skin of her wrist, the exact spot I would massage beneath her cuffs to make her forget, then I bring it to my lips, trying to kiss away her pain. I pepper delicate kisses up and down the length of her arm, paying extra attention to the wound.

"Please don't." Cora tries to tug herself free and redirect my mouth to hers, but I don't let her. She collapses against the wall with frustration. "Let me go, Dean."

I close my eyes, kissing my way up to her fingertips. "Tell me you don't hate me."

"No."

She moves to escape, but I pull her to me, pressing our foreheads together once more. "Tell me."

Cora locks her eyes on mine, trembling in my grip. She shakes her head. "I do hate you."

"Dammit, Cora." I clench my jaw as my fingers curl around her upper arms, clinging to her. Begging for a different answer. "Please."

"I…" She's still looking me in the eyes when her breath catches and her face crumples. "I hate myself."

Cora goes limp in my arms with a heart-wrenching sob. I don't catch her before she falls—no, I let her fall, and I fall with her. Our legs buckle and we hit the floor, Cora in my lap, her face buried against my chest. I hold her so fucking tight I'm afraid I might break her, feeling her tears seep through my shirt and bleed into my skin. She clings to me, raining her own kisses along my torso in between her tears and hiccups, and I glide my fingers through her hair, down her back, letting her release.

"I've got you," I whisper into her hair. "Always."

She can pretend to hate me. If it diminishes even a fraction of her pain, she can fucking pretend all she wants.

But I know it's love… It *has* to be, because if this isn't love…

Then I'm certain it does not exist.

22

I WALK DOWN THE LONG HALLWAY, passing closed doors on either side of me. All of them are adorned with artwork, pretty wreaths, or homemade crafts. Most of the art is childlike, made by grandchildren and great-grandchildren and displayed with pride.

My feet stop at the one door that is blank and empty. Cheerless.

Sad.

She doesn't have any grandchildren. She doesn't have anyone except for me, and I'm too much of a coward to visit her more than once a year.

I knock against the frame as I let myself in, spotting her across the small condo, watching television from the foot of her bed in a nightgown.

"Leave it by the door, Frank," she says without looking away from the TV screen.

I swallow, taking hesitant steps inside the room. "It's me, Mom."

She doesn't move. Doesn't blink or flinch.

Holly Asher was a strong woman. Kind and soft in so many ways, yet there was always fight in her eyes. Her spirit burned bright with fierce protection for her family and love for those she deemed worthy.

My mother loved my father with the fire of a thousand suns, and he loved her back just the same. My childhood is riddled with vivid memories of them madly in love, kissing, chasing each other around the house, tickling, and dancing in the kitchen to Hootie & the Blowfish. I'd get embarrassed when my friends came over because I knew my parents would act like fools with their terrible dance moves and off-key singing. Mom would always try to pull me into the dance party and I'd run away, shouting, "You guys are so weird!" They would laugh and laugh, immune to my humiliation, and then they'd kiss, not giving a damn.

But they would fight, too. *Oh*, they would fight, and I'd hear them from the other side of the house in the middle of the night as I clutched the bedcovers to my chin.

"You're an idiot, Mark!"

"You drive me crazy, Hol!"

Their stomping feet and hostile words would vibrate right up to my room and tickle my heart. It always sounded so *bad*, like I'd wake up the next morning and Dad would be gone.

But that never happened.

Things would go back to normal by sunrise, as if I'd dreamt the whole thing.

Then there was the day I woke up and Dad *was* gone. It was two days after my high school graduation. I was yanked out of bed by my mother's horrified screams that still linger in my mind to this day. He'd passed away in his sleep from a heart attack.

So sudden.

So quick.

So fucking unfair.

My mother never really recovered from the loss and her mental state deteriorated over the next few years. Her memory began to decline at only fifty-two years old, and I always thought to myself, *"How horrible it must be to forget the love of your life."*

Now, I can't help but wonder if it was the only way for her to cope.

Maybe there is no recovering from something like that. Maybe there is no healing or moving on. There is no forgetting.

Not unless you truly *forget*.

I approach my mother, her light-brown hair dappled in silver and cut just above her shoulders. She glances up when I'm standing a few feet away, my hands in my pockets. "You look good, Mom."

She smiles, a warmth washing over her baby-blue eyes, almost like she recognizes me. "Randall. I'm so glad you came to visit."

I try not to take it personally. The doctors all say she can't help it. My father could be standing here, fresh from his grave, and she'd still be all mixed up. "Mom, it's Dean. Your son."

She nods her head. "Come sit." Mom pats the embroidered quilt beside her, encouraging me to join her. "Frank brought tea. It's by the front door."

"Thanks."

We sit in silence for a moment, my mother's attention back on the television. She sighs wearily. "It's such a shame the way those towers fell down. So much fire and destruction. So much loss." My mother shakes her head from side to side, her eyes glistening as images play out on the screen.

I glance at the TV. It's a commercial for dish soap.

My fingers weave through my dark hair, recalling the way my mother used to stroke my scalp with her fingertips to alleviate my stress or calm my nerves. I miss that sometimes.

I clear my throat, shifting my weight on the bed. "I know you're not going to understand what I'm saying, but I think I just needed someone to listen. I went through some pretty crazy stuff a few months ago, and I don't think I'm handling it very well. I'm confused about a lot of shit. I still have nightmares. It's taking all my willpower not to drink myself to death. And…" I close my eyes, grinding my teeth. "I think I'm falling in love with the only damn woman in the world who's completely off limits. I know she feels it, too, which should be great, right? This is the shit people write books about."

She sits very still, staring at the television screen as if she didn't hear a word I said.

"But there's no story like ours, Mom. People don't write about what we went through. They don't write about how we were abducted in the middle of the night by a sick motherfucker, handcuffed to pipes for three weeks, hungry, dirty, and scared out of our damn minds while I was forced to violate her with a gun to my head.

"They don't write about how I shredded a man's face with my bare hands until I cut my knuckles on his skull. They don't write about what the hell we're supposed to do after something like that, when life goes back to normal and everyone around us is smiling and happy, but we're still stuck in that hellhole, clinging to each other because we're all we have." I lower my hands to my face as I try not to break. "And the real kicker is that I was engaged to her *sister*. What the hell kind of twisted shit is that?"

Jesus Christ. What a goddamn mess. Part of me is glad my mother has no clue what I'm saying.

I breathe deeply into my hands, my elbows on my knees. I jump when I feel familiar fingers trail up the back of my neck and into my hair, massaging my scalp, quelling the pain that's tearing me apart inside.

I inhale a shaky breath, sitting up and looking over at my mother. Her focus is still on the screen, but her fingers continue their soothing trek along my scalp, forcing my eyes to close in contentment.

"Every love story is worth writing, no matter how messy it might be," she says absently, still stroking my hair. "I would like to read your book."

My brow creases into a frown, confused, wondering if she was absorbing my words after all. My mother used to have many moments of clarity, but they have become few and far between. The last time I visited her—in March, for fuck's sake—she wasn't at all lucid. She called me Gator the entire time, which was the name of our beagle who died ten years ago.

Mom reaches for my hand resting on my thigh, clasping it inside her cool palm, still enamored by the pictures on the television. "I had a terrible nightmare once. It was a lot different than yours, though." She squeezes my fingers and releases a small sigh. "I was all alone."

I wait for her to continue.

I wait for the story to unfold, the horrors to play out, the nightmare to come to life.

But she doesn't say anything else and I realize…that *was* the nightmare.

We sit in silence as her words pinch me. My insides ache and twist with something I don't exactly understand.

And then my mother lets go of me, smiling pleasantly as she folds her hands in her lap. "I should have the paperwork all filled out by the end of the day. I do appreciate you coming by."

As I drive home that afternoon, I think about the things I said, about the things *she* said, and about how sometimes all we need is a good dose of perspective.

There are worse nightmares than this.

I could be all alone.

I decide right then and there that I will start visiting my mother more often. No more hiding. No more fear. No more guilt.

Because as sad as my mother's condition is, there is nothing sadder than walking up to that blank, empty door.

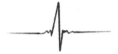

It's a little after 9:00 p.m. when the power goes out. My television flickers off, as do the lights, and I'm left sitting on the couch in complete darkness.

The first thing I think about is Cora.

She doesn't like the dark. She keeps the lights on at night, even in her bedroom, and I don't blame her.

I'm on the other side of town, but I reach for my phone just in case. Just to check on her.

Me: Did your power just go out?

I wait for her reply.

It's been another week since I last saw her—since we kissed and cried and held each other on her bedroom floor until reality crept back in and I drove myself home.

And that was it. We haven't spoken since, and it fucking sucks. I'm not sure what to say to her now that she feels responsible for my breakup with Mandy. I'm not sure what to think after she told me she hated me over and over, even though I know it's the furthest thing from the truth. And I sure as hell don't know what to do now that we've tasted each other again, voluntarily, *desperately*, and were likely one more kiss away from doing a lot more than that.

It's a mess.

My phone buzzes in my lap, and I quickly open the message.

Cora: Yes

Shit. She's probably terrified.

Me: Do you have candles or something?
Cora: I can't find my lighter. I'm using my phone's flashlight, but my battery is almost dead. Shoot me.

I run my tongue along my teeth, weighing my options. There are only two options, and it doesn't take long for me to pick one.

Me: On my way.
Cora: That's not necessary.
Me: You're afraid of the dark.
Cora: I'm afraid of a lot of things. You're one of them.

I stare at her text, my heart sinking into my stomach.
She's scared of me? What the hell?

Me: Wow. Ok then.

A few minutes tick by before her response comes through.

Cora: I didn't mean it like that. I'm afraid of the way you make me feel.

I should have figured that's what she meant. I tap my finger against my phone and shoot back a reply before grabbing my shoes and coat.

Me: I get it. But I'm starting to realize there are things much scarier than that. See you in 15 mins.

Cora opens her front door in a tank top and cotton shorts that I can hardly make out through the veil of darkness. I hold my phone screen up for light, illuminating the hesitant look in her eyes.

"You didn't need to come over, Dean."

I offer a small smile. "I didn't want you to be alone."

She steps aside, sighing softly, and allows me to enter. I take tentative steps inside, holding out my hands so I don't bump into anything. "Shit. It's really dark."

"That's generally the consequence of no light."

I make a humming sound, turning toward her when the door clicks shut. We stand there in silence for a few beats as our eyes adjust and find each other's faces.

Cora clears her throat and sweeps past me, heading toward the kitchen. "It figures the power goes out the same day I drop a small fortune on groceries. Do you want anything?"

The moon is our only night-light, and I can make out her vague outline reaching into the refrigerator to pull out a bottle of something. "I'm good."

"Well, I'm going to have a glass of wine and try to pass out."

I make my way into the kitchen, only bumping into one side table along the way. I hear the jangle of a dog collar from across the room and glance over to see four eyes glowing at me through the dark fog. "How are the dogs doing?"

I hear Cora rummage around a drawer, likely looking for the wine opener. "Really great, actually. Jude already knows how to give me his paw. Penny follows him around everywhere. It's adorable."

"That's awesome, Cora. I'm glad it's working out."

"Yeah, I definitely haven't gotten any vibes that they want to turn me into puppy chow. I think I'm in the clear."

I quirk a smile, sidling up beside her and watching as she pours the wine. She sets the bottle down and cups her glass, bringing the rim to her lips and flicking her eyes up to me as she takes a sip.

Cora nibbles on her bottom lip, lowering her glass. "I didn't hear from you all week."

Her tone is accusing, but her eyes spear me with something softer. "Oh…" I scratch my head, then rub my hand down my face. "I didn't know you wanted to hear from me."

She blinks over the glass, then dips her chin. Cora turns away and ambles into the living room, plopping down onto the couch without responding.

I follow, sitting down beside her. "Cora, you told me you hated me—like, a dozen times. Then you told me you hated yourself, which I can only assume is because of me."

She shrugs her shoulders and takes another sip. "I was upset."

"Well, I didn't want to make you more upset."

"We kissed, Dean." Cora glances at me through fluttering lashes. If I could see her better in the dark, I'm almost certain her cheeks would be flushed pink—and not from the wine. "A real kiss. You didn't have a gun to your head."

"I know."

Cora starts picking at her sock, averting her gaze. "I figured that would warrant a follow-up call, or a text or something."

I study her shadowed outline.

Her waves of hair spilling over her shoulders. Her eyes lowered to the wineglass she's spinning between nervous fingers. Her lips pressed together in contemplation. Her nipples pebbled through her cotton tank top.

Damn.

I lean back against the couch, my hands on my knees. "If it makes any difference, I wanted to call you. I wanted to see you." I wait until she's returning my gaze before finishing, "I wanted to kiss you again."

There's no mistaking the way her fist grips the stem of the glass, and a small gasp escapes her mouth. "That's not a good idea."

"No," I agree. "It's not."

But my eyes cut to her mouth anyway, and hers trail to mine. We look back up at the same time.

Cora chugs the rest of her wine and places the empty glass beside her. I think she's going to start scratching her wrist, but a fresh bandage provides a barrier, so she runs her hand along her arm instead, almost like she's cold. "I should get to bed. I haven't been sleeping well lately."

She glances at me, and I'm not sure if that was supposed to be an invitation or not. *Shit.* I realize I have no idea what I'm even doing.

But I came here for a reason, so I reply, "I can lie with you until the lights come back on."

Cora bites her lip, grazing her teeth back and forth as she processes the offer. Then she gives me a small, agreeable nod and rises from the couch.

I must not scare her quite as much as the dark.

Standing up, I watch as Cora saunters down the hallway, her white tank and shorts the only thing visible as she heads toward the bedroom. I make my way over to the bed, careful not to trip on anything in the process, and run my hands across the sheets as I slide in. I feel her body heat from the center of the bed, so I scoot my way to her and sling my arm around her middle. Cora stiffens for a moment, as if she's surprised by the contact. "Sorry… Is this okay?"

She responds by moving in closer, nuzzling into my chest like she's done so many times before, and letting out a long breath. "It's okay."

I can almost feel the tension leave us both, my nose nestled in her soft hair, her warm body pressed into me like she's the missing piece to my puzzle. Cora lies on her back with my lips to her ear, and I feel her shiver every time I exhale. She dances her fingers up my arm as we embrace the darkness together.

"Do you want to know the worst night of my whole life?" she asks suddenly, her voice merely a whisper, yet so loud in the silent room.

The truth is, I don't think I want to know…but I assume she wants to tell me. "What was it?"

Cora tickles my arm as her fingers glide back down, inciting goose bumps to sprout all over my skin. "It was the night after we… Well, the first time you had to…" She swallows. "You didn't talk to me. You didn't sing. And it was so dark."

God, she's going to rip my heart out. I close my eyes and squeeze her closer to me, my fingertips unconsciously dipping beneath the hem of her tank top. She lets out a squeaky sound when I trail them along the skin just below her belly button. "That was the worst day, and night, of my whole fucking life, Corabelle. I didn't know what to say to you." I inhale her freshly washed hair, burying my face into the crook of her neck. "What could I say?"

"I wasn't mad," she responds in a breathy tone, pressing herself even closer to me. "I understood."

"No." I shake my head, her golden locks tickling my nose. "You couldn't possibly understand. I spent the whole night wishing I'd let him kill me."

Cora jerks her head to her left, pinning her eyes on me. "Don't say that."

"It's the truth."

"No… Dean, don't ever say that again. Don't even think it." She twists around until we're facing each other, and my hand slides up behind her top, caressing the small of her back. Cora maintains my gaze for a long time before dipping her chin and sucking in a choppy breath. "Remember when we were trading confessions?" she asks, still avoiding my gaze.

I nod, and our noses almost kiss. "I remember."

Her tongue slicks over her lips and her eyes close as she pieces together her words. "You told me two confessions and I only told you one."

My hand instinctively rises up her back, massaging her spine, then curves around to her front. I splay my fingers along her stomach, feeling her body melt into me, and my breathing picks up to match my racing heart. "Do you have another confession?"

Cora nods timidly, her lips parting as she arches into my roving hand. I slide it up her middle until my fingers graze the underside of her breast.

Fuck, I'm getting hard. I should probably stop touching her.

But I want to keep touching her. The last time we were trapped in the dark, we couldn't even touch our toes together.

"Tell me," I whisper, lowering my hand and curling it around her waist. I leave it there, waiting for her to speak.

Cora's eyes are shimmering with moonlight seeping in through the adjacent window, and it looks like it takes all of her courage to let them meet mine. She inhales sharply, then lets it out, her breath skimming my lips. "The only time I felt safe was when you were inside of me."

Her words shoot straight to my groin. My cock twitches in my jeans, remembering exactly how it felt being inside of her. Only…I thought she was repulsed. Outraged. *Horrified.*

"Me too." I manage to get those two words out as my hand crawls back up her body and cups her breast, forcing a moan from her lips. Her pelvis thrusts against mine, and I grab her face in my hands and start kissing the fuck out of her. When my tongue pushes past her lips, it's just as desperate as before. Just as wild and untamed. We are pulled together, fueled by our memories and trauma and desire and *need*.

Cora hoists her leg up around my hip as her arms encompass my neck, pulling herself impossibly close. Her tongue is in my mouth, hot and demanding, and her hands start fisting my hair, tugging it until I moan. I roll her onto her back, our mouths only parting so I can slip her tank top up and over her head, her long hair falling down to the pillow like a golden halo.

Like an angel.

I capture her lips again as I tug down her shorts and panties until she's wearing nothing but the necklace I gave her for Christmas.

Cora grips my T-shirt, her legs linking around my hips. "I need to feel you…" She discards the shirt, and her hands drift up and down my bare chest, over my shoulders, along my arms, then back up again. She leans up to kiss my neck, nicking her teeth on my skin—like a claim.

It fucking does something to me.

A sound pitches in my throat, almost a growl, and I loosen my belt buckle and kick off my boxers and jeans, descending on her again with maddening urgency. My mouth takes hold of her nipple, dusky and taut, and my tongue laves over each one as I feel her writhing beneath me. Her hands are in my hair again, her nails digging into my scalp, and it only drives me wilder. "You're fucking beautiful," I murmur against her skin, trailing my lips down over her flat stomach, then lower, until I'm between her legs. Her scent alone fuels me, but the way she bucks her hips against my face, still pulling my hair, has me diving into her heat with a hunger I've never felt before. Cora arches her back and lets out a cry of pleasure that electrifies me. I palm her inner thighs, then push her legs further apart, spreading her as wide as I can. I want her to be fully exposed to me—utterly *vulnerable*.

I push two fingers inside her as my mouth works her clit. The sweet, intoxicating taste of her, mixed with how goddamn wet she is, has my cock throbbing, yearning to be inside her again. I glance up at the stretch of her body, bowed and trembling, and reach up to palm her breast as she rides against my face. I thrust my tongue over her slick folds, sucking her clit, until she's chanting, "Dean, Dean, Dean…"

Jesus.

I've heard my name expelled from her mouth so many times, in so many ways: anger, annoyance, outrage, humor, audacity, fear, confusion, grief, heartache…and I swear to God, *love.*

But not like this.

Never like this.

I crawl back up her body before she spirals, and Cora squeaks in surprise when I leave her unfulfilled. But before she can protest, I hook her thighs around my waist and whisper against her ear, "I want you to come when I'm inside you."

Cora pushes at my chest and flips me onto my back, climbing on top of me and straddling my hips. My cock grazes the crease of her ass, and I want to lift her onto me, but she reaches behind her and starts stroking me. She drags her fingernails down my abdomen with her opposite hand, then leans down to kiss me.

Feeling her hand grip my cock as her tongue plunges into my mouth is too fucking much, so I flip her again until she's on her back, like we're in some sort of power play.

But I want to be in control.

I kneel in front of her and grab one of her legs, tonguing and nipping along her thigh before hooking it over my shoulder. My other hand reaches up to grab her breast, tweaking her nipple between my fingers until she whimpers. Then I situate myself between her thighs, my cock just teasing her entrance. Cora moves her hips downward and releases a gasp-like moan when the tip pushes inside.

Fucking hell, this is really happening.

We're going to have sex.

By choice.

There are no guns, no chains, no shackles, no evil eyes watching us from across the room, tainting us like poison.

It's just *us*.

I lean forward as Cora's ankle curls around my upper back, her leg still draped over my shoulder. She's spread wide and waiting.

A trace of moonlight brightens her face, and I can see that her eyes are closed. I pull all the way out of her, and she lifts her hips with frustration. "Look at me, Corabelle."

Cora's eyelids flutter open beneath her long lashes, and we are face-to-face. Chest to chest. Heart to heart. I could never look her in the eyes when I entered her before. There was too much shame and guilt. Too much heartbreak. Too much I was afraid I might see.

Now I want to see it all.

When our gaze is fixed and holding tight, I push my cock inside her. We both cry out with a tapered groan, and I watch her eyes glaze over, widening slightly, as we are swept up together in the culmination, the *pinnacle*, of the last fifteen years. We are frozen for a heartbeat, taking it all in, absorbing it for everything it is.

And then we let go.

I pull out and push back in, hard and demanding, and it's teeth and nails and moans and sweat. Cora scratches at my arms, meeting me thrust for thrust, her neck arched back against the pillow as she whimpers and gasps. I glide my hands up her chest to her neck, my fingers catching on her necklace and gently curling around her throat as I plunge into her. My lips caress her ear, biting the lobe.

Cora grabs my ass, spearing me with her fingernails, tightening her legs around me while she moans, "Yes…"

Goddamn.

I pull out completely, flipping her around until she's on her stomach, and reenter her from behind. She cries out, fisting the bedsheets as I slide my arm under her stomach and yank her up, driving into her with zero restraint. I tug her hair back until she's fully flush against me, back to chest, moaning and mewling. One of my hands roves over her breasts, twisting each nipple, while the other finds her throat and tilts her face toward me. Our mouths collide over her shoulder, and I can taste every beautiful fucking sound I'm ripping out of her, our tongues tangling and hungry as our bodies crash together.

My lips make their way to her ear again as my right hand slides between her legs and finds her clit. "You're mine, Corabelle," I breathe out, claiming her, branding her, marking her as my own. Her wetness slicks my fingers as I massage her into a frenzy, feeling her shuddering, spinning, begging for release. "Say it. Tell me you're mine."

Cora snakes one arm behind my head, holding my face to the crook of her neck where I pull the tender flesh between my teeth and bite down. She gasps, squeaking out more sounds that drive me fucking mad. "I'm yours," she says, whispery, laced with lust. "You know I am. You've always known it."

"Fuck…" Does she really believe that? Do *I* believe that? I'm overcome with the need to look her in the eyes, so I pull back out and spin her around, pushing her down onto the mattress. I climb over her until we're face-to-face, my arms resting on either side of her head. My cock grazes her entrance, and Cora jerks her hips up, craving me, needing me to fill her.

"Please," she tells me, grinding herself against my length, making me crazy.

I love teasing her. I always have. "Please what?"

She whimpers. "Please fuck me. Please make me come."

Jesus.

I curl my hands around her wrists and press my forehead to hers, pushing in slowly, our eyes locked. Desire is the color green, and it floods me, bathing me in emeralds and jades and the waves of the sea. I lean down to kiss her mouth, puffy and pink, and Cora arches up, wrapping her legs around my waist and locking her ankles. I reach down to grab her thighs, palming and squeezing, as she rakes her nails down my back, then back up to tug handfuls of my hair. I pick up the pace, drowning in the madness. Drowning in *her*.

I never honestly believed we would be in this position again, voluntarily. Not really. I thought about it, of course. Fuck, I thought about it a hell of a lot more than I care to admit. And when I pictured this moment, being inside her again, feeling her pulsate around me, I envisioned something softer. Slow, gentle lovemaking that wiped us clean of all that violence. Of all that *darkness*.

But this is anything but soft.

This is rough and raw and dirty, and we're animals clawing at each other, biting, all primal growls and desperate thrusts.

It's fitting, I decide.

After all, we were created in darkness.

It's in our blood.

I angle my hips so I stroke against her sensitive bundle of nerves as my fingers dig into her thighs. I ram into her over and over, quicker and harder, until I feel her body tense beneath me, her breaths hitching and halting as she begins to peak.

The last time she moaned with pleasure as she came, my mouth found hers before the sound could touch the air. As much as I wanted to hear it, as much as I wanted it to sweep right through me and claw its way inside my bones, I couldn't let *him* hear it. I couldn't let him have it. So, I kissed her instead and swallowed it down.

But this time I watch her let go; I let her cry out with shameless abandon, and she's so fucking loud and wild and stripped down, I can't hold back any longer. My orgasm takes over and I come inside her, burying my face into that perfect, familiar curve of her neck and groaning as my body shudders and releases.

We cling to each other, her legs stretching out underneath me, her toes tickling their way down my calves. I bring my hands up to her hair and weave my fingers in the soft strands, breathing in her scent with a long sigh. I feel her arms wrap around my middle as she pulls me close, and I lift my head to meet her eyes.

And then the lights flicker back on, like a spotlight, illuminating our tangled limbs and flushed skin. Our bite marks and scratches and sweat. Disheveled hair and wide eyes. All of our flaws and cracks and weaknesses are spread out between us, visible and raw.

We don't speak. I pull out and roll beside her, sliding my arm around her waist and tugging her toward me. She curls up against me, her back to my chest, and we lie there silent and spooning, wondering what the fuck happens now.

But then I feel her start to tremble, shivering in my arms as she tries to hide her tears from me. I hold her tight, kissing her shoulder and whispering soothing words into her ear.

I told her I would stay with her until the darkness passed, and I did not lie.

23

Morning afters are confusing when you have no idea what's supposed to come after.

The sun shines in through a nearby window, setting her milky skin aglow as she rests a few inches away from me. After watching her fall in and out of sleep so many times in that basement, I can tell she's awake just by the way her body swells and deflates with every uneven breath. I stare at the expanse of her slender back, the bedsheet dipping off her hip, and I vividly recall every glorious detail from the night before.

But considering she's pretending to still be asleep after slipping out of my embrace, I'm wondering if she's trying to *forget* those same details.

I decide to brave the inevitable and slide my way over to her, scooping her up with one arm and pulling her to my chest. "Morning," I whisper, noting the shiver she produces when my lips graze her ear. I trail my fingers up and down her belly, in between her breasts, and stop just short of her neck. I play with the heart pendant on her necklace as I wait for her response.

Cora stiffens at the contact. "Hey."

"You don't seem quite as excited to see me as I am to see you," I tease, nudging my growing erection against her bottom as I kiss her shoulder.

Silence.

I go still, trying to read the mood. It's feeling more like an awkward one-night stand and less like the best night of our lives. "Cora?"

Cora rolls onto her back and peers up at me with tired eyes. She scans my face, worrying her lip between her teeth as she pulls the bedsheet up over her chest. "I have some errands to run today."

"What?" I blink at her, not expecting such flippant words to be the first thing out of her mouth after the night we just shared. "Right now?"

"Yeah," she shrugs. "It's Sunday. It's errand day."

"It's also the day after we had mind-blowing sex, and we should probably talk about it."

Cora sits up, her cheeks staining pink, and begins to move herself to the edge of the bed as she drags the blankets with her. "I don't want to talk about that, Dean."

What the fuck?

"Seriously?"

"Yes. Seriously."

I watch her collect her discarded clothes from the floor, slipping the tank top over her head and looking around for her bottoms. I do the same, pulling on my boxers and jeans as my heart clenches in my chest with rising emotions. "You can't just pretend that didn't happen."

Cora glances at me over her shoulder, just briefly, and steps into her cotton shorts. "I'm going to hop in the shower. I forgot to pick up more dog food yesterday, and the store opens at nine."

Ouch.

I gape at her, standing on the other side of the bed, shirtless and gutted. "Cora…you're killing me."

She falters midreach for her cell phone charging by the side of her bed. Her shoulders heave up and down with a weighted sigh, and she sits down, tugging her hair back with her fingers. "We weren't even…*safe*."

My fingers curl around my hips as I stare at the back of her head. I can't argue with that. She's absolutely right. "I'm sorry. That was my fault." I approach her with hesitant feet, coming up beside her on the bed. "Are you on the pill?"

"Yes, but…I've missed a few doses. I've been forgetful with a lot of things lately, and I wasn't expecting…" She sighs again, and this time, tears spring to her eyes. "It's my fault, too. I should have stopped it from getting that far."

I scratch my cheek. "I'll give you money for the morning-after pill. Just in case."

Cora swallows, sparing me another quick glance. "Are you…?"

"Am I what?" My eyebrows go up. "Clean?"

She nods.

Normally, this question wouldn't offend me. It's a responsible question to ask your sexual partner, albeit, a little late. But this is *Cora*. She knows I was with her sister for the last fifteen years. Plus, I got tested after our captivity and everything came back clean, so I know that fuckhead didn't give *her* anything. "Of course I'm clean. Do you think I cheated on Mandy?"

A shrug.

A fucking shrug.

"Wow. I never thought you *actually* believed that shit." I spin away from her, trying to hide the hurt creeping onto my face. "I was faithful throughout our entire relationship, Cora. Even when we separated for those few months back in college. I've literally only had sex with one person my whole life…until you."

I turn back to see tears quietly tracking down her cheeks as she keeps her gaze fixed in front of her. "My tests came back normal, too. Shockingly. They sent me home with antibiotics just in case, but…" Cora ducks her head as she lets out a breath. "This is such a mess."

She pushes her hair back, revealing multiple pink splotches along her neck, along with a colorful bruise from where my mouth had been. I swallow. "Yeah."

"I'm a horrible human being. Mandy will never forgive me for this."

A wave of guilt pinches my gut as reality starts seeping in. One week after breaking off a fifteen year commitment to Mandy, I sleep with her sister. There's not a single explanation we could come up with that would make this sound even remotely acceptable.

Then again, there's not a single explanation that would adequately describe our relationship either. Our dynamic. Our history. Our connection. None of it's normal; none of it's relatable—all of it's confusing as fuck.

I take a seat beside her, and Cora's breath catches when my bare arm grazes hers. "Corabelle, I'm sorry for not being stronger. I hate that you're feeling like this, and I hate that it's my fault. I just… I'm fucking *crazy* about you." She tips her head to me, her eyes swelling. "I can't turn it off. And I can't stop caring about you just because the circumstances aren't ideal."

"It's more than 'not ideal,' Dean. It's *wrong*. It's beyond the realm of appropriate."

"But it's *real*, and it's intense, and it's swallowing us whole."

"Is it, though?" Cora inhales a shuddering breath. "Is it real?"

"What?" I frown, thrown by the question. "Of course it is."

She looks away, fisting the hem of her tank top between sweaty palms. "Maybe this was simply born out of trauma and survival. We think we still need each other even though we made it out. We wouldn't be having this conversation if we didn't go through what we went through."

"I disagree," I say, shaking my head. "Maybe not right now, but…I think this was inevitable."

"No. When the trauma fades away, *we* fade away. This is temporary."

My anger flickers. "That's not what you said last night when I was inside you. You said you've always been mine."

Cora sets her jaw, her cheeks flaming. She rises to her feet and storms away. "I was in the heat of the moment, Dean. I can't believe you brought that up."

I stand to follow, grabbing my shirt off the floor and tugging it over my head in the process. "Why not? You said it."

She whirls around with a fresh set of emotions ready to fly. "I can't do this!"

"Cora…"

"No! Don't try to change my mind or feed me that fairy-tale, always-meant-to-be bullshit. You were engaged to my sister as of a *week* ago. You were with her for *fifteen years*." Her tears spill out, catching on the corners of her mouth. "Then you dumped her for *me*, and now I have to live with that."

I reach for her hands, but she yanks them away. "I already told you. Ending my relationship with Mandy had nothing to do with you. Or us."

"Lies."

"Stop, Cora. You could walk away from me right now and tell me it's over, and I wouldn't go back to Mandy. It ended because *we* ended. You don't change that."

Cora stares at me with flushed skin and crossed arms. She nods her head slowly, deliberately, and pins her eyes on mine. "I guess we'll see." She takes a step back and drops her arms to her sides. "It's over, Dean. I can't do this to Mandy."

She continues to walk backwards, away from me, and I shake my head with a bitter laugh. *Unbelievable.* I reach into my pocket, pulling a wad of cash out of my wallet as I pace over to her. I lean in close, then tug her wrist toward me and open her palm. "You probably should have thought about that before you fucked me." I slap the money into her hand, trying to ignore the pain that flashes in her eyes. "For the pill."

I grab my coat off the back of the couch, slip on my shoes, and slam the door shut behind me as I walk out of her house.

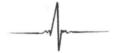

Morning fades to night, and I don't hear from Cora all day.

I've been pissed off and resentful since I left her house, alternating between taking power naps to try to forget all the bullshit swimming through my head, and binging Netflix to try to distract myself from all the bullshit swimming through my head.

So far, neither have worked. I'm plagued with bullshit.

I never thought this would be easy. I never assumed we'd hop into bed, wake up the next day, and our magical, new life would begin. Fuck, no. There is nothing easy or magical about any of this. It's messy and dirty and confusing and *hard*.

But I knew that. I'd considered all the bumps and curves we'd hit along the way, and I was willing, *prepared*, to brave the fallout every time with her. We've already survived so much together. We've weathered through the most turbulent storms. We've faced things that would keep the most fearless person up at night. We've looked death in the eye and persevered.

And yet, she runs from this.

From *me*.

But I suppose matters of the heart can be the scariest thing of all.

I stretch out on the couch, pulling up my blanket and calling in an order for Chinese food. I glance at Cora's name and our last string of messages, and I notice a text from her that I never opened. It was in response to me telling her that I'd be at her house in fifteen minutes:

Cora: That's not a good idea

Would that have stopped me from driving over there in the middle of the night to try to comfort her in the dark?

Probably not.

But she tried. She tried to stop it.

I feel like a guilty asshole, even though I know what happened between us was real and inevitable and consensual. We both wanted it. We both *craved* it.

But I know her heart. I know that her loyalty to her sister will always be a jagged wedge between us. Maybe I pushed too hard. Maybe it was too soon. I swipe at her name on my screen and type out a message I'm sure I'll regret instantly.

Me: I don't want to fight with you. I understand why you're scared and I totally fuckin get it. But whatever is between us isn't gonna go away. Last night was everything, and I know you felt it too. We can go slower. We can start over. Just don't shut me out...we're in this together :)

I add the smiley face because Mandy always said it was the key to texting in order to get your proper feelings across. One time she had an entire conversation with me using only emojis, and it was strange and confusing.

The message shows Read almost immediately, so I hold my breath and wait. I wait for those little bouncing dots to appear, telling me she's thinking, telling me she's responding…but they never come.

I check my phone periodically in between my kung pao chicken and *Sons of Anarchy* marathon, but there's still no response.

Dammit.

I glance at the time on my phone, noting it's already after 10 p.m. I have to be up for work in six hours. Groaning with frustration, I toss the phone beside me on the couch and run both hands through my hair, letting out a weary sigh of defeat. I stand up, dragging my blanket to the bedroom with me, when I hear my phone ring from the couch.

I pause. Then I drop the blanket and jog toward my cell phone, my heart thundering with anticipation and relief when I see Cora's name light up the face.

I swipe to accept. "Hello?"

It's silent for a beat, and then her groggy, slurred voice reaches my ear. "You're…incorrigible."

"I suppose I am." I bite down on the inside of my cheek, a tingle of concern poking at me. "You okay, Corabelle?"

"No…no, I'm not okay. But I think *you're* pretty okay. Even though you're incorrigible."

Her voice is raspy. Sluggish. She sounds drunk. "Have you been drinking?"

"I've been *thinking*."

"Okay…"

Cora sighs, and I hear clatter in the background like she knocked something over. "I think we could have been the best thing to ever happen to me."

I zone in on her use of *could have been*. "We still can, Cora. This doesn't have to be over."

"It does have to be over, Dean, because you're a lion and I'm a mouse."

"What?"

A stretch of silence passes, and I wonder if she spaced out or fell asleep, but then she replies softly, "You're a lion, fearless and strong, and I am just a mouse." Cora pauses again, then continues, "I'm small and weak, afraid of everything lurking in the dark. The things I want are disguised in deadly traps, and yet, I'm still tempted."

"Cora…" I start pacing around my living room, my stomach unsettled.

She sighs, long and lingering, her heavy breaths like an ominous soundtrack to her words. "'The trouble with mice is you always kill them.'"

I recognize that quote from the book *Of Mice and Men*. It sends a chill down my spine. "That's not true. Are you sure you haven't been drinking?"

Cora laughs a little, and it's just a fleeting, foreboding chuckle. "Goodbye, Dean."

"Wait. I'm worried about you, Corabelle. Talk to me."

"I do think we could have been great," she finishes. "If you weren't a lion, and I was not a mouse."

The call disconnects, and I'm left staring at my phone, my insides twisting into knots and my heart telling me that she is not okay.

Something's off. Something's *wrong*.

I realize I might come off like a stalker driving to her house in the middle of the night to console a woman who clearly wants her space. But I'm willing to take that risk because my instincts are screaming at me to *go*.

I'm knocking on her front door ten minutes later, after speeding my way over, blowing two stop signs. The happy, turquoise door is a deceiving camouflage to the dejected woman residing on the other side of it. "Cora!" I call out. My knuckle taps turn into pounding fists when she doesn't open the door. "Cora, open up. I'm worried about you."

All I can hear on the other side are animal claws pacing the entryway, mingling with squeaky whines. I try the doorknob and heave in a breath of relief when it opens. But then I realize Cora never leaves her doors unlocked, and my relief fades back into concern.

Jude and Penny Lane greet me at the door for the first time, pacing around in circles. As I step through the threshold, both dogs go running down the hallway toward Cora's bedroom, like they are beckoning me to follow. "Cora?" I try to make my presence known so I don't startle her. "Cora, it's me. I'm just here to check on you."

Nothing.

Fuck. I make my way through the living area, down the hall, and stop short of Cora's room. Her light is on, but she's clearly not awake. She's lying on her back on top of the covers, one arm hanging off the edge of the bed, while the other is sprawled across the mattress, still clutching her cell phone. Both dogs are pawing at the side of the bed and whimpering.

"Cora."

I step inside the room, my feet cautious at first. Unsure.

"Corabelle."

She doesn't move. She doesn't flinch.

Is she even fucking breathing?

"No, no, no, no, no…." I feel like the air leaves my own lungs the moment the thought crosses my mind, and I dash over to her bedside, shaking her. "Cora. Cora!" She doesn't respond. "Holy fuck…. Jesus…" My eyes catch sight of an empty bottle of sleeping pills tipped over on her nightstand and I fucking lose it. I climb on top of her, straddling her waist with my knees, and I press my ear to her chest as I continue to shake her.

This isn't real.

This is a prank—a practical joke, just like that time I gave her the cornstarch doughnut and she pretended to faint. She's about to wake up and say, "Gotcha." Then she'll laugh and laugh, and I'll be so pissed off at her, but so, *so* relieved that she's okay.

But that doesn't happen.

She is still, lifeless, and I flash back to Blizzard lying on that dog bed in the middle of the hospital room looking eerily similar.

"No…God, no, Cora. Come back to me. Fucking *please* don't do this…"

I pull my phone out of my pocket, almost dropping it as my hands start violently trembling. I punch in the numbers 9-1-1 and ramble off the situation to the dispatch operator, sounding like a crazed, desperate man. And I am.

I am.

I'm instructed to perform CPR. I carry her from the bed and lay her down on the floor, pressing against her chest like I've seen in the movies. Then I tip her head back, pinch her nose, and breathe my life into her mouth.

"Is she breathing?" the operator asks over the speaker.

I reach for her wrist and try to find a pulse. I place my ear to her heart again. God, I can't tell.

"I don't know. I don't fucking know…."

"Okay. Just stay on the line and help will be there soon. Continue the chest compressions, fast and hard…"

The voice fades out as I continue to press against her chest, occasionally stopping to search for a sign of life. "Don't you leave me, Corabelle. I fucking *love* you. Don't you dare leave me." I gather her petite frame in my arms, bringing her up to my chest, sobbing into her hair. I cling to her, trying to zap her with my life force, trying to bring her back to me with nothing but my tears and words and love. "Come back," I whisper through my grief, then lay her back down to continue the chest compressions.

The sirens sound in the distance as I break down on top of her, weeping and shaking.

What have I done?

What the hell have I done?

PART 3

WAVES

24

CORA

"YOU PROBABLY SHOULD HAVE THOUGHT about that before you fucked me."

Dean smacks a handful of money into my palm like I'm some kind of hooker. I stare at him, wide-eyed and wounded.

"For the pill," he adds.

I watch him storm out my front door, and he slams it so hard, it rattles on its hinges and the dogs leap up from their place on the giant dog bed. My feet remain frozen to the wooden planks of my living room floor, and my eyes are glued to the door, secretly hoping it will swing back open and he'll come running through.

And secretly hoping it doesn't.

I swallow the acrid lump in my throat before I choke on it. A tiny paw jabs my bare calf, and I'm reminded that I've been staring at the door for at least five whole minutes with a wad of crumpled bills in my hand that Dean gave me to purchase the morning-after pill.

Because we had sex.

Because I had sex with Dean.

The reminder almost knocks me off my feet. I realize he's not coming back, but I haven't decided if I'm okay with that or not. I blow out a slow breath, making a humming sound. It's the sound I make when mind-numbing pain is crawling its way up my throat, looking for a way out.

Dear God, I had sex with Dean Asher.

And then I told him it was over because I'm weak and unprepared to deal with the consequences of my own selfish actions.

I pace backwards until I reach the couch, collapsing onto it as the pain comes spewing out. I toss the money on the coffee table and draw my legs up to my chest, burying my face between my knees. Sobs pour out of me in waves and my ribs start to ache.

Jude appears in front of me, sitting at the edge of the couch with perky ears and a swiftly moving tail. Penny hops up beside me with her little legs, resting her chin against my hip bone. This only makes me cry harder, knowing these sweet animals are trying to console me when I don't deserve it. I made my bed.

I made my bed, and then I screwed my sister's ex-fiancé in it.

And *holy crap*, it was good. So, so good. Hot, intense, rough—unlike anything I've ever experienced before, physically and emotionally. *Mind-blowing* is the term Dean used, and I wholeheartedly agree, despite the fact that I couldn't tell him that because even acknowledging what happened between us feels like a slap in the face to Mandy. And to my own dignity.

I run my fingers between Jude's ears as I scoop Penny onto my lap, stretching my legs back out. I've never been so torn like this before, so split in half, pulled in two different directions. I've never wanted something so badly, while rejecting it at the same time.

Dean is like the ocean.

Compelling, calling to me, within reach…

So much magic. So much beauty.

Something I want with every aching layer of my soul.

But I'm that little girl again, frozen in the sand, afraid of the dark waters in front of me. There's so much uncertainty. There's so much I can't see. I'm scared I'll lose myself to the tumultuous waves and drift away, barely treading above water, hardly able to breathe.

I'm scared I'll lose everything—my sister, my parents, myself.

I'm scared I'll drown.

It's safer here at shore.

I tell myself this as I go about my day, running out to grab dog food and plan B. I try not to die of embarrassment as I keep my oversized sunglasses on at the pharmacy, while tugging my beanie down as far as it will go in case I have the words *Totally Banged Dean* scrawled across my forehead. I don't check my phone as I clean the house later. I already cleaned yesterday, but I vacuum again and wipe down the windows just to distract myself.

I don't text him. I don't call him.

I don't go near the bottle of wine in the fridge in fear of texting or calling him.

I can do this.

But when my sister shows up unexpectedly with Mexican food that evening, I almost faint from crippling anxiety.

"You look like hell." Mandy breezes through the entryway also looking like hell, and I can't help but feel like one common denominator is responsible for our mutual hells. "I brought a shit ton of tacos. Cilantro has cleansing powers."

"That's because it tastes like dish soap."

Mandy scoffs at me as she slips out of her knee-high boots. She saunters through the living room to the kitchen, tossing the brown paper bags of food onto the dining table. Then she wavers, taking a few steps back, and glances toward the corner of the room. She looks up at me. "You have dogs."

I shrug, my arms crossed. "You would have known that if you hadn't dodged my calls and texts all week."

A bleak silence stretches between us. I take in the way Mandy's eyes lower to the floor, lacking their usual sparkle, rimmed with dark circles. Her hair is pinned up in an ultra-messy bun, her roots growing out. She blows back a strand of hair that has come loose from her bun and leans her hip against the back of the couch. "I've been avoiding you."

"I noticed." I dig my fingers into the fuzzy fabric of my sweater, my insides clenching with unease. I'm not sure how I'm going to get through this night without confessing all of my dirty sins to Mandy. I clear my throat, braving a few steps forward. "How are you?"

Mandy flusters a bit and shrugs her shoulders, her eyes flickering back to me. "I'm guessing Dean told you?"

Just the mention of his name makes me flush. "It's all over Facebook. You changed your relationship status to 'single' and have been posting sad, depressing quotes every few hours."

"Helps me cope. So, you're saying he didn't mention anything about it?"

Something in my chest pitches and my cheeks flare with heat. "I didn't say that."

"I figured as much," Mandy says flatly, turning back to the kitchen to sort through the food. "He said you had a connection. A bond. He said you were both forced to do fucked-up shit."

Oh God.

Bile rises up my esophagus, and I choke it back down. "It-it's complicated."

"He said that, too." Mandy spins around, holding out something wrapped in tinfoil. "Two steak tacos, no cilantro."

I swallow, taking a few more hesitant steps toward my sister, and reach for the tacos. "Thank you."

Her smile is strained. Forced. Mandy unwraps one of her tacos and takes a bite, nodding her head at Jude and Penny curled up in the corner. "What made you get two dogs?" she asks, swiping a dollop of sour cream from her lip. "Protection?"

I set my food down on the kitchen island, feeling too queasy to eat. "Companionship, I guess. I planned on getting a dog before…well, before everything happened." I scratch the back of my head. "They're the dogs that were confiscated from his property."

Mandy pauses midchew. "That psycho's property? You adopted your kidnapper's dogs?"

"Sort of."

"That's fucked up, Cor." She resumes her chewing and hops up onto my table, swinging her legs back and forth. "You seem to be having a hard time letting go of the things that connect you to that basement."

Her eyes cut to me, knowing and pointed. She's not just referring to the dogs. I slink back like the coward I am. "It's not like that. They needed a home, and I needed a distraction from the pain."

"There are a million other dogs out there you could have taken."

Pretty sure she's still not talking about the dogs.

Shit.

"Mandy…"

She hops off the table. "Your food is getting cold."

I watch my sister parade around the kitchen, pulling a wineglass from the cabinet and digging through my refrigerator. I feel hysterical tears stabbing just beneath the surface, ready to blow. I gather a slow, calming breath, trying so hard to rein in my fear and nerves and guilt as Mandy saunters back over with a full glass of wine. She leans forward against the kitchen island, elbows to countertop, facing me as I stand behind the opposite side.

I wring my hands together as she stares at me over the rim of her glass. There is only a small kitchen island between us, but it feels like a continent. "I appreciate you stopping by with dinner. That was nice of you."

God, I'm pathetic.

Mandy arches an eyebrow, sipping on her wine. "You haven't touched your food."

"I'm not that hungry. I'll bring it to work tomorrow for lunch." I smile as sweetly as I can, but I'm pretty sure I look like I'm about to start ugly crying.

Mandy taps a perfectly painted fingernail against the glass, her gaze shifting between me and her beverage as if she's trying to string together her next sentence. Her eyes are hazel and hollow as they linger on mine, her head tilting slightly to one side. "So, what fucked-up shit were you forced to do?"

She asks the question so casually, so nonchalant.

But it thunders through me like a typhoon, wreaking havoc on all of my fragile insides. My skin tingles, my hands clam up, my legs start to wobble in place. I latch onto the edge of the countertop to keep myself steady as I hold my breath. I hold it for a long time, afraid that my oxygen alone will spill out all of my secrets. I hold it until I feel dizzy and sick and light-headed, and then I let it out like a harrowing confession. "I–I don't want to talk about it, okay? It's personal and traumatic, and I'm trying to forget those three weeks ever even happened…" I bite down on my lip to stop the words from flowing.

Mandy's eyes narrow as she chugs down the rest of her wine. Then she slams the glass down on the counter, making me wince. "Something happened down there, Cora. I need to know."

"Nothing. It doesn't matter."

"*Tell me.*"

"I can't!" The tears start spilling, my voice catching and breaking. "I can't."

Mandy is about to bite back when my cell phone vibrates between us on the island, resting only a foot away. We both look at it.

Dean's name lights up the screen with a text message.

I glance at Mandy. She glances at me.

Then we both lunge for the phone at the same time, with Mandy coming out victorious. I practically scream in defiance. "No!" I race around the island to where Mandy is reading the message with her back turned to me. I wait for her to face me, my shoulders heaving, beyond horrified and nauseated by what she may be discovering right now.

Mandy lets out a gasp that sounds an awful lot like betrayal. She whips around, her eyes watering, gleaming with rage. "You *bitch*."

I rip the phone away from her, my hands shaking as I skim over the message in a panic.

Don't want to fight. Scared. I get it. Last night was everything. Slower. Start over. In this together.

Last night was everything.

"What happened last night, Cora?" Mandy demands, her tears erupting like rainfall. "Did you sleep with him?" Her voice changes in pitch, sounding more desperate and shrill with each word. "Did you fuck my fiancé?"

"I…"

"Tell me!"

I shake my head, a cry breaking through my lips.

"I want to hear it from your lying, filthy mouth."

I've never seen Mandy so upset. I've never seen her radiating blind *hate* like this. I feel like I'm going to throw up or keel over and die from abject humiliation and all-consuming *guilt*. "We…we were forced to have sex in that basement."

Mandy pales, her eyebrows creasing. "What?"

My chest expands, up and down, hard and fast. "Earl put a gun to Dean's head and made him do it. We didn't have a choice. We…" I dig my fingers into my scalp and tug my hair back. "It was awful and sick and beyond depraved, but…"

"*But…?*" Mandy sounds horrified. Appalled.

As she should.

"But something happened, okay? Something changed between us, and I can't explain it. I thought the feelings would go away when we returned to our normal lives, but the connection is still there. We can't shake it. I never wanted this to happen, Mandy…" I continue to crack and break and splinter, my entire body shutting down. "I never wanted *any* of this!"

Mandy's eyes assess me with a quiet rage. Her chest is beet red, the heat climbing up her neck and staining her cheeks and ears. "Did you have sex last night?"

I pull my lips between my teeth to keep them from quivering. Then I lower my chin, unable to look her in the eyes as I whisper, "Yes."

Only a heartbeat passes when her hand flies out and connects with my face. I inhale a sharp, startled breath, the sting of her slap rattling my bones.

Mandy has never hit me before. I've never hit her.

We've argued and bickered and not spoken for weeks, but…this is different. This is *unfixable*.

My eyes are glazed with disbelief as I look up at her, wishing I could erase the heartbroken, forsaken expression staring back at me. My fingertips lift to brush against the welting handprint on my cheek, my remorse and regret eating me alive. "I'm *so* sorry, Mandy."

She takes a step back, shaking her head furiously. "I can't believe you're my sister. I can't believe you were going to be my *maid of honor*." Mandy wipes at the stray tears lingering on her cheekbones. "You're disgusting. You're *trash*. You're the most selfish person I've ever met, and I never want to see you again. Mom and Dad will disown you over this."

I gape at her, my mouth parted with incredulity.

Mandy spits out one final barb before storming away: "I hope his dick was worth it."

The front door slams for the second time that day, another person I care about walking away from me, angry and betrayed. I collapse onto the kitchen tiles, a panic attack creeping into my lungs and taking over. I sob hysterically, manically, ashamed and astounded by the damage I've caused. I'm a broken pile of bones and failure, crumpled on the floor, wanting to die.

I just want to die.

All those weeks fighting so hard to live, and for what?

Hell followed me home.

It lives inside me, housing all of my demons and ghosts and unforgivable flaws.

Two wet dog noses tickle my cheeks, and then my tears are kissed away by worried tongues. I stare up at the ceiling fan spinning in circles above me.

Around, around, and around.

It could spin forever, spiraling out of control, until I decide to turn it off.

I try to catch my breath, choking on ugly hiccups as I wipe at my nose and rise to unsteady feet. The dogs follow me around the kitchen while I fill their bowls with food and water. I don't bother to lock the front door as I head toward the hall bathroom, flipping off the ceiling fan before I round the corner.

I open up the mirrored medicine cabinet and reach for my sleeping pills. I snap the door shut, gazing at my reflection, feeling totally numb. My eyes are red and swollen, my nose puffy. I'm marked and bruised all over.

Dean's teeth and tongue carved into my neck.

Mandy's slap of scorn across my face.

I blink slowly, then glance down at the pill bottle clasped inside my fist.

My whole life I've been terrified of the ocean. I've been scared of being dragged down into a cold, dark sea, swallowed by waves, clutching my chest and gasping for air.

But this sea is not made of water.

And maybe drowning is the only way out.

25

"CORABELLE."

I can hear my name being called from the other side of the shoreline.

I hate that dreadful name, and yet, it sounds so much sweeter flickering across his tongue. My hands wave around in the air, trying to grab his attention. "Dean!"

His head twists in every direction, until he spots me running toward him in the sand. "There you are," he says, a devilish grin lifting on his mouth. "I thought I lost you."

I leap into his arms and he catches me right beneath my thighs. Our noses kiss, my smile matching his. "You can't get rid of me that easily."

"Promise?"

My head bobs as I lean in to caress his lips with mine. I pull back, searching his eyes. "Are we going to be okay?"

Dean plants another kiss against my forehead, then sets me back down, my toes disappearing into the sand. He places his hand over my heart, while reaching for my own hand and placing it against his. With my hand to his chest, and his to mine, our heartbeats vibrating through our fingertips, he whispers down at me, "They're still beating. As long as they're beating, we're okay."

My smile broadens as tears coat my eyes. I'm about to reply when I hear my name being echoed across the beach again.

"Corabelle."

Dean releases a sigh, and it evaporates on a salty breeze that sweeps through. "It's time to go," he says wistfully.

"But I like it here."

He cups my cheek in his palm, grazing his thumb along my skin. "We'll come back."

"Corabelle."

My eyelids flutter, rejecting the artificial light spilling into my irises. The poetic sound of ocean waves transforms into angry beeps and buzzes, humming machines, and jumbled voices. My lips are dry and chapped as I part them to speak. "Dean?"

I'm met with a moment of silence before a familiar touch strokes my hair back. "It's me, sweetheart."

"Dad?"

Another presence nears the edge of my bed where I'm lying beneath itchy sheets, hooked up to needles and monitors. "Oh, Cora, baby," my mother says as she sits beside my father.

I blink, willing their blurry faces to come into view. "How did I get here?"

I try to remember the events leading up to this moment. I try to recall the reason I'm lying in a hospital bed with my parents looming over me with tearful faces.

"You overdosed on your sleeping pills. Dean went to your house to check on you and found you unconscious. He called 911," my mother tells me. "Oh, sweetie."

She drapes herself over my stomach and starts sobbing as nurses begin to filter in, poking and prodding me.

Oh God.

Memories trickle through me, and I feel sick.

I wanted to die.

I genuinely wanted to *die*.

Tears brim in my eyes, and I can hear my heart monitor start to climb as my breathing escalates. I lie there, dazed and horrified, while a nurse relays information to my parents in a voice that sounds like the adults in the Charlie Brown movies. I wonder if I'm still underwater.

After the nurses check my vitals and file out, I glance up at my mother standing at my bedside. "I–I'm sorry. I'm sorry for everything."

"Honey, none of that matters right now," she replies, placing her hand against my shoulder. "We'll talk later. You just need to get better."

"Where's Mandy?" I ask, my voice fracturing. "Did she want me to die?"

My father lets out a long sigh, somber and weighty. "Of course not, Cora. Your sister has been worried sick. She's just down getting coffee."

I swallow back an acidic lump. I want to ask my next question, but I can't get the words out. They don't seem at all appropriate. But the words must be written in my eyes because my mother dips her head, squeezing me gently.

"Given the situation, we thought it would be best if he weren't here, honey. But he's extremely worried about you."

My cheeks burn with shame. I shouldn't be wanting him here with me. I shouldn't be silently begging for Dean to be holding me in his arms, kissing away my tears, and singing away the darkness. My parents shouldn't *know* that's exactly what I want, just by looking at me.

My father takes my hand in his. "Your sister filled us in on what happened. She feels responsible. I know this is going to be an uphill battle for both of you, and your mother and I are not taking anybody's side here. We love you both. Our hearts are breaking for each of you." He kisses my knuckles. "We're just so grateful you made it through."

Tears streak my cheeks, moistening my parched lips as I inhale a choppy breath. "How long have I been here?" Panic sets in, and I wonder how much time has slipped away. Is it a new year? A new decade?

"You've been unconscious for four days," he responds.

I soak up the fact that it hasn't been longer, but then my eyes widen with dread. "M-My dogs. Jude and Penny. Are they okay?"

My mother quickly nods. "They're just fine. Lily has been house-sitting for you."

Thank God.

I'm nodding my relief when Mandy walks in with a cup of coffee. She does a double take when she notices I'm awake. "Oh my God…"

I turn my head to the opposite side, unable to look at her.

My father clears his throat. "Bridge, let's give them a few minutes."

I'm still looking out the window at the dreary winter day, listening to my parents shuffle out of the room. It's a fitting backdrop to my new nightmare. I feel the bed shift as my sister takes a seat to my left.

Mandy leans down to hug me, her cheek pressed to my covered chest. "I never wanted you to hurt yourself," she murmurs against me.

I close my eyes, swallowing a fresh set of tears. I never used to cry much, but now I feel like it's all I do. "You said you never wanted to see me again, and I don't blame you."

"That doesn't mean I wanted you *dead*," she insists, straightening with a sniffle. "I can't believe you did that."

"We can just add it to the growing list of fucked-up things I do now."

Mandy's sigh reverberates through me. She hesitates before saying, "Dean was here that first night. He was a mess."

My heart picks up speed, involuntarily.

"The doctors said he found you just in time. A few minutes longer and you'd be dead."

Dean saved my life.

Again.

I wipe my wet cheeks. "I'm so sorry, Mandy. I'm so sorry I hurt you."

A few silent beats pass by, and I'm afraid to look at her. I'm afraid to see her wounded, scornful eyes.

The bed moves as Mandy rises to her feet, and I finally spare a small glance in her direction. She tucks her tangled hair behind her ear, twirling her coffee cup between tense fingers. "I love you, Cora, and I'm glad you're okay, but… this doesn't wipe the slate clean. I'm still processing everything. It's…a lot." She squeezes the cup, her eyes closing. "A lot of damage was done, and I'm not sure when I'll ever be able to forgive you."

I nod, tears falling free and dampening my shoulders. "I understand," I squeak out.

Mandy opens her eyes and pins them on me, her expression sober. "But seriously, Cor, don't you ever pull that shit again. Get help. Find a new therapist if you need to. Join a support group. Get on medication. Just…don't ever feel like we'd be better off without you."

I nod again.

Mandy ducks her head. "I'm trying to understand, trying to put myself in your shoes, trying to sympathize with everything you went through that could have led to…" Her jaw tightens and she swallows. "But I'm still mad. I'm so mad at you, Cora."

"I know." I sniff. "You have every right to be furious with me. I'll never be able to explain what happened because I don't even understand it."

Mandy nibbles her lip, glancing my way, then dips her chin. "I'm sorry I hit you. I had no right to put my hands on you."

"I deserved it."

"No," she says. Then she sighs, dropping one arm to her side and taking a slow sip of her coffee. "Anyway, I'll let you rest. I'm glad you're okay. Don't ever think otherwise."

A watery smile breaks through. "Thanks, Sis."

She doesn't return the smile, but her eyes aren't flaring with hate, giving me hope that maybe there is hope for us someday. Maybe we can fix this.

Mandy takes a few steps backwards and turns to leave the room—but her feet falter. She looks back at me over her shoulder, her eyes glossing over, glowing with fresh pain. "I'm not sure if this makes it better or worse, but…I think he really loves you."

Mandy walks out, a small cry escaping her lips, and I start sobbing into the itchy bed covers.

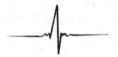

I have no idea where I am for a moment when the mattress sinks with a new weight and an arm slinks around my midsection. I have one foot in a dream and the other in reality as I breathe in the familiar scent of cedar and leather. My body recognizes him, and I instinctively snuggle in closer to the warm body on my left, still not sure if he's real or not.

"My sweet Corabelle."

His breath against my ear makes me shiver. I blink myself awake as the room comes into focus, and my head tilts to the side, finding his eyes.

He's real.

"Dean." His name tumbles out like a broken whisper, our gaze locking, our emotions rising. *God*…to think I would have never seen these eyes again if he hadn't found me. "I'm sorry."

Dean touches his fingertips to my temple, then glides a loose strand of hair behind my ear. He looks tired and distraught—but there's a distinct glimmer of relief swimming in his baby blues. His hand settles against my neck, his thumb skimming my jaw. "I thought I lost you."

His words are familiar and they cause my brows to pull together. I force a smile. "You can't get rid of me that easily."

"Promise?"

My breath catches as déjà vu tickles me from head to toe. I think this is the part where I'm supposed to lean in for a kiss, but I press my lips together in resistance and nod instead.

"You scared the hell out of me, Cora. I had no idea you felt like that—which fucks me up even more because the signs were all there. I feel like I failed you." Dean tightens his hold on my neck, desperation lacing his words as he swallows back his grief. "If you need space, I'll give you space. If you need time, I'll give you time. If you never want to see me again, I'll pack my bags and move to fuckin' Mexico, all right? But don't you *ever* try to take away the one thing you fought so goddamn hard to keep."

Dean places his hand against the swell of my breast encased in a hospital gown, closing his eyes as he revels in the feel of my heartbeat against his palm. I touch my hand to his, tears welling in my eyes. *So many tears.* I roll onto my side, trying not to tangle myself in cords, and press our foreheads together. "Mandy found out about us. She saw your text. She…she was *so* mad, so furious, and I flipped out, Dean. I was out of my head." I inhale a rickety breath. "It was the lowest moment of my life. I thought I'd lost everything."

He exhales, slowly and deliberately, pressing his hand more firmly onto my chest. "You only lose everything when you lose this, Corabelle."

I nod, and it takes all of my willpower not to lean up and capture a kiss.

We lie like that for a while, pressed together, face-to-face, his lips trailing tiny kisses along my hairline, my eyes, my nose, my chin. He avoids my mouth, and eventually we hold each other in silence, just staring and thinking. I ask him at one point, "How did you get in here?"

Dean smiles softly. "Your mom texted me. She said you were awake."

"My mom was okay with you seeing me?" I wonder through a frown.

"She saw what a wreck I was. I was losing my damn mind the night they brought you in. I thought you were gone." He shifts on the bed, pulling me closer. "Your mom took me aside and said it would be better if I stayed away for Mandy's sake, but she'd keep me updated on your condition. Trust me, Cora, if it were up to me I wouldn't have left your side."

I raise my hand and press the pads of my fingers to his cheek, grazing them down his jawline. I watch his eyes flutter in contentment. I'm overcome by the feelings sweeping through me, wondering how something so beautiful, so powerful, so *right*, could be so very wrong.

But right or wrong, I know one thing is for certain. "This is real, isn't it?"

I've been trying to deny it. I've been pushing away the blinding truths, telling myself we're still trapped in that emotional prison of Earl's basement. These feelings aren't genuine, they aren't *real*. They were manufactured by trauma and isolation. This was all a part of Earl's twisted plan, and he succeeded tenfold.

Only…it's getting harder and harder to believe that. The truth is in the way Dean holds me, the way he sings me to sleep and silences my demons with a gentle stroke of his hand. It's in the way my heart beats differently when he's near. It's in the way I envision a future, a future I can never have, and he's *there*. He's always there.

It's in the way he's looking at me right now.

Dean studies me, his eyes darting over my face, memorizing every fine line, every crack and crease. A smile touches his lips, as if we're finally coming to terms with what we both already knew. "Yeah, Corabelle. It's real."

I bury my face in his chest, nuzzling my nose to his shirt and breathing him in. "Can you hold me until I fall asleep?"

"Of course."

He hums a song against my hair like a soothing lullaby as I soak up his warmth and let it fill every cold, empty pocket inside me.

I cling to what will never be mine.

As my eyes close, my body calm and my mind in a temporary state of peace, I find myself drifting out to sea. I'm back on that beach, running into his arms, watching the seagulls fly overhead as he spins me around beneath the setting sun.

I'm still not sure where the words came from.

Were they a whisper in the wind in a magical dream? Or were they spoken into my hair, a soft confession, a haunting promise of everything that will never come to be?

Either way, I let the words sink in. They breathe new life into me as I fall into a restful sleep.

"*I love you.*"

26

"Y OU SHOULD COME OUT WITH me tonight."

I'm sitting with my best friend in our favorite local coffee shop, sipping on a latte like I didn't just attempt suicide two weeks ago.

I glance up at Lily, cupping the warm brew between my palms, considering her offer while nibbling my lip. "I don't know. I go back to work on Monday. I should probably just rest up and relax this weekend."

Lily fiddles with her long, dark braid hanging over one shoulder. "I think it will be good for you. You've been a hermit ever since…" She lowers her eyes. "Well, you know. I feel like it's only been taking you down a black hole of despair. You need fun and friends."

I instinctively reach for my wrist, catching myself before I start scratching at it. I finger my necklace instead. "I'm sorry, but I don't know those words. Are they new?"

She shakes her head with a laugh. "Come on, Cora. I'm meeting Amy and the guys at the new brewery downtown. Everyone would love to see you."

"I'm a mess, Lily. This morning was the first time in weeks I put on pants that didn't have an elastic waistband and nautical dog patterns."

"Exactly. It's time to put yourself back out there." Lily shoots me a mischievous wink from across the bistro table. "Jason will be there."

Ugh. Jason.

"That's not a good idea. I know you're just trying to help, but…" I squeeze my coffee cup a little too hard and cappuccino starts leaking out the top. "I'm kind of emotionally involved with someone else right now."

Crap. I finally said it. I finally admitted my awful, salacious truth.

Lily doesn't know about Dean. She's about to flip out and do that thing with her mouth.

"What? Who?" she wonders, craning her neck back with disbelief.

I cough into my hand. "Dean."

"Irene?" She blinks. "The science teacher with the sideburns?"

I cough again. "Dean."

"Stop coughing!"

"Dean," I finally say, loud and clear, then sink back into my seat with reddening cheeks.

Lily does that thing with her mouth, gaping at me with her eyes bugged out. "Please tell me this is a *Supernatural* reference. I know those Winchesters seem so real sometimes when we're all alone at night with our vibr—"

"*Dean*. Dean Asher. Dean, my sister's ex. My almost brother-in-law, my longtime nemesis, the source of nearly every single migraine I've ever had over the last fifteen years, the reason I have a complex about spaghetti…and the only reason I'm still alive right now rambling off my sinful secret to you." I say it all in one breath, placing both palms against my flushed face. I inhale deeply, shame and longing battling it out inside me.

The shame is for dodging his calls ever since I was released from the hospital, even though he's the only person in the world I long to hear from. I've sent him a few texts to let him know I'm doing okay so he doesn't worry, but I keep them brief and unemotional. And I completely ignored his text from last night asking if we could grab lunch this weekend and talk.

Lily is rendered speechless, which is uncommon. She stares at me with copper eyes, processing the absurdity I just spewed at her. "Wow."

"Yeah. Wow."

"That's…" She blows out a breath.

"I'm broken." I slouch further into the chair, hoping it'll swallow me up. "I'm broken, right?"

"Maybe a little."

Oof. I pick at the fuzzy snags on my sweater, then pull the sleeves down over my hands. "I don't even know how it happened," I whisper softly.

Lily takes a sip of her chai tea and sets the cup down on the table. "I got some vibes at Mandy's New Year's party, but I figured it was just tension bubbling over from everything you guys went through. I never thought…" She fills her cheeks with air and lets it out, then averts her eyes with consideration. "I mean, I guess I can see it. He's hot as sin and he's always been weirdly protective of you."

I frown. "No, he hasn't. He's always been an ass."

"Yeah, but in a cute way."

"No."

"Come on, Cora. You guys have always had chemistry. You just acted on it by torturing each other." Lily shrugs, tapping her nails against the side of her paper cup. "And obviously, circumstances wouldn't allow for much else."

My jaw starts to ache from gnashing my teeth together. I look down at my latte, hoping the little design made in foam will reach out and pull me in since the chair was a disappointing failure. "This wasn't supposed to happen."

A sympathetic smile pulls at her lips, and Lily leans forward on her elbows. "Is this the point in our friendship where you come to me with a terrible dilemma and I'm supposed to offer you super-sage wisdom and give you all the answers?"

"Yes. Definitely."

She shrugs. "Well, shit. I'm not prepared at all. I've got nothing."

I groan as my face falls into my hands. "Awesome."

"It could be worse?" she offers, giving me a triumphant thumbs-up.

I peer at her through the cracks in my fingers, shaking my head, and grumble, "No, it can't. This is *literally* rock bottom."

"Ooh, so…it's only up from here."

"You would make a terrible therapist."

Lily falls back against her chair with a soft smile, and I know she's just trying to cheer me up and make a horrible situation lighter.

She crosses her arms over her V-necked sweater and sighs. "You really want my advice?"

"I'm not sure anymore."

She chuckles, reaching for her tea. "I would go for it, woman. Get the guy, have some hot sex, and forget about everything else."

"That's terrible advice," I say, pursing my lips together with narrowed eyes.

"Yeah, well, that's why you're my only friend."

I gawk at Lily for a moment, then burst out laughing, the sound of it startling me.

Lily winks at me over her cup. "You know it's true. But for real, Cora, do what makes you happy. You've gone through stuff I can't even imagine and you deserve a little happiness. Dean might not be the smartest choice on paper, but it's *your* life. You can't tiptoe around your heart in fear of pissing people off or hurting their feelings. Sometimes we need to be a little selfish in order to avoid a life of complacency."

My fingers curl around my beverage, tightening their grip. "That was a little bit profound."

"Right? I think I nailed it." Lily performs a dramatic bow, then smiles over at me. "Also…just between you and me? If roles were reversed, Mandy wouldn't hesitate."

This grabs my attention and I jerk my head back up. "What makes you think that?"

"Call it a gut instinct." Lily flips her braid over her shoulder with a shrug. "Let's put it this way: did she or did she not sleep with that guy you were crushing on during those few months she and Dean split up?"

I scrunch up my nose. "Benjamin, the attorney? That was different. I was never *with* Ben—it was just a crush. Mandy has been with Dean for half her life."

"I get it," Lily replies, holding up her hands. "It's not exactly the same… I'm just saying. She never even considered your feelings and she *knew* you liked the guy. I always thought it was shady."

I twist the hem of my sweater between my hands. "That was also a long time ago. She's grown up a lot since then."

"Okay," Lily says dismissively. "You're right. My point is, no one is perfect. Everyone is a little selfish sometimes when it comes to matters of the heart."

I lower my head, my chest constricting.

"Speaking of…I'm going to be selfish and drag you out tonight. I miss you."

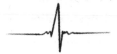

I wasn't ready for this.

The lights, the noise, the music, the *attention*.

Everyone is looking at me. Everyone *knows* me. My face comes up in their newsfeeds. I'm on their television screens. My name slips from their mouths in casual conversation. My trauma is a trending story on their social media accounts.

My body freezes as I look around the crowded bar, squeezing my wrist with my opposite hand and massaging my pulse point. Hurried breaths escape my lips, and I can hear my heart beating in my ears.

Lily links her elbow with mine, tugging me forward. "You okay?"

I lie with a nod. "I'm fine."

"You seem tense."

We approach a group of friends, and I know all of them except for one: Amy and her boyfriend, Trevor, and a nameless man with ebony eyes and long, black hair.

"Where's Jason?" Lily wonders, leaning into Amy for a hug.

Amy is a petite tomboy, dressed in a baggy T-shirt and black leggings. She smiles brightly as she embraces Lily. "He canceled at the last minute. I'm not sure." She shifts her attention to me with wide, curious eyes, her smile lingering. "You look great, Cora. I'm so happy to see you."

Amy doesn't give me a hug, and I wonder if it's because she thinks I'm dirty. Tainted in some way. *Contagious.* I force a pleasant expression and offer a wave. "Thanks. It's definitely been a tough few months."

I shake Trevor's hand, having met him a few times in the past, then face the mysterious man to the right.

"That's Lars, one of Trevor's friends," Lily introduces.

"Hi, I'm Cora." I hold out my hand and he takes it, his gaze flickering to my chest, then drifting back up. "Nice to meet you."

"Hey," he says.

I tug my blouse up. I tried to wear something cute since I've been slumming it in sweatpants and pajamas for weeks on end, but I didn't want anything too revealing. However, my sweetheart blouse is hanging low on my frame due to the weight I have yet to put back on, revealing more cleavage than I'd intended.

The evening presses on with idle conversation and a few rounds of drinks. I nurse a rum and Coke the entire time, trying to be invisible as the friends catch up and joke around. Lars is quiet, not saying much, but his stare is piercing— and often fixed on me. It makes me nervous, prompting me to start scratching my wrist again, even though I told myself I would stop.

"I like your eyes. They look like lily pads," Lars says at one point, earning my full attention.

Lily perks up at the sound of her name. "What about my pads?"

"Not you, girl," Amy says, swatting at her arm.

I send Lars a half smile, clearing my throat and forcing a small laugh. "Thank you. That's sweet."

Something tells me Lars is anything but sweet.

"Wanna dance?" he asks, not waiting for my reply and snaking his fingers around my wrist.

I jump back and drop my glass.

Everyone stops talking to stare at me, and I wonder if they would forget I was ever here if I made a mad dash to the exit right now. "S-Sorry, I'm such a klutz," I mutter. I lean down to pick up the glass, but a bartender is already headed over with a broom.

Lars's fingers are still curled around my wrist. My reaction didn't seem to faze him, and he pulls me over to the dance floor with an impish smile stretched across his wide jaw. I catch Lily winking at me as I blindly follow the stranger out into the crowd, his large palm reaching behind my back and resting there. Tension and nerves sweep through me as the music blares louder, the crowd grows bigger, and the lights flash around me like a strobe, making me dizzy.

"Relax, doll," Lars whispers, his voice buttery smooth.

It's just a dance. You're fine. You're safe.

I rein in a sharp breath, trying to let go of the apprehension.

This isn't me. I've always been fun and flirty, unafraid of male attention. I'm social and outgoing. I've never shied away from dancing, or casual touches, or compliments.

"I heard about your story," Lars says, pulling me to his barrel chest. He's a huge man, well over six feet, with muscles and tattoos. "You're a fighter."

I inch back, keeping a gap between us. "It's been hard," I respond, feeling his hand squeeze mine. "Sorry if I seem on edge. I'm still adjusting."

"No need to apologize, kitten."

My blood runs cold, and I glance up at him through timid lashes. Lars smiles down at me, his fingers skimming up and down my spine with sensual strokes.

Suddenly, I'm in that basement again. Earl is violating me while Dean talks me through it.

Look at me. Focus on me. It's just you and me, Cora.

These hands on me feel strange and unfamiliar. His eyes are much too dark, his voice missing that playful edge. His skin is too rough and his hair is too long.

This is wrong. It's all wrong.

I feel like everything is spinning, and I'm not sure if I should hold on for dear life or run away.

"You all right?" Lars asks, tipping his head back to study me.

I'm certain I've gone ashen, and my chest feels like it's going to explode. "I–I can't do this."

"Need some water?"

I shake my head, taking hesitant steps backwards. "I think I need to go."

I don't wait for Lars to respond. I make a quick stop over to Lily to let her know I'm not feeling well; then I call an Uber and get the hell out of there.

Ten minutes later, I'm standing on his front stoop.

I knock four times before the door swings open and Dean is standing in front of me, tired and disheveled, with a look of utter confusion creasing his brow. "Cora? Are you okay?"

My gaze trails over him and I feel safe again. He's only wearing sweatpants, no shirt, and his hair is tousled from sleep. His eyes, *his eyes*, are beautifully blue like a summer sky, and his hands are perfect and soft and reaching for me. "Dean…" I whisper, and I'm not sure what it's supposed to mean. Relief? Longing? Sadness?

Love?

Those hands graze up and down my upper arms, the worry in his face etched tight. "Are you hurt?"

I shake my head as my eyes fix on his bare torso, well muscled and lean. Smooth to the touch, yet rough and powerful when he's holding me, moving with me, our bodies intertwined. I glance back up to him and note the flash of desire that flickers across his face when he catches my unabashed perusal.

It's all I need.

I place my palms against his chest, pushing him back gently until we're both walking inside his town house. I kick the door shut with my heel, and then I'm all over him. Dean intakes a gasp of surprise when my hands clasp his face, pulling him to me, and my mouth collides with his. I kiss him hard, furiously, full of need and want and everything inside me I'm able to give. When our tongues meet, it's like I'm home.

Dean pulls back slightly, one hand cradling the back of my head, his fingers threading through my hair, and the other grasping my upper arm. "What are you doing?" he asks through a stunned breath.

My palms skim up the expanse of his chest, curling over his shoulders. Our eyes lock and I respond, "Being selfish."

I don't miss the subtle frown, the hint of perplexity, but I capture his mouth again before he can reply. I keep walking him backwards through the living room, my hands in his hair, tugging and pulling, my tongue going to war with his. His groans only make me want him more. I remove my hands from his skin to discard my coat and my shoes, then unbutton my pants, sliding my jeans and underwear down my hips and kicking them off as we continue our trek to the nearest piece of furniture.

We find the couch first.

I give him a small shove until he collapses back onto the cushions, then I crawl on top of him, straddling his thighs with my knees. My fingers hook inside his waistband and he raises his hips on instinct, allowing me to yank the sweatpants down. His erection springs free, and I take him in my hand, drowning in the sounds he makes when I stroke him up and down, swirling my thumb along the wet tip. I kiss him hard as I pump my hand.

"Fuck, Cora…" We pull back to breathe, but our lips stay connected, our teeth pressed together as his hands slide up and down my back, long fingers dipping beneath my blouse. "I missed you so much."

"I missed you," I reply, the words escaping like a rogue whimper. I lift up and position him at my core, squeaking out a moan when he grazes my entrance. I need this. I need *him*. He's the only calm to my madness, the only light to my dark, the only sweet to my bitter remains.

He tames me.

He *heals* me.

I lower myself onto his cock, watching his head fall back, his eyes closing, his jaw tightening. His hands drop to my hips, holding me firm, feeling the way I slide down on him, taking him all the way in. *God*, he feels good. He's big and thick, filling me completely. *In every way.*

I rock up and down, clasping my hands behind his neck and fusing our mouths back together. Dean opens willingly, digging his fingers into my waist when my tongue brushes against his. It's tender for a moment, languid and soft, but my movements pick up as desperation floods me, and our mouths go hungry. His teeth nick my lips, and I clench my internal muscles as I ride him, causing him to tug my hair back and devour my neck. He sucks and bites as I cling to him, my pace increasing. His mouth travels up to my ear and he nibbles the lobe, asking breathily, "You still mine?"

"Always."

I don't hesitate. I probably should, but I don't.

A raspy growl escapes him, something possessive and raw, and he drags his fingers backwards until he's cupping my ass, squeezing me as I cry out from the pleasure of it all. His cock is hitting all the right places, sending euphoric tingles through me, pushing me toward the edge. I skim my fingers through his hair and drop my forehead to his, locking our eyes as I grind against his groin until my body begins to shudder. I come hard, mewling and whimpering as shock waves light me up and send me spiraling. "Dean, Dean… Oh God, Dean…" I chant through my climax, inciting him to squeeze me harder, pull me closer, and ram his hips up, spearing me deep with his hard cock.

"I fucking love it when you say my name like that," he says raggedly, strained and heady. He thrusts into me three more times before tensing up and releasing, pulling me to him and clinging hard, his hands in my hair as he comes.

I hold him tight, my mouth pressed to his neck as his body tremors, a throaty groan escaping him. I kiss him then, tasting how much he wants me and burning it into every aching part of me. We come down together, our bodies slicked with sweat and the evidence of our lovemaking.

Dean wraps his arms around my middle, linking them behind my back and sighing deeply into my mouth. "Goddamn, you're sexy. You drive me crazy."

I smile against his lips, giving him a quick kiss before pulling back. I reach for the box of tissues on the side table to clean us up, then I drag the comforter toward us, lifting myself off of him and wrapping the big blanket around my shoulders.

Dean lies down and pulls me with him, and I spread the blanket over both of us as I snuggle into the crest of his arm. My legs intertwine with his, my hair haloing his chest and shoulder, and I feel him press a kiss to the top of my head.

Peace.

This is what peace feels like.

And as our bodies relax and melt together, I realize I don't need him to sing to me or massage my wrist, or offer any kind of escape from the dark cloud that hovers over me.

He is enough.

His heartbeat is all I need.

27

Dean: Umm...?

I wake up the next morning with a fluffy dog tail in my face as my phone vibrates on the nightstand beside me. Nipping the inside of my bottom lip with my teeth, I stare at the text message that just came through.

Me: Good morning :)
Dean: Where are you?
Me: Home. I had to let the dogs out.
Dean: Ok. You should have woken me up to say goodbye.

I swallow, inhaling a heavy breath.

Me: You looked so cute and peaceful. I didn't want to wake you :)

A few minutes pass by without a reply, so I start scrolling through Facebook as I roll onto my side. Jude scoots over to the opposite pillow, and I prop my head up on one hand, idly skimming my newsfeed.

Dean: You could have left a note or something. I wasn't expecting to wake up alone.

I blink slow, my eyes staying closed while I string together my response. Guilt cinches my gut as I recall waking up in a panic, half-naked and entangled with Dean Asher.

I booked it.

Me: I'm sorry. I wasn't expecting to stay out so late and I panicked. I didn't mean to worry you.
Dean: Panicked because of the dogs or panicked because of me?

Shit.

I turn off my phone and roll back over, my fingers running through my hair as I fill my cheeks with anxious breaths. I want to tell him that everything feels so perfect, so right, when we are wandering through the dark nights with our walls down.

But in the cold light of day, reality pinches me, waking me up like a bucket of ice water. The walls go back up—brick by brick, layer by layer, protecting me and keeping me safe.

However, walls are man-made. They crack and they crumble.

They are destined to fall.

And I'm terrified to see who is still clawing their way through the rubble when the dust settles…and who has just given up.

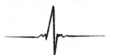

Man escapes abductor after twenty-two years in captivity

The headline stops my breath as I sit with my parents around the dinner table, distracting myself with my phone.

The partially nude man discovered on the side of Abbington Road near Pembrooke has been identified as thirty-year-old Oliver Lynch, the Libertyville boy who

went missing on the Fourth of July almost twenty-two
years ago.

The article is accompanied by a photo of a man lying shirtless on the side
of a snowy street in the fetal position, covered in blood.

My heart clenches.

Twenty-two years.

Twenty-two years.

"Cora, sweetheart? Are you okay? You've hardly touched your food."

I swallow, glancing up at my mother with wide eyes. Bile sticks to my throat
as I try to form words. "Did you see this news story about the missing boy who
was found after twenty-two years?"

My parents pierce me with empathetic eyes and my father clears his throat.
"We saw that on the news this morning."

"How awful," my mother adds, scooping peas onto her fork. "It's a miracle
that boy survived."

I blink.

Is it, though?

I can't help but wonder if he wishes he never survived at all. I was only gone
for three weeks, and I still can't shake the nightmares and haunting memories.
I tried to take my own life.

How can he ever move past his trauma and have a normal existence?

"Excuse me," I mutter, pushing myself away from the table and making
a hasty retreat upstairs to the guest bedroom. I curl up under the covers and
screenshot the article, sending it to Dean. I never replied to his last text, and it
hovers between us like so many other unanswered questions and frightening
unknowns.

He reads it right away, but I don't get a response for another ten minutes.

Dean: That's fucked. Really puts things in perspective.
Me: To him, we would be the lucky ones :(

Another few minutes pass before my phone zings again.

Dean: Speaking of... Did you see the new development in our case?

I freeze as I stare at his question, my body going numb. I haven't seen anything—in fact, I generally scroll right past all posts and articles that have the
name 'Earl' attached to them.

Me: No...

Only five seconds pass when a screenshot comes through, the picture slowly
loading. I zoom in to read the headline:

> Victim of Earl Timothy Hubbard, also known as the
> Matchmaker, comes forward

I read it again.
Then again.
My insides churn with disbelief. There's another victim out there...*alive*? I
don't even read the corresponding article. I call Dean immediately.
He picks up on the second ring. "Hey."
"Oh my God." My hand flies up to grasp my neck, scratching at my collar-
bone as I try to regain my composure. "Holy crap, Dean."
"Yeah. I was reading all about it right before you texted me."
I swallow. "What did it say? Did she give an interview? How did she escape?"
I hear him moving around on the other end with a faint rustling in the background. "Her name is Tabitha Brighton. She claims she was abducted by Earl
last spring, along with her college professor. They were kept in the basement
for two months before Earl killed the guy and let her go."
"Let her *go*?" I repeat, dumbfounded. My heart is rattling my ribs and I start
to tremble. "She's lying. She's got to be lying. That man didn't have a single
shred of decency inside him. There's no way he'd let one of his victims go."
"I don't know, Cora. It's still a developing story, but the professor checked
out. His name was Matthew Gleason and he was one of the confirmed bodies
found on the property."

"It-it can't be true. There's no one else…" My breathing escalates as I lean back against the decorative pillows, staring up at the ceiling and clutching my chest. "There's no one else."

"I mean, it makes sense," Dean replies. "There were eleven bodies found, yet he took his victims in pairs. I just figured there was either someone they hadn't discovered, or he'd practiced his sick shit on someone solo first."

"But…why wait all this time to come forward? So many victims could have been saved. *We* could have been saved." I stand from the bed and start pacing the room. "She must be lying. She's looking for attention, or…or money, or to see her name in history books one day. She's a fraud, Dean."

"Corabelle…" His voice softens, trying to soothe me through the speaker. "I'm sure more details will come out, but why does it even matter? What's done is done. There's no changing anything."

"Because!" I exclaim. "Tessie and her stepbrother would still be alive, along with countless others. We wouldn't have been abducted from your car in the middle of the night, shackled like dogs, forced to do…" My breath hitches, my fingers still curled around my neck, my emotions peaking. "Everything would be like it's supposed to be. We'd still hate each other, you'd be married to Mandy, and I wouldn't be standing here wondering how the hell I'm supposed to stop falling for you."

I cup my hand around my mouth as a small cry breaks out, my eyes squeezing out hot tears. My strangled breaths echo throughout the small guest room, and I wish he'd say something, *anything*, just so my anguish isn't the only sound humming in our ears.

"Cora…everything *is* the way it's supposed to be. This is how the cards fell. And the sooner you come to terms with that, the sooner you can heal."

I suck in a calming breath, allowing his words to sweep through me. He's right, of course. I've been stuck in a perpetual state of "what if" and "what should be" instead of accepting *what is* and working through it. This new development of a surviving victim is only heightening my warped thought process. I exhale through my nod. "Yeah. You're right," I whisper. I smooth back my hair and finish, "I should get going. Good night, Dean."

Dean pauses, then lets out a sigh that sounds like disappointment. "You don't think we should talk about last night?"

My cheeks burn from the memory. "Not tonight. I'm sorry."

"Cora, I can't do this."

I bite down on my tongue and fiddle with the pendant on my necklace. "Do what?"

"*This.* Whatever this is."

"I don't know what this is," I admit.

"Well, I can't do it—this push and pull with you. It's fucking me up."

I close my eyes, processing my response, when my mother appears in the doorway, tapping her knuckles against the frame. She mouths to me, *"Are you okay?"*

I nod, swallowing down my words, and reply to Dean. "I have to go."

Another sigh of frustration filters in my ear, and it feels like a dagger to my heart. "Yeah. Good night."

He disconnects the call, and it takes all of my willpower not to break down.

My mother is quickly by my side, rubbing her hand up and down my back. "Are you okay, honey? Do you need to talk?"

Yes. I probably do.

My parents have been nothing but supportive, despite the heinous crime I committed against their favorite daughter. But I'm not sure if it's because they truly sympathize with me, or if they're afraid I'll attempt to take my life again if they ostracize me.

I *should* talk… Lord knows I could use some motherly advice right about now.

But I'm not ready.

"No. I'm fine," I murmur with a shake of my head.

Her grip tightens as her palm moves up to my shoulder. "Sweetheart, I know we did everything we could to avoid inpatient treatment after you were released from the hospital, but if you think that's what you need to help you through this, please let me know."

"I don't need to be thrown in the loony bin, Mom. I'm just trying to adjust."

I was grateful I wasn't transferred to an inpatient facility post-release. Since it was a first-time offense with no history of mental disorder and no suicide note or indication of premeditation, I was allowed to go home. And I know I won't ever do something like that again. As low and scary as things might get, I *do* want to be alive. That night will forever be a stain on my memory. It will always be my biggest regret.

"Cora, there's no shame in needing help. That's what those services are there for. You've suffered immense trauma over the past few months—not just the abduction and the overdose, but you were *pregnant*, sweetie. It's all so much... so heavy."

I stiffen. I try not to think about the pregnancy. I bury it down, along with every other inconceivable blow I've been dealt since November. I don't think about how it could have been Dean's. I don't think about how it could have been *his*. I want to be a mother more than anything one day, but not like that. No child deserves to be born out of the horrors of that basement. "I told you, I'm fine. I just need to get some rest," I insist, escaping my mother's grasp and moving past her. "Thank you for dinner."

"Cora..."

I shuffle through the loft and down the stairs, grabbing my coat and keys. "Good night," I shout, disappearing out the front door.

When I pull out of the driveway and head toward the main intersection, I hesitate before I choose a turn lane. My heart starts to thump with nervous beats as I contemplate *not* going home. The sun has set and darkness is hovering, disguising what I know is wrong.

I don't think too hard and swerve to the left, heading to the opposite end of town.

For the second night in a row, I'm walking up his cement sidewalk, unable to stay away. Only, this time he's sitting on the front stoop smoking a cigarette. I halt my steps when our eyes meet and he blows a plume of smoke up toward the stars.

"You're smoking again," I note softly, stuffing my hands into my coat pockets.

His jaw sets as he takes a long drag, the embers flickering to life. The last time I saw him smoke was in his Camaro that night, right before Earl shattered my window.

And my soul.

"I need something to take the edge off."

I duck my head, pressing my lips together. "Am I the edge?"

Dean stares right at me as puffs of smoke trail from his nostrils; then he kicks at a loose stone. "Yeah, Cora. You're the edge." He watches carefully as I take a few slow steps toward him. "Why are you here?"

I was really hoping he wouldn't ask me that question. I offer a shrug in response.

He blinks through another drag. "What the fuck does that mean?"

"Can we go inside?"

"No. I'm smoking."

I quell my defenses and continue to approach him on the stoop. I perch myself between his legs, pushing his knees apart and reaching for his cigarette. I pluck the rolled paper from his loose grip, replacing it with my lips. Dean melts into me for one brief, exquisite moment, before pulling back and standing to his feet.

"I can't… It's getting late. You should go home."

He turns to head inside, not expecting me to follow, but I do. I stomp out the cigarette and trail him through the entryway, closing the door behind us. "I missed you."

This seems to trigger something in him and he whirls around, storming over to me frozen in the doorway. "Bullshit. You're here to scratch an itch."

I jerk back, thrown by that assumption. "You know that's not true."

"We both know that *is* true. Otherwise you wouldn't have skipped out on me this morning. You wouldn't have ignored my texts all day. You wouldn't have declined my invitation to talk." Dean tosses his arms in the air with aggravation. "I won't be your dirty little secret, Cora. I won't be your fuck toy or your goddamn escape."

Hurt sparks inside me, prickling my skin, but I shove it back down. I unbutton my peacoat and let it fall off my arms as I step out of my boots. I approach him standing there in the middle of his living room, hands set loosely on his hips, chest expanding and deflating with each arduous breath. When I'm only a foot away, I tug my blouse up and over my head. His jaw ticks as he watches, his eyes casing me, darkening and curious. I reach behind my back and unclasp my bra, letting it slip to the floor, my eyes still hooked on his.

His nostrils flare and his fingers dig into his hip bones, but he doesn't drop his gaze. "Stop."

"You don't want me?"

I'm playing with fire, but the flames are the only thing keeping me warm.

Dean sucks in a deep breath. "I want all of you, Corabelle."

I close the gap between us, grasping his hands in mine and placing them over my breasts. I release a tiny moan when his thumbs graze my nipples. "I'm right here."

"No." The word comes out forced, almost painful. His right hand slides up my chest until it's directly over my heart. "I want *all* of you."

I want that, too.

I want dinner dates and movie nights and homemade breakfasts after long, magical nights of lovemaking. I want to hold hands in public. I want to go on road trips, see the ocean, and laugh until our bellies ache.

But he's Dean.

And I'm Cora.

And we are not meant for any of those things.

I drag his hand back down until he's cupping my breast. I arch against him, my head tipping back as our groins touch together and he starts to palm my breasts, his desire taking over. "Please."

This puts him over the edge and he growls out, "Fucking hell."

His arms link underneath my thighs and he hoists me up, my legs curling around his waist. He carries me to his bedroom, our mouths locking together, our bodies ready to go, but our hearts desperate for so much more.

This is enough. This is okay.

I tell myself this as Dean fucks me doggy style on his bed, pulling my hair, nicking my skin with his teeth, and whispering dirty words into my ear.

If I can't have all of him, I'll settle for some of him.

28

"Miss Lawson?"

I straighten out my pencil skirt and turn from the whiteboard, discovering far too many eyes on me. Questioning eyes. Curious eyes. Some worried, some fascinated. I give a tug to my ponytail and force a smile. "Yes, Jenna?"

It's my first day back in the classroom. *Again.* First it was an abduction, then it was a suicide attempt. If my students learn anything from me, I hope it's some valuable life lessons—that, and the greatness that is Gatsby.

"You're bleeding."

I suck in a breath and glance down at myself. My white button-down blouse is dappled with red droplets. My eyes shift to my wrist, where I notice blood is dripping out from beneath my bandage. I didn't even realize I was scratching it. I clear my throat, flustered and embarrassed, as I reach for a tissue on my desk. "Goodness, I didn't even realize. Thank you, Jenna."

I excuse myself for a moment to clean up, the whispers and chatter lingering in my ears long after I've walked out of the classroom. I lock myself in a bathroom stall to collect my bearings, pressing my palms against the door and leaning forward, taking in deep, steady breaths. My gaze drifts to the bloodstains seeped into the white fabric of my blouse, branding me with a sinister reminder of my pain. It laughs and mocks me, telling me this will never be over.

Deep breath. Deep breath.

Before my tears break through, the bathroom door creaks open and two fellow teachers march inside, gossiping among themselves. I go still when my name escapes their lips.

"Feel sorry for her. It's got to be tough getting back to normal after something like that."

"Suicide, though? I mean, really. Way to completely botch up your second chance at life. I can't imagine surviving something like that and then trying to throw it all away."

I watch through the stall crack, clutching my necklace in a clammy fist as the two women fluff their hair in the mirror and reapply lipstick.

"You're being way too harsh. I can't imagine surviving something like that, *period*. I have no idea how I would cope."

"With alcohol and ice cream like normal people? Besides, Maryann heard from Kara that it wasn't even about the kidnapping. She started banging her sister's husband, the guy who was trapped with her, and the sister found out. She went psycho and OD'd."

"Whoa. Seriously?"

"That's what I heard."

"Shit…Cora doesn't seem like the type. She's so sweet."

"Well, you heard about her liaison with Troy Adilman years back. The girl gets around."

The women share a laugh, and I think I might get sick.

"I don't blame her, really. That guy Dean is *delicious*. I totally creeped on his Facebook page. Honestly, I wouldn't say no to being chained up with him for three weeks…"

The conversation fades out as the teachers retreat from the bathroom, leaving me heaving into the toilet bowl. My necklace remains in my hand, tears streaking down my cheeks, and I tell myself over and over, *I'm okay. It's still beating. I'm okay.*

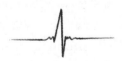

I didn't plan this.

Call it insanity, call it some kind of twisted closure—regardless, it wasn't planned.

I park my car along the side of Hawthorne Lane, an older subdivision with no sidewalks and an abundance of leafless trees. My boots crunch against the thin layer of snow turned icy from the colder temperatures. I wrap my scarf around my neck as I saunter up the walkway, my nerves the only thing warming me up. When I reach the front door, my hand stops midair before my knuckles reach the metal screen. There's still a Christmas wreath mounted, proudly displayed, even though it's the end of February.

She is still holding onto something cheerful, long after it has passed.

My eyes close tight and I grit my teeth together, my arm falling to my side. *I can't do this.*

But before I can make a quick escape, the door pulls open, revealing a beautiful, young woman with long hair made of obsidian silk. Her skin is as white as the snow beneath my boots, and her chocolate eyes flash with something akin to recognition, despite having never met her before.

And then I see something *else* in those eyes—something I am all too familiar with. Something haunting, raw, and painful…something that tethers and binds us like blood.

I know right then that her story is true and guilt eats away at me for even doubting it.

"I had a feeling you would find me. Come in."

My lips part to speak, but only my breath escapes me, hitting the frosty air like a puff of smoke. I nod, stepping through the threshold as she holds open the screen door. "I'm so sorry to drop by unannounced. I wasn't sure how to contact you. My name is—"

"Cora Lawson. I know." Tabitha offers a small smile, closing the door behind us. We share a poignant look, a knowing look, and she guides me to a brown love seat in the main living area. "Sit down. I'm sure you have questions."

I pluck my mittens off, one by one, then slide the beanie from my head as my hair frizzes out. I smooth it down and take a seat. "I'm really sorry. This is probably so inappropriate."

"Nothing is too out there for me," she says, her smile still lingering. Tabitha sits across from me in a rocking chair. "I thought about reaching out to you, but I know your wounds are a lot fresher than mine. I didn't want to hinder your healing process."

I pucker my lips, feeling like a jerk. I had no problem showing up on her doorstep, barging into her life, hindering away. *Oof.*

Tabitha catches my eyes, her head tilting slightly. "Don't feel bad, Cora. Maybe it will be good for us to talk through it. Therapeutic, you know?" She wrings her hands together in her lap, releasing a sigh. "No one really understands what we went through."

I study her with a nod. Gosh, she's pretty—like a porcelain doll or Snow White…if Snow White had eyes like pain.

A thousand questions swim through my brain, but I bite my lip and ask first, "Did you fall in love with Matthew?"

Tabitha's almond eyes widen and gloss over, startled by my initial question. "Oh, um…" She heaves in a jagged breath and bobs her head, averting her gaze. "Yes. Very much so."

Oh God.

I want to start crying and I'm only one question in. "I'm so sorry."

"Me too," she whispers softly, her own eyes tearing up. "Matthew was my rock the whole time. He gave me hope. He made me feel safe. He was truly my…"

We say the word at the same time: "Lifeline."

Our eyes meet, hollow and bereaved.

Tabitha pulls her lips between her teeth, taking a moment to regroup before she faces me again. "This is going to sound awful, Cora, so please forgive me, but…when your story broke, I was incredibly jealous of you."

"You were?"

"Yes. You *both* made it out. Together." Tabitha pushes her hair behind her ear and glances just over my shoulder. "I saw that picture of you holding hands. It looked like the end of something terrible, but the start of something beautiful."

I don't even realize tears are sliding down my cheeks as I shake my head back and forth. "He's my sister's fiancé—or *was*, at the time. There's nothing beautiful about that." I inhale a painful breath. "It's been a nightmare."

"I would give anything to live in your nightmare. Mine is very lonely." She dips her chin, her emotions climbing. "I can still hear him whispering '*I love you*' over and over as he bled out on the cement, chained to that pole. I was completely helpless to save him."

No. I rise from the sofa with a strained gasp. "I–I don't think I can hear this."

"I'm just trying to show you how it *could* be. You're truly blessed, Cora. You both survived."

I feel queasy and light-headed, and all I want to do is throw my arms around Dean and hold him tight. I imagine *him* lying on that basement floor, his life slipping away. It's too much.

I try to reroute my thoughts and center myself. "Did…did you have feelings for each other prior to the abduction?"

Tabitha watches as I sit back down. "Not really. I mean, he was my teacher and he was gorgeous. He wore these black-rimmed glasses during our lessons that made him look like Clark Kent. All the girls swooned over him." She smiles wistfully, replaying memories in her mind. "We shared a few stolen glances here and there. There was a connection. A chemistry, you know? But he was off-limits. He was walking me to my car one night after I stayed late working on an assignment, and that's when…"

She goes quiet and I close my eyes. "How did you get out?"

Tabitha wraps her arms around herself, hugging tight. "Earl developed feelings for me. He couldn't kill me."

"God…I never got that impression from him. He seemed entirely void of feelings."

"I thought so, too, but I worked hard to establish a connection with him. I pretended to enjoy it when he would…" She clenches her jaw. "Well, you know. I developed a rapport with him. I manipulated his emotions—what little he had, anyway. He told me I was his favorite pet."

My stomach twists with nausea. "Why didn't you come forward sooner?"

She fiddles with the gold fringes on her long-sleeved tunic, a silence settling between us for a few beats. "I did. I tried."

"What? They didn't believe you?"

Tabitha leans back in the chair, rocking it with her feet. "Earl never told us his name, so I had nothing to go on. I had no idea where I was. He knocked me out and dropped me on the side of the road thirty miles away. I gave my story to detectives and did a composite sketch, but they didn't have any leads. The only thing I had was that basement."

I lower my head, nodding, feeling awful for branding her a liar and a fraud before I even knew her story. I think back to those two teachers in the bathroom, women I'd formed a friendship with over the last few years, passing misinformed judgments over me. Belittling my trauma to fit into their petty gossip train. I look up at Tabitha, finding her zoned out as she stares at her colorful area rug. "You're very brave," I tell her gently, waiting for her eyes to lift to mine. "I couldn't go through this alone."

Tabitha slips a faint smile, then nods her head over my shoulder to the corner of the room. "I'm not entirely alone."

A frown pinches my brow and I twist around, gasping out loud when I catch sight of a baby swing. A tiny infant lies perfectly asleep, quiet and still, bundled up in a pink teddy bear blanket. I swipe away tears with my fingertips, my chest burning with both joy and anguish. "Is she…?"

"She's Matthew's," Tabitha confirms. "Matthew told me he'd always be with me, no matter what. He was telling the truth." Her watery smile blooms as she admires her daughter. "Her name is Hope."

I crumble.

My face collapses into my palms, my tears leaking through my fingers. I shake and sob without breaking for air, not even when I feel Tabitha slide up beside me on the love seat and wrap her arms around my shoulders. I cry for this brave woman, raising her lover's baby alone. I cry for Matthew who never got to meet her. I cry for little Hope, a product of something so horrible, yet so tragically beautiful.

And I cry for my own baby who never came to be.

Tabitha fingers my locket as I harness my breaths and wipe my face with the back of my hand. I glance down at her careful touch as she pops open the heart. "Still beating," she voices, her tone somewhat whimsical.

I sniffle with a smile. "Dean got it for me for Christmas. He would tell me that as long as my heart is still beating, I'm okay. It's a reminder when things get hard."

"Wow." Tabitha beams, grazing her finger over the engraved letters. "What an amazing gift."

My sights shift to the little bundle on my left. "We both have some pretty amazing gifts."

We spend the next hour sharing stories—some heartbreaking, some sweet. I have made a friend in this young woman, so strong and brave. A vision of healing and perseverance. A kindred soul. We exchange phone numbers and promise to keep in touch, and it's a promise I intend to keep.

As she walks me to the door and we say our goodbyes, Tabitha calls after me. "Hey, Cora. Can you give Dean a message for me?"

I turn to face her on the snowy pathway. "Sure. What is it?"

"Tell him I say thank you for pulverizing that evil son of a bitch."

We lock eyes, and I can't help but smile.

29

A VOIDANCE HAS BECOME MY NEW favorite word.

Parents want to see me?

Avoid.

Lily wants to go out for drinks?

Avoid.

Mandy posts ambiguous memes about broken trust and betrayal all over Facebook?

Avoid.

Dean wants to talk?

Well…

Nope. Utterly avoid.

It's Friday night and there's a knock at my front door. I'm wondering which one of my avoidances has had enough of my shit and is coming over to smack me. The dogs follow me to the door as I peer out through the small, square window to see Lily with her heart hands pressed up against the glass. She blows into her palms, leaving behind a fog-shaped heart.

I pull the door open, planning to look irritated, but my smile betrays me. "I thought you were going to a party tonight."

"I am." Lily reaches for the bag resting near her feet and holds it up proudly. "You're the party, Cora. I've got cheap Aldi wine that will give you such a bad headache, everything else in your life will seem like a magical fairy tale, consisting of Henry Cavill riding on a unicorn naked through fields of endless cookie-dough ice cream and orgasmic bliss."

I blink. "The unicorn is naked? That's awkward."

"No, dumbass."

"Okay, well, you should have worded it like 'a naked Henry Cavill riding a unicorn.'"

Lily swings her head back and forth as she pushes through the entryway with her migraine bag. "Dude. Don't English-teacher me."

"I mean, that whole mental image sounds very unsettling if I'm being honest…"

She smacks me with the bag, slipping off her boots. "I also brought microwavable popcorn and a box of Kleenex for when we inevitably give in to our wine emotions."

I watch as Lily traipses through my living room to the kitchen, setting the bag down on the table and pulling out wine bottles. I can't help but soften at the gesture, secretly grateful for the company. Avoidance has the unpleasant side effect of extreme loneliness. *Shocking.*

After three glasses of wine and two episodes of *Dead to Me*, Lily turns to me on the couch and gives me her gossip eyes. I glance at her, then quickly avert my attention back to the television, tossing a handful of popcorn into my mouth. "Stop looking at me like that."

"Like what?"

"Like you're ripping secrets right out of my soul."

Lily pulls her feet up onto the couch, still staring at me. "So, you're saying you have secrets."

"No."

"Liar. Tell me what's going on with Dean."

I shovel more popcorn into my mouth.

Avoid.

I try to distract myself with the show, but James Marsden kind of resembles Dean with the hair and the gorgeous blue eyes, and dammit, Lily is still staring at me. "No. Go away."

"Fine. But I'm taking the wine with me."

"Fine."

She groans in protest, nudging my knee with her toes. "I'm not taking the wine. I wouldn't do that to you. And I'm too invested in the show to leave right now, but still—tell me."

Avoid.

"Cora, I swear to God…"

"Okay, whatever, fine." My cheeks start to warm as thoughts of Dean poke through my armor. "What do you want to know?"

"Um, did you land feet first in the boneyard?"

I spit out my wine. "I have no idea what that means, but it sounds depraved."

"Are you doing the mattress mambo?"

"Just stop."

"Is he throwing the hot dog down?"

"I literally hate you."

Lily breaks into a fit of wine giggles, tipping over, her head colliding with my shoulder. "Don't be such a prude," she teases, smacking me with her free hand.

I let a grin slide across my face, my eyes drifting to my friend. "I wouldn't say I'm a prude…"

"Okay, *now* we're getting somewhere." Lily sits up expectantly, fully facing me. "You are, aren't you? Holy shit, Cora. You and Dean? Holy shit."

"You said that twice."

"I'll say it again: *holy shit.*" She bounces up and down like we're two teenagers swapping our first-kiss experiences. "You know I need all the gory details, starting with penis size. Go."

I just can't with her.

I shake my head through a sigh, riddled with giddy nerves. "It's a mess, Lily." I duck my head, stretching a smile. "A *hot* mess."

"Lord, it's probably *fire.* All that built-up sexual tension with life-and-death situations thrown into the mix?" She releases a slow breath, fanning herself dramatically. "So, are you guys together? Like, official?"

Cue the ice water. "No. *No.* Of course not… It's just sex."

"How can it *just* be sex after all you went through together? There are no feelings?"

Oh, there's feelings. A crap ton of feelings. In fact, those feelings are climbing up my chest right now, lodging in my throat. "It's…really complicated. There's definitely feelings, but there's nothing I can do about them. I'm sort of keeping him at arm's length."

Lily squints at me as if she's trying to read between the lines. "So, you just bang and bolt?"

"Your vocabulary concerns me," I joke, avoiding the question.

Avoid, avoid, avoid.

But it's kind of hard to avoid someone sitting a foot away, staring you down in Taylor Swift socks. "I guess that's one way to put it," I relent. "I basically show up on his doorstep a few times a week and we have crazy, amazing, rough sex. Then I skip out before sunrise and avoid him until the next time. In the beginning, he would try talking about it, but I think he's just accepting our fate at this point."

I worry my lip between my teeth, sounding like a giant hooker when I word it like that. I'm far from slutty—not that there would be anything wrong with that, really. I enjoy sex, but I've only been with three guys prior to Dean. Two of them were serious relationships with men who cheated on me, and then there was Troy Adilman, who was just kind of a drunken, weird, virginity-losing one-night stand. And Dean… Well, he's in his own category.

Lily's eyes are getting extra squinty, which means she's still trying to read me *and* trying to conjure up some kind of best-friend advice that will probably be terrible. "That sounds equally hot and depressing," she says after a few minutes of consideration. "Does Mandy know?"

My stomach pitches at the sound of Mandy's name, sending waves of nausea right through me. "She knows we had sex, but not that we're *still* having sex. I haven't even spoken to her since the hospital. I…don't really know what to say."

"What about your parents? Whose side are they on?"

I shift uncomfortably on the couch. "They claim to be Team Both Daughters, which I'm sure is code for Team Mandy But Can't Tell Cora. I've only seen them once over the last few weeks, and it was an awkward dinner without much conversation."

"You've always thought your parents loved Mandy more than you, but I've never gotten that impression and I've known you a hell of a long time. They probably *are* on both of your sides."

I try to squash the bitterness that tickles me. "Mandy can do no wrong in their eyes. She was the perfect prom queen with the perfect high school sweetheart, and I've always been the stubborn, nerdy kid who refuses to conform. Mandy always got the lavish birthday parties and the over-the-top praise: *Congratulations! Mandy learned to tie her shoes even though she's nine. Oh my God! Mandy got a B minus on her final exam. Wow! Mandy got her driver's permit and only crashed once, and it was just a little crash.*" I pause to catch my breath, my resentment bubbling to the surface. "All I ever got was a pat on the back. Now, I'm the stain on the family—the daughter who gets kidnapped by a psychopath, the daughter who sleeps with her sister's ex, and the daughter who overdoses on sleeping pills."

Lily cowers away, holding up her hands. "Touched a nerve. Got it."

"Sorry." I cringe at my oversharing rant. "It's the wine talking."

She holds up the Kleenex box. "That's why I brought these," she quips. "And for the record, literally your only flaw has ever been liking NSYNC over Backstreet Boys. Otherwise, you're pretty perfect."

We share a smile, the compliment washing away all of my inner turmoil for the time being. Before I can reply, my phone starts vibrating in my pocket.

It's a text from Dean.

Dean: I miss you.

Lily yanks my phone away and reads the message, swooning instantly. "Dear God, that's adorable. Guys only text me when they miss my vagina."

"I'm sure that's what he's implying," I shrug.

"It's not."

Lily starts texting back a reply and I panic, lunging for the phone. "Absolutely not. Give it back."

She dives from the couch laughing, her thumbs frantically swiping over the keyboard. I chase her around the living room and almost tackle her like a linebacker.

"Okay, okay. Don't be such a psycho. Here."

Lily tosses me the phone and I check for damage.

Lily: I need your baloney pony.

"Lily! Damn you!" I curse, glaring at the message, then watching as my friend doubles over with laughter. "I hate you *so much*."

A zing comes through and I force myself to open the message.

Dean: Hi, Lily

My head is shaking back and forth, embarrassed by her immaturity, as I text my own reply.

Me: Sorry. She's awful.
Dean: It was kind of funny
Me: No

Ugh.

I toss my phone onto the sofa cushions as Lily comes down from her laugh attack. "How are you the worst *and* the best at the same time?" I ponder, plopping back down with a huff.

Lily shrugs, joining me. "One of my many talents, along with singing the alphabet backwards and gardening."

I try to return my attention to the TV show that we've been completely missing when Lily's elbow pokes me in the ribs. "Ouch. What?"

"Well?"

I stare at her, unblinking.

"Are you going to invite him over?"

I scoff, returning my focus to the screen. "No. It's a bad idea."

"So is drinking Aldi wine, but we do it anyway."

"One bad decision is enough for me tonight."

Lily lets out a sigh but doesn't push the matter, curling up with one of my throw pillows and whispering, "If you say so."

An hour later, Dean has me bent over the kitchen table, pounding into me from behind as my fingernails scratch along the wood. He tugs my hair back, twisting my face to his, and I chant his name against his lips. I know it drives him wild.

He snakes his hand around my middle, sliding it down my stomach until it reaches its destination between my legs. With my sweatpants around my ankles, I arch into his touch, moaning when his fingers find my clit. "Oh God…"

Dean works me into a frenzy, trailing his lips from mine and attacking my throat with his tongue. "You're always so wet. I fucking love it."

I gasp out loud, already edging toward release as I press myself against the table. Dean sweeps his fingers up the nape of my neck, collecting my long hair between them and squeezing his fist, ramming into me harder, while still fingering me with his other hand.

Holy, holy, holy crap.

This shouldn't feel this good.

Why does this feel so good?

"Come for me, Cora," he demands, leaning forward on top of me, his chest to my back, thrusting his hips with impossible intensity.

I shatter.

I dig my nails into the kitchen table, surely leaving marks, as my body convulses around him, a cry escaping my lips.

Dean whispers against my ear as I come down, brushing my hair aside and slowing his pace. "That's my girl."

I'm hardly recovered when he pulls out of me and spins me around, lifting me onto the table and settling between my legs. He kisses me as he pushes back inside, hands planted on either side of me as I link my ankles behind his back. His thrusts are slow and even, and I already feel the pressure building again when he breaks the kiss to hold my eyes.

God, his eyes. They will be my undoing.

I look away, the feelings swirling inside me proving too much. Too intimate, too powerful, too *real*.

This can't be more than sex.

Dean pinches my chin between his thumb and finger, gently turning my face back toward him. "Why can't you look at me, Cora?" He's still moving inside me, but not as hard. Not as fast. His strokes are languid and deliberate, almost like he's trying to tell me something.

But the last thing I want to do is talk about our feelings when he's balls deep inside of me, so I clasp his face between my palms and crash our mouths back together. I push my tongue between his lips and he lets me in, his hips moving quicker when our tongues begin to dance. I'm an arrow to his heart—a dagger to his defenses. He knows what I'm willing to give and he takes every piece, every breath, every accidental crumb.

And then we're grinding against each other, nails scratching, tongues vicious and angry, bodies full of raw desperation. I open my mouth to speak, suddenly craving more. I'll never know if it was the goddamn wine, or maybe I'm just irrevocably fractured, but three words spill from my mouth that make Dean go still: "Tie me up."

He looks at me, a light sheen of sweat casing his brow, his blue eyes wide and troubled. He halts all movement, and even his breathing goes shallow. I stare up at him, wishing I could swallow those words back down.

He deflates then, like a child's balloon or a wounded animal. Like I stole something precious right out of his hands. Dean pulls out of me and drops his forehead to mine as I sit there in silence, my legs still wrapped around him. "Fuck," he mutters, but not out of anger, not out of spite. It sounds like hopelessness. He untangles himself from me and steps back, tugging his jeans up over his hips.

Heat flames my cheeks as I rest propped up on my elbows, spread-eagle and exposed. I feel like he can see right through me, right into my tormented center, where my guts and ghosts and darkest parts are utterly vulnerable. I snap myself into action and slip down from the table, pulling up my sweatpants without meeting his eyes.

"What the hell, Cora?"

I spare Dean the tiniest glance as I smooth out my hair. He's facing me, fingers perched on his hips, his gaze riddled with heedful regard. "It was nothing.

Forget it." I storm past him, making my way to the bedroom. "I assume we're done here, so feel free to let yourself out."

He's hot on my heels. "No. We need to talk about this."

"There's nothing to talk about."

"Are you kidding me?" He grabs my wrist, spinning me around as we enter the bedroom. His tone turns sober, his shoulders dropping. "This isn't okay."

"Then go. I'm not keeping you here."

Dean's jaw clenches as he tries to hold back his frustration. "I thought I could do this. I thought I could live with whatever the fuck this is, whatever scraps you were willing to give me…but this is *killing* me. It's killing both of us."

I repeat my statement slower, putting emphasis on each word. "*Then go.*"

"Is that what you want?" His hands rise, resting on my shoulders, and his breath catches. "Because when I walk out that door, I'm not coming back."

His words do something to my heart. They wrap around the bleeding organ, squeezing the life out of it. "I can't have what I want," I say, my voice weak and frayed.

Dean lets out a breath, dipping his chin. "This isn't healthy, Corabelle. We can't thrive like this. We can't *heal* like this. You told me in your car that night at the Oar that I was holding you underwater, that you couldn't breathe, and I made myself believe it wasn't true. I wanted to believe that we *needed* each other. That we had to cling and fight and claw our way out of this together." He shakes his head with surrender in his eyes. "But you were right. We're drowning here…and I'm gonna fuckin' lose you if we don't come up for air."

My emotions start to soar like waves crashing down, drenching me in bitter truths. "I don't want to lose you, but I don't know how to keep you." My tears fall fast, landing on my lips, tasting like the salty sea. "I'm just sinking."

"That's why we have to stop, Cora." Dean tightens his grip on my shoulders and the pain is evident in his eyes. "I need you healthy. I need you put back together, smiling and alive and glowing. I think you're still living in that basement, and as long as you're tied to me, you're tied to *it*. You need to get the hell out of there. You need to be free."

I'm shaking my head, my face a mask of heartache. "I can't let go of you."

"Then let *me* let go of *you.*"

"No. Dean…please." I reach for his shirt, clutching the fabric in my fists. Holding on for dear life. "You said we could start over. Maybe we just need a few days to think and regroup, and then…"

"It's too late." He kisses my forehead, inhaling deeply. "It's too late to start over."

I lift my chin, finding his lips and pressing a kiss to his mouth. "But I…" My voice trails off. I drift away, choking on the words.

Dean frames my face with his hands, kissing me again, light and tender. "You what?" He pulls away to search my eyes, smoothing back my hair.

"I love you."

I think both of our hearts skip a beat—the *same* beat. And I feel like that must mean something.

Dean's eyes slowly close, as if he's absorbing those words, replaying them over and over in his mind. Carving them into the deepest layer of his soul. "Shit," he mutters quietly. "You're making this so damn hard."

I inch up on my tiptoes to capture another kiss, only this one is brimming and burning with everything that's in my heart. Passion, possessiveness, love, desire, *need*. I can taste his hesitation as he goes to battle with himself. Right and wrong. Yes and no. Stay or walk.

Dean envelops me in a fierce hold, his arms wrapping around me and pulling me to him, our mouths feasting and yearning. His tongue kisses mine, and for a moment, we are lost. We're okay. We're still swimming.

But he jerks back with a heaving chest, scrubbing both hands down his face as he retreats. "Goddammit. I need to go, Cora. I need to fuckin' think about this."

I step forward. He steps back.

"Dean…"

"I have to think. I'm sorry."

I lower my eyes, forcing back an ugly meltdown. I fold my hands together, my knee bobbing with anxiety. "Fine. Just go."

"Cora, don't make this harder. I'm trying to do the right thing here."

"*Go.*" Everything comes bubbling to the surface—rage, disbelief, sorrow, rejection. I confess my love and he still wants to walk away. I feel shredded. Dismantled. "Go, go, go! Just get out."

I try to avert my gaze, try to keep my eyes off his, but I can't help myself. I glance up as Dean takes two steps backwards. His head is swaying side to side, his features pinched with conflict, and I swear I see tears rimming his eyes. But he keeps backing up. He keeps going.

He keeps walking away.

And when the front door closes shut, I break down.

Dean said we needed to come up for air, but I don't understand. It doesn't make sense.

He's gone…and I can't breathe.

30

THE ENSUING WEEK IS A blur. I put my brain in autopilot mode to get through work without a breakdown, slapping an overly forced smile onto my face. My students are restless and distracted with spring break quickly approaching, which works in my favor, because I don't think they notice the dark circles under my eyes and my hands that are constantly shaking.

I make my way through the school parking lot that following Friday afternoon, releasing a long breath when I hop inside my car. My fingers clench around the steering wheel as the tension I've been holding onto all day—the *facade*—begins to dissolve.

It's just me and my emotional demons now.

But we are interrupted when my phone lights up with a new text message. I'm taken aback when I see Mandy's name.

Mandy: Meet me at the ice cream shop @ 4:30

My brows furrow, my knees starting to tremble as I sit and stare at the screen. I glance at the time, noting it's already quarter after four, then turn the car on and head into town. I spot my sister's Kia Soul parallel parked in front of the familiar building, so I pull into the space behind it. I haven't spoken to Mandy in over a month. She's refused dinner invitations from our parents and has ignored the few texts I've sent her since my hospital release.

I don't blame her. Not at all.

Which is undoubtedly why I'm terrified to face her right now.

I inhale a breath of courage as I slide out of the driver's seat and make my way inside on shaky legs. The sun is shining warm and bright today, melting the lingering patches of sidewalk ice and offering a welcome taste of spring.

I can't help but hope for another change of season today.

Mandy is sitting at a corner booth on her cell phone, her eyes lifting when the little bells on the door chime, alerting her of my presence. She stands to face me, then approaches the counter to order our ice cream cones—the birthday tradition we missed in November when I was busy being kidnapped and falling in love with her fiancé.

My throat tightens as we stand shoulder to shoulder and give the clerk our orders. We wait in silence while the treats are made, then handed to us over the counter. Like always, we take a quick bite—hers, strawberry, and mine, cookie dough—and head outside toward the nearby playground. We skip the secret handshake and the selfie in front of the building.

Our go-to swings are vacant as usual, likely due to the melting ice chunks dampening the seats. We swipe our hands over the puddles and sit down; then I wait with nervous anticipation for what happens next. I want to say something to break this belly-churning silence, but words are being elusive, stuck inside me like bubble gum.

I glance over at my sister who is swinging at a leisurely pace to my left. Her hair is in a perfectly coiffed bun on top of her head, her makeup impeccable. Her beauty has always taken my breath away. I never understood why she wanted to hide behind all the heavy foundation, loud colors, and fake eyelashes.

"I cheated on him, you know."

I almost drop my ice cream cone. "What?"

"Last summer at Allie's birthday party. Dean had the flu, so I went by myself. I had too much to drink, and…" She licks her hand as melted ice cream drips between her thumb and finger. "It was a huge mistake. I felt like shit. I betrayed a person I truly loved, all because of stupid insecurities—because of this desire to feel wanted and appreciated, even though I already was. I don't know why it wasn't enough… I don't know why *he* wasn't enough."

I'm staring at her, my mouth open wide as ice cream spills onto my lap. I'm stunned by her confession. I don't know what to say.

"I feel like all of this is karma smacking me in the face. And part of me knew, deep down, I had sealed our fate with that one stupid decision, even though Dean never found out about it. I just… I never thought it would be *you*." Mandy looks over at me, her eyes glossed over and spearing me with both guilt and disappointment. "You've always been the strong one. The lucky one. The *good* one. Everything you worked for, you got. Everything you put your mind to, you succeeded at. You had the smarts and the good grades, the quick wit and sense of humor, the respectable job, the *house*. You have your own house, Cor… You're not even thirty and you're killing it.

"I had to take a GED just to pass high school. I'm barely making ends meet at the hair salon. I've lived in the same crappy, two-bedroom apartment since college because Dean never wanted to pull the trigger on moving in together. He told me he liked his space and wanted to wait until we were married, and I respected that, but maybe…maybe it was because he knew we were never meant to be."

"Mandy…"

"Anyway," she swallows, glancing at her feet. "All I had was Dean. He was my only trophy, my only success story." She inhales a quick breath, then finishes. "I couldn't handle the fact that you had him, too."

God.

I'm absolutely dumbfounded, sitting slack-jawed on the swing with ice cream dribbling down my arm. I have to look away before my emotions boil over. "I–I never knew you felt like that. I've always had the complete opposite perspective. I've envied you my whole life—your beauty, your popularity, your bubbly personality. You always got your way. You were always celebrated and adored…the center of attention. I've just been hiding in your shadow."

An abrupt laugh escapes her. "It's funny how different things look on the other side."

I'm not sure how to respond to that, so I sit quietly and process it instead. This whole time, Mandy has been jealous of *me*? The thought alone is preposterous.

Mandy continues a few minutes later after our truth bombs have sunk in. "This isn't me forgiving you, Cor," she says, biting her lip as she stares down at the patches of grass peeking through the melting layer of snow. "Not yet, anyway. I'm not ready…just like I'm not ready to forgive myself for my own actions. But I can recognize the fact that we're all human and we all screw up. We all make big, messy, life-altering mistakes, and sometimes it's for selfish, superficial reasons like what I did…and sometimes it's because the universe throws you a curveball, forcing you in a direction you never saw coming.

"And while I can understand that, Cora, I really can, I just can't accept it yet. I can't handle the thought of family dinners with Dean at the table by *your* side, holding *your* hand, kissing *your* lips. I can't imagine holidays or social gatherings or double dates, or *God*, becoming an aunt when I thought I was about to become a mother."

Tears mix with ice cream as I close my eyes, sucking in a breath that singes my throat.

Mandy's own tears leak out, streaking down her pink cheeks. "But what I *can* accept is the fact that we weren't meant to be and what's done is done, regardless of how or why. Dean deserves to be happy, and if that's with you, I won't stand in the way. But I can't stand by your side either…not now. Not yet. Not until my heart fully heals." She raises her chin, glancing up at the cloudy sky, one hand holding her cone and the other gripping the swing. "Maybe someday."

Maybe someday.

I fiddle with the heart pendant around my neck with sticky fingers, swallowing hard, letting her words fill me up.

Maybe someday sounds a lot like hope, and hope is all I have right now.

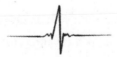

It's 7:00 p.m. and I'm cuddled up on the couch watching HGTV with Penny in my lap and Jude curled into a ball beside me. It's almost like I'm expecting his text to come through as I reach for my phone at the same time it zings to life with a new message.

Dean: Can we talk?

We've seen each other every Friday night for the past few weeks. Only, there hasn't been much talking involved.

Me: Sure. I was thinking the same thing. Can I call you?
Dean: I'd rather talk in person.

Oh. Well, maybe talking is code for sex, after all.

Me: Okay.
Dean: I'll be over soon

I run into the bathroom to freshen up, taking my hair down, brushing my teeth, and spritzing a few pumps of perfume onto my neck. The dogs alert me of his arrival fifteen minutes later, pawing at the door when he knocks.

"It's open," I call out, applying a touch of lip gloss before joining him at the front of the house. Dean is crouched down in the entryway, scratching Jude's stomach like he always did with Blizzard. Penny is circling his leg, begging for attention that he quickly provides. I can't help but smile at the image. "Hey."

He glances up, his expression disguising whatever it is he may be thinking, then rises to his feet. "Hey."

Usually, this is the point where we pounce on each other. But since I actually *do* want to talk first, I'm not sure how to proceed—so I just kind of stand there, awkwardly playing with my hair and tapping my bare foot against the wooden floor.

Dean takes the lead, letting out a sigh as he approaches me. "Thanks for letting me stop by. There's some stuff I wanted to discuss with you."

"Me too… I was actually going to text you about grabbing coffee this weekend. But this works." Our eyes are holding tight, making me nervous. I gulp. "Um, have a seat."

We make our way to the couch, Dean trailing behind me and sitting farther away from me than I'd prefer. All I want to do is jump into his arms and kiss him senseless. We lock eyes again, both of us out of our element. Neither of us fully prepared to face the fallout from last week. I lower my head and we both speak at the same time.

"So, I—"

"I wanted to—"

Dean clears his throat. "You go first."

I gather up my courage and nod, twisting on the couch so I'm facing him, one leg pulled up in front of me. I curl my fingers around my ankle as my heart thumps wildly in my chest.

Just be honest. Tell him what you want. Don't hold back.

"I, um, just wanted to say how sorry I am for dragging you down into my dark hole for the past few weeks. Hiding you in the shadows. Keeping you at a distance. Letting you in, then pulling away. It wasn't fair because I know you wanted more… I've just been so ashamed, so confused, and I haven't been handling it right."

I watch as his gaze floats over my face, his jaw tight, his eyebrows creased. He doesn't say anything, so I keep going.

"I talked to Mandy today. She invited me out for ice cream—our traditional birthday cone at the park. We had a long talk, and I think it's going to be okay." I scoot closer to him on the couch, reaching for his hand. "I'm not saying it's going to be easy, but I'm hopeful Mandy will accept everything one day. She even said she was talking to this new guy and there's a spark, and maybe someday we can both move on and—"

"Cora, I'm leaving."

His words flip me upside down and I drop his hand. "What?"

A look of pain stretches across Dean's face as he blows out a hard breath. "A job transfer opened up and I'm taking it."

Disbelief rips through me, cinching my chest. I turn away from him, pulling my lips between my teeth as I try to process what he's telling me. The heart that was beating so rapidly from nerves, from excitement, from the possibility of actually *being* with the man I love, is now cracking in two. "Oh." It's hardly a whisper, barely a breath. "Where are you going?"

He pauses, glancing away. "Bloomington."

I feel blindsided. "That's three hours away."

"I know."

"When?" I'm almost afraid to ask.

Dean replies, still gazing off over my shoulder. "A week. I start next Monday… I'm putting my town house up for rent and getting an apartment until I'm settled."

A small sob breaks through, despite my best efforts to hold it in. Dean takes my hand, but I pull away as if he struck me with a match. "Please don't try to comfort me when you're the one breaking my heart." I rise from the couch and walk over to the bay window, desperate to get away. Desperate to hide how much he's hurting me.

"Corabelle…"

I whip around, finding him standing a few feet behind me. "Don't call me that."

"Listen to me," he says, taking cautious steps toward me, like I'm either going to bite or run. "This is the hardest decision I've ever had to make and I'm doing it because I know, I *know*, it's for the best. I've tried so hard to be the one who pulls you through this, but I'm only holding you down. I'm preventing you from healing."

"That's bullshit. You've been the only thing keeping me going."

Dean paces forward, closing the gap, and reaches out his hands to cup my face. "You're right. And that's why I have to go." He lowers one of his hands until it's pressed up against my splintered heart. "*You* need to keep yourself going. It's the only way."

I pull back sharply. "You don't get to touch me anymore."

He looks wounded, like I just shoved a blade through his chest. "Cora, please. Try to understand."

"Oh, I understand. You've made yourself perfectly clear." My legs are trembling as I wipe away the fallen tears. "You've had your fun, and now you're moving on."

His face flashes with fury.

Shit.

I move back on instinct, afraid of the words he's about to cut me down with.

"*Fun?*" Dean repeats, advancing on me, his eyes alight with incredulity. "You think being abducted by a serial killer, shackled to a pole for three weeks, forced to rape my fiancée's sister at gunpoint, and murdering a man in cold blood with my bare fuckin' hands has been *fun?*" His fingers are balled into fists at his sides, his face a mask of anger. "Or do you think falling for you has been fun? Falling in love with the only woman in the world I can't have, watching her slip through my fingers, little by little, day by day, only to find her nearly dead from an overdose?

"Or maybe you're referring to the sex. Sex is always fun, right? It's been so fucking *goddamn* fun trying to reach you the only way I can, making love to you while you can't even look me in the eyes, and trying to collect all the little bones you throw at me without ever truly *having* you. It's been loads of fun waking up every morning to an empty bed with my sheets reeking of you, mocking me with the reminder that you're not there. And it's been especially fun having to uproot my whole life because I care about you so damn much, I can't bear to keep watching you suffer."

I'm breathing heavily, almost as hard as he is, my guilt battling it out with shock and rage. I used the wrong word, yes, but this still feels like a slap in the face to everything we've been through. "Don't play the martyr, Dean. If you really loved me, you would stay."

"I *do* love you." He's on me again, his hands on my shoulders. "I love you. *Madly.* But with mad love comes madness, and what you need right now is *peace.* Don't you get it, Cora? Don't you see?" His grip on me tightens, his face directly in front of mine. "I'm leaving *because* I love you."

I don't get it.

I don't see.

All I see is him not choosing me.

All I see is abandonment.

"I'm a big girl. You don't get to decide what's best for me."

Dean drops his head, breathing out through his nose. "You asked me to *tie you up.*"

"So?" I push him away and cross my arms. "A lot of couples do that."

"Not us. Not you and me." He runs both hands through his hair, linking them behind his neck. "Jesus, Cora…that was a huge, fucking red flag. How could you ask me to do that after what we went through? How could you *want* that?"

"I don't know!" I throw my hands up. "It just came out. Why is it such a big deal?"

"Because…" Dean closes in on me again, tears in his eyes, hands still behind his head as if he needs to hold himself back from touching me. "Because you have a hole you're trying to fill. A void. And this is going to sound totally messed up, but I think a part of you misses that basement."

My eyes widen. My stomach drops. "How dare you."

"I'm serious, Corabelle. Nothing else mattered down there but you and me and trying to survive. I was all you had, and we clung to each other, and we were *allowed* to. We had to. But now we're back in the real world and everything's different, and I think you miss that."

I'm shaking my head through his words, rejecting every single one. "That's sick. You don't know me at all."

"I do know you. I know you pretty damn well." Dean sighs, pinching the bridge of his nose as a look of defeat washes over him. "I don't want to end things like this. I don't want you hating me."

"Well, you don't get a choice in that, Dean," I say through a bitter laugh. "*You're* the one ending it. You don't get to control the fallout, too."

He steps back, running his tongue along his teeth and shoving his hands into his pockets. "Yeah. I guess that's fair."

"It's probably best if you leave now."

So I can go sob into my dogs for the next decade.

Dean flicks his eyes up to me. There is so much pain there, so much uncertainty. But he's doing it anyway. He's leaving me alone to pick up the pieces of our shared trauma. I turn away, afraid I'm going to collapse with grief if I keep looking at him.

And then he's scooping me into his arms, holding me tightly to his chest, his mouth against my ear. "God, I'm so sorry. I didn't want to walk out your door without making you understand why I *need* to do this…but I realize you won't understand until I'm gone. And I'm so fucking sorry, Cora. The last thing I want to do is give you more pain, but I *promise* this is the right thing to do." Dean clutches me, squeezes me, his hand cradling the back of my head and threading through my hair. He peppers kisses along my neck as I start to cry uncontrollably. "Don't cry. Don't cry, my sweet Corabelle. I love you so goddamn much."

I can't stop crying. I don't know if I'll ever stop.

Dean pulls back slowly, his hands lifting to my cheeks and wiping away my tears. He kisses my forehead, my nose, landing on my lips with a final goodbye. "You're still my girl. You'll always be my girl."

Then he releases me, turning around and heading to the front door.

I'm overcome with emotion—with love and sorrow and regret and anger—and I call out to him as his hand reaches for the doorknob. "Wait."

Dean hesitates and faces me.

I reach behind my neck and unclasp my necklace chain, moving toward him. His eyes drift from my face to the gold locket I'm holding out as I approach him. He's shaking his head, not wanting to believe what he's seeing.

I take his hand in mine and outstretch his fingers, delicately placing the locket into his palm. He closes his eyes, fisting it, and heaves out a deep breath.

I leave him with parting words before I turn away: "I wish you fought for me as hard as you fought to get out of that basement."

I should have turned around sooner, walked away faster, and disappeared down the hallway…but I waver. I glance at him before I retreat, catching his reaction.

I have seen my fair share of horrors, and many of them still keep me up at night.

But I fear nothing will ever haunt me quite like the look I see in Dean's eyes before he steps out my front door and walks out of my life.

31

I MAKE IT THROUGH THE WEEK, just barely.

I called into work on Monday because I hadn't quite recovered from the bomb that was dropped on me Friday night. Now, after days of self-isolation and ignoring all of my texts and phone calls, I finally venture out and land on my parents' doorstep that following Sunday afternoon.

My mother opens the door and I quite literally collapse into her arms.

"Cora...sweetheart," she says in that familiar, soothing tone as she strokes my hair. "What happened?"

Oh, nothing much. Just suffered through the worst four months of my entire life, only to have my heart smashed to smithereens just when I finally see a break in the clouds.

I blubber like a sobbing idiot against her shoulder as she pulls me into the house and shuts the door.

"He left," I croak.

I shouldn't be doing this. I shouldn't be falling apart in front of the woman who was almost Dean's mother-in-law—through *Mandy*. It's twisted, and it just makes me cry harder.

But I really need my mom right now.

"Cora, honey, let's go upstairs and talk."

I collect myself enough to wobble up the staircase and dive beneath the covers of the bed in the guest room. My mother slides in beside me, wrapping her arms around me and just letting me cry for a while. It feels good to be stripped down and comforted after a week of braving the storms alone.

Dean used to be those comforting arms, but he's gone now.

My hair is damp from tears as she brushes it away from my face, whispering words of solace against my forehead. "Do you want to talk about it?"

I nod. I do, I *really* do—but I don't know how. "I'm just not sure how to talk to you about this. I'll sound like a huge hussy."

"I'm your mother, Cora. I would never think of you like that. Dad and I are very aware of the situation that unfolded, and while it was an unexpected shock, we never judged you or thought any less of you."

"How?" I glance at her through bloodshot eyes. "*I* judged me. I'm still judging me."

"Because we love you…unconditionally."

I swallow a sticky lump in my throat, nuzzling against her warmth. "None of this was supposed to happen. It's not supposed to be like this."

My mother continues to caress my hair, my cheek, all the way down my arm and back up again. The motions tame my erratic heart. She lets a few moments slide in silence as I soak up the temporary peace, and then she speaks. "This reminds me of your junior year of high school when you were bedridden for six days with mono," she reminisces, her hand continuing its climb and descent. "You were so sick. You could hardly get out of bed."

"You would hold me like this every night and sing me lullabies. I was so embarrassed and told you to leave because I wasn't a baby anymore, but I secretly loved it." A wistful smile washes over me. "It made me feel better."

She nods. "And every day at dinnertime, I'd bring homemade chicken noodle soup up to your bedroom."

I still remember that soup. It was *so good*. I began to look forward to it every day. Even on the days I had no appetite, that soup warmed me up and made me smile. "I remember that. I loved it."

My mother pulls back to find my eyes, a knowing smile stretching across her pretty face. She leans in to kiss my hairline, then whispers, "That soup was from Dean."

My chest tightens, the air escaping me with a sharp gasp. "What?"

"He would come over every day after school to study with Mandy, and he'd bring you soup. He never made a big deal about it. He acted like it was nothing." She squeezes my arm, noticing my watery, wide-eyed stare. "He's always cared about you, Cora."

My mind is spinning and reeling, careening back in time to our early days of teasing and loathing. The only things that stand out during my high school years with Dean are elaborate pranks, like when Dean stole the tarantula from the science lab and hid it in my gym shoe.

That was on my *first day*.

That was after sharing a sweet look with him across the room in Mr. Adilman's class, thinking maybe he would become my friend.

Nope. Cue the hairy spider in my shoe that traumatized me so hard, I spent half the day in the nurse's office recovering.

There were no heroic gestures or kind words.

There was no soup.

I slick my tongue along my dry lips, feeling confused. "Why didn't you tell me?"

My mother glances up, leaning back onto the pillow with a sigh. "I'm not sure." She turns her head to look at me and I'm still staring. Processing. "But I started noticing things after that. Little things. Just the way he'd look at you sometimes. His eyes held such… I don't know. Admiration. Endearment. I don't think he even realized it. Neither of you did."

"You think…you think we've always had feelings for each other?"

No. That can't be true. I *hated* him, and he hated me.

"Subconsciously, I think there has always been a special connection between you two," she says with a thoughtful expression. "I never questioned his loyalty to Mandy. I know they cared about each other very much. But as the years went on, I noticed the differences between them. They grew into different people who were not as well suited as they were in the beginning. Of course, I never expected anything like this, but…I can't say I'm entirely surprised by the outcome."

I blink, my stomach in ropes. "You don't hate him?"

My mother tucks a strand of hair behind my ear. "I don't hate him, honey.

Dean has always been like a son to me, and your father and I both know none of this was intentional. This wasn't a nefarious plot to hurt your sister. It's been a horrible situation for everyone, and we knew there would be tough roads ahead with even tougher choices. Your sister and I have had plenty of long talks, and it's going to take time, but I'm confident you will all find your way." She kisses my forehead. "We hurt for Mandy. We hurt for you. We hurt for Dean."

Tears track my cheeks in quiet streams, and I roll onto my back with a deep breath. "He left, Mom. He said he was holding me back from healing, so he took a job transfer in Bloomington, just to get away from me. He claimed it was because he loved me, but that doesn't make any sense…" Those quiet tears turn loud as reality hits me once again. "I don't know how to get through this without him."

Her arms tuck around me once more, pulling me in. "Cora, sweetheart… love doesn't exist without sacrifice. Sometimes those sacrifices are waking up ten minutes early to make your partner coffee. Sometimes it's taking on a second job to support your family. Sometimes it's staying up all night with a newborn so your significant other can finally sleep. Sometimes it's shoveling the other person's car out of the driveway after a snowstorm." She places her palm against my wet cheek and smiles softly. "And sometimes it's making the ultimate sacrifice and walking away for the greater good."

I shake my head through the gut-wrenching sobs. "I don't want to be the ultimate sacrifice. I want to be the coffee one."

"Oh, honey." My mother holds me tight, a chuckle slipping out. "You need to think of it as an act of love, and not as an act of betrayal. And I think you should take this time to do some soul-searching and put the pieces of your life back together. I'm here to help with whatever you need, and so is your dad. This isn't necessarily an end… Think of it as your chance to start over."

I sniffle, thinking back to my final conversation with Dean in my living room last Friday.

Thinking back to that look in his eyes when I returned the locket—the most precious gift I've ever received—and hurled my angry words at him. That was our final moment together. Our last dance. And I allowed my demons to take over and strike him down when he was hurting just as much as I was.

Maybe my mother is right. Maybe this *is* all about love.

Maybe love is singing her favorite song in the dark, just so she can sleep. Maybe love is giving away the shoes on your feet to help keep her warm. Maybe love is coming over in the middle of the night when the power goes out because you know she's afraid of the dark.

And maybe love is walking away because it's the only way she'll find the light again.

I wanted to believe our situation was the *reason* our feelings changed—shifted and swayed like a high tide. But feelings like this cannot be built in the course of three weeks. They are created over time, blooming and growing, manifesting into something bigger than us both.

Our ordeal may have opened a door, but it opened a door that was already cracked. Dean and I have always had a connection—a unique chemistry. It was disguised with banter and jokes, hostile words and silly pranks, but there was always *something*. And if I were to play the last fifteen years out like a film reel in my mind, I'd see the signs. I'd notice the things I'd blatantly ignored due to circumstances, ignorance, and our battle of wills.

I'd recognize the look in his eyes in the rearview mirror after we rescued Blizzard in the middle of a snowy highway.

I'd see his mask of horror and guilt when he thought he'd hurt me with the cornstarch doughnut.

I'd pick apart his winks and smirks and the twinkle in his eyes whenever I was around.

I'd feel his careful arms around me at the animal hospital as he filled me up with hope.

I'd recall the way he came to pick me up that fateful night in November at almost 2:00 A.M.—no hesitation, no questions asked.

I'd hear his noble words in that basement: *"Do what you want to me. Leave her alone."*

I'd go back to my living room on Friday and listen, truly *hear* him, and I'd do it all so much differently.

A desperate whimper escapes me and I sit up in bed, wiping both eyes with my wrist and facing my mother. "I–I have to go."

She strokes her fingers through my hair one last time, giving my shoulder a tender squeeze as she pulls away. "I know."

I lean in for a hug, holding her tight with both arms, burying my teary face into her neck and soaking up her vanilla perfume—a scent that is entirely my mother. "Thank you. I'm sorry for everything I've put you through."

"Oh, Corabelle…" She kisses my cheek before she lets me go. "Just get better. There's no shame in the struggle, but you can't stay there forever. We're all here for you."

We share a final hug before I race down the staircase, out the door, and hop into my car. It's a little after 1:00 p.m. and there's a chance he hasn't left yet.

I want to say goodbye. A *real* goodbye.

I fly across town, likely breaking at least eleven traffic laws, and park in front of his town house, my car door left hanging open as I jump out. I run up the familiar walkway, peering in through the side window as I knock on the door. I squint my eyes through the dusty glass, but everything looks empty. It all looks vacant. Hollow and cleared out.

No.

I'm too late.

I turn around and slide my back down the door until my bottom hits the cement stoop. I think about calling him. Texting him.

But I don't even know what I would say.

I'm afraid everything would come out sounding like,

I want you.

I need you.

Come back.

And I know now, I *know*…the one who really needs to come back is me.

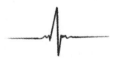

I wander through my front yard fifteen minutes later like a zombie, drained and exhausted. I'm so distracted by my emotional distress that I almost miss the envelope taped to my turquoise door with my name scrawled across the front.

Corabelle.

I lose a breath as I reach for the white envelope, plucking it off the door and grazing my forefinger along my name written in black ink. I swallow hard as I tear open the seal, then a gasp squeaks out between my lips.

My locket is tucked inside, along with a handwritten note:

> It's still beating.
> You're still okay.
> And I still love you.
> Dean

The words blur through my tears as I choke on a sob. I reach into the envelope and pull out the familiar golden chain with a trembling hand, pressing the envelope between my knees as I fasten the necklace behind my hair. The pendant falls between my breasts, heart to heart, and I smile at the feel of the tiny weight against my chest. Then I press my fingertips to my ribs and close my eyes, letting my heartbeat vibrate through me and fill me with peace.

Love is so many things I never thought about, never expected, never *knew*… and one of those things is being the best version of yourself you can possibly be, no matter how many obstacles stand in your way. No matter how dark, how hard, or how painful the road to recovery may be. No matter how many blows or setbacks try to drag you back down into the mud.

We can't give our heart to another without loving our own first.

And that's exactly what I plan to do.

32

EIGHT MONTHS LATER

I'M GRATEFUL FOR THE MILD November so I can still get on my bike and feel the breeze hit my face as my hair whips around me, tickling my nose.

It's the little things that make me smile.

I pull up to the quaint, downtown coffee shop, locking my bicycle to the metal rack and smoothing down my windblown hair. It's been an exhausting week at work, wrapping up first-quarter assignments and prepping for exams before we head into Thanksgiving break. I've been looking forward to our monthly coffee date ever since my alarm clock tore me from an idyllic dream this morning, consisting of sand in my toes and his laughter dancing off each rippling wave.

I shake the reverie away, adjusting my sweater dress and plucking a rebel leaf from my knee-high boot. I sling my purse strap over one shoulder and push through the entry door, casing the small café for my dates.

"Cora!"

I glance to my left, spotting them in a corner booth, and I wave with a smile. "Sorry I'm late," I say, still slightly out of breath from the five-mile trek. "I hopped on my bike last minute—the weather was too nice."

Tabitha beams up at me as I approach the cozy booth. "Only you could pull off looking like a movie star after a twenty-minute cardio session."

"Hardly. I flashed a dozen people on the way over and ate half my hair," I tease. I tug my V-necked sweater dress down, regretting the fashion choice, as I slip into the seat. I shift my gaze to baby Hope, who is still secured inside her car seat, playing with the dangling rattles and toys in front of her. "She's getting so big."

"She just turned ten months on Tuesday. It's wild, right?"

"Wow." The baby is absolutely gorgeous with tufts of silky black hair, just like her mother's. Her eyes are like sapphires, her cheeks round and pink. I look back to Tabitha across the table and find her gazing at me with a thoughtful expression. "What? Is there a bug in my hair?" I frantically swipe at my golden-blond tresses, while Tabitha laughs at me.

"You're bug-free. I was just admiring you."

I lower my arms, my features relaxing. "Oh."

"You're absolutely glowing, Cora. You look incredible," she tells me, folding her hands around her coffee cup and tilting her head to the side, studying me further. "I'm proud of you."

I let her words wash through me like a calming cleanse, my own smile blooming. The truth is, I *feel* incredible. Lighter. Softer. Free and weightless.

The last eight months have been nothing short of challenging, filled with uphill battles, hours upon hours of counseling and mental health struggles, and a promise to myself every single morning that I will be better than I was the day before.

I joined a meetup group for PTSD survivors and have made an abundance of new friends and connected with kindred spirits. I took up bike riding as a form of therapy and have put on a healthy amount of weight and muscle mass, spiking my confidence levels and prompting me to splurge on a new wardrobe. I have monthly coffee dates with Tabitha, weekly dinners with my parents—along with Mandy and her new boyfriend—and regular girlie movie nights with Lily and the occasional coworker. I take my dogs for a long walk every morning. I picked up summer hours at the school to keep myself busy and distracted. I listen to inspirational podcasts and audiobooks. I drink smoothies. I take my vitamins.

I even got a tattoo.

I won't lie and say things are perfect now. I still have nightmares. I still sleep with the light on because the dark makes me uneasy. I still jump when someone touches me in an unfamiliar way, and I still mentally retreat sometimes, zoning out in the middle of a conversation when I don't even realize it.

And…I still miss him.

But I'm healing. I'm learning. I'm growing. And there's no going back to the person I was eight months ago—not ever.

"Thank you," I reply softly, tucking a lock of recently highlighted hair behind my ear. "You look great, too. I swear you get prettier every time I see you."

Her cheeks fill with rosy blush as she ducks her head, then nods to the lone coffee sitting beside me. "I ordered for you."

"Ooh, thank you." I reach for the drink, bringing it to my lips and sighing deeply. "Vanilla cappuccino with an extra shot of espresso. You're my hero."

It really is the little things.

Tabitha fiddles with one of her loose bracelets as she eyes my wrist. "Your tattoo looks great. It healed up nicely."

I glance down at the simple design peeking out from under my long sleeve. I lift my arm to give her a better look, grazing the pad of my thumb over my pulse point. It's a heartbeat tattoo, a little EKG symbol, etched across the tiny scars I carved into my wrist with my own fingernails. It's drawn along the exact spot Dean would comfort me, giving me a daily reminder of everything I've suffered through and have overcome. It's trained me to stop scratching myself—an anxious habit I picked up post-rescue. And, well…it makes me think of him.

"Thanks," I say. "I love it. It keeps me present—in the moment, you know?"

She nods. "I've been thinking about getting a tattoo to honor Matthew. Maybe Hope's name weaved into a butterfly. Butterflies make me smile." Tabitha takes a sip of her coffee, swallowing it down and braving her next question. "Have you talked to Dean recently?"

My heart beats faster at the mere mention of him. *Oy.* "Here and there," I tell her, shifting back into the booth and fidgeting with my dress belt. "He texts me sometimes to see how I'm doing. He left me a nice voicemail on my birthday in August." I chuckle then, thinking about our last interaction on social media.

"He recently tagged me in this article showcasing the world's greatest pranks and practical jokes. He said he was taking notes."

Tabitha grins over her cup, tickling Hope's toes when the baby squeals beside us. "That's great, Cora. I'm glad it hasn't been complete radio silence."

Me too. I wasn't sure what to expect in those initial months after he left. I wasn't even sure what I *wanted*. They say "out of sight, out of mind" is the key to healing, but I never felt like I needed to heal from Dean. I needed to heal from myself. And I couldn't imagine a future in which he simply didn't exist anymore.

So, the occasional contact has been refreshing. We never let our conversations get emotional or veer into any intimate territory. He checks in. I check in. We send a funny meme here and there.

We stay connected.

Tied, but with a loose grip.

It's enough for now.

I'm just not sure if it always will be.

Tabitha gives Hope a wafer to gum when the baby begins to fuss, and we continue our chat over coffee and giggles. Time runs away from us, as it usually does during our monthly get-togethers, and Tabitha needs to head out for a doctor's appointment. When we hug goodbye, I feel her arms encompass me in an extra tight squeeze, her breath whispering against my ear.

"You're such an inspiration, Cora. The true meaning of hope."

Tears rim my eyes as we pull back, and I offer her a watery smile. "The feeling is very mutual."

I watch the two girls depart the café, returning the wave Tabitha sends me as they disappear down the sidewalk. I grab my purse, about to follow her out, when I remember I wanted to bring Jude and Penny home puppuccinos— basically cups filled with whipped cream.

Want to know what else is whipped? Me.

I laugh at the absurdity of carrying home cups of whipped cream in my purse for my dogs and shuffle over to the counter. I hear the door jingle behind me as I order, then move off to the side and wait. When I collect the two cups and make sure the lids are sealed tight, I spin around and collide into a hard body.

"Oh! I'm so sorry."

"Shit. Sorry."

That voice.

We both look up, making eye contact, and I freeze.

Then I drop one of the two puppuccinos, sending a spattering of whipped cream all over my boot. I feel like I should probably clean it up, but I can't seem to take my eyes off him, and moving in general is definitely out of the realm of possibility.

Dean's face is a mask of surprise, a little bit of wonder, and a hell of a lot of *oh, shit.* "You dropped something."

I blink, registering his words very slowly. When they sink in, I can't help but release a small smile that only brightens when his own smile begins to stretch. "Did I?" I squeak out, feeling a strange mix of disbelief, awe, confusion, and potent familiarity.

"According to my pant leg, you did."

I glance down, my face flushing with embarrassment as I take in the whipped cream dappling the leg of his jeans. When I look back up, the humor has faded, and neither of us make any attempt to clean up the mess.

"You look amazing, Cora." He breathes out, his eyes scanning over my healthy curves and shorter hair, and settling on the renewed sparkle in my eyes. "I didn't even recognize you when I walked in."

I duck my head somewhat bashfully. "You're just not used to seeing me in anything other than sweatpants," I joke.

Dean is still studying me head to toe, but not in a sleazy way. It's almost like he's soaking me up. Reveling in all of my put-back-together pieces. "It's not that."

We both know it's not that.

I swallow, trying to find the words I've so desperately wanted to say to him for eight long months, but now that he's here, I feel tongue-tied. I nibble my lip, our eyes drawing back together. "You look good, too."

Well, he does. He *really* does. He's wearing a crisp, black button-down over a white band T-shirt with dark jeans. His hair is mussed and slightly overgrown, and a light stubble shadows his jaw. And I think his eyes are even bluer—*is that possible?*

I clear my throat when he doesn't reply and attempt more words. "What are you doing back in town?"

Dean finally seems to be swept from whatever daydream he was lost in, and he scratches the back of his head, shuffling from one foot to the other. "I was visiting my mom. Also, my buddy, Reid… He had something he wanted to talk to me about, so I'm on my way over to meet him."

I hate that I wish his answer had simply been…*you*.

I flick my fingers through my hair, brushing it over to the opposite side. I have a feeling I know what Reid wants to talk to him about, but it's not my place to tell, so I just nod and stand there in awkward silence. I seem to have run out of words.

"I wanted to see you, Cora." Dean presses his lips together, his cheek ticking as he lets out a low breath. "A lot. I just… I didn't know if you wanted to see me, and I didn't want to disrupt your life. I didn't want to pass through and shake you up, only to walk away again. It seemed easier to keep my distance."

"I get it," I quickly nod, forcing an agreeable smile as my hand clings to the surviving puppuccino cup. My sweater sleeve slips to my elbow, catching Dean's attention, and he stares at the small tattoo along my wrist. I don't miss the sharp intake of air he sucks in when he spots it. I hold it out to him, proudly displaying my new piece of art. "Do you like it?"

Dean seems to drift for a moment, somewhere far away, and I wonder if it's the same place I go to sometimes. He clears his throat through a nod. "Yeah. I like it a lot."

I can tell he wants to touch it. He wants to reach out and press his thumb to the sensitive underside of my wrist, tracing the little design, sending goose bumps up my spine. I see it in his eyes. But he resists the temptation and slides his hands into his pockets instead.

"Well, I won't keep you. I'm sure you're not in town long," I blurt out.

Those were literally the last words I wanted to say to him, but they just spilled out.

Judging by the tensing of his jaw and the shift in his gaze, I think they were the last words Dean wanted to hear, too.

"Right," he says, tousling his dark hair with one hand and dipping his chin to his chest. "I should get going."

"Okay." I chomp down on my lip, keeping it from releasing more lies.

He strains a smile. "This was a nice surprise. You really do look good."

"You too."

This isn't us. We're more than trivial conversation and superficial dialogue. *Dammit.*

But then he starts walking away with his whipped-cream jeans and eyes full of missed opportunity, and my feet stay glued to the coffee shop floor, unable to do much more than watch. I feel helpless. Stuck. Conflicted.

Dean glances over his shoulder at me before he steps out the door. So many unsaid words pass between us with that one striking look. It's brief. It's here and gone within a blink, and yet, it clenches my heart like a tight fist.

I let out a hard breath and lean down to pick up the fallen cup, reaching for a napkin to swipe the mess off the tile. I toss the garbage into the trash can near the door, watching Dean saunter down the sidewalk, pausing just once. He stands there for a moment, faltering, his hand massaging the back of his neck as he glances down at his boots. Then he keeps on walking.

I close my eyes.

I take a deep breath.

Then I say, *Screw it.*

I force my feet into action and push through the doors, jogging down the busy sidewalk with my hair and my inhibitions trailing behind me. "Dean!"

He stops in his tracks, spinning around, his mouth tipping up into a grin when he sees me running toward him. There is distinct relief mingling with his surprise.

I come to a slow stop in front of him, fluffing my hair back and laughing lightly. "Can we do that over?"

"Please." He chuckles, his hands on his hips, his eyes twinkling beneath the autumn sun.

"Should I drop the whipped cream again?"

Dean pretends to ponder this, scratching his jaw. "I think we can skip that part."

I nod, then lean up on my tiptoes to circle my arms around his neck, pressing my chest against his, my heart against his, my mouth grazing the skin of his throat. I breathe him in, and I feel like I am home.

And holy hell, what is that cologne he's wearing?

Is it new?

Is it legal?

"Hi," I whisper, feeling the way he shivers against my lips.

Dean's arms wrap around my waist as he pulls me closer, his tension draining with mine. He inhales deeply, exhaling his doubts and regrets against my temple. "Hi."

It's a hi. It's a hello. It's a welcome back. *I missed you.*

We don't pull apart right away. We savor the feel of our warm bodies melded together in a way that makes my knees tremble and my belly flutter. I try to memorize the way he feels in my arms, hard and safe, buzzing with heat and energy and undeniable chemistry.

I only step back when my toes feel like they're going to fall off from leaning up on them for so long. I straighten out my dress, unable to hide the tiny smile that feels permanently engraved into my cheeks. "That was better."

His smile matches mine as we stand there toe-to-toe. "Much better."

"Do you want to go to dinner tonight?"

Oh, hello, word vomit. There you are.

I inch backwards just a step, my face heating up from the bold request.

Dean's eyes flash with something playful, something almost wicked. "Are you asking me out on a date?"

"Ew, no. Never." I look away, pursing my lips before glancing right back at him. "But do you?"

"Yes."

I grin. "Okay."

"Okay."

We stare at each other, enchanted and bewitched, temporarily speechless as we absorb the implication of my invitation.

A date. With Dean.

We've gone from mortal enemies to two people thrown into the black pits of hell together. We've shared tears, trauma, angry words, and a lot of hot, toxic sex. We've been through it all, and yet, we've never gone on a date before.

Such a simple thing is filling me with a plethora of tiny sparks, like lightning bugs fluttering around inside my heart. I smile up at him—a little shy, a little nervous, a little flirtatious. "Pick me up at seven?"

Dean nods, pacing backwards with a wink. "See you then, Corabelle."

I watch him turn around and head down the sidewalk once again, but this time, there is a bounce in his step. There is no hesitation.

This time, he knows he's coming back.

33

LILY IS HOGGING MY HAIR straightener as we squeeze together in my tiny bathroom. She has her own date she's getting ready for…with Lars. The towering tattoo guy from the brewery the night I tweaked out and landed on Dean's doorstep.

I can see it. He was dark and brooding—a little intimidating, maybe, but Lily can hold her own. I think they would make a sexy couple.

"Okay, so, underwear or no underwear?" Lily wonders, running the wand through her chocolate tresses.

I crinkle my nose. "How frisky are you planning on getting on the first date?"

"You tell me. I was asking you."

I smack her shoulder, snatching the flat iron from her hand. "I'm planning on taking things slow, for your information. I don't want to jump into bed with him right away, only to have him drive home to Bloomington tomorrow and settle back into his new life."

"Oh, please," Lily counters, reaching for the makeup bag and skimming through it. "You ended a hot and heavy sexual relationship cold turkey, then haven't seen each other for eight months. There's no way you're not getting freaky tonight. Insertion is inevitable."

"Insertion is inevitable? You frighten me sometimes."

She puckers her lips in the mirror, debating on a lipstick color. "I vote for no underwear."

"Noted. Thanks." I shake my head, half-irritated, half-amused—my general reaction to every word that comes out of Lily's mouth. Then my insides start to warm at the prospect of…insertion.

Dammit. That's a terrible word.

And a terrible idea.

I flip off the straightener, fluffing out my hair and gauging my appearance in the bathroom mirror. My makeup is natural but flattering, accentuating my champagne slip dress and my still lightly bronzed skin from the warmer months. I touch my finger to the locket around my neck as nervous energy climbs up my throat. Then I turn to Lily and ask, "Is this a bad idea?"

My friend doesn't hesitate as she pops the cap back on her cherry-red lipstick choice. "Nope. You need to get laid, girl. You've been in vagina limbo."

Oy.

"I'm not talking about sex, Lily. I meant…spending time with Dean. Reconnecting." I shoot her a warning glare. "Do not make a joke about the reconnection of body parts, please."

"Jeez. How immature do you think I am?" She winks, then turns to face me, giving me her full attention. "You want honest?"

"Of course. I know you're good for it."

Lily runs her tongue along her teeth, leaning her hip against the sink. "I think it's been a long time coming. You two are *meant* for each other, Cora. And you're in such a better place now. *God*, I can't wait to be a godmother to your adorable babies one day."

"Okay, that escalated a bit." I frown, but a grin peeks through despite myself. "You really think so? You think there can be a happily ever after for a story like ours?"

"Are you kidding? A story like yours just makes the happily ever after that much sweeter."

I smile.

Then I picture it: me and Dean.

A future.

Dinner dates, cuddling, movie nights, vacations by the beach. Children. Dogs.

More dogs.

Even more dogs.

I can picture it all—and for the first time ever, I can truly *see* it.

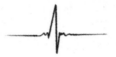

The knock at my front door makes the butterflies in my stomach take flight.

Lily left twenty minutes ago, and I've been sitting on the couch practicing how to breathe.

Breathing is good. Breathing is important. Breathing keeps us alive.

Jude and Penny beat me to the door as I traipse across the living room in my black pumps, repeating the mantra to myself. I close my eyes for just a beat, collecting my nerves, then I pull the door open.

Dean goes completely still when his eyes find me, his gaze trailing me up and down, slowly and purposefully. His Adam's apple bobs in his throat as we stare at each other for a few moments, unsure of what to say.

Finally, Dean sucks in a deep breath. "Holy shit. You look…"

Penny skips out onto the porch and starts pawing at his ankle, circling both of his legs. This seems to snap him out of whatever daze he is in, and Dean crouches to give both dogs attention. But his eyes keep flicking up to me as I linger in the doorway, biting my lip.

I clear my throat, calling for the dogs to retreat so Dean can step inside. "Hey, you," I mutter with a smile, happy to have found my voice. "Looks like they missed you."

He rises to his feet and steps through the threshold, his stare still hot and pinned on me. He swallows again, sliding his hands in his pockets.

I feel my skin start to singe from the fire in his eyes, so I turn away, wringing my hands together and walking toward the coatrack to grab my jacket. "So, where did you want to go? I'm up for anything. We can even do the Oar for old time's sake, even though I'm—"

My breath catches in my throat, possibly indefinitely, when I feel two warm hands capture my waist from behind with a featherlight touch. And then his lips are up against my ear, his heartbeat pressed into my back, his proximity a painful reminder of everything I've been missing for the last eight months.

"I promised myself I'd be good tonight, but I feel like you might make a liar out of me."

His low, gravelly voice tickles my ear, sending the butterflies in my belly into overdrive. In fact, they may have exploded. My stomach is now a butterfly graveyard.

Breathe. Breathe. Breathe.

Those breathing exercises were garbage.

I force myself not to shut down completely and slowly turn to face him. His hands fall from my waist when he takes a step back.

Dean shoots me a grin and a wink, likely to lighten the mood, but all it does is murder more butterflies. "The Oar sounds good to me."

"O-Okay. Great."

Lord. It's going to be a long night.

Or a very short one.

I manage to slip my coat on, all too aware of Dean's eyes on me as I fasten the buttons and reach for my purse. I suck in a replenishing breath and lead him back to the front door, giving Jude and Penny ear scratches before we step outside.

Dean places his hand against the small of my back, then points through the dark veil of night. "Check it out," he says, averting my attention to the vehicle in the driveway, parked behind mine. "I got my baby back."

His hand gives my hip a tiny squeeze before he pulls away, and I can't help but wonder if he's still talking about the car. My eyes widen as we approach the black Camaro. "Oh my God. Is it…*the* car?"

"Nah. I'm pretty sure that asshole liquified it somehow, but she's an identical replacement."

I make my way to the passenger's side, sliding in as Dean hops into the driver's seat. My senses are inundated with leather, nicotine and cedar, and a torrent of haunting memories that zap me right in the gut. "It's a beautiful car," I whisper through a breath, clicking my seat belt into place.

Dean hesitates before placing the key in the ignition. His shoulders deflate as he presses his lips together, turning his head to look at me. "Monday is November 8th," he says softly.

I nod, our eyes holding, the air charged with emotion. "Yeah. The timing is not lost on me."

It's almost our one-year anniversary.

But we're not celebrating an engagement, or a marriage, or some kind of superficial milestone. We're celebrating survival.

And I *will* celebrate on Monday. I'll celebrate by waking up extra early, watching the sunrise with my dogs and a hot cup of coffee in hand, and breathing in the crisp November air.

Then I'll smile.

Because I have a hell of a lot to smile about.

Dean reaches over the console to my lap, clasping my hand inside his palm. He brushes his fingers over my knuckles and says, "We fuckin' made it."

A grin spreads across my face—a real, big, genuine grin. "Hell yeah, we did."

He returns the smile and lets go of my hand, starting up the car and reversing out of the driveway. Fifteen minutes later, we pull into the familiar parking lot of The Broken Oar. We both stall as we stare at the front of the building, swarming with groups of people, smokers, and loud laughter. I worry my lip between my teeth, remembering my first interaction with Earl against the building. I think about that uneasy feeling in the pit of my stomach as he leered at me. I recall Dean's car cruising into the lot while I watched him hop out with a glimmer of mischief in his eyes, totally unaware of the horrors we were about to face.

I exhale a choppy breath, my anxiety spiking, when Dean finds my hand again. He squeezes it gently. "You know what? I've got a better idea."

Twenty minutes later, we're sitting at the edge of a grassy ravine, looking out at the lake with bags of fast food scattered around us. We're side by side, shoulder to shoulder, munching on greasy cheeseburgers and french fries, feeling totally ridiculous but even more liberated.

"I'm a little overdressed for this date, Dean," I tease, popping a fry into my mouth and nudging his shoulder with mine.

He eyes my bare legs stretched out beneath my peacoat, and his eyes flicker with heat. "You are a little overdressed."

Another wink. Another dead butterfly.

Dean chuckles as he continues. "I'm not usually such a cheap date. I just figured the occasion called for something…simple."

"It's perfect," I smile up at him, truly meaning that. These are the things I took for granted one year ago—fresh air, ripples on the lake, blades of grass between my toes, cheap fast food. I would have given anything to experience even one of those things.

I gaze out at the dark water, hugging myself when a breeze sweeps through.

"Penny for your thoughts?" Dean asks, wiping his hands along his jeans.

I turn to him, blinking through the memory. "Do you have a penny this time?"

"No."

"Unfair trade," I say, quirking a grin.

"A thought for a thought, then."

"Or a confession for a confession…"

Dean leans back on the heels of his hands, his leather coat parting and falling to his sides. He spears me with a devilish look, his eyes dancing beneath the moonlight. "I got myself into all sorts of trouble last time."

"Ah, yes," I agree, pretending to conjure up the memory, even though it has never left my mind. "You fell in love with me when I walked into Mr. Adilman's class looking like a deer in headlights, wearing a hideous purple blazer that I may have burned." My eyes narrow. "Then you showed your love by hiding Terrance the Tarantula in my gym shoe."

"Shit." Dean can't hold back his laughter. "I was such a fuckin' idiot, Cora. I'm sorry."

"Yeah, well, I feel like I've gotten you back just as good," I sigh, lying down, my hair splaying out across the grass.

"You have. I'm not sure if I had more fun pranking you or anticipating your retaliation." Dean leans back all the way, resting beside me and twisting his head to face me. We glance at each other, his expression soft and thoughtful. "You go first."

"Okay…" I avert my eyes, rolling a thin button on my coat between my thumb and forefinger. My heart rate increases when I meet his gaze again, and I whisper softly, "I haven't been with anyone else."

Dean studies me, unblinking, and replies, "Neither have I."

My eyebrows rise, reflecting how startled I am by the admission. I was certain he was out there enjoying the bachelor life. "Seriously?"

"Of course I'm serious," he says, rolling onto his side to face me fully, propping his head up with his elbow. "I don't give a shit about other women."

"Oh." I gulp, turning to look up at the starry sky. I can't deny the relief that washes over me, even though we were never *officially* together. Dean had every right to date around and sleep with other people. We both did.

But we didn't.

Dean continues, returning to his back and linking his hands behind his head. "I saw Reid today. He said he wanted to talk to me about something personal. Something he was afraid I'd get pissed about."

I know exactly what Reid wanted to talk about, but I let him finish.

"He told me he started seeing Mandy back in May. Things got serious pretty fast and he's thinking about proposing, but he wanted my blessing first."

Oh, my God…*proposing*? I knew they were dating and that Mandy was over-the-moon happy, but I had no idea they were *that* serious. It's only been six months. It took Dean fourteen years to propose to Mandy. They never even moved in together.

I can't help but wonder if those were red flags. Maybe there was always some uncertainty there.

"I knew they were together," I reply, taking a moment to process his words. "I had no idea Reid wanted to propose. That's so exciting."

"I know," Dean says. "I'm happy as hell for him. For both of them. He honestly thought I'd punch his lights out. He said it goes against 'bro code' or some shit like that."

"I think we're all past *codes* at this point."

He chuckles, catching my eyes. "Yeah. We are."

We lie like that for a while, silent and comfortable, watching the stars twinkling above us as the wind picks up, sending the tree branches into a mesmerizing dance. Then we talk about the last eight months, swapping stories and laughs, somehow inching closer and closer to each other on the grass. At one point, my head makes its way to the crook of his arm, and I take solace in the feel of his voice vibrating through me as he speaks.

Before we know it, two hours have swept by and my legs are starting to freeze from the crisp air. We collect our bags and wrappers, discarding them in a nearby trash can, and Dean hands me a piece of nicotine gum as we make our way back to his car.

"You're not smoking anymore?" I wonder, plucking the piece of gum from his fingers and studying it.

"I quit a few months back. Just doing the gum now."

I pop it in my mouth. It tastes pleasant at first, but then my throat feels like I swallowed a beehive. "Ack, it burns. It's awful."

Dean laughs, holding open the passenger's side door for me. "It's a good burn. It'll give you a little buzz." He winks, then closes the door after I'm situated inside.

Damn him and his winks. Like I need any more of a buzz right now.

When we pull into my driveway, my nerves reappear, uncertainty looming in the air. We glance at each other at the same time, and I lower my head, gnawing my lip between my teeth.

"I'll walk you to your door," Dean says, that raspy edge returning to his voice.

Walk me to my bedroom, you say?

I shake my head, knowing we shouldn't. Knowing my stitched wounds will only rip wide open when he heads back to Bloomington come morning.

We saunter up to my front door, dead leaves crunching beneath our shoes. My heart starts to thump inside my chest as we linger on the porch, turning toward each other. The porch light illuminates the conflict in his eyes and the heady unknowns that are surely reflecting in my own.

Dean raises his hand to my face, his thumb skimming along my cheekbone and causing me to inhale a sharp breath.

"What do we do now?" I wonder out loud, nuzzling my cheek into his palm.

The gesture seems to awaken him and he moves in closer, until our bodies are almost touching. His hard gaze caresses my face, trying to read me. Trying to pull answers out of my eyes—like if he looks close enough, he'll find them.

He will.

Dean lowers his hand to my neck, his fingers catching on my hair. He leans down to press a light kiss to my forehead, his lips hovering against my hairline as he whispers, "I'm not sure, Corabelle. All I know is that I want to kiss you more than I want air."

My knees start to quiver and I tip my chin up to meet his eyes. "I don't usually kiss on the first date."

He tightens his hold around my neck, his fingers curling around the nape. "Would you consider making an exception?" he asks, inching forward until I'm leaning back against the brick pillar and Dean's chest is pressed to mine.

I lick my lips, grateful for the support behind me. "I suppose I can be persuaded."

"Yeah?" Dean moves in, dipping his mouth to my neck, breathing in my scent and peppering heated kisses up along my jawline. Our groins are touching, prompting a whimper to escape my throat. Dean lets out a small groan near my ear. "Tell me what I have to do."

"You're doing it."

He raises his other hand until he's cupping my face, then pulls our mouths together, arching me back against the brick post. I cling to him for support, out of necessity, out of desire, and his tongue pushes past my lips, invading me and making me mewl. I expect the hunger and raw need to overtake us, but Dean remains soft and careful. His tongue kisses mine with gentle strokes, his hands clasped along my jaw, cradling gently—*lovingly*.

Dean pulls back and presses our foreheads together. "Inside?" he suggests breathily, my fingers curling around his leather coat.

I nod, taking him by the hand and leading him to the door, my own hand trembling as I insert the key into the lock. Dean hovers behind me, so close, brushing my hair aside and kissing the curve of my neck as I try not to collapse. The door pushes open, happy snouts and tails greeting us as we stumble through the threshold, then come back together like magnets as soon as the door closes. I unbutton my peacoat with shaky fingers, Dean's lips on mine, and let it slide from my arms before they encircle his neck. Dean moves back to look at me, taking in my slip dress that resembles a sexy nightgown.

He makes a possessive, growly sound, his fingers reaching down to fist the hem of the silk fabric. "Fuck, Cora…you almost killed me when I saw you in this dress."

My head drops back as he ravishes my neck with more kisses, his hand trailing up my inner thigh. I part my legs instinctively, desperate for his touch. "Mmm…"

That's all I've got.

Dean stills his movements when his hand reaches between my legs, and lets out a groan. "No underwear?"

I shoot him a naughty grin that has him kicking off his shoes, yanking his coat off, and diving back into me. I try to tug him toward the couch, but he picks me up instead, carrying me down the hall to my bedroom.

"I want to make love to you in your bed."

I kiss him as we shuffle into the room, landing clumsily on the mattress, our mouths still fused. We only break apart to discard more clothes, until the only thing between us is my gold locket. Dean fingers it for a moment, his eyes drifting up to mine as he hovers over me, a tenderness seeping in. I sift my fingers through his hair, my touch soft and delicate. "Thank you for bringing it back to me," I say, rising up to press a sweet kiss against his lips.

Dean kisses my nose, then my forehead, his arms resting on each side of me. He pulls my gaze to his, holding it as he says, "You said I didn't fight for you, but that's so far from the truth."

I almost choke on a breath, my wrists linking behind his neck, trying to pull him back to me.

He resists, keeping our eyes locked and stroking his knuckles along my cheek. "Corabelle…that *was* me fighting for you. That was me fighting for your healing, your joy, your smile, your laughter…your beautiful, broken spirit. I never stopped fighting for you and I never will."

My heart swells, my eyes water with tears, and my soul surges with absolute *love*. A small cry passes through my lips, and he catches it with a kiss. We lose ourselves in each other, in the moment, in the time lost—in the possibility of a real future. And when he pushes inside me, his mouth raining kisses along my face, my neck, my breasts…it's *different*.

He's slow and steady. I don't look away. Our bodies move together with a perfect certainty. There are no desperate touches or fear-infused kisses, and we aren't clinging to each other, holding on tight to the idea of something more.

We just are.

And maybe we always have been.

Dean holds me that night in steadfast arms, our bodies exquisitely entangled, relaxed and content. He holds me like a lover. Like my own personal defender.

Like my savior.

After all, he saved me from a serial killer.

He saved me from an overdose.

He saved me from myself.

34

DEAN

*C*ORABELLE.

A single sunbeam peeks through her lace drapes, lighting up the golden glints in her hair. She's still asleep, as peaceful as I've ever seen her, and my heart constricts with each quiet breath. I'm trying not to be a total creep and stare at her, but I'm hypnotized by the rise and fall of her chest, her slightly parted lips, and the way her eyelashes flutter as she dreams.

I'm painfully in love with this woman, and I'll be damned if I don't soak up every fleeting moment with her while I'm here.

Her hands are tucked beneath her cheek, and I swear there's a tiny smile creasing her mouth. I can't help myself. I lean in, placing a soft kiss against the corner of her lips. Cora stirs, nuzzling into her hands, her hair dipping down across her face as she moves. I brush it aside with my fingers, my touch lingering until her eyes blink open.

It takes a minute, but then her smile brightens as recognition and relief fill her eyes. "Hi," she whispers, her voice cracked and sleepy.

"Hi." Fuck, I could get used to this—waking up every morning to her drowsy, love-laced stare and rosy cheeks. "What were you dreaming about? You were smiling."

Cora stretches out her arms, the bedsheet falling further down her hip and catching my attention. "Shakespeare."

I squint at her. "Hmm. Is that code for all the new ways I used my tongue last night?"

She blushes, burying her face into the pillow with a laugh. I pull her to me until her nose is pressed to the top of my chest, her head right beneath my chin. Then I whisper against her hair, "'Shall I compare thee to a summer's day?'"

Cora lifts her head with a grin. "You know Shakespeare?"

"We've never met. But I do know a sexy English teacher who often quotes him."

Her smile widens and she pecks a kiss to my chin. "I always used to think you were dumb, you know."

I laugh as my hand trails down her arm and lands on her hip bone. "Yeah. You would get so fired up when I'd pretend not to know something. It was cute as hell."

"You were the worst."

"Incorrigible."

Cora giggles as she wraps her leg around my thigh, her eyes twinkling. "We should make love. Then we should take the dogs for a long walk, come home and cook breakfast, and crawl back under the covers until you have to drive home."

All of that sounds fucking fantastic—minus the last bit. The thought of heading back to Bloomington to my eerily quiet one-bedroom apartment all alone, reeking of Cora Lawson, seems unfathomable. But I realize there's no way around it right now. And I sure as hell don't regret the choice I made eight months ago to accept the job transfer, uproot my life, and put distance between me and the woman who desperately needed it.

It was *hard*.

It was the hardest thing I've ever had to do. It was harder than everything we went through during those fateful twenty days in a madman's basement, because it was a choice. It was *my* choice. And I had the power to say "fuck it" and be weak and stay, and it would have been so damn easy to do that. I *wanted* to do that.

But the only thing I wanted more was to see her smile.

I wanted to see her glowing and thriving and truly living her life.

I wanted to see her just like this, just like she is *right now*: happy and healing and learning to love herself again.

So, it's all been worth it. I just don't know where the hell we go from here.

I swallow, trying not to let the unknowns spoil this blissful morning after. The last time we woke up together ended up being the worst day of my life.

I reach for her arm that's entangled around my neck and tug it down, turning it palm-side up. I gaze at the small tattoo inscribed onto her wrist, brushing my thumb over the heartbeat symbol. Her skin is soft and lightly puckered from the tiny scars beneath the design, a permanent reminder of her past. I massage my thumb over her pulse point in the same way I used to do when my touch was the only solace I could give her.

Cora inhales a quick breath, her eyes closing as she lets the feelings sweep through her. The memories. The flashbacks. The thoughts and sensations. When her eyes open, hazy and glossed over, I press my lips to her wrist, sprinkling soft kisses along her vein.

She lets out a sigh of contentment and says, "I love you."

I've replayed those three words over and over in my mind for eight torturous months, wondering if I'd ever hear them again.

Nothing beats the real fucking thing.

I squeeze her to me, inhaling her daffodil hair and skin made of citrus that still lingers with remnants of our lovemaking. "I love you so damn much, Corabelle. I've thought about you every single day since I left, craving your kiss, your touch, the smell of your hair. You never left my mind. I drove myself crazy not knowing if you were really okay, or wondering if you'd moved on with someone else. It's been hell." I kiss her forehead, hesitating before I pull back. "But seeing the light in your eyes again is *everything*. And even if you had moved on and found happiness with some other guy, it would have fucking sucked, but it still would have been worth it to see you like this."

Cora places her fingertips against my cheek, trailing them down the stubble along my jaw. "I've thought about you, too. Every day. Every night. I dream about us at the ocean sometimes, listening to the waves roll in, feeling the water mist our faces." She kisses my lips, wrapping her leg tighter around me and hitching it over my waist. "It's my happy place."

I smile against her mouth. "My happy place is wherever you are. And I want to make this work, Cora. No more hiding, no more holding back. I'll wait for a job position to open back up here, and I'll put in for a transfer. It might be a few months; it could be a year. But I'll spend every goddamn weekend with you until I'm back for good."

Tears well in her green eyes, her lips parting with wonder. "You're coming back?"

"If you want me to. If you want this like I want this."

She quickly nods. "I want this, Dean. I want *you*. I want everything I told myself I didn't deserve."

"You deserve it all, Corabelle, and I'll spend my whole damn life giving it to you."

She kisses me again, then again and again. "I'll talk to Mandy this week. There might be tension at first… It might still be weird. But we're in a better place now, and she's moved on and is crazy happy with Reid, and I just know it's going to be okay. My parents still love you." Cora pulls herself even closer to me, tears trickling down her cheeks. "I know we can do this."

I grin, my heart flipping the fuck out inside my chest. I wrap her up in my arms, whispering against her neck, "We escaped from a serial killer, Cora. We can do anything."

Cora pulls my face to hers, capturing a kiss that tastes somehow different from all the rest.

It tastes like a new beginning.

After we finish making love that morning and lie basking in the afterglow, I have one more question to ask her. I catch her eyes, drunk with happiness, and I twirl a soft strand of her hair around my finger as she faces me on the bed. "Are you still mine?"

Cora doesn't hesitate. She reaches for my hand, placing it above her heart. "It's still beating," she says. Her face lights up with a radiant smile that looks exactly like how her heartbeat feels. "As long as it's beating, I'm yours."

Epilogue

CORA

Aunt Mandy and Uncle Reid are here!"

Aiden and Brooklyn charge toward the front door, the dogs trailing behind them. I frantically try to zip my suitcase, sitting on it, then bouncing up and down as Dean saunters up behind me pulling a T-shirt on over his head.

"Shit, Cora. It looks like you packed for the end of days."

"Well…" *Bounce.* "You know I just like to…" *Tug.* "Be prepared."

"For Armageddon?"

"For vacation with two children." *Bounce.* "Who knows how many outfit changes we'll need, and I packed the good camera because, you know, memories, and then the books take up a ton of space."

"How many books are you bringing?"

"Five."

"Jesus…"

I huff. "It's a series, Dean."

Dean chuckles, relieving me of my struggle and nudging me off the suitcase. He places his palm against the top and presses down, successfully zipping it on the first attempt.

I flip my hair back, puckering my lips together. "That was kind of hot."

"Only you would get turned on by me zipping up a suitcase." He winks.

I narrow my eyes teasingly. "Let's hope so."

We're about to lean in for a kiss when Mandy and Reid shuffle up behind us with four dogs at their feet.

"Sorry we're late," Mandy says, scooping Penny Lane into her arms and peppering kisses along her snout. "Are the beasts ready for us?"

Jude, Lucy, and Rigby sit patiently, tails wagging, as Penny is placed back down between them. Mandy is the resident dog-sitter. She and her husband, Reid, take the animals back to their house once a year when we go on our annual vacation.

Mandy and Reid have been married for seven years now. Reid proposed on New Year's Eve, just a month after his conversation with Dean, and Mandy walked down the aisle one year later. I finally got to stand up in my sister's wedding as her maid of honor and with Dean as Reid's best man, and there was a hell of a lot of tears, joy, forgiveness, and full circle. Then Mandy and Reid stood up in *our* wedding six months later, and we all cried some more.

"The beasts look ready," I smile, reaching for the leashes hanging along the wall and turning around to look for the kids. "Speaking of beasts, where did Aiden and Brooklyn disappear to?"

Dean slides over to us, giving Mandy a quick hug and fist-bumping Reid over her shoulder. "They're in the kitchen grabbing snacks."

"Mom!"

The sound of my name pulls me into the kitchen of our two-story house, locating both kids carrying hot mugs of coffee around the island in their unsteady hands. *Yikes.*

Aiden, our six-year-old son, holds up the cup as hot liquid splashes over the rim. "We got your coffee ready. It's already after eight o'clock, and I know how you get."

Well.

He's not wrong.

I try not to panic as the dark roast seeps into my hardwood floors and accept the offering. "This is so thoughtful of you. It's very hot, though, so grab me or your dad next time."

Our five-year-old daughter, Brooklyn, sets the other mug down on the table. "Here's yours, Dad!"

Dean steps away from his football-infused conversation with Reid and joins us, shooting me a wink as he reaches for his mug. "Thanks, Princess. Such service."

Dean and I take a sip of our respective coffees.

Then we simultaneously spit it out.

Everywhere.

I start gagging as Dean wipes at his shirt. We're both looking at each other accusingly, our eyes brimming with blame, when both children break out into hysterical laughter beside us.

"Gotcha!" they shout, doubling over in a fit of giggles.

Dean and I share another glance. Our mouths tip up into smiles that grow bigger and brighter as we absorb the fact that we have raised devious little pranksters, much like ourselves. Then we race to the sink and start wiping the salt coffee off our tongues with paper towels, while chugging down water.

I wonder if Mandy and Reid would mind taking an extra two beasts with them.

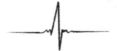

"Do you think we can bring some seashells home for Nana Asher?"

Brooklyn skips over to me across the shoreline, her arms full of delicate seashells.

On the way to the airport, we made a quick stop at the assisted living facility to visit Dean's mother and to deliver homemade masterpieces from the children. Aiden and Brooklyn love spending time with Holly, despite her memory loss. Her door is now completely covered in construction paper, crafts, and love notes created by the kids. We spend hours with her a few times each month, singing songs and telling stories. Holly has moments of clarity here and there, more so lately, especially when we sing.

She knows every single word to "Hey Jude," and I can't help but wonder if the song helps her cope with the darkness like it did for me.

I smile down at my daughter, bobbing my head. "I think that's a wonderful idea. She'll love them. Make sure to grab some for Gram and Gramps, too."

"Yes! Gram loves shells. We can make necklaces with them."

She scurries away to join her brother in the sand, her auburn hair floating behind her and catching on a breeze.

I'm taken by the moment, lost in a daydream, as I study my two babies filling buckets with sand on the scattered beach towels. And then I feel Dean's arms slide around my waist, his fingers dipping just slightly into my bikini bottoms. I melt into him, my back to his chest, his chin finding the crook of my shoulder. We stand like that for a long while, both soaking up the feel of each other, both reminiscing, both being fully present in the blissful moment.

I turn in his embrace, grazing my fingertips down his bare chest. The sight of him alone, shirtless and lean, all toned abs and broad shoulders, has me swooning as I teeter on both feet.

Dean ducks his head, planting a kiss on mine. "You have that look in your eyes," he whispers against my hair.

My arms snake around his midsection, clinging tight. "What look?"

"Like you're falling in love with me all over again."

I grin into his chest, pressing soft kisses to his sea-swept skin as his hands travel dangerously low on my hips.

He's very familiar with that look.

Dean reaches for my hand and tugs me toward the water. "Ready?"

My heart dances inside my chest, my nerves tingling. I follow him to the edge of the sea, where sand touches water, and we slow our steps, gazing out at the roaring waves.

It's November 8th.

Every year on this day we go to the ocean. I still recall our very first trip together one year after we made our relationship official. Dean was finally able to secure a job transfer back to his original union location after eleven, agonizing months of waiting and only seeing each other on the weekends. But the distance just made us stronger and more certain of our future.

Three weeks after moving in together, we hopped on a plane and headed out to Santa Monica, so I could finally dip my toes in the sea. It was an emotional moment, made that much more potent with Dean by my side. We ran into the waves, hand in hand, side by side, and I screamed when the cold water engulfed me.

And then I broke down.

I collapsed against his chest, overcome by the power of it, the *beauty* of it—the reality of finally conquering my lifelong fear. And as I sobbed in his arms, shaking from the cold and from the sheer intensity, Dean dipped down onto one knee and proposed. Right there in the middle of the ocean as I cried my heart out, tears mingling with seawater, and my skeletons washing away for good with the crest of each wave, disappearing to the ocean floor.

I jumped into his arms, my legs wrapping around his waist as I shouted *yes* over and over and over into his neck, holding onto him as the waves tried to take us down.

But we held tight, fighting each surge, standing strong like we always do.

Like we always will.

Dean and I both inhale a sharp breath as we stare out over the horizon at the setting sun. And then his knuckles graze against my own like a soft kiss, a knowing touch, a *promise*. I feel his fingers interlace with mine. We stand there, hand in hand, much like we did all those years ago as we awaited rescue, unsure of what our future held.

I glance at Dean, soaking up the smile lighting up his face as his eyes linger on mine. He squeezes my hand with his trademark wink. "Happy anniversary, Corabelle."

"Happy anniversary," I whisper back, the tears already threatening to spill.

I reach for my locket with my free hand, fisting the heart pendant between my fingers as my other hand clings to my husband.

And on the count of three, we rush into the ocean, tears mixing with laughter, love swelling higher than the tide, and we jump into the water.

Together.

Bonus Scene

TABITHA

S HE WON'T STOP CRYING.

Anxiety trickles through me as Hope squirms in my grip, her cheeks a deep, blotchy pink. Tiny cries sound louder than the firework display overhead, highlighting her dark tufts of hair with magenta and orange. "There, there," I coo, cradling the back of her head. "It's okay. It's okay."

I bounce her along my hip, but it's futile.

She wails.

Everyone stares at me, their conversations fading out as my child turns tomato-red beside the patio pillar. Even the fireworks go silent, enhancing my mortification.

Mandy races through the grass in a periwinkle dress, her arms extended toward my fourteen-month-old daughter. "Give her here! Right now," she commands through a smile, fingers wiggling at little Hope. She glances over her shoulder at her fiancé, who is jogging up behind her. "Reid, take my drink. My ovaries are imploding, and I need to squeeze her."

In an instant, my arms are weightless.

Hope flails against Mandy's chest, her legs kicking as she tries to break free. She isn't walking yet, even though all the other babies her age at daycare are walking.

"I think the fireworks spooked her," Mandy says, bobbing her knees as she sways side-to-side, stroking the back of Hope's head.

She's right. A bustling Memorial Day party in Cora's backyard is not the ideal place for a baby.

I didn't have a choice.

My babysitter fell through at the last minute, and there was no one else to watch her. Mandy is my usual go-to for last-minute social outings, but her loyalties were here with her family.

Cora and Dean shuffle out through the patio doors, beelining toward me as I run my fingertips through my hair. Humidity and embarrassment have my skin sweltering, my hairline frizzing with sweat. I greet them with a shrug, looking sheepish.

Cora's face is painted with worry when she slows to a stop and curls her hand around my forearm. "Hey, sorry. Dean and I were just…" Trailing off, the couple shares a heated look that tells me exactly what they were doing. "We ran inside for a minute. I didn't mean to ditch you."

"No worries." I sigh through a floaty chuckle. "Hope was just having a meltdown over the fireworks."

"She's a drama queen, just like me." Mandy grins, swinging Hope up into the air and giving her a playful shake. "Aren't you, little one? Too much time with Aunt Mandy, huh?"

The image tickles my heart.

A few beats pass, and Hope quiets, resting her cheek to Mandy's bare shoulder.

Reid snakes an arm around his fiancée's waist. "You're a natural, babe. Makes me want one of our own." His eyebrows pulse with implication.

She scoffs. "Pass. Managing the salon is grueling, and I hardly have enough time for Hope as it is." Flashing her full set of teeth at my baby, she nuzzles their noses together. "Maybe someday."

"Hmm, yeah. I probably shouldn't be talking about babies when we're not even married yet. I guess I'm just—"

"Excited? Eager?" she provides.

Reid's dirty blond curls glow with orange against the tiki torches as he drags his hand to Mandy's jaw, twisting her face toward him. Then he whispers, "In love."

They kiss, and I pan my gaze over to Cora and Dean perched beside the couple. It's like they don't even hear them, lost in their own little world. Lost to each other.

Dean bends to whisper something against Cora's ear, and she throws her head back with laughter. It's easy. Effortless. It's not hard-fought. I watch the dynamic between both couples, remembering how different it was over a year ago.

When everyone breaks apart, Reid pulls Dean over to the patio for a sports-infused conversation, while Mandy whisks Hope away to the kitchen to retrieve a juice cup.

Cora nudges my shoulder with her own. "How have you been lately? I feel like we haven't seen each other in forever." She fiddles with the heart-shaped locket around her neck, her eyes drawing up to me with fondness.

Sadly, it's true.

I'm working extra hours just to make ends meet, and Hope is going through a clingy, fussy stage. It's been hard enough trying to keep my head above water, let alone carve out time for social get-togethers and self-care. Even coffee dates are few and far between.

Loneliness has been suffocating me. Being a single mother is all-consuming, especially with my full-time work schedule. I'm a constant provider, one-hundred percent of the time. It's rewarding, sure—a gift. But I won't lie and say there aren't days when it feels like a stack of heavy bricks resting atop my shoulders. Those are the days I close my eyes at night and pretend he's lying beside me, alleviating a semblance of that weight.

I link my arm with Cora's as we stroll away from the patio, halting beneath a sprawling oak. "I've been so busy lately," I admit, chewing on my cheek. "I miss you guys. I'm trying to work on my time management. My mother keeps pushing me to start dating, but…"

My stomach pitches at the notion.

It's been two years, and he still haunts me.

No man should have to compete with a ghost.

Our eyes meet, that familiar tether pulling us closer. Cora's grip on her necklace tightens, a tangible reminder that she's not alone.

Not anymore. Never again.

"Yeah," she nods. "Trust me, I get it. Everyone tried to rush me into dating again after…well, everything." Swallowing, she glances up at the sky as a burst of light paints the stars in violet and indigo. "They didn't know how to deal with me. And I can't fault them for that, you know? People don't have a manual that details how to manage someone else's trauma. They were only trying to help me move past it. Their intentions were in the right place."

That's all too relatable.

If I've learned anything from the aftermath of my ordeal, it's that surviving the event itself was only half the battle. Surviving every day since has been decidedly just as hard.

I'm about to respond, unlinking my arm from Cora's and letting out a shaky breath, when a query sounds from a few feet away, stealing the words from my lips.

It's a question, a memory, an awful echo.

"Have you seen my car keys?"

Mandy.

Her voice resonates across the lawn, trumpeting over the laughter and chatter.

It's a simple question. Nothing profound.

And yet my breath sticks in the back of my throat like I swallowed a spoonful of paste.

Everything around me starts to spin. I freeze, the muggy late-May breeze turning to frost and freezing the blood in my veins.

Cora is speaking to me, but I don't hear her.

I don't hear anything except for Mandy's words and the newfound ringing in my ears.

"Have you seen my car keys?"

That day slams into me like a bottle rocket of pain.

His face flickers behind my eyes. Dark, dark hair and blue-gray eyes. A light stubble that morphed into a full beard as we spent weeks staring at each other from across the dimly lit cellar.

So handsome. So brave.

I think I hear his voice.

"I'm getting you out of here. I swear to God, I'm getting you out of here."

My mind starts to dizzy with buried memories. My heart stutters. My lungs feel smothered as I inhale a sharp breath and forget to let it out.

And then I'm there again.

The basement.

Matthew.

The space is dank and full of ghosts. A rat skitters along the edges of the walls, making my skin crawl, as my bare feet scrape along the cold cement. I skate my eyes back and forth, drinking in the shadows, wondering how this could possibly be happening to me.

I'm scared. I'm so, so scared…

But I'm not alone.

Familiar chains jangle across from me, metal against metal. It's a grating sound, but it sends a shot of warm comfort to my chest.

"Tabitha, listen to me. Listen carefully, okay? I'm going to tell you how to get out of this. You have to trust me."

"What about you?" I croak.

"Don't worry about me."

Images flash behind my eyes, grisly and painful.

Nightmares.

But they aren't nightmares…

They're real. They're memories.

And they're mine.

He's kissing me, he's protecting me, he's brushing tears off my cheeks, murmuring words of solace into my hair.

"I'm getting you out of here. You know that, right?"

I know. I trust him.

He's going to get us out of here. There's still hope.

And then…

My stomach drops, heart jack-knifing between my ribs. My world shatters—erupts—ashes and black confetti spilling at my feet.

Blood oozes from the corner of his mouth, and a tortured sound falls out of him.

A grunt. A goodbye. His eyes ping wide open with disbelief as he staggers back, away from me.

"No." *It's a whisper at first, and then it's a roar.* "No!"

He collapses.

He collapses, and I can't breathe.

"Matthew!"

My captor only laughs as he drinks in his handiwork, his belly jiggling with disgusting joy.

I scream.

"You're all mine, now, kitten. All mine."

I scream, and I scream, and I—

"I got you. Shh. I got you."

The past fuses with present, sickly tendrils of trauma bleeding into everything I've worked so hard to rebuild.

I'm confused. I'm lost. I don't know where I am.

"Matthew," I weep, falling against a hard body, holding on for dear life.

As reality seeps back into my psyche, I realize it's not Matthew whispering into my ear.

It's someone else.

It's Dean.

I'm latching onto Dean, my nails digging into his biceps as he keeps me from collapsing to the grass beneath a sky of fireworks.

"Whoa, shit, hey," he says, panic lacing his words. "Tabitha. Hey. You're okay."

I'm a ragdoll in his arms, half here and half there.

I'll always be half there.

"Cora!" he yells over his shoulder before jerking his attention back to me. Light blue eyes shimmer with concern.

With understanding.

With kinship.

Cora is a blur of golden blond hair and a red-and-blue romper, racing toward me with a cup of water. It splashes over the rim, spilling onto my sandals when she reaches me. Their voices are muddled as the backyard party spirals back to life like a white-knuckled fist through my chest. I heave in a giant breath, almost as if I've been pulled from a swamp, choking on ropes of algae and muddy water. My lungs rattle, clogged with murk and grit.

I wheeze, fighting for clean air.

"Tabitha…oh my God…" Cora shoves the glass of water into my hand as she untangles me from Dean and pulls me into her arms. "You're okay. I promise, you're okay. It's over." She repeats it, and she repeats it again. "You're having a panic attack. It's over…it's over."

I fall into her warm embrace, my gaze tangling with Dean's over her shoulder as he scrubs a hand up and down his jaw.

Worry, empathy, anguish.

It all shines back at me.

And for an irrational, shameful moment—I feel envy.

I'm envious.

The insidious feeling that clawed its way through me the moment I heard about Cora and Dean's survival story comes careening back in red-hot waves.

He's here.

He made it out.

They made it out…together.

But Matthew didn't.

My lover was forever entombed in that monster's backyard, buried right along with my whole heart.

It's not long before guilt overrides the jealousy, and I feel sick inside. Sick and sorry. I feel like an awful, terrible person, condemning someone whose one and only sin was survival.

And that's not a sin at all. That's a beautiful, beautiful thing.

I bury my face into Cora's neck, clinging to her as the cup of water drops to the grass.

She holds me for a long time, the party music finally eclipsing my heartbreak, and the sound of Hope's little giggles tethering me to solid ground.

"I'm sorry," I say, pulling back and drinking in a lungful of broken breaths. As I swipe two fingers under my eyes, I exhale the lingering remnants of my breakdown and strain a smile—the smile I've spent months practicing, getting

just right. "I don't know what happened. Something triggered me, I guess…
I just—"

"You *know* you don't need to explain anything to me." Her own smile
stretches, and it's brighter than mine. A little more authentic. She doesn't need
to practice because she has Dean to keep it alive and thriving. Cora grips my
shoulders, giving them a tender squeeze. "I'm here for you. We all are. You
know that, right?"

"I'm getting you out of here. You know that, right?"

I nod quickly so my chest doesn't cave in again, harnessing that smile. "I
know. Thank you."

Dean extends a hand, rubbing it up and down my arm. "Why don't you go
lay down for a bit? We can keep an eye on Hope. Mandy is entertaining her."

I glance to my right, spotting Hope sitting near the patio, playing with a
set of car keys as Mandy watches me with troubled eyes. Clearing my throat,
I shake my head. "No, thank you… I appreciate it, but I'm all right. I'm fine
now." The smile sticks, and I'm thankful for that. "Really, I'm sorry. It's been a
long time since I've had a panic attack."

They both take a small step back, their arms instinctively draping around
each other. Dean sends me a soft nod as he presses a kiss to the top of Cora's
head, rubbing his hand up and down her spine.

It's almost like they're holding on to each other even tighter after watching
me come apart.

Returning a look of gratitude, I move away and trek toward Hope, catching the way Cora's heart pendant reflects off the moon and glints with muted
starlight.

Their wishes came true.

Another memory flares to life as I shuffle across the yard. Matthew used to
tell me to stare out the small, narrow window lining the wall across from me
as I lie slumped against a metal pole with my wrists chained behind my back.
That window was the only source of light brightening our cell. It was our only
glimpse into a world still waiting for us.

He told me to look at the stars whenever I got scared, and whenever that
monster violated me, turning me into his sick plaything.

"Look at the stars, Tabitha," Matthew would tell me. *"Let them be your anchor. Let them give you comfort."*

Stars were made for wishing, after all, so that's what I did.

I wished, and I begged, and I pleaded, and I purged, unleashing everything I had left.

But those stars were always just out of reach, stuck on the other side of that dirty pane of glass. They twinkled in a sky that was no longer mine, deaf to the wishes I foolishly whispered to them.

The stars never answered me.

They couldn't hear me.

As I glance up at the shimmery night sky, illuminated with stars and firelight, I don't make a wish this time. I pluck my daughter from the grass and pull her to my chest, pressing a kiss to her cheek as I make my way back to my friends.

Those stars were never on my side.

PROLOGUE

G ET OUT OF THE ROAD, freak!"

I jump back. Vehicles speed past me, loud and obtrusive, flashes of colors and lights. Panicked breaths climb up my throat as I stumble along the side of the roadway.

This is a dream.

There are humans behind the wheels of these vehicles, some hanging out of their windows, pointing a device toward me. They are breathing the air. They are gawking and laughing and shouting clipped words into the dusky evening.

This can't be right.

I break out into a run, a shot of dizziness funneling through my veins. The sound of my heartbeats nearly detonating in my ears has my legs weakening with every urgent step. There is so much noise, so much chaos. I unzip my hazmat suit midrun, my insides suffocating, and pull it off as I reach for my mask.

I falter.

The sound of a blaring horn startles me, and I almost trip on the plastic bunching around my ankles, revealing my blood-soaked chest and pants. The cold air shocks my skin.

Before I can think it through, I yank off my mask—my final barrier of protection.

I inhale giant gulps of oxygen, breathing in deep, letting the ice fill my lungs for the first time in decades. God, it is glorious. Unrivaled. I drink it in like water, like sustenance, basking in the earthy winter musk I had long since forgotten.

Then I smell what lies beneath—something astringent. Fumes of some sort. My heart rattles with dread.

Oh God...fumes.

Bradford was right.

I have made a fatal mistake.

Clutching my neck, I wait for death. Chest tight, lungs wheezing, I fall atop the gravel when my knees give out, hitting hard. Vehicles continue to pass, spraying me with sludge and dirt. Through blurred vision, I see one of them decelerate beside me, feet appearing in my line of sight a few moments later. The feet grow closer, my breaths quickening.

"Sir? Are you all right, sir?" It's a male voice, similar to Bradford. "I think you're having a panic attack. I'll call 911."

The voice fades out as I fully collapse, struggling for air. The toxic fumes are consuming me, snuffing out my life. I curl my legs up into the fetal position and whisper raggedly as everything goes dark, "Lotus..."

The Black Lotus has been defeated.

1

SYDNEY

I DIDN'T MEAN TO FLASH THE neighbor.

I was only running out to grab the mail, so my robe seemed like an acceptable amount of coverage. My neighbors are used to seeing me in paint-smeared pajama pants, assorted beanies, mismatched socks, and oversized T-shirts with nineties prints on them. Usually, all at the same time.

So, the robe seemed like a step up. I felt good about it.

But then I slipped on a patch of ice and fell spread-eagle on my driveway, facing Lorna Gibson's house. I was wearing underwear at least, but the tie came undone, and a boob popped out, prompting the old woman to clutch her rosary and perform the sign of the cross a dozen times.

I tuck the girls back into place and climb to my feet, groaning at the throbbing ache in my tailbone. I wave to Lorna, who dropped her own mail and is staring up at the heavens, surely praying for God himself to strike me down. "I'm okay!" I call out with forced cheerfulness. She ignores me, still chanting her Hail Marys. "The leopard print panties are on sale at Victoria's Secret if you were curious. Super breathable!"

Lorna gasps with a hand over her heart, shaking her head at me from across the yard. She looks like she wants to personally give me an exorcism. "Blasphemous child," she mutters before scooping up her mail and racing into the house.

Sydney Neville. The sacrilegious tramp of Briarwood Lane.

I chuckle under my breath, unfazed. Lorna has hated me ever since I politely declined her offer to join her Bible club a few years back. I'm assuming it's like a book club with only one book—the Bible.

Considering I like to read dark romances with lots of graphic sex and explicit language, I'm certain I would have been sitting there bored, wondering when Adam and Eve were finally going to get freaky.

"You okay, Sydney?"

I massage my backside, then tighten my robe, turning to face the house on the opposite side of mine. Gabe is poking his head out through the screen door with a worried frown.

I grin through my shrug. "Oh, you know, just pissing off old ladies before I've even had my morning coffee. The usual."

"Troublemaker." He winks, propping his elbow against the frame. "You hurt yourself?"

"Just my pride and sparkling reputation."

"So, you're good, then."

"Fantastic." I smile wide. "*Always Sunny* marathon tonight?"

He points a finger at me. "Make that taco dip and it's a date."

I give him an agreeable salute and watch as he disappears back inside.

Gabe Wellington is my best friend. We're like siblings, having grown up together over the past twenty-six years. I moved into this house with my parents when I was only three, then bought it from them last year when Dad retired and wanted to pursue his lifelong dream of living on a golf course. Gabe grew up in the house next door with his father and stepmother.

And Oliver.

But we don't talk about Oliver anymore.

Gabe's stepmom passed away a decade ago, and his father, Travis Wellington, remarried and transferred the title of the house over to his son.

So, we're still neighbors, still friends, and still making terrible decisions together.

I wander into the house, flipping through my credit card statements and utility notices. I push my dark-rimmed eyeglasses up the bridge of my nose, reminiscing over the days I would look forward to getting mail—back when I was on the receiving end of a *Teen Beat* subscription and money-filled cards from Grammy.

My tabby cat, Alexis, purrs as she circles my ankles, and I tug at my messy bun before leaning down to scoop her up. I make my way into my office with the orange cat tucked under my arm, prepared to sort through emails and get to work. I'm primarily a graphic designer who focuses on building websites for clients. That's what pays my bills, anyway.

I also paint.

Painting is my true passion, and I'm grateful that it provides an additional financial cushion to help support my coffee habit and dirty-book collection. I've had a few pieces shown in art galleries, as well as auctions. I attend craft fairs and vendor shows, and I take on personal requests through my Etsy shop.

It's a dream life in a lot of ways. I'm independent, and I work from home doing what I love. I even bartend on the occasional weekend so I can pretend I have a social life outside of Facebook and my cat.

But I won't lie and say it's perfect—loneliness creeps in more often than not. My parents live an hour away, and my sister, Clementine, has her own life with a young daughter as she battles through a messy divorce.

After powering up my laptop and settling in with my mug of coffee, I get to work, scrolling through emails and corresponding with one of my favorite romance authors who I have the privilege of designing a website for.

While I reach for my cell phone to turn on a Lord Huron playlist, I accidentally elbow Alexis, who jumps from the desk and knocks my coffee over in the process.

"Shit!" I curse, realizing my Arabian mocha has just toppled onto a stack of paintings I had carelessly placed beside my workstation. "No, no, no…" I act quickly, grabbing a discarded T-shirt and rushing back over to the scene of the crime. My breath catches when I notice the painting that caught the brunt of the mess.

It's a painting of Oliver Lynch.

My childhood best friend.

Gabe's stepbrother.

The little boy who went missing on the Fourth of July almost twenty-two years ago, never to be seen again.

I frantically begin dabbing at the portrait, tears springing to my eyes.

Not this one. Please not this one.

I spent eight months working on this painting. It was based off the computer-generated, age-progressed photo of Oliver released by the media. It's an image of what he might look like today if he were still alive.

The shirt soaks up the dark coffee, and I watch it seep into the cotton fabric before setting the shirt aside to trail my finger down along Oliver's jawline. It's been over two decades, but the wound feels fresh. My heart still aches when I think about the boy with light-brown hair and eyes like a burgundy sunset. I can still hear his laugh and picture his dirt-smudged overalls.

Sometimes, I swear I *feel* him or hear him whisper my name…

Syd.

Oliver's old bedroom is adjacent to my office, which used to be a playroom when my sister and I were kids. I have vivid memories of shouting knock-knock jokes from window to window, playing "telephone" with a string and two tin cans, and telling ghost stories with flashlights underneath our chins. On that final day, July 4, 1998, we made plans to go see *The Parent Trap* when it released later that month. Our mothers were best friends and loved taking us to the movies. We'd giggle through our popcorn and gummy candy, while my mom and his mom, Charlene, snuck wine into the theater and giggled more than we did.

I never did see *The Parent Trap*.

To this day, I still haven't seen it. It never felt right seeing it without him.

With a final glance over to Oliver's window, which is now dark and filled with boxes and junk, I finish drying off the portrait and move it to a safer location in the corner of the room. I choke down my emotions and try to refocus.

Before I can settle in again, my ringtone goes off. It's the *X-Files* opening credits music, which means it's my sister. I send her to voicemail, flustered that I've made zero progress with my deadlines and it's already almost 3:00 a.m.

She shoots me a text instead.

Clem: Answer me, hoochy

I groan.

Me: I'm working, skank
Clem: I need you to watch Poppy this weekend. Pretty please. No cher-
ries on top because I ate them.

A grin slips as I sigh and text her back.

Me: I'm working at the bar this weekend, but I can bring her with me.
We can make fabulous memories and learn about what choices not
to make when she grows up. Plus, Brant is sure to teach her some
colorful new words, AAAND there's a wet T-shirt contest going on.
#auntniecebondingherewecome
Clem: I'll ask Regina.

Clem follows up her text with an abundance of aggravated emojis, and I can't
help but laugh, silencing my phone and running downstairs to make another
pot of coffee.

That asshole stood me up.

Gabe and I decided on seven o'clock for our *It's Always Sunny in
Philadelphia* binge fest, and it's almost eight. The taco dip is dwindling
with every scoop of my tortilla chip, while Alexis lies perched in my lap.
I pluck off my glasses and reach for my cell, prepared to blow up Gabe's
phone with David Hasselhoff memes. He probably found a hot girl to cozy
up with tonight, which is perfectly fine, but he could have filled me in on
his change of plans.

Instead, I see a missed text from Clementine.

Clem: Sis. Turn on the news.

I frown. She knows I don't have basic cable—only Netflix and Hulu like most millennials these days. I'm about to open Facebook, my preferred news source, when I notice flashing lights reflecting in my television screen. I pull myself up to my knees on the couch and peek through the curtain, my mouth going dry.

Gabe's house is surrounded by police cruisers.

What the hell?

At first, I wonder if he's having one of his parties, but there are no other cars in the driveway, and I didn't hear any music or loud noise.

Shit. Something's wrong.

Nausea sweeps through me like a windstorm, taking my breath away. I don't think twice before pulling on my winter boots and running out the front door in nothing but my sweatpants and *Rugrats* T-shirt. The crisp air is a welcome contrast to the heat prickling my skin.

My head twists to the right, spotting Lorna Gibson standing on her front porch, taking in the scene. One hand clasps her cross pendant while the other cups her mouth, and her eyes aren't filled with their usual scorn and judgment. They are filled with tears.

Heart racing and knees begging to buckle, I gather my courage and trudge through the thin layer of snow coating my lawn. The police lights are blurry as I make a clumsy trek over to Gabe's, realizing I forgot to put my glasses back on. When I reach his front stoop, I don't bother to knock. I yank open the screen and push inside, almost hitting an officer with the door. Three unfamiliar faces turn to look at me with pinched brows and tight lips.

"Are you a friend of the family?" one of them asks.

My voice trembles as I respond, "Where's Gabe? Is he hurt?"

But then I see him.

An officer steps aside, revealing my friend. Gabe is sitting on the edge of his couch, elbows to knees, his hands tented in front of his face. His eyes are red and bloodshot, rimmed with tears, and he gazes up at me with the most haunting expression I've ever seen.

My heart clenches through chaotic beats, confusion and fear battling it out inside me. "Gabe…what the hell is going on?"

Gabe stands, scrubbing his face with his palms as he takes slow steps toward me. His dark-blond hair is stuck to the sweat glistening on his forehead. "Sydney."

I stare at him, waiting with wide eyes and quivering limbs.

"Sydney…" he continues, then heaves in a deep breath. "It's Oliver. They found Oliver."

The air leaves my lungs with a giant *whoosh*, and I teeter on both feet, wondering if I misheard him. My foggy vision becomes even more hindered as fresh tears coat my eyes. "Wh-what?" A strangled gasp escapes me, the words registering one at a time.

They found Oliver.

They. Found. Oliver.

I manage to get one more question out: "Where was his body?"

His body. His bones.

His dirty overalls with Popsicle stains.

Gabe takes a few more steps forward, his throat bobbing as he swallows hard. He reaches out to squeeze my shoulders, and I'm grateful for that, I'm so grateful, because his next words rip the rug out from under me.

"He's alive."

I collapse.

2

SYDNEY

A POWDER-BLUE HOSPITAL CURTAIN IS THE final barrier hovering between me and my childhood best friend—the man discovered on the side of a snowy highway thirty miles west of his hometown, shirtless and bloody, with a protective hazmat suit gathered around his ankles.

It's the only *physical* barrier, anyway.

My sneakers pegged to the sticky hospital floor provide an equally effective excuse to remain on the opposite side of that curtain, chewing on my fingernails. Hands shaking violently, eyes closed tight, I can feel the dense lump in my throat that refuses to budge.

Much like my feet.

I'm not sure what I'm expecting to find when I walk through that curtain, and that's exactly why I'm stalling. That's why I'm scared shitless, near tears, tongue-tied and teetering. Part of me thinks I'll see that same little boy from twenty-two years ago with freckles on his nose and shaggy hair, bangs cloaking two curious eyes. We'll share a Popsicle and a knock-knock joke, then everything will go back to the way it was before.

The way it's supposed to be.

Another part of me expects a ghost.

Oliver Lynch can't be real… He can't be *alive*, walking and talking, warm flesh, blood flowing. He can't be more than a pile of brittle bones and soil.

A beautiful memory.

The last twenty-four hours have overthrown everything I thought I knew, shattering the walls I've constructed over the years, dismantling each and every misaligned theory I force-fed myself, just so I could *cope*.

Just so I could move forward with my life without him.

But part of me knew—part of me fucking *knew* he was still out there, and I hate myself for not looking hard enough.

Gabe's hand floats to the small of my back, causing me to jump in place. "You okay?"

I forgot he was even standing beside me.

As I nod through a watery smile, my lie is as transparent as my nerves. My hands continue to tremble, nail beds raw from my teeth, legs hardly holding up my weight.

God, what am I supposed to say to him?

Will he even remember me? I look nothing like the seven-year-old girl he left behind with sun-kissed pigtails and chubby cheeks. I'm a grown woman now.

And he's a man.

"What did he look like?" The question squeaks out as a whisper, my gaze fixed on the curtain as if my eyes might gift me with X-ray vision, allowing me to steal a peek at him.

I know all I need to do is pull back the drape and step inside, I *know* this… but if he doesn't remember me, if he doesn't look at me and see fireworks and oatmeal cookies and laughter beneath the summer sun, I swear my heart will shrivel up and die.

Gabe's hand travels up and down my spine with languid strokes, curling around my shoulder and offering a comforting squeeze. He replies in an equally strained whisper. "Lost. He looked…lost."

My insides twist and ache as I fight off tears. "They still don't know what happened to him?"

"Not yet. He's confused and not entirely coherent. The doctor wouldn't even let me see him right away because they didn't know if he was violent, or…" Gabe falters through a pained gulp, dipping his chin to his chest. "He didn't recognize me."

No.

I realize Gabe was only in preschool at the time of Oliver's disappearance, but Lord help me, I want him to remember *everything*. Every single detail from our magical childhood that has been carved inside me, permanently engraved.

"Do you want me to come with you?"

My dismissal is quick, despite the fact that my feet are still rooted in place, idle, refusing to press forward. "I got this."

"Yeah?" He quirks a grin amid the emotional turmoil swimming between us. "Because I'm literally holding you up right now."

Gabe lets go of my shoulder to prove his point, and I stumble, almost plowing through that ugly curtain like a human wrecking ball. He catches me by the wrist before I make an overly dramatic entrance. "Ugh, point taken," I bite out, inhaling a giant breath of courage and slamming my eyes shut. "But I need to do this alone."

"I get it, Syd." Gabe taps his knuckles along my upper arm with a light punch before stepping back. "I'll be in the waiting room. Text me if you need me."

Gnawing my bottom lip between my teeth and resisting the urge to drag Gabe into the room with me as a security blanket, I bob my chin, seeing him off.

And then I inch toward the curtain, counting to ten, chanting words of encouragement under my breath as I try to zap away the rattling nerves.

I raise my hand, bunching the stiff, itchy fabric between my fingers to move it aside.

That's when I see him.

That's when my eyes land on Oliver Lynch for the first time in twenty-two long, devastating years. The curtain drops from my fingers as my hand shoots up to cup my mouth, preventing a strangled cry from escaping. I'm frozen in the entryway with Oliver directly in front of me, lying partially covered beneath a white blanket. He's hooked up to various cords and monitors, and I'm thankful they are beeping and buzzing, filling the air between us. Otherwise all we would hear is the sound of my heart screaming and choking with the weight of each breath.

Oliver doesn't look at me. His eyes are trained on the popcorn ceiling, a slight frown marring his forehead. Maybe he doesn't realize I'm in the room, or maybe he's lost inside his head, but while his focus is elsewhere, I take a moment to drink him in, my gaze soaking up every incredible inch of this man—this stranger, in a way, and yet…*so much more.*

He is beautiful.

That same light-brown hair falls at his shoulders, shaggy and untamed, infused with hints of amber. A shadow of scruff lines his sharp and masculine jaw, emphasizing sleek cheekbones and a sallow complexion.

My gaze slips lower, and I'm surprised to discover a man who seems to have been well cared for. Despite whatever circumstances he's endured, Oliver is not overly thin or malnourished as I had anticipated—the opposite, in fact. Biceps peek out from his hospital gown encompassing broad shoulders and a strapping chest that heaves with his own weighty breaths.

Tentative feet carry me closer to his bedside, his name croaking out between my lips and addressing him for the first time in decades. "Oliver."

My God, those three syllables caressing my tongue force out a sob that finally catches his attention. Just barely.

Oliver blinks. Long eyelashes flit and flutter, his gaze still pinned on the ceiling, his fingers gripping the bedcovers between tight fists.

Moving closer, I pull my lips between my teeth, unsure of what to say or do. I don't want to startle him. I don't want to spook him.

I just want him to look at me—to *see* me.

"Oliver," I repeat. My own hands move behind my back, wrists crossing as a way to prevent them from reaching for him. "I'm Sydney. Do you remember me?"

I monitor his micro-expressions carefully. The subtle twitch of his mouth. The tensing of his jaw. The muscle spasm in his right bicep.

The slight widening of his eyes—so quick, I wonder if I imagined it.

I continue forward, stepping closer until the front of my sweater grazes the guardrail and I can feel his body heat warming my skin. Curling my fingers around the rail, I mutter softly, "It's me, Oliver…It's Syd."

AUTHOR'S NOTE

Thank you so much for reading my dark romance novel *Still Beating*!

This book was a HUGE labor of love, and it took me to a very emotional place. I put off writing this story for a long time, and I had even planned on publishing it under a pen name due to some of the taboo content in the beginning. I also anticipated it being nothing more than an erotic novella. Then I gave it a little heart, then a little more, and all of a sudden, this beautifully tragic love story began to unfold. I sent a few chapters off to my trusted beta readers, and they begged for me to publish this under my own name. I'm so glad I did.

Cora and Dean wrote this story for me, and I hope you enjoyed the ride.

If you would like to chat about this book, feel free to check out the *Still Beating Discussion Group* on Facebook:
facebook.com/groups/1830681193755622

If you or anyone you know suffers from suicidal thoughts, please seek help.
You are wanted, and you are loved.
National Suicide Prevention Hotline: 1-800-273-8255 or direct dial 988.
If you or anyone you know is a victim of rape or sexual assault, please reach out.
You are not alone.
National Sexual Assault Hotline: 1-800-656-4673

PLAYLIST

"Hey Jude"—The Beatles

"Bag of Bones"—Silversun Pickups

"Shimmer"—Fuel

"Haunted"—Poe

"Angel"—Theory of a Deadman

"Change (In the House of Flies)"—Deftones

"Overfire"—T.H.C.

"Carnival of Rust"—Poets of the Fall

"Lucky Now"—Ryan Adams

"The Otherside"—Red Sun Rising

"Starlight"—Muse

"Head Above Water"—Avril Lavigne

"Blind"—Lifehouse

"Hold Back the River"—James Bay

"Through Glass"—Stone Sour

"Blessed Be"—Spiritbox

"Especially Me"—Low

"Watch Over You"—Alter Bridge

"Breathing"—Lifehouse

"Hold"—Built for the Sea

ACKNOWLEDGMENTS

First and foremost, my undying love and eternal gratitude must be given to my incredible husband, Jake. I assure you, this book would not exist if it weren't for him. I basically crawled into a black hole of darkness for thirty-three days straight as I devoted full- time hours to the completion of this book. I'm a mother of three, so my husband kicked into Super Dad mode and held down the fort while I brought this story to life.

Jake also deserves the biggest shout-out of all shout-outs for creating my book cover. Y'all.

Picture this: A living room cluttered with toys, a toddler pulling at our pant legs and demanding chicken nuggets, a camera on a tripod that almost got knocked over a dozen times by said hungry toddler, a wife complaining that her arm was going to fall off, and 938,749,324,234 different takes as we tried to properly center and frame the photo with our arms chained together.

I have no idea how we managed to get the shot, but we did. Then my husband edited it and turned it into the book cover that hundreds of thousands of people have now seen. Phew.

Thank you, dearest husband, for your unconditional support and your role in making my dreams coming true. You are my rock, my inspiration, and my sounding board.

And my savior.

You may not have saved me from a serial killer, but you certainly saved me from a life of complacency. Thank you for believing in me and my writing dreams before I did. ♥

Huge thanks to my early beta readers who got to read this story as I was writing it: Amanda Jesse, Rachel Wanland, Vanessa Sheets, and Lyndsey Farrar. You ladies were essential contributions to this book in so many ways. You kept me focused and on track. You kept me inspired. You encouraged me to step outside my comfort zone and not hold back. You rooted and cheered for these characters right along with me. You convinced me to own these words and publish this book under my real name. I am forever indebted to you.

Thank you to all of my additional beta readers who provided feedback, suggestions, love, and kind words: E. R. Whyte (your little notes made me smile), Nicole Marie, Stephanie Goodrich, Emily Gutzmann, Gisell Butler, Ashley Marie Santorius, Amber Pardue, Megan Lick, Nicole Vaughn, Autumn Black, and Ali Herlihy. And thank you to all of my early ARC readers for leaving incredible reviews that made me sob into my coffee.

Thank you to my incredible group of Queens in my reader's group for cheering me on with my writing journey and with life in general. I love my community of inspiring women. You guys always make me laugh, lift my spirits, and keep me focused.

Thank you to my amazing children and family for always pushing me, and for being my biggest cheerleaders. I love you all so much.

It takes a village, and I'm so thankful for mine.

ABOUT THE AUTHOR

Jennifer Hartmann resides in northern Illinois with her devoted husband and three hooligans. When she is not writing angsty love stories, she is likely thinking about writing them. She enjoys sunsets (because mornings are hard), bike riding, traveling, binging *Buffy the Vampire Slayer* reruns, and that time of day when coffee gets replaced by wine. Jennifer is a wedding photographer with her husband. She is also excellent at making puns and finding inappropriate humor in mundane situations. She loves tacos. She also really, really wants to pet your dog.

Follow her at:

Instagram: @author.jenniferhartmann
Facebook: @jenhartmannauthor
Twitter: @authorjhartmann
TikTok: @jenniferhartmannauthor